DOCTOR DOGBODY'S LEG

BOOKS BY
JAMES NORMAN HALL
in collaboration with
CHARLES NORDHOFF

FALCONS OF FRANCE

MUTINY ON THE BOUNTY

MEN AGAINST THE SEA

PITCAIRN'S ISLAND

THE HURRICANE

THE DARK RIVER

NO MORE GAS

DOCTOR

DOGBODY'S LEG

BY JAMES NORMAN HALL

With Drawings by
Warren Chappell

LITTLE, BROWN AND COMPANY

BOSTON 1940

Published July 1940
Reprinted July 1940

THE ATLANTIC MONTHLY PRESS BOOKS
ARE PUBLISHED BY
LITTLE, BROWN AND COMPANY
IN ASSOCIATION WITH
THE ATLANTIC MONTHLY COMPANY

TO

Messrs. ATWATER, BAIRD, BEECHER, BRANDER, CHIDSEY, COBB, CRIDLAND, CROSS, CURTIS, FRISBIE, GUICHARD, GUILD, HIRSHON, JONES, KELLUM, MERSMAN, MURPHY, NIELSON, NORDHOFF, O'BRIEN, RASMUSSEN, SAGE, SEABROOK, SMITH, SPIES, STARK, STIMSON, STONE, SWIFT, THOMSON, TRENN, WOONTON, and WORONICK

In memory of chance meetings at various island taverns through the thickness of the Globe from Portsmouth, and some light-years distant from the Cheerful Tortoise.
And to the hosts at four of the taverns:

Messrs. BOHLER, MAUU, RIVNAC, and STURGIOS.

Manuia Tatou!

CONTENTS

DOCTOR DOGBODY'S LEG

I

THE CHEERFUL TORTOISE

On a dreary autumn evening when the clouds hung low in the heavens and the masts and yards of the tall men-of-war in the harbour were obscured by a chill drizzle of rain, there was no more inviting spot in Portsmouth than the taproom of Will Tunn's Cheerful Tortoise. But times were dull, now that Napoleon had been safely exiled to Saint Helena; half the fleet was paid off, ships laid up, and the Royal Dockyards, which had hummed with activity two years before, were reduced to the peace-time establishment.

The Cheerful Tortoise had suffered with the rest of

the community from the return of peace, although the creature which gave the inn its name smiled down upon passers-by with its old-time air of wistful geniality. The inn sign, as Mr. Tunn himself was willing to admit, was a veritable work of art. Carved from a huge slab of oak by an old seaman, many years before, it was impervious to wind and weather; only the strongest gale would cause it to swing slightly on its heavy gilded chain. Many a thirsty seaman, just ashore, would stop short to gaze in admiration at Will Tunn's tortoise, touch his hat to it with a grin, and seek no farther for refreshment. The carapace was a bright sea-green, the calipee pale blue, and the flippers yellow, while the head, with its eager smiling face, was richly ornamented and picked out in gold leaf. But the tortoise was greater than the sum of its parts, thanks to a happy stroke of seaman's genius. Its attitude of absorbed interest as it craned its neck to one side, as though to gaze past the lintel of the doorway into the taproom, combined with its smile, in which sadness at thought of its own deprivations seemed to be mingled with unselfish delight at thought of the good cheer and good company within, had made it a famous tavern animal amongst innumerable swans, blue boars, cocks, dogs and ducks, red lions, green dragons, white harts, and horses that adorned the highroad between Portsmouth and London.

Mr. Tunn's house stood on a corner a short distance from the waterfront. Although not one of the great posting-inns of the time, it was a place of call for some of the principal London coaches, and was especially frequented by men who followed the sea. It was a brick building of three stories which had been raised in the substantial manner of the period, to last for centuries. A door studded with brass nails gave directly upon the taproom with its dark paneled wainscoting, its floor of red bricks, well worn and scrubbed, its casks on trestles with a line of bright spigots behind the high old-fashioned bar, and its comfortable recesses with oaken tables, the chairs and settees upholstered in breeches-polished leather. One such recess alongside a mighty fireplace at the far end of the room was reserved for the "props" of the house, as the landlord called them, old friends and steady patrons who well deserved the name.

Beyond the taproom and connected with it by a wide passageway was the kitchen, an apartment equally spacious, whose dusky rafters were festooned with sides of bacon, hams, sausages, strings of onions, and parcels of dried herbs. Pots and pans polished to a degree of brightness something past perfection hung on pegs about the fireplace, where an entire bullock might almost have turned on the spit. At one side of the kitchen stood a long deal table, scrubbed white, where guests of the humbler sort were furnished with food and drink. On the floor above, reached by a staircase from the taproom, was the handsome apartment in which Tunn's famous dinners were served, and where four tall windows looked to the westward toward the Royal Dockyards and the shipping in the harbour. Along a carpeted passageway were the sitting rooms and bedchambers for travelers. On the third floor, where mullioned windows projected from the steep slope of the roof, were the quarters for postboys, coachmen, and hostlers, and for the landlord and his staff.

Mr. Tunn was a stoutly built, muscular man of sixty, with a clear ruddy complexion, a solid paunch, and a fringe of iron-grey hair framing a bald head. His had been a blameless, useful life, and he deserved well of the world if any man did; but on a certain evening in November his thoughts were as cheerless as the autumn day. He stood in the kitchen, superintending with little of his wonted relish the preparations for supper. Bilges, the kitchen boy, was seated on a stool opening a cask of oysters fresh from Newport. Another boy stood at the spit where a stubble goose and a splendid saddle of mutton were turning under the landlord's direction. So pleasant a prospect would have caused Tunn's mouth to water at another time.

His worries were unselfish ones, for he was not a man to permit his own troubles to weigh heavily upon him. Mr. Tunn was a widower who revered the memory of his wife. A cousin of hers, a Mrs. Quigg, had done well with a lodginghouse during the long years of war, and although times grew hard after the defeat of the French, she had clung to her lease, waiting and hoping for lodgers who seldom came. Mrs. Quigg was a sturdy independent woman who would accept no help from her kin, and it worried Mr. Tunn to see a connection of his beloved Sarah reduced to such straitened circumstances. Thinking of this, he sighed, wiped his hands on his apron, and walked along the passage to the taproom, just in time to see one of his drawers toss off a pint-pot of ale. Tunn stopped short.

"Tom!"

The drawer, a spindle-shanked cadaverous fellow with a colourless face and a surprisingly round belly, turned his head with a grin, half guilty, half impudent.

"Tuppence in the till, ye rogue!" said the landlord, indignantly. "Tom Tapleke! Curse me if ever a man was better named! It's so ye help your master, is it? And custom fallen away to naught in these days! Tuppence in the till, I say!"

Tapleke, who knew to a shade his master's moods, sighed with the doleful air of a deeply wronged man, produced the coins with reluctant ostentation, and dropped them in the till. Tunn was about to say more when the drawer nodded toward the window. Dimly discernible through the frosted panes, a hackney coach was drawing up outside. The landlord turned in that direction as a smallish active man flung open the door and stumped in on a wooden leg. He wore a cocked hat of a style somewhat past the fashion, a handsomely embroidered waistcoat, and a coat which, though plain, was well cut and of the best materials. The buckle of the single shoe below the white silk stocking was of silver.

"Mr. Tunn?" he asked, briskly.

"Will Tunn, sir, at your service."

"Doctor Dogbody, at yours, sir. I was directed to you . . . but damme, I'm parched! You've good rum here?"

"The best old Port Royal, sir."

"Then I'll thank you to take a glass with me while I tell my errand."

The visitor seated himself at a table and removed his hat, displaying a head of thick white hair, brushed neatly back and gathered in a queue. Doctor Dogbody's eyes, of the clearest blue, twinkled with shrewdness and good humour, in a face as ruddy as a winter sunset. It would have been difficult to guess his age with any exactness, although he appeared to be on the latter side of seventy. But the vigour of his movements, his erect carriage, and his small, well-shaped, muscular hands were those of a much younger man. Taking up the small glass of spirits the drawer had set before him, he nodded to the landlord and drained the contents at a gulp.

"Hah! That's better!" he exclaimed. "Ahoy, you at the tap! What's your name?"

"Tom, sir."

"Another of the same presently, Tom. And draw a pint of ale for yourself."

"Thankee, sir," said the delighted Tapleke, with a malicious grin for the landlord's benefit. The doctor turned to his host.

"Of all the drawers, Mr. Tunn," he said, "in all the inns between London and Portsmouth, five in six are named Tom. On the Dover road the ratio is seven Dicks to four Toms, whilst on the Exeter road there's naught but Joes as far as the King's Arms, Salisbury, whence, curiously enough, the Toms begin again and continue without break to the Elephant, in Exeter itself."

"You're a great traveler, sir?" Mr. Tunn asked, politely.

"By sea, yes. By land, no. But when I do travel, ashore, there's little I miss by the way, sir."

The doctor lifted his refilled glass, holding it toward the light as he examined the contents, critically.

"A prime old spirit, landlord. It has made a new man of me, I declare! Now, sir, to my errand. But before I proceed, just send out a tankard of your best to the coachman. The fellow's waiting for me and looks as dry as ashes.

"For some fifty years, Mr. Tunn, I've been a surgeon in His Majesty's Navy. For the moment I'm ashore, but London doesn't suit me. Damme, no! Portsmouth's the place for an old seaman, where he can cross tacks with shipmates now and again. At the Angel, in Town, the landlord told me that Will Tunn, of the Cheerful Tortoise, was the man for me. It's lodgings I'm after, with a well-found inn, like yours, sir, close at hand. Now then, do you know of a snug berth near by? My compliments once more!"

Tunn raised his glass with a pleased smile and pretended to reflect for a moment before he spoke. "I know the very place, sir. A quiet house, and kept by a decent woman, a Mrs. Quigg."

"I'm no ordinary lodger, Tunn. It's not every woman would put up with me. I might make a bit of a noise abovestairs, getting about on my larboard leg. Then, it's not easy to cook for me, and there'll be times I want to dine in. Not that I demand any fiddle-faddle fare. I'm an old seaman; I've been nourished, and well nourished, on pease, oatmeal, good salt beef, cheese, and such simple food, but I'll have it dressed as I want it, in the best old Navy fashion. Would this Mrs. . . . what's her name again? Quigg? — would she be the woman for my money?"

"The very one, Doctor Dogbody! Her husband was a warrant officer, and as choice a man about his victuals as ever I see. You could ransack Portsmouth from the waterside up without finding a woman with her knack for making a man comfortable."

"There's another thing. I'll have no bed. I must have my hammock battens made fast to the wall."

"No trouble about that, sir. Mrs. Quigg's lodged none but seamen since her house was opened."

"Then, Tunn, if you'll show me there, we'll board the coach." The surgeon fumbled in his waistcoat pocket and tossed a sovereign on the table. "Credit me with the balance of that," he said. "You've not seen the last of me, here."

"I trust not, sir, indeed," said the landlord in a pleased voice; then, taking his hat from a peg on the wall, he glanced from Tom Tapleke to the line of spigots with a look conveying a warning and a menace, and followed the surgeon out through the door.

*

The hour had gone six before Mr. Tunn again appeared in the taproom, entering from the kitchen with the air of a man who has dined well and is deeply content with the world. Two old patrons of the house came

in at this moment, and with a nod to the landlord went
to their customary corner at the left of the fireplace. The
first, Ned Balthus, was a burly man of middle stature,
dressed in a worn and weather-stained coat, with anchor-
buttons of silver, and wearing a wig of the kind called
"Grizzle Major." There was not a better old fellow in
Portsmouth, nor one with a kinder heart, but his face
was marked with the scar of a deep cutlass slash that
gave him a most forbidding frown. He had been a Navy
gunner for nearly half a century, and now, at the age of
retirement, some small employment had been found
for him at the Portsmouth Arsenal. His companion,
Mr. Ostiff, engraver of charts to the Admiralty, was a
tall spare man in middle life, whose small mouth, sharp
nose, and long upper lip gave him an air of solemnity
belied by a pair of nearsighted grey eyes with a twinkle
of mischief in them. As the drawer was attend-
ing to their wants, the landlord joined his two old
friends.

"Gad, Tunn," Mr. Ostiff remarked, drily. "You look as
though you'd come into a fortune."

"And so I have, Mr. Ostiff," said Tunn, taking a seat
at the end of the table, with a comfortable sigh. "I do
believe it! A landlord's fortune is the guests who choose
his house. I've had the luck to add one to-day, a rare
gentleman, if I'm a judge. If ye'll allow me to say so,
he'd make a companion to those of ye who favour this
corner."

"We'd best decide that for ourselves," said Ostiff, still
more drily.

"I'd be far from wishing to foist him amongst ye, Mr. Ostiff," Tunn replied; "and he'd be the last to permit it. But he's to lodge close by, at Mrs. Quigg's, and he's done me the honour to say the Tortoise will suit him well for his evenings."

"What name?"

"Doctor Dogbody."

Mr. Balthus set down his pot with a bang.

"Dogbody!" he exclaimed. "Not F. Dogbody?"

"There could be only the one, surely," said Ostiff. "You mean to say it's the man's true name?"

"Tunn, is it F. Dogbody?" Balthus repeated, eagerly.

"I'll not be certain as to that," said the landlord.

"One leg?"

"Aye. His left one's off above the knee."

The gunner brought his hand down on his thigh with a resounding smack. "Damn my eyes! He's here? In Portsmouth?"

"He was in this room not two hours gone. Ye know him, then, do ye, Mr. Balthus?"

"Know him!" said Balthus. "God's rabbit! Where's the old Navy man that don't know Doctor Dogbody? I'm astonished at the pair of ye who've not heard of him till this day. But there's this to be said: he's none of your half-pay surgeons. I'll warrant he's not spent six weeks ashore in a quarter of a century. A better-loved man never trod a ship's deck."

"How did he lose his leg?" asked Tunn.

Balthus sat back in his seat with a look of pleased recollection on his face. "Well may ye ask, Tunn! I've heard him tell the tale a dozen times if I've heard it once, and never twice the same."

"The man must be the very king of liars," said Ostiff, testily.

The gunner smiled. "Say ye so! I'll say naught. My belief is that *all* his tales are true! And mark ye this, Mr. Ostiff! If ever a man lost his leg in some strange way and survived the loss miracle-fashion, as ye might say, that man is Surgeon F. Dogbody. There's nothing humdrum about him. If he no more than spits to leeward he does it with an air of his own."

The door opened at this moment and another old patron of the Tortoise entered. Captain Thankful Runyon was a merchant from Boston, in America, who owned two Nantucket whaling vessels commanded by his sons. He was also half-owner of a vessel which plied chiefly between Boston and Portsmouth with sperm oil, for which the British Admiralty was an excellent customer. Captain Runyon, whose business it was to dispose of the oil, spent most of each year in Portsmouth, and, despite his being a Yankee, was well liked at the Tortoise. He was in his early sixties, rawboned, wiry, with a sunburned leathery face and neck. Although he had spent much of his life at sea, he was a man of excellent education, most of which he had acquired himself.

"Here's one will bear me out, I'll warrant," said Balthus, as Captain Runyon took his place amongst them. "Mr. Runyon, ye must have heard of one of our old Navy surgeons, F. Dogbody?"

"Never, Balthus, never," Runyon replied, in his curt manner. "Hot pot for me, Tom," he added to the drawer, who stood at his side. He turned again to the gunner. "Peabodys, yes; ye can raise three or four in a ten-minute walk anywhere in New England. I know a Fairbody or two, and one Angelbody in the West India trade. But a Dogbody or a Catbody it's not been my fortune to meet. Friend of yours, Balthus?"

"I'd wish him to think me one," the gunner replied, gravely, and the reproach implied by his manner was obvious.

"No offense, Balthus," Captain Runyon replied. "We've names on our side as odd as any of yours. My partner, in Boston, is Ralph Soilbibb, and well he lives up to the allegation. And the best friend I had in the world, in my younger days, was George Pigwart. Lost at sea, off Cape Horn, poor fellow! But what did ye wish to say of Surgeon Dogbody?"

"He's here, gentlemen!" Tunn put in, in a low voice. The street door swung open, admitting the surgeon himself, and a gust of damp air that made the lamps flicker for a moment. Balthus half rose from his seat, thought better of it, and dropped back once more. "Wait!" he cautioned the landlord. "Say naught!"

After a sweeping glance around the room, Doctor Dogbody was about to take a seat at a vacant table on the other side of the fireplace when Balthus roared out: "Clean sponges, damn your eyes, and be quick about it!" The surgeon stopped short, spun round on his peg, and brought down his bushy eyebrows as he peered through the dimly lighted room. Then he stumped across to the table, his blue eyes twinkling.

"Not Ned Balthus?" he exclaimed. "Not that corny-faced gunner of the old *Minerva?* Gentlemen, does the man call himself Balthus?"

"Aye, that he does!" said the gunner, heartily. The surgeon took him by the shoulders and held him at arm's length. "By God, Ned! I've mourned ye as dead these five years! D'ye mind Captain Farshingle, of the *Trent?* 'Twas him that told me. You were back on the West India station, he said, and went off with the yellow fever."

"He might well have heard it, Doctor," Balthus re-plied. " 'Twas a near thing. I was in the *Acteon* that year, and a good half of the ship's company left their bones in the cursed place. But let me make ye known to these gentlemen."

There was a gleam of honest triumph in the gunner's eyes as he noted the reception accorded the surgeon. That the others approved of him was plain, and it was Ostiff himself, hard to please in company, who invited him to take his place amongst them. The surgeon, sens-ing the sincerity of these overtures, needed no further urging.

"So ye've come ashore at last, Doctor?" Balthus asked, when the drawer had attended to the wants of the com-pany.

"Ashore? Damn my eyes! Who says it?" the surgeon replied, with a snort.

"I understood as much from the landlord here."

"Begging your pardon, sir, if I took your meaning wrong," Mr. Tunn put in, hastily. "I was telling these gentlemen ye'd honoured the Tortoise with a call this afternoon, and I'd the notion ye'd retired from the service."

"Temporarily, sir, but not for good. No, no! There's a score of years' use in me yet. But I won't say I'm not pleased with a bit of a holiday, now that old Boney is safely caged."

"And well ye might be, Doctor," said Balthus. "Ye've not been ashore long, then?"

"Six weeks, come next Thursday. I was paid off out of the *Bedford*. She's to be broken up."

Mr. Ostiff shook his head. "Many's the good ship will go that way now," he said. "I wish we may not live to regret them."

"As to that, sir, I'm of the same mind as yourself," said the surgeon. "It tears my heart to see them go. But since go they must, the Admiralty might better have scuttled 'em all, off soundings. The oldest and the least of them deserve a better fate than the breaking yard."

"Your Admiralty Board had fewer for that end at the close of the American War," said Runyon, with a sly grin.

"Pay no heed to this Pompkinshire Yankee, Doctor," said Ostiff. "By God's grace, the Americans managed to raise up one seaman amongst them — Paul Jones, and even he was born on this side. But Runyon will boast of him, in season and out. To hear him you'd think Paul Jones had destroyed the entire British Navy."

"I'll do them the honour to say they'd more than one of his mettle," the surgeon remarked.

"Handsomely admitted, sir!" said Runyon, warmly. "I've never had such an acknowledgment from Ostiff. You've met them at sea, I take it?"

"Aye; to both my pleasure and my sorrow."

Captain Runyon turned to Ostiff, with a triumphant smile.

"There, sir! The best of testimony for the defense!"

"For the defense?" said Ostiff. "Gad, sir, I like the way you put it! I'll leave it to Balthus, here, if you've ever taken a defensive position."

"He'll not acknowledge, Doctor Dogbody," said Runyon, "that an American ship of war ever came off best, in a battle against odds. There was the old *Protector,* for example. You may have heard of her?"

"The *Protector?* Captain John Foster Williams?"

"The same, sir! You knew her, then?"

"From truck to keelson," the surgeon replied, quietly. "Oddly enough, it was the *Protector* that cost me my leg."

"You don't tell me!" said Runyon, an expression of keen interest upon his face. "Would you be willing, sir, to favour us with the circumstances?"

"Quite, if these other gentlemen are of the same mind as yourself."

"We'd esteem it a privilege, Doctor Dogbody," said Ostiff, with a slight bow. Balthus stole a cautious glance at the surgeon, who was gazing before him with a grave, musing, abstracted expression.

"You'll mind, Ned," the surgeon began, with a glance at the gunner, "the first time we were on the West India station together, and *I* came so near to a taking-off with the cursed yellow jack?"

"Aye, well, sir," said Balthus, with an emphatic nod. "And how grieved we was at thought of leaving ye behind."

"I need say nothing of the two months that followed. I took what comfort the place afforded in the way of convalescence, and when recovered was appointed surgeon for the homeward voyage to a Company ship, the *Admiral Duff,* returning to England with a cargo of sugar and tobacco which we'd taken on at Saint Kitts. The *Duff* was a well-found ship. We had a crew of two hundred and fifty, and, for the weight of armament, thirty-six twelve-pounders on the gun deck. Her captain was Richard Strange — Mad Dick he was called behind his back, and well he deserved the name! But mind you, he was mad in the way of genius. His men worshiped him; it was a happy ship, and we'd not been a week at sea when I was perfectly recovered, and as content as an old Navy surgeon could be in a merchantman.

"Well, sir, Dick Strange thought no more of the valuable cargo he was taking to London than did his men. It was so much ballast, and his owners could whistle for it. He was a born fighter and I saw how matters stood before we'd lost the land. We were for prizes, so I spent my time with my loblolly boys preparing sponges, dressings, tourniquets, and the like, certain that we'd have use for a plenty before Dick Strange would consent to sail home.

"We took two Yankee brigs the first week and a third the week after, and sent all to Saint Kitts; then, b'gad, you'd have said the seas had been swept clean. Not a sail did we spy, though we were in the direct track of shipping up and down the Atlantic coast. We had dirty easterly weather and could scarce see a mile; even so we'd expected better luck than that.

"We got well north, and crept to within ten leagues of the American coast. On a morning in June, after a thick fog had cleared away — this was in 1780 — a sail was sighted to the eastward not two leagues off. We made sure he was a Yankee by the cut of his royals and were ready to eat him up. Damme, I had my share of the prize money already spent! But we had to reach him first, and there was not wind enough to lift a feather.

"In ten minutes we'd four boats out, towing. The men put their backs into it, but you'll know what headway they made with a thousand-ton ship. Nevertheless, we moved. Captain Strange was halfway up the mizzen ratlins, egging them on, one minute with his eye to his spyglass, the next, roaring out encouragement to the seamen. Then he made out that the Yankee was towing as well, and in our direction, so we felt easier. It was clear they wanted to engage.

"So it went for near an hour, but the breeze came at last. The Yankee had it first, and as soon as we spied their boats at the falls, in came ours. Being to windward, they edged down toward us, and it was a near thing but they'd have caught us without so much as steerageway, the breeze was that light. But the *Duff* felt it at last. Long before this we had the hammocks up and stuffed into the nettings, decks wet and sanded, matches lighted, and the bulkheads hooked up. They flew the English ensign, but Strange was not deceived by that. As we passed him, Strange called out, 'What ship is that?' The only reply was from their sailing master bawling out orders to his men. They steered to cross our stern and hauled up under our quarter. At that moment up went their true colours and their captain replied: 'Continental ship, *Protector!* Come on! We're ready for you!'

"B'gad, gentlemen, they were! But no more ready than ourselves. We'd caught a tartar, as we learned, directly we were abreast of him once more. He let go every gun on his starboard side, and every shot hulled us, I'll take my oath! The *Duff* was a higher ship, and our gunners were hard put to bring their guns to bear where they would do the most damage. But the noble fellows performed prodigies, and, for all the advantage of the Yankees, our fire was near as murderous as their own.

"The action began within easy pistol shot, and it was yardarm to yardarm from then on. We were fairly matched as to armament, but they had seventy marines amongst them whilst we had none, and seamen are no match for marines in the use of small arms. They killed our topmen as fast as we could replace them, and they'd not forgotten, the rascals, that there were fair targets, aft. But Dick Strange's quizzing-glass never dropped from his eye, save for an instant when the ribbon to it was cut by a musket ball. He caught the eyepiece before it could fall, twirled it carelessly by the bit of frayed ribbon, and replaced it just as our lads let go a broadside that might have taught them better manners.

"Aye, it was warm work, but the end of it was that they made a sieve of us from wind to water. Down came our foremast, then the main, and, b'gad, the mizzen followed! There was nothing left a yard high to hoist our colours on. The Yankee thought we'd struck and ceased firing. Little he knew Dick Strange. D'ye know what he did, sir?"

Doctor Dogbody paused and took up his glass. Finding it empty, he turned to the drawer, who was standing near by, forgetful of his duties while he listened. "Here, Tom, you rascal! I might positively die of thirst with you looking on!" Tapleke, galvanized into action by the abrupt summons, was away to the bar and back in an instant. The surgeon then resumed.

"Well, sir, Strange was fairly beside himself, though you'd not have guessed it by his manner. To have been thought to have struck was an insult so rank he could scarce bear it. He glanced coolly around the quarterdeck — the place was a shambles of the dead and dying — and his eye fell upon a lad standing near by. 'Fetch me a boat flag,' said Strange, 'and be quick about it!' The lad was back with one in twenty seconds. Strange fastened it to his cane, for he fancied his little stick even on shipboard. With this he sprung onto the bulwark and roared out to Williams: 'I've not struck, sir! Tell your bloody bang-straws to try and hit my stick!'

"Gentlemen, I give you my word: he stood there, holding that small flag aloft for a full ten minutes. But in the end, hit it they did. The shot from a carronade clipped off the stick within three inches of Strange's hand. Meanwhile, our three remaining guns continued to fire when they could be brought to bear, but without a rag of sail left you can imagine our situation.

"I and my assistants were at work on the orlop, but with the best will in the world we could not keep pace with the stream of shattered bleeding fellows that were carried or came crawling down to us. Aye, it was rawmeat day, one of the worst in my experience; the tubs were heaped high with arms and legs. Busy as we were at the bloody work, we'd no time to know what was taking place above us, and you can imagine my astonishment when one of the lieutenants came with orders to move all my wounded to the gun deck. We were sinking. It was the first intimation I'd had of the seriousness of our situation.

"Serious, do I say? Damme, it was hopeless, as I saw a moment after, but Dick Strange would not call it so. And there was that in his spirit to have made a ravening lion out of the veriest sheep in his ship's company, had there been any such, which there were not. By God, they fought like devils, even the lads of fourteen. The Yankee was right alongside, and we'd not carried above a dozen of our wounded up from the orlop when, even above the uproar overhead, we heard Strange bellow out: 'Boarders! Boarders! Every man on deck!'

"There was no more thought of the wounded then,

nor would they have wished us to think of them. My cutlass and pistols were in my cabin, and I seized the nearest weapon that came to hand, a tomahawk, and rallied with the others at the starboard bulwarks. There were not above a score of us left, but with Strange to lead us we felt equal to a gross of Yankees. He'd a pistol in one hand and a cutlass in the other, and his quizzing-glass with the frayed ribbon was still at his eye. I was pleased that he should have a word for me at such a moment, with the Yankee closing in, not twenty yards off. 'Dogbody,' said he, coolly, with a nod toward the *Protector,* 'we'll have a noggin of rum directly, in my cabin yonder.' And I've not the least doubt that he was perfectly convinced we should.

"There had been no time to get out our nettings, and the Yankees swarmed into us the moment they grappled. They were five to one, and the *Duff* had settled to such an extent that our bulwarks were now lower than their own. Two stout fellows were upon me at once, to their cost, if I may be permitted to say so. The third I did not see until too late, else I might have lost both legs in the place of one. I had my right foot raised and resting on a casing by the bulwark, when I felt a most peculiar numbing sensation in my left leg, and immediately fell back on my buttocks. As I did so I beheld my severed leg lying beside me, and a gigantic Indian, — he looked all of eight feet high, although I later found he was but six feet six, — who by this time had rushed by me, drawing back his cutlass for a swing at the man beyond. Him he fairly cut in two, at one ferocious blow.

"I spare you the details. It is enough to say that we were taken, but the Americans had little good of their prize. There was no surrender. We sunk under their very feet, not five minutes after they had boarded. Strange went down with his ship, by a miracle unwounded, but he was not one to suffer the humiliation of capture. Lacking his delicacy of feeling in this respect, I seized the first floating object I could get my hands upon in the swirl of waters that closed over the *Duff*. Fortunately, I had had the presence of mind, after my leg was off, to tie up the femoral artery with a bit of marline, and had then plunged the stump into a bucket of tar, else I should have died before I could be taken up. As it was, I'd lost a deal of blood by the time I was laid amongst the wounded, both ours and theirs, aboard the *Protector*.

"Their surgeons were working at top speed, but with so many to be served, they were obliged to choose those most likely to live. Two of their dressers were about to take up a fellow, one of their own men, lying beside me, but the surgeon said, 'Let Little lie. Attend to the others first. He will die.' Indeed, he might well have thought so, for the poor fellow had been horribly wounded in the face by a charge of grape. I rose on my elbow and turned to look at him. The man was perfectly sensible, and I saw that within his eye which gave me a most vivid impression of indomitable courage. It was curious: as our glances met, something passed between us — complete sympathy, mutual respect, and I was convinced not only that the man would not die, but that I could learn to love him like a brother.

"My professional interest in his case was immediately aroused. I have a brusque way with me in my capacity as surgeon, and in an instant I had one of their dressers fetching for me. He brought me a basin of water, sponges and lint, and, managing to raise myself to a sitting position, I proceeded to dress Little's wounds. Strangely enough, I then felt no sensation of pain in my severed leg, and suffered but little inconvenience from it.

"Little had been wounded by three balls: one between the neck bone and windpipe, one through the jaw, lodging in the roof of his mouth and taking off a piece of his tongue, and the third through the lip, which had destroyed nearly all of his upper teeth. I worked over him for an hour, removed the lodged ball, cleansed the wounds, sewed up his lip, and staunched the flow of blood. The event of it was that he perfectly recovered."

Doctor Dogbody rose abruptly. "I ask you leave for one moment, gentlemen," he said; then, turning to Tapleke: "Tom, your necessary-house."

"This way, sir," said the drawer, leading him toward a passageway to the left, and the surgeon followed him out with great dignity.

Mr. Ostiff looked after him with a faint smile, in which puzzlement and admiration were mingled.

"Balthus," said he, "I can scarcely believe our friend to be the liar you've pictured him."

"A liar!" said Runyon. "The tale has the very stamp of truth upon it! Some of the details are inexact, but I've often heard, at home, of the fight between the *Protector* and the *Duff,* and I'll take my oath that the latter was conquered as the surgeon has related the circumstances. What's this, Balthus?"

"I said naught of his being a liar," Balthus replied, warmly. "What I did say was that I've heard him tell the tale of his lost leg a dozen times, and never twice . . ." He broke off, for the surgeon was again approaching. Captain Runyon waited with impatience for him to be seated.

"Sir," he said, "the man whose wounds you dressed could have been no other than Captain Luther Little."

"So it was, sir," said Dogbody, "though he was not a captain at this time. He was a young man on the *Protector* and served in her as midshipman and prize-master. An older brother, George Little, was a lieutenant in the same vessel. They belong to a family, Little in name only, from the town of Marshfield, in the Massachusetts colony."

"I've no doubt that you became excellent friends, after such a meeting?" said Runyon.

"The very best, sir. Mr. Luther Little was considerably my junior, but the small service I was able to render him whilst wounded, combined, as I have said, with something compatible in our natures, served to draw us together upon terms of sincere liking and deep understanding. His elder brother, George, became no less my friend. For the next eight months I was a guest in the Little home. I was, to be sure, a prisoner-of-war, but not the least restraint was put upon my liberty, nor upon my sentiments as a loyal Englishman. And I came to understand the sentiments of our late colonists better, perhaps, than many an Englishman who has never had occasion to live amongst them. They are an admirable nation, and I have little doubt will be a great one in the course of time. It could scarcely be otherwise when one considers the stock from which they sprung."

The surgeon paused to give Captain Runyon a keen glance. "You are acquainted with the Littles, sir?" he asked.

"I have not that honour," Runyon replied, "although I have more than once passed through the town of Marshfield. The place was as famous at one time for a gigantic Indian follower of the Little boys as for the family itself."

"Of the name of Powana?" the surgeon asked.

"Bless my soul! The very same! . . . Jehoshaphat! Could it have been . . ."

"Yes, sir. It could have been, and was, Powana who deprived me of my leg, and a cleaner blow was never given with a cutlass. I could not have made a better amputation at leisure, with my saws and razors, than was done by the Indian before I could have said 'Oh!' His name, Powana, signifies 'whale' in the Natick tongue, and a whale he was in stature. He carried me about like an infant at Marshfield, whilst my stump was healing, and when it had healed he made me a very serviceable wooden leg to replace that he had taken."

"Is it the one you are wearing, Doctor?" Will Tunn asked.

"No, Mr. Tunn, it is not. Curiously enough, Powana's leg was to serve me but a short time, as I shall explain

in a moment. . . . Nine months, almost to a day, from
the time of our first meeting, Little and I were again at
sea, though not, to be sure, as companions-in-arms. He
was now in virtual command of the letter-of-marque brig
Jupiter, carrying twenty-one guns and one hundred and
fifty men. I say in virtual command, for the owner and
nominal captain was a merchant of the town of Salem,
in Massachusetts, a man of the name of Gorme. My
status was still that of a prisoner-of-war. Little had gone
bail for me to the American authorities, and whilst he
would have liked nothing better than to release me, that
he was in honour bound not to do until I could be exchanged for some American prisoner of my own rank.
He meant to arrange for this at sea, at the first opportunity.

"We cruised for a full three weeks, in a southerly direction, without any particulars worthy of mention, but
I am bound to say that this result was due to the exces-
sive timidity of Captain Gorme. We often sighted English vessels, whereupon Gorme would examine them
through his spyglass with the fluttery apprehension of
an old woman, and would not allow Little to approach
nearer than two leagues. His mouth watered for prizes,
but he could not bring himself to take the least risk in
obtaining them.

"One morning whilst crossing the Gulf Stream not far
off the American coast, we sighted an object a mile or so
distant to leeward which Gorme, for once, was willing to
approach for a nearer view. There was a light breeze
from the northeast, and a curious popple, due perhaps

to the action of the Gulf Stream itself. We soon made out the object to be a floating log of considerable size, and clinging to it were three men whom we first took to be Indians. They were dressed in skins resembling that of the raccoon, though there were but three rings on the tail instead of five. Their hair was long, straight and black, like that of the Iroquois, but strangely enough their eyes were of the deepest blue, and their skins almost as light as those of Englishmen. They were nearly dead when picked up, and in spite of my ministrations and those of my Yankee colleague on the *Jupiter,* they lived but a few days. Powana, who was, of course, on board, was unable to exchange a word with them, either in the Natick tongue or in any of the other Indian dialects with which he was familiar. But, astounding as it may seem, a Welsh quartermaster discovered that they spoke a language closely akin to his own. To the great loss of science, they died before he was able to learn whence they came.

"But what I wished to say was that we took on board the log as well as the Indians, if such they were, who had clung to it, for Captain Gorme hoped that it might be useful for spars. We found it to be of a nature as strange as the mysterious castaways. No one on board could identify the wood. The heartwood was almost as hard as iron, and yet it could be worked. When sawn, its peculiar fragrance attracted clouds of butterflies from the main; they appeared in countless thousands, so that, for some days, the ship could scarcely be navigated. I discovered, later, that this heartwood sank like lead in the water, and, strangest of all perhaps, it was impervious to the teredo worm, the ruination of our ships in warm seas.

"The log, though useless for spars, was a valuable find, and Captain Gorme was beside himself with vexation that he had not been able to learn, from the Indians, whence it came. From a morsel of the heartwood, Mr. Colbarch, the ship's carpenter, fashioned me a leg to replace the temporary one made by Powana, and a more comfortable, serviceable peg, once I was accustomed to it, I have never had the pleasure of wearing. It is the one I have on at the moment.

"We proceeded on our voyage, and, as the days passed, my friend Little and the entire ship's company became more and more impatient with their fainthearted captain. At last the captain himself, finding himself incapable of making a resolute decision, placed Little in command. Thereafter, Gorme kept to his cabin. As the event proved, he had not long to keep it.

"The following morning, at dawn, we sighted a schooner which showed no colours, though Little was convinced, as well as myself, that she was English. 'Dogbody,' said he, 'if she proves to be such, and has American prisoners on board, you shall be exchanged immediately.' He then ran up a signal of a parley and we bore down on the vessel. As we approached, we made her out to be a smart little privateer of eighteen guns. I went to my cabin to prepare for quitting the *Jupiter,* and whilst there, I heard the parley which followed.

" 'What ship is that?' Little roared through his speaking trumpet.

" '*Lion*, of London,' came the reply, so clearly that, though I could not see the schooner, I knew that she was right alongside. 'Who are you?'

" '*Jupiter*, of Salem,' Little replied. 'Have you prisoners to exchange?'

" 'That's as may be,' replied the British captain. 'What d'ye offer?'

" 'A one-legged surgeon,' said Little, 'and better with one than any you've got with two.'

" 'A sawbones? What name?'

" 'Dogbody.'

" 'Dogbody!' came the reply. 'Ye don't mean F. Dogbody, late of the *Duff*?'

" 'Aye, the same,' said Little.

" 'You mean ye've got him there, on board?'

" 'Aye,' said Little, 'all but his larboard leg.'

" 'By God, sir,' said the British captain, 'for Dogbody I'll give ye two Yankee lieutenants, a boatswain, a gunner and a gunner's mate, three quartermasters, and a half-dozen reefers for a makeweight. Will ye trade?'

" 'Send 'em across. He's yours,' said Little, and within the quarter-hour the boatload of Yankee prisoners came on board, the *Lion's* captain with them. I knew him well. We'd served together three years earlier in the *Lowestoffe*, frigate, under Captain William Locker. His name was Irons, and he had been a lieutenant in the *Lowestoffe*.

" 'Dogbody,' said he, clasping my hand warmly, 'I hate to buy ye home at so cheap a rate, but these' — with a nod toward his prisoners — 'are all I have on hand at the moment. I sent threescore off, a fortnight since, in one of my prizes. Well, sir,' he added, turning to Little, 'for once I've got the best of a Yankee in a trade, but a bargain's a bargain, as your countrymen say.'

"He had a provoking way with him, did Irons. He was tough as an old lanyard knot, and, fine seaman that he was, I regret to say that he had no delicacy of feeling. Indeed, he had a deep respect for the seagoing American, but he took pleasure in showing the contrary.

"Little nodded, with a grim smile. 'I'm content,' said he. He then clasped my hand. 'Good-bye, Dogbody, and God bless you!'

" 'Little,' said I, 'I would not have believed that a prisoner-of-war could ever leave the hands of his captors with any degree of reluctance, but so it is in my case. I respect you as a man, sir, and, if you will permit me to say so, esteem you as a friend.'

" 'Then why leave him, Dogbody?' said Irons. 'Shall we take his little ship with us?'

"Little's eyes blazed. 'By God, sir! Will ye fight?' he asked.

"Irons, who was a short thickset man, bristled up like a bulldog. 'Have ye ever met an Englishman that wouldn't?' said he.

" 'Then get ye gone to your vessel,' said Little, 'for ye've not long to command her.'

"Captain Gorme, who had come out of his cabin meanwhile, stood by, pressing his hands together with an expression of perfect anguish on his face, but Little paid no heed to him. The *Jupiter* buzzed like a nest of hornets before we were down the side. 'Irons,' said I, as we were being rowed across to the *Lion,* 'you've a wild-cat by the tail this time.' 'Never ye mind, Dogbody,' said he. 'I'll have him by the throat, directly.' He was silent for a moment, then he added: 'I must make him strike within the half-hour, for I'm damned short of ball.'

"And, b'gad, gentlemen, we did! 'Twas a miracle, no less, for we deserved to have been taken. Irons had told the plain truth: he'd powder a plenty, but only sufficient ball for six charges for each of his guns. But the man was a veritable firebrand and would have used his own head for ammunition had it been necessary. We were overmatched, both as to men and guns, but the *Lion* had a picked crew and was a worthy foe for a ship twice her size. I've never seen a vessel better handled; every shot from our guns went home. The *Jupiter's* mainmast went over the side in the first five minutes of the action, and the mizzen followed shortly; and whilst the *Lion* re-ceived her share of punishment, she'd lost nothing in her sails. Little performed prodigies with his disabled ship. He was tearing to board, but we kept clear. Damme, I was more than glad, for I could see Powana towering above the *Jupiter's* bulwark, and I knew he'd as soon cut off my other leg as look at me. What cost them the victory was, past question, the cowardice of Gorme. He was for running away, and gave orders counter to those of Little, which confused the Yankee seamen. But hav-ing shot and to spare, they poured them into us at an appalling rate. More than half our company was either dead or wounded.

"I'd removed my wooden peg directly upon boarding the *Lion,* for the stump of the limb was still tender. I could not bear the heavy peg for long at a time, and so would make shift, for an hour or two, with a crutch. Fortunate it was that I did so on this occasion, for it was the indirect means of victory.

"The *Lion's* gunners had fired their last broadside, and a murderous one it was, but we'd not a ball left. One shot had all but shattered their foremast, and Irons was dancing round our quarter-deck shouting, 'Fall, blast ye! Fall!' At this moment the gunner came aft; he was dripping with sweat and breathing heavily. 'Sir,' said he to Irons, 'we've fired our last shot.' 'What's that to me?' Irons bellowed at him. 'Get back to your guns! Use marlinspikes! Get back to your guns, damn your blood! Use deadeyes, chain plates! Get back to your guns, I say!'

"And, b'gad, gentlemen, he did! All the rusty raffle in the ship went into the guns and on to the *Jupiter,* and with it my new peg which might well be classed as hardware. One of the gunners, seeing it resting by the bulwark, seized upon it and rammed it down the muzzle of his piece amongst iron spoons, bolts, nuts, and fragments of brick prized up from the galley floor. I was told afterward, upon unimpeachable authority, for I was, of course, then at my own bloody work below, that it was my leg that cost the Yankees the day. It caromed off the *Jupiter's* tottering foremast and then struck my friend Little a glancing blow on the head, which, thank God, only knocked him unconscious. The other oddments of the charge worked great havoc as well, amongst the ship's company, and Gorme, who was then forced to take command, immediately struck his colours."

Doctor Dogbody broke off, refreshed himself at his glass, and touched his lips with a richly coloured silk bandana.

"And what then, sir?" Will Tunn inquired, when it seemed apparent that the surgeon had no intention of proceeding.

"What then, Will Tunn? Why, nothing then. What more could there be save that, when we had made temporary repairs on the two ships, we carried our prize to the West Indies? It was a sad blow for Little, but he took it like the man he was, and whilst he must have despised Gorme with all the strength of his being, no word of censure crossed his lips. I was not surprised, later, when Gorme jumped his parole. Little refused to give his. Despite my protestations, he insisted on being put aboard the *Regulus,* a dismantled seventy-four, moored in the harbour of Saint Kitts, and used to confine prisoners-of-war. 'Never fear, Dogbody,' said he. 'I shall not remain long aboard of her, and I refuse that you should be compromised by my escape.' Two days later, when I went aboard the *Regulus* to visit him and to bring him some delicacies from shore, he was gone, and Powana with him. I have never heard of either of them from that day to this."

"It is my pleasure, sir," said Runyon, "to tell you that he is still living, and an honoured citizen of the town of Marshfield. Powana, as well, survives."

"I am profoundly glad to hear it, sir," the surgeon replied.

"You have said, Doctor Dogbody," Ostiff put in, "that the strange wood of which your peg was made was impervious to the teredo worm. How could you be certain of that?"

"It was a piece of good fortune for me, sir, that the peg was not lost when fired into the *Jupiter*. After wounding Little, it struck the bulwark, and the smaller end penetrated four inches into the oak. Captain Irons recovered it for me when he went on board to receive the ship. Some months later, whilst we were lying at Port Royal, in Jamaica, I lost the leg overboard, having unstrapped it, as my custom then was of an evening, to rest my stump. I offered a hogshead of the finest rum the island produced to the man who could fetch it up. During the next fortnight, scores of negroes attempted to secure it, and one poor fellow was taken by the sharks. I immediately withdrew the reward and ordered that no further search should be made. Imagine my surprise, six months later, upon returning from Barbadoes, to find that one persevering fellow had dived it up! He was a veritable sea otter, else he could never have reached bottom at such a depth. Needless to say, I rewarded him handsomely. The peg was as good as upon the day I'd lost it; not the mark of a worm appeared upon it. It was like meeting an old friend to strap it on once more, and my stump being perfectly hardened by that time, I never again exposed myself to the risk of losing it. . . . Bless me, Tunn! What's this?"

A great commotion was heard in the kitchen, and a few seconds later a huge black rat came running into the taproom, followed by Hodge, the dwarflike waiter, Bilges the kitchen boy, and several others, all in a mad chase after the rodent. Doctor Dogbody, who had already donned his hat and coat in preparation for going home, skipped across the taproom with the agility of a boy, and, with a dexterous side blow with his wooden leg, caught the rat fairly in the middle and sent it hurtling through the air against the tavern wall, where it fell lifeless. Then, with a slight bow, "Gentlemen," he said, "I bid you good evening," and a moment later the door closed behind him.

II

THE SILVER BUCKLE

DOCTOR DOGBODY, entering the taproom of the Tortoise
on a wet, blustery evening early in November, paused
at the doorway to survey the comfortable scene before
him. A fire of splintered oak beams was blazing on the
great hearth, the light flickering upon the walls and casting grotesque shadows of tables and settles across the
floor. The place was empty save for half-a-dozen seamen,
warrant officers, who sat in a far corner, and Tom Tapleke, the drawer, drowsing on a high stool behind the
bar. The latter looked up at the surgeon's entrance, and,
taking a cone-shaped Venetian glass from a shelf behind

him, filled it at a small cask and carried it to the table
to the left of the fireplace.

"Thankee, Tom," said Dogbody, as he removed his
hat and coat. "Take these to the kitchen to dry. There's
half a hogshead of rain soaked into 'em, I'll be bound."

"Ye'd best be furnished with one of the umbrella
things, sir, that's comin' into use so fast," said Tapleke,
with a grin. "I've heard say they'll shed a mort o' water."

"An umbrella!" said Dogbody, with a snort. "Be off
with you, trapsticks, and mind you don't roast my coat!
. . . Pawl there! Mr. Balthus is coming. You can take
his at the same time."

The surgeon seated himself with a grunt of pleasure,
held his glass to the light for a moment, and took a
generous swallow. "What cheer, Ned?" he remarked, as
the gunner handed his own dripping coat to the drawer
and took a seat at the opposite side of the table. "God
bless me!" he added, with an admiring smile. "A fine
figure ye make in your best band and bib!"

The gunner glanced down apologetically at his coat
of blue broadcloth with its gold anchor-buttons and the
wide expanse of white silk waistcoat beneath.

"Thought I'd best wear it," he said. He shook his head
uneasily. "I wish the evening was well over."

"Over! A man loving good company and good cheer
as you do, wishing it was past and done with? Here's the
best part of it, to my notion: us sitting by a good fire,
with the whole of it before us."

"Aye, if it was us to ourselves, Doctor, with a two-three
of old cronies alongside," said Balthus. "But to draw up

to meat with an admiral at one end of the table . . ."
He shook his head once more. "I can't think what Mr.
Ostiff was about, to ask me."

"Tut, man! An admiral's naught but a fellow creature: flesh and blood like ourselves."

"Flesh and blood! Sir Nicholas Trecothick? Ye've
never served under him, Doctor Dogbody. I have. He's
known as Old Nick in the service. Flesh and blood? Aye,
if fire and brimstone can be called such!"

"He'll be wearing his land face, take my word for it,
Ned. Taut hand that he is, at sea, I've heard say there's
no better company on shore than this same Old Nick of
yours. Ostiff himself says so, and he knows him well."

"Mebbe so," said the gunner, doubtfully. "For all that,
I wish he was come and gone."

"We'll survive; I'll go bail for it." The surgeon rose.
"Let's step into the kitchen before they come. My mouth
waters to see what Will Tunn's got on his spits."

The scene in the great kitchen was of the liveliest
description. The landlord came forward at once at sight
of the surgeon, wiping his damp face with a napkin.

"Will Tunn, a fairer sight than what I see here could
not be found this night in the whole of England. There's
a noble bird on spit, yonder."

"Ye may well say so, Doctor," Tunn replied, with a
pleased smile. "The country was scoured for it, and I
chose it from scores that was offered."

"And what's to come before and after?"

"Well, sir, there's oysters to begin. Then I've half-a-
dozen fat grilse, baked, and basted with egg sauce. The

roast turkey's to follow, stuffed with minced veal, ham, and chestnuts, well spiced and seasoned, and roast potatoes to go with the fowl. As for the joint, ye'll agree, Doctor, that ye never set teeth into better-flavoured meat, and that tender 'twill part at the least touch of the knife. There's a bean tansey to come with the beef, for Mr. Ostiff told me Sir Nicholas Trecothick is very partial to it."

"A bean tansey? Better and better," said Dogbody. "The admiral's not alone there. But there's more than one way of making a tansey."

"Aye, so there is," said the landlord, "and the best is this, to my notion: first, you bruise your beans and season with pepper, salt, cloves, and mace. Then you mix in well the yolk of six eggs and a quarter of a pound of butter, and put all into a deep dish on layers of well-streaked bacon, sliced as thin as a sharp knife can do it. This you bake, and when . . ."

"Say no more, Tunn," said the surgeon. "My belly yearns for it! Ned, ye might face the Lord High Admiral himself for such a feast as we're to have."

"Aye," said the gunner, "but it grieves me to think I can't relish it as I'd like with Old Nick not three paces to windward."

"Ye've not heard me through, Doctor," said Tunn. "There's the pasties and puddings . . ."

"Let them come *when* they come, Will Tunn," the surgeon interrupted. "I can scarce bear the mere report at the moment, empty as I am. . . . No more! You'll have us eating the roasts off the spits."

The two friends returned to the taproom, and Balthus stopped short at the entrance. "God's rabbit! He's here!" he exclaimed, under his breath. Mr. Ostiff, Captain Runyon, and Sir Nicholas Trecothick, Vice-Admiral of the Blue, were standing in conversation in front of the fireplace. The admiral was a man of sixty, tall and solidly made, with a carriage so erect that he gave the impression of leaning slightly over backward. His voice was loud and hearty, and his hawklike nose and rather prominent blue eyes gave him something of a predacious look. His complexion, of a deep claret colour, seemed to take on a richer hue from the firelight which played upon his face. He was dressed in a blue coat with white facings, none too clean, ornamented with tarnished gold braid, and his lemon-coloured waistcoat and breeches, dingy with long use, contrasted strangely with those of the immaculate Ostiff.

The latter made haste to present the surgeon and gunner to his distinguished guest, who greeted them in a manner so free from any hint of arrogance or formality that the astonished Balthus could do no more than mumble a scarcely audible, "I'm proud, sir," and he gazed in mute awe at the surgeon, who was as much at ease as the admiral himself.

"Surgeon Dogbody, Mr. Balthus," said Trecothick, "here we are, three old Navy men, toasting our carcasses at a fire of ship's timbers. Like enough we've trod the decks of those same ships, times without number."

"I'll take my oath we have, sir," Dogbody replied. "That length of worm-eaten strake yonder," with a nod toward the fireplace, "could have come from no ship save the old *Bedford*."

"Damme if I don't think you're right, sir," the admiral replied, with a hearty chuckle. "Rotten as she was, at the last, it passes belief that the *Bedford* could have been kept afloat to reach the breaking yard. But a noble ship she was, in her time."

"Shall we sit, Sir Nicholas?" Ostiff asked. "We've time for a whet before dinner."

"By all means!" said the admiral. "Mr. Ostiff, it does me good to have a run ashore now and again, where there's no need to stand on my dignity. A dog's life we lead, aft, and no mistake."

Of a sudden his eyes blazed with a baleful light, and there passed over his face an expression of such concentrated ferocity that Balthus all but dropped his mug. "But, by God, sir, it's necessary that we should!" Sir Nicholas added, glaring from one to another of them. "The service requires it!" Immediately he resumed his easy affable manner, the abrupt change being as startling to the gunner as the first had been.

Tom Tapleke shuffled in from the kitchen with a platter of sliced roasted turkey's gizzard, rubbed with cayenne pepper, which he placed upon the table.

"Ostiff, did you order this for me?" the admiral asked, with a pleased smile.

"I would have, Sir Nicholas, but it chances to be a specialty of the house," Ostiff replied.

"And an excellent one, from every point of view," said Trecothick, chewing with an expression of rapt virtuosity on his face. "A better thirst-provoker has yet to be found. Not that I've ever needed one," he added, with a smile.

Will Tunn now appeared in the doorway, his face scrubbed and polished and a fresh blue apron covering the broad expanse of chest and belly. "Dinner is ready, gentlemen," he announced, "if ye'll please to step upstairs."

Admiral Trecothick drained his glass and rose with alacrity, followed by the others. "We'll not say nay to that, landlord," he said, heartily. "My guts was beginning to think my throat was cut."

"I trust they'll make ye a better report, sir, afore the evening's over," said Tunn. "Asking your pardon, gentlemen."

Gazing proudly to right and left as he crossed the now well-filled taproom, the landlord led the way up the staircase to the first floor, and, standing by the door, bowed his guests into the dining room, where Hodge, the tiny waiter, and his assistants, had already put wine and oysters on the table. The admiral took his seat at one end of the board and Mr. Ostiff at the other. Doctor Dogbody was seated at the admiral's right, with Balthus and Runyon opposite. Balthus, to his great relief, soon discovered that little was required of him in the way of conversation. A lively exchange was kept up amongst the others. The wine was as excellent as the food, and as generously supplied, and before the meal was half over all were in the mellowest mood; even the gunner had, by this time, overcome a little of his awe before the distinguished guest. At

length, when all had eaten to more than comfortable re-
pletion, the cloth was removed, the port brought up, and
nuts and raisins set upon the table. Healths were then
drunk to the King and the Fleet, and Mr. Ostiff next pro-
posed the admiral, who returned the compliment. Sir
Nicholas, filling his glass once more, then turned to the
surgeon.

"Dogbody, your health, sir! Your name is known
throughout the service. It is only fair to add, and favour-
ably known."

"It is handsome of you to say so, Sir Nicholas," said the
surgeon, with a gracious bow.

"You've never served under me, I believe?" said the admiral, wiping his lips.

"I've not had that honour, sir, though, oddly enough,
I came as near to it as may be, in 'ninety-seven."

"Near to it? How is that, sir?"

"You force me to a personal reference, Sir Nicholas.
You may have observed that I am shy a larboard leg?"

"I have, sir."

"Well, sir, curious as it may seem, had I joined your
squadron in the winter of 'ninety-seven, which unfore-
seen circumstances alone prevented, the leg would not
have been lost."

Admiral Trecothick, who was in the midst of a gulp of
wine at this moment, choked, sputtered, set down his
glass hastily, and seized his napkin just in time to prevent a shower of aerated port from deluging Mr. Ostiff,
at the other end of the table.

"Damn my eyes, Dogbody!" he gasped, when he could

speak again. "I've seen arms, legs, hands, feet, and other human appendages go over the sides of my ships by the tubful, times without number, during action; but this is the first I've heard of a man losing a limb because he had *not* served under me. Explain yourself."

"The story is a long one, Sir Nicholas, for the leg is attached at the very end of the chain of circumstances I spoke of. I would not wish to weary you with it upon this occasion," the surgeon replied.

"Come, I'll have it, chain and all! Every link! Rot me! What should old seamen do in company but listen to one another's yarns? We'll have it, shall we not, Mr. Ostiff? But you've heard it, perhaps?"

"Never, sir," Ostiff replied, promptly. He exchanged glances with Runyon, while Ned Balthus stared gravely at the opposite wall, his brown hands clasped lightly around a mighty beaker of port.

"Then, Surgeon, no excuses," the admiral replied, brusquely. "Draw that leg in to me at the end of whatever length of chain. But first tell me when you lost it."

"I began to lose it, if I may so speak," said the surgeon, "on the fourteenth of February, 1797 . . ."

Admiral Trecothick sputtered once more. "*Began* to lose it?" he asked. "There *was* a leg, that lost itself by degrees! But forgive me, Surgeon. I'll not interrupt again."

"Curiously enough," the doctor proceeded, "the statement is one of simple fact; for, had I but known it, my leg was as good as off on that very fourteenth of February, though it was then attached to me as solidly as its fellow. I need not remind you, Sir Nicholas, of the glorious victory that date commemorates."

"I should think not, indeed," the admiral remarked, drily. "The battle of Saint Vincent. It was my accursed luck to have been in the mid-Atlantic at the time. Proceed, sir."

"I was serving in the *Excellent,* Captain Collingwood. As you will recollect, the *Excellent* performed the greatest service during the engagement by extricating Nelson, in the *Captain,* from a devilish bad situation. The *Captain* was being fired into, at this time, by no less than three first-rates, in addition to the *San Nicolas* and a seventy-four. But no more of this. It is enough to say that we saved Nelson, and, as might have been expected from so noble a man, he gave us the credit which was our due.

"At the close of the battle I was transferred to the *Raven,* Captain Starte, which was ordered home with wounded. We had some three hundred poor fellows on board, and you will understand that I had my hands full until we anchored at Deptford, where the wounded were disembarked and a strict guard put upon the *Raven,* none of her company, save a detachment of marines under a captain, being permitted to remain aboard of her. The reason was that we had brought home with us, besides wounded, some four thousand ounces of platina, a metal of the colour of silver, and about one eighth heavier than gold, which had been taken from one of our Spanish prizes. This metal had never before been seen in Europe outside of Spain, where it was consigned to the Crown from some of her South American colonies. It was said to be worth no less than thirty pounds the ounce."

"Thirty pounds the ounce!" Admiral Trecothick put in. "Damme, sir! What ship took it?"

"Ours, sir, the *Excellent,* although the matter was kept in the strictest secrecy at the time. I was privy to it, as it chanced, Captain Collingwood himself, of course, and no other save Admiral Sir John Jervis. The treasure was taken in charge by the Admiralty, and the decision of the Prize Court, which sat upon it, was delayed because of the difficulty of estimating the true value of the platina.

"Meanwhile, I had come ashore with but ten pounds in my pocket, which I lost in a night at Boodle's Club. In a night, do I say? Damme, in the fiftieth part of a night! In less than five minutes I was cleaned out. The play at Boodle's is said to be less ruinous than at Brooke's or White's, but, b'gad, *I* found it ruinous enough! I had gone there with Captain Starte, and the pair of us came away without sixpence between us.

"I might easily have borrowed a sum sufficient for my immediate needs, but this I would not do. I have always made it a practice to be in no man's debt — no, not for a farthing. Except to tailors, who are not to be classed as human. Astounding as it may seem, it was one of these bloodsuckers that cost me my leg.

"The *Raven* being the first ship home, after Saint Vincent, His Majesty had expressed, through the Board of Admiralty, the desire to meet and converse with some of her officers. Captain Starte, two of his lieutenants, and three warrant officers, myself amongst them, were commanded to an audience.

"You will understand, sir, the greatness of this occasion to an obscure surgeon in His Majesty's Navy, and, as well, my profound chagrin at being without funds at such a time. Nevertheless, I went at once to a tailor for a costume suitable to the occasion. I resolved not to stint myself in the matter of expense, though not, of course, to dress above my station. I was measured for a handsome coat, full mounted, of cut velvet, trimmed with silver lace, and with silver buttons and bindings, a waistcoat of blue satin, embroidered with silver, breeches, also of blue satin, a pair of white silk hose, and two fine Holland shirts and neckcloths. My hat, while plain, was elegant, and my shoes had silver buckles rather than gold, to carry out the modest general effect. Oddly enough, one of those buckles I still have. I am wearing it at this moment."

The surgeon paused to take a generous sip of port.

"Damn your eyes, sir! 'Twas a gay rig for a ship's surgeon," Admiral Trecothick remarked. "It must have cost you a pretty penny."

"Fifty guineas, sir, eleven shillings, ninepence ha'penny, though the true value was no more than half that, if as much. I was indignant upon receiving the bill, though there was naught I could do. In my impoverished condition I could not, of course, pay it, but gave my note for it in thirty days, fully expecting to have my share of the Saint Vincent prize-money by that time.

"I will now, sir, pass over those thirty days. The audience with His Majesty was, for some reason, put off, so that my note to the rascally tailor was due a good fortnight before the final date set for our appearance at Whitehall. Meanwhile, Sir Nicholas, I received orders to join one of the ships of your squadron, though I was not to proceed thither until the day following the audience with the King. Nor could I receive the back pay due me until I joined my ship, so that I had not one penny to rub against the other on the morning when we were to appear before His Majesty. Therefore, I was constrained to walk in all my finery through muddy streets, in a drizzling rain, to the place of our assembly.

"I had not gone far when, to my amazement and indignation, I was set upon by two Robin Redbreasts, accompanied by my tailor, an insect of the name of Chizbeak."

"Robin Redbreasts? What may they be, Doctor?" Captain Runyon inquired.

"You mean to say that you are not cursed with the tribe in America?" said the surgeon. "They are Bow Street runners, sir — constables, and it was a pair of these ruffians that attempted to seize my person for the debt owed to the tailor. Needless to say, I resisted stoutly, and I had the satisfaction to knock the rat, Chizbeak, into the gutter, with such force that he lay there, stunned. Whilst the pair of runners were picking him up, by good fortune a hackney coach came by, driven by as odd a little creature as might have been found in the confines of London. He was no taller than Hodgepodge, there."

The surgeon nodded toward Hodge, the waiter, who was standing by the wall: a tiny man of uncertain age, whose alert, cheerful face and raised eyebrows gave him an expression of perpetual astonishment. His large bald head, vastly out of proportion to his diminutive body, was covered with a moth-eaten wig, three sizes too big for him, and he was continually adjusting it as he served at table.

"Hodgepodge, how tall are you?" Dogbody inquired.

"Fower fut two, sir," Hodge replied, in a husky whisper.

"Quite so," the surgeon resumed. "Well, this hackney coachman was much of a size with Hodgepodge, and curiously like him, now that I think of it, though a much younger man. He took in the situation at a glance, drew up his lean horse with a jerk, and with a wink and a nod invited me to enter. A friend in need he was, though I owe to him the loss of as good a larboard leg as ever followed its fellow across the threshold of an inn. Chizbeak and the constables lost no time in taking up the pursuit. They hailed another hackney coach and followed in hot haste, but my little fellow was worth a dozen of theirs. Never have I seen a coachman get so much out of a horse that had nothing in him to begin with. B'gad, we fairly soared through the air! You would have said that bony Pegasus had human intelligence and was resolved to perish rather than permit one of His Majesty's warrant officers to suffer the ignominy of capture by the sheriff's men.

"We had near a cable's length the start of them, and

my little coachman increased it by three times the distance before we reached Westminster Bridge. When we had crossed to the Surrey side, I made sure we'd lost Chizbeak and ordered my coachman to proceed at a more leisurely pace. And then, b'gad, half an hour later, here they came again! Where they'd been in the meantime I couldn't say, but they were now so close I feared I was taken. But once more my coachman got prodigies of speed from the bag of bones that drew us. The distance was again increased, but at last the poor animal was at the end of his strength and I saw that Chizbeak and the constables were gaining. I had taken small notice of direction until, upon turning a corner, I found that we were passing the Royal Victualing Yard at Deptford. For the moment we were out of sight of the pursuers, and, realizing that I must leave the coach or be taken, I hastily cut off one of the silver buckles to my shoes and passed it to my coachman, for I had nothing else with which to pay the gallant fellow. Meanwhile, without a word having passed between us, he drew up with a jerk, opposite the gateway to the Victualing Yard. I leaped from the coach and was out of sight on the instant, whilst the little fellow was off as quickly, leading Chizbeak and the constables, who passed at a gallop a moment later, away on a false scent. I have not laid eyes upon any of them from that day to this."

Admiral Trecothick, who was leaning back in his chair with his glass of port in one hand, banged his knee with the other fist.

"Dogbody," said he, " 'twould have been worth a

man's losing his dinner to have seen ye scampering into the King's Victualing Yard with your finery on. Did ye go in at the main gate?"

"No, sir; I went by the wagon gate," said the surgeon, "and glad enough there was none I knew to see me. It was then one o'clock in the afternoon, the very hour appointed for the audience at Whitehall. And, b'gad, Sir Nicholas, instead of going on my knee before His Majesty, down I went on my behind before one of His Majesty's butchers in the Royal Victualing Yard! The entranceway is paved, but there was greasy muck four inches deep on top of the cobblestones and I fell in that. The name of the butcher I remember to this day — Joe Thurst; he chanced to be passing as I fell. Thurst was as thick through the body as three boatswains and as thick in the head as an Admiralty clerk, but, damme, the fellow had a heart of gold! He did me no small service, though with the best intentions in the world he cost me my leg. It was gone from the instant I met him. Had he taken me, mucked as I was from head to foot, straight to his chopping-block and lopped off the leg with his meat-axe, he could not more surely have deprived me of it."

The surgeon broke off to treat his gullet to needed refreshment. "Honest Joe Thurst," he said musingly, as he set down his glass. "Where will he be now, I wonder? . . . Sir Nicholas, you must have had some small commerce with the Victualing Yard in your younger days?"

The admiral leaned forward abruptly, his blue eyes

blazing, the blood all but bursting from the pores of his skin through violently aroused passion.

"In my younger days?" he roared, in his deep voice. "In *all* my days! Where's the King's officer who has not had to defile himself through commerce with the King's rogues? Rogues, do I say? By God, I flatter the sly, thieving villains! England has made Herself mighty in spite of them!" The admiral wished to proceed but the violence of his anger prevented this. He sat breathing heavily for a moment, glaring around the table until his eye fell upon the gunner. He leveled his forefinger at him like a pistol. "But mind you, Mr. Balthus! The food in His Majesty's ships, bad as it is, is good enough for seamen! I've et it my life long. I've fought my ships on it. I fare no better, aft, than my men forward, and by God, sir, I'll have no complaints! None!"

"Quite so, sir, indeed," the gunner muttered, apologetically, as though he were, somehow, to blame for this outburst. "Hearty fare and welcome, Sir Nicholas."

The baleful light died once more from the admiral's eyes. "Damn your heart, Dogbody," he added, with a laugh. "'Twas you that set me off. I thought I was aboard ship, listening to a seamen's deputation complaining of the beef. D'ye mean to say ye found one honest man at the Victualing Yard? What was his name again? Thurst?"

"Aye, Sir Nicholas; so simple a fellow he'd no notion of the rascals he was thrown amongst. And, of course, he saw naught of those in authority where the great rogues are. His duty, and his only duty, was to chop beef, and he'd do it and do it well, whether that beef was horse, dog, cat, or whatever the carcasses provided by the contractors for English seamen. But I was about to say that this Joe Thurst picked me out of the mud and wiped me down as best he could with his own apron. Then he took me to a kind of shed in one corner of the yards where he and some of his fellows were lodged, and there I had a good wash at the pump. B'gad, I needed it!

"I don't know what the honest butcher thought of my predicament, for I made no explanation save that I needed shelter for some days, perhaps a fortnight. There's no doubt that he considered me a lord, no less. He couldn't do enough for me. He'd a little cabin of his own, for he was on night duty at the yards, and there I sheltered. He found me, somewhere, a pair of seaman's trousers, shoes, a flannel frock, and a low tarpaulin hat such as is worn in the merchant service, all of a size too large for me, but they would do. Then he took my court costume out to a cleaning shop, paid for its renewal out of his own pocket, and brought it back as good as ever. I didn't put it on again. My plan was to lay low where I was for a bit. I've feared but one thing in my life, the debtors' prison, and I'd no wish to give the worm Chizbeak the pleasure of putting me there.

"Meanwhile, in seaman's clothes, I could go where I would in the Victualing Yard, as though on duty. Not a question was asked of me. The place is so vast, and the numbers employed there so great, that a man might easily roam the yards for years without being brought to book. Would you believe it, Sir Nicholas? There's sheds and warehouses in the yards filled with stores and clean forgot by His Majesty's commissioners. They're not looked into, I'll take my oath, from year's end to year's end. But *I* looked into 'em! 'Twas such a chance as don't come often to a Navy man, and I was bound to see all I could."

"Are such houses for stores not under lock and key, sir?" Admiral Trecothick inquired.

"Some were, sir," the surgeon replied, "but after a manner that accords well with what I have seen elsewhere of Admiralty methods. There were doors locked and double-locked at one entrance, and doors agape, half rotted off their hinges, at another entrance to the same apartment."

"Damn their blood!" the admiral exclaimed. "I'd surmised there were fools as well as rogues in the yards, but I would scarce have believed in such incompetence as this. What did ye see there?"

"For the most part, food for His Majesty's ships, sir. Food that will, some day, find its way aboard those ships for men like ourselves to break their teeth on. Old salt junk that dates back to the mythical domestication of the horse. Ship's bread that was baked in the reign of Harry the Seventh. B'gad, Sir Nicholas, I'd have liked well for some of the admirals, captains, and lieutenants of His Majesty's Navy to have seen what I saw. There's hundreds of casks of beef and bread in the stores that go back, I dare say, to the time of Eleanor of Aquitaine and will be served to British seamen yet unborn."

"Blast me, Dogbody," said the admiral with a chuckle. " 'Tis my loss not to have had ye aboard my ship these twenty years past. Many a weary evening I might have been spared, with you to spin a yarn opposite me at a meal of that same salt junk. But heave in on the chain of circumstances ye spoke of. Where's the leg I'm waiting for?"

"I'm at the windlass, Sir Nicholas, but the leg is still down the depth of the tale at a good twenty fathom. I'll leave it there if you tell me to."

"No, damn your eyes! I'll have it though we call the morning watch before it breaks water! Mr. Ostiff, Captain Runyon, we'll have it, shall we not?"

" 'Tis but the blush of the evening, Sir Nicholas," said Ostiff. . . . "Hodge, look sharp! Fill the admiral's glass."

"Aye, and welcome," said Trecothick, as the waiter sprang to obey. "Damme if I've ever tasted better port. Commend me to the landlord here. Now, Dogbody, proceed. The leg is already four times off in prospect. First, indirectly, through my fault; then, thanks, in turn, to a tailor, a hackney coachman, and a butcher at the Victualing Yard. Who next deprived you of it?"

"You must bear with me, Sir Nicholas. I can but tell the tale as the events fell out, and I'm still at the Victualing Yard," said the surgeon, with great dignity.

"Bear with you? That I will, sir! Heave ahead, Dogbody, at your own good pleasure," the admiral replied, apologetically.

"It was at night that I saw the yards at their busiest," the surgeon proceeded. "I gave particular attention to the slaughtering and salting department, for, having been reared on the King's beef, you will understand my curiosity to see that beef on the hoof. It was quite as I had surmised: a good half of it had never walked on hoofs. There was brought in before my very eyes, sir, an assortment of four-footed animals that would strain my ingenuity to describe. Dogs and cats were, of course, the foundation on which the beef was built up in the casks, and the butchers were so skillful in cutting up the carcasses that the best anatomist in London could not have been certain of the nature of the beasts from which they came. But there was variety enough beyond. In one evening I saw disappear into the casks three bears which had been baited in London within the week; a most curious animal called a *kanguru* sent from Botany Bay, a gift as I understood from the Governor of New South Wales to Lord Casstoby, but which had only just survived the voyage to England; a camelopard dead of old age in His Majesty's Tower Gardens, and a bison from the American colonies which had wasted away to skin and bone in our uncongenial climate. But skin and bone was good enough for seamen's beef and in he went. Hackney-coach horses, no longer good enough even for hackney coaches, were, of course, common. The very evening of my arrival at the yards, one horse with a whitey-brown mark on the haunch was dragged in from some place near by. I recognized him at once; 'twas the poor beast that had saved me from the constables, and had, apparently, only just managed to do it. I felt truly sorry for my little coachman who had lost his all in my service. Many a time since have

I wished that I might reward him, but, as I have said, I never saw him again.

"Aye, there was enough and to spare to interest a Navy man at the Victualing Yard, and I would often roam about the place until a late hour. Joe Thurst was on duty until dawn, and the pair of us would then go to a tavern hard by for a morning whet, the honest fellow paying the score for both. But 'whet' is scarcely the word with respect to Thurst's morning refreshment. His name suited him precisely. He could drink, and hold, three gallons of beer before breakfast.

"One morning we were at the tavern as usual. Thurst still wore his butcher's apron and I was in my borrowed seaman's costume. I was to leave Joe that same morning, and I had my court suit in a parcel beside me. Of a sudden the door was flung open and a lieutenant with a dozen men, well armed, rushed in. Unbeknownst to us there had been a hot press up and down the river throughout the night; all the waterside taverns had been scoured and scores of poor fellows seized for service in His Majesty's ships. Now the boats were returning down river with the miserable captives. It was my misfortune that one press gang, not yet having its full quota, was still on the search.

"The lieutenant and his men surrounded us at once. 'Come along, my hearties,' said he. 'Will ye go quiet, or do ye choose the butt end of a musket?'

" 'Ye can't press me, your honour,' said Joe. 'I'm a butcher at the Royal Victualing Yard.'

"The truth of that was plain to be seen, and when the

landlord of the tavern vouched for it, Joe was let off. 'And who's this George Brightbolt with ye?' the lieutenant asked, looking me up and down. 'He's the cut of a good seaman about him, off that merchant ship yonder, I'll lay to that! Take up your parcel, Brightbolt. The King needs such handy fellows as yourself.' Poor Joe Thurst stood with his mouth open, fairly sweating at the effort of thought, but he was on the nail.

" 'He's my helper in the yard, your honour,' he said, 'so please to spare him.'

"The lieutenant laughed at the notion. 'Aye,' said he, scornfully, 'no doubt of that. Come along, Brightbolt. Ye can butcher the King's meat, such as it is, with your teeth, in future.'

"Little he knew the years I'd been at that work, but I said naught of it. There was a kind of fate in the event, and I let it take its course. There was nothing else I could have done at the moment, for he'd never have believed the truth, so I said good-bye to Joe and off I was marched to the river.

"I'll not weary you, Sir Nicholas, with the log of the next few days. We dropped down to Sheerness where the pressed men were collected on His Majesty's sloop *Bengal*, for transporting to the fleet at Spithead. And there the lieutenant who'd taken me received a surprise he'd not expected, for the captain of the *Bengal* proved to be no other than my old friend Bob Fingott. Fingott had been lieutenant on the *Shoreham* when I was surgeon's mate of her, and a more scatterbrained fellow never drew the King's wage. He was a rare companion, but not a man to be trusted with authority, for it went straight to his head, which contained little more than a donkey's breakfast. But I loved the man, though he cost me a leg within the next forty-eight hours.

"He had his fun at my expense. An old Navy surgeon taken up by the press gang! Nothing would do but he must call up his lieutenant and threaten and bedevil him for seizing one of His Majesty's warrant officers. The poor fellow all but sweat blood till he found it was play, for Bob Fingott can be as downright as an admiral when he chooses. And he'd a voice to carry from here to London. Damme, the whole ship heard the rating the lieutenant got, but 'twas all made up to him later.

"Well, Fingott had the story of my misadventures whilst we were under way for Spithead, with one hundred and fifty poor devils below hatches, food for the French guns, once they'd been licked into shape. I learned from Fingott that the *Excellent* prize-money award had been passed by the Admiralty Board. He had the *Gazette* with the notice of the award in it, with the amounts due all ratings. Mine came to fifty-three pounds, seven and fourpence. Sir John Jervis, of course, got the lion's share. His cut went into the mythological numbers, but I was well pleased with my own, and I could touch it as soon as we reached Portsmouth.

"But we were not there yet, and with Bob Fingott in command of the *Bengal* I was prepared for any mishap save the one that came. We were a day out from Sheerness, not far off Dover, so Fingott thought, and making about two knots in a fog so thick you couldn't see the foremast from the quarter-deck. I'd changed into my finery once more, and, somehow, I felt uneasy in that rig. 'Dogbody,' thinks I, 'mark my word, ye'll have no luck in your court suit. Ye'd no business to buy such gay feathers in the first place.' Nevertheless, I made a brave show, especially up against Fingott. There never was a man more careless in his dress; he'd wear a suit of sailcloth at sea if he chose, and be damned to appearances. He chaffed me no end about my court suit.

"Well, sir, along about three in the afternoon came a sharp hail from the lookouts: a ship on the lee bow. We saw her near as soon as they did. The fog was as thick as furmity and she looked enormous, and so she was compared with the sloop. I could have sworn she was a first-rate, though we soon found that she was the *Duguay-Trouin,* a French seventy-four. The breeze was the merest sigh; we'd no more than steerageway. . . . Sir Nicholas, what would you have done in that situation?"

"What would I have done? On a sloop against a seventy-four? Damme, what any sensible man would have done: melt into that fog once more as fast as the breeze would let me. You don't tell me that Fingott wanted to engage?"

"Wanted to and did, b'gad! The man was as bold as brass, and as little able to make a sensible decision; but I must do him the credit to say that he thought he could damage her and make off into the fog. We had twelve carronades on the upper deck and six were let go before the Frenchman had his hail out of his mouth. Luckily for us, her guns could not be brought to bear for a moment, else we should have been blown out of the water. Before they could, we fell afoul of her; her yards caught in our rigging and we were dragged right alongside. They grappled and poured into us like water. Damme, they were twenty to one; our decks were so filled with them that they took us by smothering.

"If ever there was a sorry ship's captain it was Bob Fingott. He'd lost a fine little sloop, commissioned only a month before, and one hundred and fifty men badly needed by the fleet at Portsmouth to replace casualties. And above this, he'd lost what little repute he had as a man of sense. Then, to top all off, when we were brought aboard the Frenchman, Fingott, who was dressed in a pair of dirty flannel breeches and a common seaman's jacket, was not recognized as captain of the sloop. My court suit got me his commission, and damme if I didn't keep it for a bit to pay him off for getting us into such a mess! He was put below hatches with his crew, whilst I was invited aft to the great cabin, where I was received with the greatest courtesy by the commander, Captain Touffet. The French, for all their new democratical notions, still have an eye for a gentleman, the more so if he is dressed to look like one, and there was naught missing in my costume save the one silver buckle I'd given to the hackney coachman.

"I speak French with remarkable fluency, and — so I have been told by Frenchmen themselves — without a trace of accent. I was introduced by Captain Touffet to his officers, and we sat at our leisure with cheese, biscuits, and excellent wine before us. One officer, I could not but observe, regarded me with a most particular attention, and with an air of studied carelessness strolled about the cabin, but all the while, as I felt certain, examining my person from different points of view. In my simplicity, or I should say, vanity, I put this down to his admiration for my court suit, for not a citizen amongst them was dressed as handsomely as myself.

"At length, when I felt that I had paid Fingott off somewhat for his stupidity, I turned to Captain Touffet and remarked in an offhand way, 'My dear Captain, I am aware of the vast social changes that have taken place in your country these past few years, but I am surprised to learn that you ignore rank at sea.'

" 'What do you mean, sir?' said he.

" 'Why, sir,' I replied, 'you have put the *Bengal's* captain below hatches as though he were a common seaman.'

" '*Tonnerre de Dieu!*' he exclaimed. 'You were not her commander?'

" 'No, sir,' said I; 'merely a private citizen en route to Portsmouth as the captain's guest' — and with these words, off went my leg as surely as though I had sawn it off in the captain's presence."

"Damn your eyes, Dogbody!" Admiral Trecothick exclaimed. "What a foolish thing to have said! Why not have acknowledged that you were a Navy surgeon?"

"Because, Sir Nicholas, I was more of an idiot at that moment than Bob Fingott had ever been. He was brought aft at once, mad enough to have eaten me alive when he first came up, but he has a heart sound and loyal toward a friend, and when he saw the hole I'd dug and tumbled myself into, he did his best to pull me out of it. For it was surmised immediately by Captain Touffet and his officers that I was as French as themselves, but a renegade, a spy of some sort in the English pay. Bob Fingott threatened them with the concentrated and destructive wrath of the entire British nation if a hair of my head were injured; for all that I was separated from the others, placed under a special guard, and when we put into Havre de Grace, I saw my last of Fingott and the *Bengal's* company."

The surgeon paused to taste his glass.

"The leg is all but off, Sir Nicholas, but the most curious part of the tale is to come. I was taken to Paris, examined before one of their Revolutionary committees, and then confined in a gaol where, for several days, I was on display in a most humiliating manner. People were brought to look at and question me. I was treated with the utmost rigour, which was understandable enough if they considered me a traitor. But there was more to the matter than this, as I was soon to learn. I stoutly defended my identity as F. Dogbody, one of His Majesty's Navy surgeons, but I succeeded in convincing only one man, an assistant keeper at the gaol. 'Sir,' said he, 'I believe you. There is that in your face and manner which perfectly convinces me of the truth of your story. Unfortunately, it is not myself who must be convinced, and nothing I might say will save your head.' 'Good God!' I exclaimed. 'Do you tell me, sir, that I have already been condemned?' 'You have, my poor Surgeon Dogbody,' said he, and there were tears in his eyes as he spoke. 'You may as well know the truth. You are to be guillotined within the week.'

"To my astonishment and dismay, I then learned that I had been positively identified, by no less than a dozen persons, as a notorious enemy of the Revolution called Le Loup-Garou, a Breton of the Chouans, who, as you doubtless remember, Sir Nicholas, are a class of people who rose in insurrection in the west of France and joined the Royalists of La Vendée. The man had been sought far and wide, and it was considered unquestionable that he had been found in my person.

"You have never been condemned to death, Sir Nicholas, and cannot be expected to know, from experience, the thoughts and feelings of a man in my situation. Try to imagine those feelings, sir, on the morning set for my execution. But I resolved to die as befits an Englishman, fighting for my rights to the very drop of the knife. I calmly bade farewell to Citizen Blanchdent, the assistant gaoler, who had been as kind to me as he dared, and took my place in the tumbrel which was to carry a dozen wretches beside myself to the Place de la Révolution where the guillotine was set up. A vast throng had gathered there, and never shall I forget that sea of heads as I viewed them, first from the cart, and then from the guillotine itself. It was like a ravening beast, that throng; a beast with myriad faces, pity in none, ferocious curiosity in all.

"The French are a methodical nation, and the executions took place in alphabetical order. I owe my life to that arrangement, for I was dying not as F. Dogbody, but as the State's enemy, Le Loup-Garou. As it chanced, the name was last but one on the list. Nine heads had fallen to the knife before my turn came. I was led up the steps to the dreaded machine. 'Sir,' I said, to the citizen in charge, 'I wish to address the populace. That right cannot be denied a dying man.' After a brief conference amongst them, the request was granted. 'Be brief, miscreant!' said the chief executioner. My arms were then unbound and held by two men who led me to the edge of the platform.

"The vast throng heard me in silence for a moment. I told them who I was and what I was, and of the enormous injustice about to be committed upon my person. But they soon burst into a frenzy of shouting, demanding my head. The very perfection of my French was, of course, against me: it was inconceivable to people of that nation that an Englishman could speak their tongue so well. I was then dragged to the dreaded block, but I resisted with the strength of indignation and the fury of despair. I used my legs to such purpose that two of my captors were pushed off the platform and fell amongst the crowd below. In the struggle that followed I wrenched myself free for an instant and fell beneath the guillotine itself. Then, whether by chance or design, the awful knife was released and fell, striking off, not my head, but my left leg. The shock of the blow deprived me of my senses for some little time."

"Blast me, Dogbody, if ever I've heard, before, of a man losing a *leg* on the guillotine," Admiral Trecothick remarked, somewhat thickly. "But how did you contrive to save your head?"

"You may well call it strange, Sir Nicholas," the surgeon replied. "I believe that I have the distinction of being the only person, male or female, who has ever contributed a leg to the executioner's basket. Whether it was held up for the crowd to see, as their custom is with heads, I do not know, but I believe not. As I have said, I lost consciousness, and when I regained my faculties I was still lying on the platform of the guillotine, and three medical men were working over me with as much concern as though my anatomy were the most valuable in France. I fancied, of course, that they merely wished to preserve me, conscious, for the execution at the other end of my person. A cup of wine, which, curiously enough, despite my desperate situation and weakened condition, I immediately recognized as Montrachet, 'fifty-nine, was held to my lips. And at that instant, Sir Nicholas, I felt a thrill of hope. I could not conceive of Frenchmen wasting half a pint of the wine of that remarkable vintage and year upon a wretch whose head was to be removed from his body a few moments later. I gazed anxiously into the faces bending over me, and amongst them I recognized that of the chief of the Revolutionary tribunal before which I had been three times examined.

" 'My poor Citizen Dogbody,' said this judge, seeing that I had recovered my senses; 'we have done you a great injustice.'

" 'Proceed, sir, to the greater one,' I replied, weakly. 'I can resist no longer.'

" 'No, no!' said he. 'You are saved! We have caught *le misérable* for whose crime you have so narrowly escaped the final penalty. See — he is there! Lift him, citizens.'

"I was tenderly raised to a sitting position, and there before me, Sir Nicholas, I beheld my own decapitated body. Believe me, sir, I was all but convinced of the fact as I gazed. The man who lay there beside his severed head was my very self: in stature, complexion, hair, features — I would add, in voice as well, had the voice not been still forever, but I was later informed that here, too, he was my exact twin.

"What had happened, sir, was this. This man, the authentic Loup-Garou, had been apprehended ten days earlier, in a distant part of France, and had only reached Paris, with his guards, on the very morning set for my execution. Upon his being brought to the gaol, Citizen Blanchdent had come in desperate haste to the place of execution, in the nick of time to save my head, though not my leg. And here, so to speak, is the leg fetched up at last, Sir Nicholas, and glad I am it is not the real leg, for the peg I have in its place suits me vastly better."

"But damme, Dogbody, the rest of your anatomy is still in France," said the admiral. "Come home, sir, to England, before you end the tale."

"The getting home was nothing. I was treated with great consideration, and the moment I was able to travel I was conveyed across the Channel by a' frigate detached for the purpose, and taken by boat, under a flag, into the harbour at Dover. There I regained my strength under the most pleasant circumstances, for I received my long-overdue prize-money within a few days of my arrival at Dover. As soon as I could walk, my first errand was to proceed to the Royal Victualing .Yard at Deptford, where I rewarded my friend Joe Thurst in a manner to make the honest fellow happy for many a day. Had I been able to find my little hackney coachman my satisfaction would have been complete, but he was lost to me forever."

"No, sir, arskin' yer pardon, sir," came a hoarse whisper at the surgeon's elbow. Dogbody turned quickly. "God bless me! What's this, Hodgepodge?" he exclaimed.

"I was the 'ackney coachman, sir," said Hodge.

"Avast, ye shrimp! Ye'll not cozen me . . ." The surgeon broke off and moved back his chair to regard the dwarflike waiter more narrowly. He took him by the shoulders and pushed back the musty wig on Hodge's bald head, that he might have a better view.

"Damn my bones and blood!" he then exclaimed. " 'Tis the very man! Hodgepodge, I recognize you now! By all that's wonderful . . ."

"Arskin' yer leave, sir; I'll be back in a tick," Hodge broke in, earnestly, and away he went, his wig askew, out of the room before the surgeon could again speak. He returned on the instant and laid on the table, at the doctor's elbow, a silver buckle.

"It's yourn, sir, the one you give me," he said. "I allus kep' it. I was give three and tuppence 'a'penny for the carcase of me' oss at the Vittlin' Yard."

"Hodgepodge, tell me this," the surgeon asked presently, when the first blush of the company's astonishment had somewhat subsided. "How could ye get such speed from so miserable a nag as that which died for my sake?"

"I feagued 'im, sir," said Hodge, "else 'e'd never have fetched ye off from the constables."

" 'Feagued'? Damme, what's that?" the surgeon asked. "Ostiff, what the devil's 'feagued'?"

"It's a good old English word," said Ostiff, "meaning 'to set in brisk motion; to whip, or beat.' "

"Arskin' yer leave, sir, ye 'asn't a w'ip w'en ye feagues a 'oss," said Hodge. "Ye 'as a feaguin' stick. Abaht three fut long, sir; and ye 'as a bit of a swab at the end, and ye dobbles the swab wif ginger and cayenne pepper. Then, sir, w'en ye 'as the charnce, ye touches the 'oss lightly in the fundament wif the feaguin' stick. It does the 'oss no 'arm, and he'll go champion for the matter of a furlong."

Admiral Trecothick, who had listened with keen interest to this explanation, so ill-timed a drink of port at the close of it that he all but choked himself into insensibility before he could recover his breath. Mr. Ostiff, with repeated apologies for taking such a liberty, pounded him on the back, and in the ensuing laugh-strangled coughing on the admiral's part, Ned Balthus, who had fallen asleep, raised his head and looked about him with a perplexed frown.

Having recovered his speech, the admiral, with an effort, struggled to his feet. "Gentlemen," said he, "we'll go home on that!" He swayed unsteadily and would have gone down again had he not reached out desperately

and put a hand on Hodge's head. Hodge braced himself
for the emergency, and, small as he was, stood fast, but
the wig, under pressure of the admiral's hand, slipped off
Hodge's bald pate, and Sir Nicholas would have fallen
had not Doctor Dogbody made haste to seize his other
arm and draw him on even keel once more. "Steady on!"
said the admiral. "Is it possible I can have had a drop
too much?" He peered down on the other side. "What's
this I've got my hand on?" "Me 'ead, sir," Hodge mur-
mured, apologetically, in his hoarse voice. "Stand fast,
Hodge!" said the admiral. "Blast me! Sand the decks!
That bald head of yours is slick as slush!"

With Doctor Dogbody supporting him on one side
and Hodge, his tiny body stiffened under the heavy pressure, upholding him on the other, Admiral Trecothick
made his way down the staircase followed by the others,
their arms linked for mutual support.

"Dogbody," said the admiral, thickly, "you're as sober
as a judge, and damme if you haven't drunk as much port
as myself! Where the devil d'ye keep it?"

The surgeon's eyes twinkled. "In my jury-leg, Sir Nicholas," he replied.

III

FOR RUSSIA

It was three o'clock of a Sunday afternoon, but already so dark that the Argand lamps had been lit in the tap-room of the Cheerful Tortoise. At a table to the left of the fireplace, a gentleman in the uniform of a naval captain was reading the *Times* over a bottle of claret. He glanced up as Will Tunn entered from the kitchen, wiping his hands on his blue apron.

"I crave pardon if I seem to neglect ye, Captain Murgatroyd," said the landlord, "but dinner's on the way, and 'tis the afternoon off for the half of my kitchen folk."

"And what's there to be for dinner?" Captain Murgatroyd asked.

"Nothing so much, sir, on a Sabbath. But I've some fine fat mackerel with a sauce of gooseberries, a brace of wild duck with mushrooms, a leg of pork with patargo new from Jamaica, a veal-and-tongue pasty, and an apple tart for the sweet, if you're partial to it."

"I'm partial to the whole of it, Tunn," said the captain. "Many's the time, these past ten years, I've dreamed of your dinners."

"Ten years . . . ye've been out of the country as long as that?" said Tunn.

"It seems double the time to me," said the captain. "I was in Petersburg the greater part of it, buying hemp for the Navy whilst brisker fellows were putting old Boney in his place."

"In Roosia? Ye don't tell me, sir! Well, honest hemp was as needful to win the war as good English oak, and the lads to man our ships. No doubt ye talk Roosian with the best of 'em?"

Captain Murgatroyd was about to reply when, glancing toward the door, he saw a burly figure approaching. After a second keen glance he got to his feet with alacrity.

"Ned Balthus, on my soul!" he exclaimed, joyfully.

"I knew ye at first sight, Captain Murgatroyd," the latter replied. "Well met, sir! I'd no idea ye was in Portsmouth, nor in England, for the matter of that. D'ye recollect the old *Prompte?*"

"That I do! The Happy *Prompte,* eh? Ned, I'd not

hoped for such luck as this! Sit ye down! Tunn, ye've time for a whet? The dinner'll keep for that, surely?"

"With pleasure, Captain," the landlord replied, seating himself ponderously. "Ye Tom!"

Tom Tapleke, having attended to their wants, returned to the bar, and the old friends were in the midst of talk when the street door opened again, admitting Doctor Dogbody, Ostiff, and Runyon. The surgeon swept off his hat, shook the rain from it, and with a nod to the landlord and Balthus stumped briskly to the fireplace to warm his hands. Runyon followed at a more leisurely pace, while Ostiff, spying the newcomer at the table in the corner, hastened forward to greet him. The landlord rose as the surgeon and Runyon joined the rest of the company.

"Doctor Dogbody, Mr. Runyon, I wish to make ye known to an old friend and patron of the Tortoise — Captain Murgatroyd." The captain greeted the newcomers with a bow, and when they had taken their places at the table addressed the surgeon, who was seated opposite.

"My memory's not what it was, sir," he said, "but I'd take my oath that we've met somewhere, years ago."

The surgeon regarded his neighbour steadily, his blue eyes twinkling.

"Damn your memory for a poor one, Inky Murgatroyd," he said. "You were a mid in the *Forester*, in 'sixty-one, when I was loblolly boy to that nature's mistake, Slatstone. D'ye mind how ye got the name 'Inky'?"

Captain Murgatroyd's face lighted up. "God bless me! Why, you're — Wait! I'll have it directly! There's a name coming . . . Furdle . . . Fardle . . . No, that's not it. . . . Damme, I've got it! Feadle! Feedle-de-dee, we called you!"

The surgeon held up his hand appealingly. "Inky, no more! For old friendship's sake, not another word in the matter of names. Here, a pinch of snuff, ye rogue, and we'll bear away on another tack."

Captain Murgatroyd laughed heartily as he helped himself at the surgeon's snuffbox. "Will Tunn," he said, turning to the landlord, "ye've a lucky house. I've always said it. I've never stepped inside your door but I found it to my good. But damme, this is exceptional! I'd hoped to find Ostiff here, moored as he is to a stool in an Admiralty office. But Dogbody and Ned Balthus — I'd never even have dreamed to find such a wandering pair."

"That's the Tortoise, Captain," the landlord replied. "It *is* a lucky house, as ye say. Many's the old friends has crossed tacks in my taproom."

"And the luckiest day you could have had is when one F. Dogbody first sailed into it."

"Aye," said the surgeon, drily, "ye'd make it up to me, would you? Be honest, ye villain! Ye'd clean forgotten my existence."

"Never, Dogbody," Murgatroyd replied, with warmth. "I've thought of you many's the time. But it's all of a dozen years ago I was told you were dead; on good authority, too."

"I'm always being killed on good authority," the surgeon replied, with a chuckle.

"Close enough ye came to it once, in the *Forester*. But

Doctor, ye'd two legs when I last saw you. Where did ye leave the larboard one?"

"Far enough from where we sit, Inky," said the surgeon. "D'ye object to the 'Inky'? Say the word and I'll be as stiff with ye as a post captain."

"Object? Never! It does my heart good to hear it again, after all these years. Ye've dropped a mort of time off my shoulders by the use of that old handle."

"Then tell me, Inky, where ye've been since I last punched your head aboard the *Forester?*"

"Aye, an active lad ye was, Doctor, in those days, but no handier with your fists than myself, as ye'll admit unless your memory's clean gone. It grieves me to see ye hampered as ye are, with but the one leg."

"Hampered? Be damned to ye, Inky! I'm better with the one than yourself with two. I'd not swap my larboard leg for a dozen of flesh and blood. Many's the time I've considered amputation on the starboard side. Did ye never stop to consider the advantage of a jury-leg? On one side I'm spared corns, gout, rheumatism, swelling of the joints, scurvy, scrofula, and other griefs past counting. No, b'gad! Never waste sympathy on a one-legged man. But where've ye been, I say?"

"In Russia."

"Russia? Damn my eyes! When?"

"These past five years, the better part of 'em."

"Inky, why couldn't it have been years before? In that case we'd have met. We'd have found each other for all the vastness of the Russian Empire."

"You've been there? You know the country?"

"Know it? Damme, I'm a part of the Empire, in a small way. I left my leg there."

"The devil you did! But how is this, Doctor? I was buying hemp for the Navy in the cursed country, but what has a ship's surgeon to do with a land-faring nation like Russia?"

"You may well ask, Inky. But the story is a long one, and I'd not weary you with it."

"Weary me? I'll take my chance of that, and it's a good hour till dinner. What d'ye say, gentlemen? Ned, you must have heard it before this?"

"Never," said Balthus. "Blessed if I knew the doctor'd ever been in Rooshie."

"He'll say next to naught of himself, Murgatroyd," Ostiff put in. "We'd be grateful if you can draw the tale out of him."

"Then, Doctor, for old friendship's sake?" said Murgatroyd. "Damme, we've not met in close to half a century. You'll not deny me so small a favour?"

"Inky, I won't, since you put it so," said Dogbody. He raised his glass of old Port Royal, inhaling the aroma with a faraway look in his eyes, as though for an aid to memory. Then, without tasting the contents, he set the glass down again.

"The West Indies are a longish way from Russia," he began; "but it's there I must take you for a start. You'll recollect that General Monckton captured the island of Saint Vincent in 'sixty-two, and the Treaty of Paris confirmed our possession of it in the following year. 'Twas done, of course, without consulting the native Caribs, a proud and warlike race, and there was a ten years' job to subdue them. They were finally conquered in 'seventy-five, and a reserve was given them on the north end of the island. I was stationed at Kingston when the treaty was made.

"I'll spare you the account of what went before — the fighting and all that, and go on to speak of my Carib friend. He was one of the principal chiefs, who had been captured after a desperate resistance when both his arms were broken by musket balls. I set the bones and adjusted the splints in a manner of my own, and within two months he was quite recovered. He'd an odd name, Pai-wari, after the native liquor of which he was excessively fond. Oddly enough, I grew almost as fond of it myself.

"Paiwari was released when the fighting ended, and nothing would satisfy the old fellow but I must visit him at his village. I was granted a fortnight's leave, for it was considered fortunate for future peace that an English-man had made friends with so powerful a chief. This had never happened before. Paiwari's village lay on the lower slopes of Mount Soufrière, and whilst we were climbing to it, I had the ill luck to give my ankle a severe wrench. The pain near drove me mad, but I hadn't to suffer it long. Paiwari sent some of his young men out for a native remedy, a most remarkable herb that belongs, I should say, to the genus Cannabis, closely related to the Indian hemp. It was from this that the remedy was pre-pared, a milky fluid expressed from the flowers and giving off an enchanting odour of spices. This was rubbed into my swollen ankle, gently at first, more strongly as the pain ceased. Incredible as it may seem, within a quarter of an hour the pain was gone.

"You will understand my interest, as a medical man, in this anaesthesia which lasted for precisely an hour and five minutes by my watch. When the time was half up, I scraped a thorn clean and drove it a full inch into the inflamed joint. The result convinced me that the anaesthesia was complete, extending as far as the bone. The soothing qualities of the herb were apparent when feeling was restored. The pain was far from acute, the swelling diminished rapidly, and on the following day I was able to walk as well as before.

"I was eager to obtain a large quantity of this invaluable addition to our *materia medica,* but my Carib friend informed me that the supply was not equal to the needs of his tribe. However, he was kind enough to have prepared a supply of the liquid sufficient to fill a pint vial which I had in my medicine case. That vial I carried home with me to England, some months later."

The surgeon broke off to take a generous pinch of snuff.

"You've heard of Lord Brasparts, Inky?" he asked, as he dusted his fingers with his handkerchief.

"Of Brasparts? I should have," said Murgatroyd, with a wry laugh. "Our hammocks were swung next to each other for the better part of a year, in the *Scorpion.* For all his wealth and noble blood, a more abominable snorer never cursed the berth. It was a relief to all when his older brother broke his neck in the hunting field. Young Brasparts then came into the title and left the service."

"Aye," said Dogbody, "he was a champion whistler through his nose, but a good fellow for all that, though a shade partial to his bottle. I came to know him well at the time when Sir George Pocock took the *Havannah*. Well, sir, it was Brasparts who cost me my leg, in a round-about fashion. We chanced to meet in London, directly after my return from Saint Vincent, and spent an evening together talking of old times on the West India station. Knowing him for a lover of curious knowledge, I told him of my remarkable Carib anaesthesia. Lord that he was, Brasparts was not one to hold his liquor well. B'gad, he led me a chase before the evening was over and wrecked three sedan chairs and a hackney coach before I got him safely back to Grosvenor Square.

"You'll mind the old saying, Inky: 'Chance calls the dance.' *I* danced far enough, b'gad, by reason of the mention, to Brasparts, of my Carib remedy. Not a fortnight later I was sent for to come immediately to Brasparts House, and there I found my unfortunate friend in bed with a severe attack of the stone. One of the most eminent surgeons in the kingdom was at his bedside.

" 'God be thanked you're found, Dogbody,' said Brasparts. 'I must be cut, and damned quick! You've still got the Indian herb you told me of? Will you operate?'

"I bowed to the surgeon standing beside me. 'With the consent of my illustrious colleague,' I replied.

" 'Oh, damn him,' said Brasparts, callously, for he was a rude man. 'He's not to touch me. It's you I want. Send for the herb, curse you, and be quick about it!'

"The long and the short of it was that my things were

sent for and I had the stone out and Brasparts patched up and resting comfortably within the hour. The London surgeon, one of the ornaments of our profession, looked on in stupefaction.

"Then, Inky, for the next three months I had the devil's own time of it, for Brasparts wouldn't leave me in peace. He couldn't do enough for me, and I was dragged from my own modest station in life to Brasparts House, where I was wined and dined in company as illustrious, in rank at least, as any to be found in England. Damme, it opened my eyes to high life! The more I saw of it, the more I longed for the peace and quiet of my waterside haunts. But there was no getting away from Brasparts. B'gad, he'd have deeded the family town house to me, had I consented to take it.

"One of his frequent visitors was Count Litnov, the Russian ambassador, a well-made fellow with a forked beard and a chest covered with stars and crosses and such ironmongery. He'd taken a fancy to me — Lord knows why, unless it was because I spoke French — and often kept me yarning with him till I could scarce keep awake.

"One evening when Brasparts and I were about to sup, alone for the first time in those many weeks, Litnov was shown in. He was in a state of powerful agitation. He joined us in a whet, but his hand shook so he could scarce hold his glass.

" 'Gentlemen,' said he, 'an hour ago I received despatches from Petersburg. The Empress — may God protect her! — has suffered an acute attack of the stone which would have killed an ordinary woman. The Court surgeon informs me that another such attack will, certainly, cost her her life. Nothing remains but to operate, but no surgeon in Russia dares undertake the task. I am commanded to secure the services of the most eminent surgeon in England. He is to leave at once for Russia. Brasparts, where is that man?'

"Brasparts leaned across the table and put a finger against my breastbone. 'There,' said he. 'By God, Litnov, it is well that you came to me for advice in this matter.' Then he told him of the operation I had performed so successfully upon his own person.

"B'gad, Inky, before I knew where I stood, I found the place of standing to be the deck of the brig *Ice Bear,* which was dropping down Long Reach with the morning tide, bound for Petersburg. Protests and excuses were useless. I was to have rejoined my ship within the week, but Brasparts put in a word at the Admiralty and I was detached for foreign service. I was hustled aboard the *Ice Bear* in such a pother that, damme, if I didn't all but forget my vial of the Indian juice! Luckily, I was minded of it in time to have it fetched.

"You've been in the Winter Palace, in Petersburg, Inky?" the surgeon inquired.

"Inside? God bless me, no," said Murgatroyd. "What would a buyer of hemp for the Navy be doing in the Winter Palace? But I've seen it from the outside often enough."

Dogbody nodded. "I was conducted directly there by a high official who met me at the Kronstadt Dock," he continued. "I was ushered into a magnificent apartment, known as St. George's Hall, with walls of snow-white marble, and columns richly adorned in gold. You could have moored three first-rates, abreast, in that apartment, with room and to spare for half-a-dozen seventy-fours and frigates and sloops without number. The shot of a long nine-pounder would scarce have carried from one side to the other.

"Whilst standing there with my conductor, who wore a general's uniform, we were approached by an imperious-looking fellow in a costume of barbaric splendour. Immediately, my general began bowing himself out like a lackey, turned, at a respectful distance, and, in time, disappeared. 'Bless me!' thinks I. 'Who can this newcomer be?' However, being an Englishman, I stood my ground. His name, I discovered, was Orlov, a man in authority in the Winter Palace, second only to that of the Empress herself. He led me to a divan in the exact centre of that enormous apartment where we were half a cable's length from the walls on either side; but even there, before addressing me, he looked about him with the greatest caution.

" 'You are the English surgeon?' said he, with an air that made me bristle a bit.

" 'I have the honour, sir, to be one of His Majesty's naval surgeons,' I replied. 'Her Imperial Majesty is still in pain?'

" 'In such pain as no mortal could bear,' said he.

" 'Then conduct me to her chamber at once,' said I, 'and I will soon relieve her of it.'

"He gazed at me with an expression of horror, as though I had been guilty of some monstrous presumption. 'Sir,' he replied, 'Her Imperial Majesty is not to be approached in this fashion. On peril of your life, inform no one of your presence here! Her Imperial Majesty knows nothing of it. We hope to lead her, by degrees, to consent to an operation, but the proposal, if it comes, must come from her. Meanwhile, you shall be lodged as befits your station, but you must by no means leave the apartment assigned to you. The moment Her Imperial Majesty has expressed her will, if this can be brought about, you shall be sent for.'

"Then, Inky, I had the honour and privilege of seeing the Empress herself, and never shall I forget the impression that extraordinary woman made upon me. Whilst Orlov and I were conversing, there entered at the remote extremity of this state apartment a procession that was all of a quarter of an hour in reaching us. Orlov fell on his knees and remained there, but I stood, though in an attitude of the utmost deference. Her Majesty was preceded by a dozen high officials of state and was followed by as many others. She was on the way to her Council Chamber.

"I could well understand the awe and reverence in which Catherine the Great was held by her subjects. She was well past forty at this time, but in the very bloom of maturity. I shall not attempt to describe her. There can never be another Catherine of Russia. That immense room with its unbelievable magnificence seemed small and mean from the moment she entered it. It was more than filled with her presence and charged with her vitality. Upon coming opposite the divan where Orlov and I had been seated, she halted to rest upon it, whilst her train waited in awestruck silence. She sat imperially erect, but I saw that her fine hands were clenched upon her knees, and, whilst she had her features well under control, I saw that written upon her face which told of all but unbearable pain. A moment later she rose, and for the first time appeared to notice Orlov and myself. I was, of course, young at this time and — in all modesty, let me add — a fine figure of a man for one of my stature. As she looked at me, I saw in the eyes of the Empress an expression of suddenly awakened curiosity and interest.

"She turned to Orlov, still on his knees.

" 'Who is this man?' she inquired, in French.

"Orlov was so terrified that he could scarce speak, but he managed to reply: 'No one, Your Imperial Majesty. An Englishman.'

"Then, Inky, I forgot myself. I well understood the deference, not to say reverence, due to the Empress of all the Russias; but, b'gad, Orlov's reply aroused my temper. Had he said, 'No one. Doctor F. Dogbody,' I should have had nothing to say. But 'No one. An Englishman,' was another matter. I could not suffer such a slight to my country to pass.

"Therefore, I bowed low and said: 'Your Imperial Majesty, my name is F. Dogbody, and I am one of His Royal Britannic Majesty's Navy surgeons. I believe that you are suffering from the stone. If Your Majesty will place herself in my hands, I will relieve you of the agony within the hour, without the least pain or danger to your person.'

"Even as I spoke, I thought: 'Dogbody, you're done for,' and there's no doubt the others thought so. But the Empress, being herself a person of great courage, knew how to appreciate courage in another, the more so as she was constantly surrounded by those who scarcely dared breathe in her presence. I met her gaze modestly but steadily. Of a sudden she turned to her attendants. 'Go!' she commanded, and, b'gad, go they did, Orlov with them! The Empress watched them dwindle down the room before turning again to me.

"I need not speak of the conversation I then had with her. I was relieved, for Orlov's sake, that the Empress had no suspicion that I had been sent for. Like all Russians, she was incredibly superstitious and believed that I had divined her illness. The end of it was that I was commanded to attend at the Imperial bedchamber at one o'clock that same afternoon.

"It was Orlov who conducted me there. Arriving at one of the remote antechambers, I found a dozen of the most eminent surgeons in Petersburg assembled in haste to examine me as to my qualifications. I perfectly satisfied them on this head and Orlov then led me into the presence of the Empress. I felt not the least nervousness, nor, apparently, did she. What a woman! What a patriot! She thought only of Russia, and, since she *was* Russia, she thought only of herself.

" 'Doctor Dogbody,' said she, 'I have perfect confidence in your ability. You promised, did you not, that I should feel no pain?'

" 'I did, Your Imperial Majesty,' I replied.

" 'Then proceed,' said she. Her smile had all the warmth of sunshine in the dead of winter on the Siberian snows as she added: 'But remember, I have already suffered enough. If I feel the slightest twinge of pain during the operation, even though it is entirely success-ful, that twinge will cost you nothing but your life.' "

"God's rabbit!" Balthus exclaimed. "That would have made lard of your vitals, Doctor?"

"On the contrary, Ned. I was never more steady and composed. With my vial of the Carib juice at hand, I worked in perfect confidence, and the result fully justi-fied my expectations.

"Catherine's gratitude at the outcome was, indeed, im-perial. She showered me with favours, but I could well have dispensed with some of them. I was commanded to remain in Russia and was given a suite in the Winter Palace large enough to have housed a regiment of foot, but I soon found that I was little better than a prisoner within it. At the doors leading from my apartments were stationed giants in the uniform of the Palace guard, and as I opened each door, they would smile and say 'Please!' in Russian, barring the way, although with the utmost courtesy. So it went for three months. I became weary of the Muscovite fashion of living, which combines squalor with magnificence. It was not to my taste.

"I had not seen the Empress since the day of the op-eration, but one night I was awakened by my *valet de chambre,* who laid out for me a rich costume of mink's fur, with boots, gloves, and hat to match. This I was told to put on at once, at the command of the Empress. I was then conducted to Catherine's private entrance to the palace. She appeared an hour later and led me outside where a magnificent sleigh, drawn by three black stallions, was awaiting.

"She treated me with the most flattering condescension, and when I had taken my place beside her would not suffer her footmen to tuck the great fur robes around me, but did it herself.

"'My little Dog's Body,' said she, for she thus delighted to corrupt my name, 'I have a surprise for you. I shall not tell you what it is for I wish your joy to be unexpected.' She then gave orders for her drivers to proceed.

"The weather was bitterly cold, but we were well wrapped, and the winter stars shone with a brilliance seen only in Russia. The Empress was charming; she tried to make me forget the vast gulf that separated us. She herself crossed it with imperial swiftness. 'I am Catherine, my little Dog's Body,' said she. 'You are to remember that until we are again within sight of the Winter Palace.' I tried. I tried my hardest. But imagine, Inky, the difficulty!

"Toward noon of the following day, we drew up before her favourite hunting lodge, sixty versts from Petersburg. When we had breakfasted, we proceeded on into the forest, escorted by a company of guards who stationed detachments in blockhouses which commanded every approach to the Imperial Lodge. Then, for two hours, we two alone followed the huntsman's sledge through the forest where the snow lay deep under endless ranks of firs. The sun was near setting when we came to a halt. Catherine's two menservants sprang down from the sleigh. One went to the horses' heads. The other helped me to alight and put a loaded musket into my hands. The Empress remained in the sleigh, tucked in amongst the fur robes. I glanced at her, questioningly.

" 'Dog's Body,' said she, laughing lightly as though in anticipation of my own pleasure, now at hand, 'my huntsmen have discovered the father of all bears. His cave is there, not two hundred paces from our track. You shall have the honour of killing him.' "

The surgeon paused and raised his eyes for a glance at Tom Tapleke, who had so far forgotten himself as to stand by the settle on the opposite side of the table, leaning his elbows on it as he listened. The drawer shifted immediately, and taking up the surgeon's glass quickly refilled it and returned. Dogbody took a generous sip.

"Inky, what would you have done in that situation?" he asked.

Captain Murgatroyd laughed. "I'd not like to say, offhand," he replied. "I'd want time to consider the matter."

"And you, Mr. Ostiff?"

"I would have presumed upon the intimacy commanded, and told Catherine she could jolly well shoot the bear for herself," said Ostiff.

"Ned Balthus?"

"There's no call for me to say, Doctor. I'd never have been there. *Me* with the Empress of Rooshia? God's rabbit!" And the gunner laughed, heartily.

"Proceed, Doctor," said Runyon. "You shot it, of course?"

"No, b'gad, but I tried. Damme, I'd not flinch. I'd too much vanity for that. I pretended to be as pleased as the Empress wished me to be, and floundered through waist-deep snow, following the huntsmen to the cave. They had already prepared the place by digging away the snow at the entrance. They now stationed me there, whilst they climbed well out of harm's way to the top of the mound that made the cave. Then they began to make a frightful din, blowing horns, beating on iron pots and the like, and yelling at the top of their voices. A few moments later there was an upheaval in the snow and there he came!

"B'gad, Inky, he was colossal! Bears such as we see baited in London would have been mice beside him. I admit it — I was terrified, but the sleigh of the Empress was in full view and I stood my ground. I raised the musket, took careful aim, and pressed the trigger, but the cursed musket missed fire. Then courage went, and dignity with it. I threw down the musket and ran. I would never have survived had it not been for Catherine. She stood in the sleigh and shot the monster at sixty paces, when he all but had me.

"It couldn't have happened better. The Empress was helpless with laughter by the time I reached the sleigh,

and she'd had the satisfaction of killing the beast herself. 'My little Dog's Body,' said she, 'you don't know
how comical you looked,' and she laughed till the tears
rolled down her cheeks. On the instant she checked herself and turned to one of her footmen.

" 'Who charged the muskets?' she asked, in a voice as
cold and pitiless as the winter evening.

" 'The keeper at the lodge, Your Imperial Majesty,'
said the man.

" 'Then he shall die,' said Catherine, but I pleaded so
earnestly for his life that she at last consented to spare
it. She went to visit the bear as the men were skinning it.
She said, and I could well believe it, that so huge a monster had not been killed since the days of Peter the Great.
She gave a heavy purse of gold to the huntsmen; then,
turning to me, she said, 'Doctor, he shall be called the
Dog's Body Bear,' and again her laughter made the forest ring.

"The moon was well up when we started back to the
lodge, with the bearskin stowed away in the back of the
sleigh. The Empress herself took the reins for the return
journey, and I sat with her on the driver's seat. The footmen were in our former places. Never in my life have I
been more deeply distressed than I was then."

"You were still suffering from wounded pride?" asked
Ostiff. "I should think you might easily have conquered
that feeling."

"Wounded pride? On the contrary, Mr. Ostiff. I suffered nothing on that score. But . . . no, I'd best pass it
over. I will merely say this: that the Empress, with the

appalling frankness privileged only to the great, had told me, in so many words, that, upon our arrival at the Imperial Lodge where we were to spend the night, she would require of me another operation, but not in my capacity as a surgeon. I was not in the least doubt as to the nature of the operation desired. But I had the greatest doubt in the world of my ability to perform it upon command."

"God's rabbit!" Balthus exclaimed.

"No, Ned. I was Catherine's rabbit, and a more frightened and timid one, under the circumstances, could not have been found in captivity. However, I concealed my anxiety as well as I could, and I can never be sufficiently thankful, in my own case, for what happened within the next half-hour.

"Presently, glancing back, I saw that one of the footmen had removed his hood, despite the bitter cold, and appeared to be listening intently. Then I heard the most dreaded of all sounds to travelers in Russia — the faint, long-drawn howling of wolves. The Empress heard it as well, and, with a grim smile, lashed the horses to a gallop. One of the footmen leaned forward, appealingly. 'They smell the fresh bearskin, little Grandmother,' he said, in the quaint Russian fashion. 'But they shan't have it,' the Empress replied.

"As she spoke, I made out the pack behind us, black shadows in the moonlight, loping easily over the snow. There were a score of them at least, and they were fast gaining. One of the footmen was loading a musket clumsily, for his hands were numb with cold. 'God preserve

us!' he exclaimed, in Russian. The bullet pouch had
slipped from his fingers and gone over the side. 'Shoot,
fool!' said the Empress, half turning her head. When informed of what had happened, she smiled still more
grimly. '*Tant pis pour nous,*' she remarked, in a steady
voice.

"The wolves were now close and their yelping mad-
dened the horses. Catherine's face showed not a trace of
fear. She laughed lightly. 'Dog's Body,' she said, 'I promised you a surprise and a reward, but I had not hoped
to give you this double one. It remains to be seen whether
or not you are to receive a further mark of my good will.'
Then, turning her head slightly, she said, in a voice there
was no mistaking: 'Feador!'

" 'I hear you, little Grandmother,' one of the footmen
replied; then, to my amazement, the poor fellow rose
without an instant's hesitation, and threw himself from
the sleigh. The yells of the pack as they tore him to
pieces still ring in my ears, but our respite was only
momentary. The brutes soon closed in again. 'Ivan,' said
the Empress, in the same firm, quiet voice. And Ivan
followed his comrade.

"The noble fellow's sacrifice enabled us to reach one
of the outlying blockhouses before we were overhauled
for the third time. As we approached, going at a tre-
mendous pace, I observed with a sinking of the heart
that there was no bonfire by the sentrybox and there appeared to be no lights in the barrack — an *isba,* or cabin,
of logs. The leading wolf made a spring, all but gained
a foothold in the rear of the sleigh, and fell back. The

Empress, who was lashing the horses furiously, glanced toward me with a smile more chilling to the blood than the howling of wolves.

"'Dogbody,' she said, quietly. . . . 'Dogbody! For Russia!'"

The surgeon paused, and gazed absently through the small leaded panes of the window beyond, through which the dusk of the winter afternoon seemed to be flowing into the taproom, deepening the shadows among the rafters and transmuting itself to the yellow radiance of the Argand lamps.

"Well, Doctor?" Captain Murgatroyd asked, when the silence had been more than prolonged.

"I obeyed, Inky," the surgeon replied. "B'gad, yes. Such was the force of that remarkable woman's character that, scarce knowing what I did, I seized an unloaded musket and sprang from the sleigh. But it was not in the resigned, exalted spirit of her two faithful servants that I leaped. No . . . an Englishman will never concede death as certain, though his chance is but one in ten thousand. I little expected to survive; nevertheless, that grain of hope leaped with me. And it may very well be that what Catherine had more than intimated as we prepared to return from the bear hunt had its part in my instinctive decision to leap.

"Our speed was so great that I rolled over and over in the snow, regaining my feet in the nick of time. The wolves were upon me. The leader I brained with clubbed musket in the midst of his spring. But the pack closed in, and despite my efforts to keep them off, one of the brutes sprang from behind and seized my leg. I was dragged down whilst beating off the others, and at that moment I saw, or thought I saw, lights in the windows of the blockhouse, and I heard a volley of shots from near the sentrybox. Immediately . . ."

The street door of the taproom was opened at this moment, causing the doctor and his listeners to turn their glances in that direction. A boy in the uniform of a midshipman, all but hidden under an enormous cocked hat, entered, and after a glance around the room he approached the table where the company was seated. Will Tunn rose. "What do ye wish, young master?" he asked.

"I'm in search of Surgeon Dogbody," the boy replied, in a thin, childish treble. "I was told at his lodgings I'd find him here."

"And so you have, young waspwillow," Dogbody replied, gruffly. "What's your errand?"

"Please, sir, I've a message for you from Captain Sudd, of the *Hector*."

"Captain Sudd?" said the surgeon, his face lighting up. "He's here, in Portsmouth?"

"We're off Spithead, sir. The Captain sent me ashore in search of you" — and with that he handed him a letter which he carried in his hat. "Captain Sudd would like a reply at once, sir, if you'll be pleased to oblige."

"With your leave, then, gentlemen," said the surgeon. He brought forth a pair of silver-rimmed spectacles, adjusted them, and opened the letter. A moment later he got briskly to his feet.

"Will Tunn, call me a hackney coach. Tom, my hat

and coat." Tom Tapleke sprang to fetch them and held the coat while the surgeon struggled into it. "I'll not wait for the coach," he added. "Tell the man to follow me to my lodgings at Mrs. Quigg's. You come with him, lad. I'll be off with you to the *Hector* in half an hour's time."

"What's all this, Surgeon?" Mr. Ostiff asked.

"I'm for service again," the doctor replied, with a beaming smile. He turned to Balthus. "Ned, d'ye mind asking me if I'd come ashore for good? Here's the answer. B'gad, yes! I'm off!"

"But where's the call for haste?" said Captain Murgatroyd. "Ye'll not leave your carcass amongst the wolves, in Russia, and us looking on till ye come back again? Finish the tale. You're at the end of it."

"The end! Inky, 'tis the mere preamble. But the end will keep. It must."

"But where is it you're going?"

"You may well ask! This much I can tell you: where my services will be sorely needed. 'Tis a pity you're so far past your prime, for there's work ahead for hardy men. Mind you send the coach, Tunn, the moment it comes."

With a nod and a wave of the hand to the company, Doctor Dogbody stumped out of the room and slammed the door behind him.

IV

THE VULNERARY WATER

"'Tɪs a day for the creature comforts," Balthus remarked as he took seat beside Captain Murgatroyd and stretched his sturdy legs toward the fire. Mr. Ostiff and Captain Runyon sat opposite.

"So it is," Murgatroyd replied. "Mr. Ostiff will be grudging us our greater joy of them, Ned."

"You've the conceit of your calling, the pair of you," said Ostiff. He turned to the American. "Why is it, Mr. Runyon? Seamen think none but themselves know the value of warmth and good cheer."

"We'll not deny ye a kind of weak pleasure in 'em, Mr. Ostiff," Balthus replied; "but the Navy's the only school.

What can landsmen like yourself know of one or the other? Ye've had naught else all your lives. I'm thinking," he added, "of the ships that sailed on Monday. They'll be rolling the Bay of Biscay by now, and every man aboard dreaming of the taverns of Portsmouth."

"Aye," said Murgatroyd; "the first week out is the homesick time, above all, in winter." He rubbed his hands gleefully. "The Lord be thanked, I'm past and done with all that!"

"You've come home to stay, then, Captain?" Runyon asked.

"For good," the other replied, with a tasting kind of relish, as though he would, if possible, increase his pleasure at the thought. "I've been up to London about my affairs Wednesday was a fortnight, and all's settled. I've my half-pay and a snug little sum in the 3 per cents for the emergencies. England's had half a century's use out of me. This tag-end is mine, if peace holds. Damme, if ever again I set foot out of Portsmouth!"

Will Tunn had entered from the kitchen during this conversation, with a great bowl of mulled wine which he set to simmer on the hearth.

"And glad we are to hear ye say it, Captain," he put in. "But never call it the tag-end. Ye've a good twenty-five years, I'll be bound, to be one of the props of the Tortoise."

"You've none of us to spare at the moment, Tunn, by the look of things," Ostiff remarked as he glanced across the taproom, empty save for themselves. "There's no lodgers in the house?"

"The ships that sailed for India has all but emptied the town," the landlord replied; "but I've two gentlemen down from London yesterday. And not a coach has come through since; they'll be storm-bound all the way along. But the mail's in — trust Joe Weddle for that. He'd deliver the King's mail though the snow lay two fathom deep. His coach is stuck fast two miles the other side of Petersfield. Joe broke a path with his leaders to the Dolphin, in Petersfield, and his passengers followed him there, on foot; then he came on with the mailbags. He was ten hours covering the eighteen miles. There ain't been such a fall of snow in England these twenty years."

"Americans, did ye say the lodgers were?" Runyon asked.

"Aye. They're to sail for Philadelphia next week, weather permitting. Ye'll know them like enough, Mr. Runyon? A Mr. Larcum and a Mr. Chubb."

Runyon shook his head. "Ours is a wide land, Tunn. We've counties and to spare to put all England in."

"And naught for company save bears and Indians," Captain Murgatroyd added. "I'd as soon live in the wilds of Russia. . . . Ned, there's no news from Dogbody? Were he with us this day, I'd call it the perfection of company."

"We'll have him here within the half-hour," said Balthus.

Murgatroyd's face lighted up. "What? He's back?"

The gunner nodded.

"And where's he been these five weeks?"

Ostiff smiled. "Don't speak of it when he comes," he said. "You'll recall how he was whisked away of a sudden by an old friend, Captain Sudd, of the *Hector*? 'Twas all a jest. The *Hector* was bound for Ireland, and Sudd intrigued him off, for company's sake. The doctor was wild about it."

Murgatroyd chuckled. "D'ye mind how he bustled off and left his carcass amongst us with the wolves of Russia devouring it? I'd like well to hear the end of the tale. But he's been there, that's certain."

"In Rooshia? Ye can lay to that," said Balthus. "Where's the land the doctor ain't seen, little or big? Aye, down to the mere crumbs, with just soil enough to bury a leg in."

The conversation was broken off as Mr. Tunn's two lodgers came down the stairway. The first was a man of portly frame, dressed in tawny-coloured coat and breeches, black shoes, and white thread stockings. His complexion was pale, his face pitted with smallpox scars, and he wore a bushy Dalmahoy wig from which the powder sifted at every movement of his head. His companion was a small man of fifty or thereabout, dressed in rather shabby black, and he wore his own hair, in a queue, tied with a bit of string in lieu of ribbon. He was, apparently, nearsighted, and would blink his eyes rapidly, a habit caused, seemingly, by a want of water with which to moisten his eyeballs. They were about to seat themselves on the opposite side of the fireplace when the landlord, at Mr. Runyon's suggestion, seconded by the others, crossed to ask the favour of their

company. The invitation was cordially accepted, and
the introductions were in progress when the street door
was flung open and Doctor Dogbody entered, his cocked
hat and greatcoat powdered with snow. His eyes twinkled
with pleasure and interest at seeing the company and he
stumped across the room to where they sat.

"Mr. Ostiff, Captain Runyon, Captain Murgatroyd,
well met! Ned, lad, what cheer? Will ye believe it? The
snow on the streets is now above the knee. From my
lodgings at Mrs. Quigg's to the Tortoise not a soul was
abroad save myself. Hearty weather, gentlemen — brisk
hearty weather, good to look out upon from as snug a
berth as this."

"We were saying it, Doctor, not five minutes gone,"
said Balthus.

" 'Twill be nothing to an American like Mr. Runyon,
from the arctic regions of Boston. But for England . . .
I don't remember a storm to equal it since the winter of
'eighty-two. This morning the mercury in my bedchamber stood at ten by the Fahrenheit scale."

Captain Runyon proceeded to do the honours with
respect to the strangers. "Mr. Larcum, Mr. Chubb, let
me make ye known to Doctor Dogbody, of His Majesty's
Navy. Countrymen of mine, Doctor, though it is only
this moment I've had the honour of their acquaintance."

The surgeon bowed to each of the strangers, then
turned to the larger one. "Not Mr. Jonathan Larcum,
the apothecary, of Philadelphia?" he asked.

The other bowed with great dignity. Though he
wished to conceal the fact, he was, plainly, flattered.

"Your servant, Doctor Dogbody."

"Gentlemen, we are honoured indeed," said the surgeon. "In the whole of England there are not two apothecaries of Mr. Larcum's eminence. Your *Seamen's Remedies* is a handbook amongst us, sir. Mr. Chubb, I am bound to admit that I hear your name for the first time."

The little man smiled with great good humour as the company took seats. "Small wonder, sir," he said. "I am a mere bookseller whose sole claim to distinction is that I am Mr. Larcum's publisher. Mr. Runyon's introduction should have been: 'Doctor Dogbody, Mr. Nobody.'"

He laughed at his own sally, which placed them all on easy terms together.

"Never, sir," the surgeon remonstrated. "A nobody has yet to come from the city of Doctor Benjamin Franklin. My belief is that you all partake of his enlightenment."

"My friend, Chubb, is far too modest," the apothecary said. "He is known in America wherever learning is esteemed and books read, which is to say, in every corner of the land."

"I have no doubt of it," said the surgeon. "And this reminds me, Mr. Larcum: in your *Seamen's Remedies* I have discovered what I think must be an error. It is to be found in your recipe for the sweating-powder. I believe I can quote your words: 'Take ipecacuanha, liquorice and opium, each one ounce. Nitre and vitriolated tartar, each four ounces. Fulminate. Beat them in a mortar with the opium, and sift through a fine sieve to the ipecacuanha and liquorice. Mix well.' It appears to me, sir, that a mistake has been made, for nitre will not fulminate with vitriolated tartar."

"Say no more, sir," Mr. Chubb broke in, smiling ruefully. "The error is at my charge, as Mr. Larcum's publisher. It was corrected in the second edition."

Launched upon a subject dear to both their hearts, Doctor Dogbody and the apothecary were soon deeply engaged, the others listening with mild but respectful interest. Mr. Larcum was describing with gusto his method of preparing antimony for his Pill-and-Drop when Ostiff, with great tact, brought the pair of them back to a sense of present company. Glasses had been set on the board, and Will Tunn, a napkin in his hands, was offering the mulled wine to the company.

"What's this, Tunn?" the surgeon asked.

"A negus, Doctor, of my ordering," Ostiff replied. "I'd be pleased to have you taste it."

"Willingly, Ostiff. We've the best of the afternoon before us. I'll have my Port Royal to come. 'Twill sit well on the negus."

The fragrant steam gleamed rosily in the firelight while toasts were drunk and responded to with great affability. Captain Murgatroyd having alluded to the antiquity of the custom, the surgeon took up the subject with zest.

"You may well say so, Inky," he replied. "The drinking of healths was common amongst the Greeks, and derived from them by the Romans. But they were all too partial to libations: wine poured *out* rather than *in,* to honour their gods. Imagine the waste, in the course of so many centuries!"

"They would have managed to save enough for themselves," said Mr. Chubb, blinking his eyes rapidly. "Ovid, that happy proficient in all the literature his age afforded, gives us reason to think so. In his *Metamorphoses,* he introduces the usage of drinking to friends and acquaintances as of very ancient origin. And Asconius tells us it was their custom to drink neat wine; nay, it was indispensable to drink *morum,* that is, wine, not only undiluted by water, but without any of the mixtures then used, as saffron, honey, and the like."

"Aye," said the surgeon, "Greeks or Romans, they'd have held their own with ourselves, no doubt. 'Twas the custom of the Roman gallants to toss off as many glasses to their mistresses as there were letters in their names. What does Martial say?

> "Let six full cups to Naevia's health go round,
> And fair Tustina's be with seven crowned.

B'gad, had I lived then, I'd have chosen one with all the letters in the alphabet to her credit. My compliments once more, Mr. Chubb. And to you, Mr. Larcum. 'Tis a pleasure indeed to drink to fellow townsmen of Doctor Benjamin Franklin."

"You knew him, perhaps, sir?" Mr. Larcum asked.

The surgeon nodded, gravely. "As a young man I had the honour of his acquaintance."

Ned Balthus and Mr. Ostiff exchanged glances, and Mr. Runyon settled his back more comfortably against the well-polished leather cushions behind him. As the surgeon seemed undisposed to proceed, Mr. Ostiff remarked: "All England knows him, Mr. Larcum, by repute, at least. The Franklin rod, against the electrical fluid, is coming into common use upon our dwellings and public buildings, and I doubt not that the Franklin stove will be as widely known, in time. Inventions, both, of the greatest value."

"You may well say so, Ostiff," the surgeon remarked. He paused, shaking his head with a wistful sigh. "And the Franklin leg might have been the chief of boons to the military, considering the perversity of mankind and our universal practice of making wars for the killing and maiming of one another."

"The Franklin leg? Bless me, I've never heard of it! What may that be?" the apothecary asked.

Doctor Dogbody sipped his wine meditatively, and set down his glass once more.

"He made but the one, more's the pity," he said. "In the midst of his universal labours, scientific, political, philosophical, I've no doubt he lacked the leisure. 'Twas an artificial limb, sir, and vastly better than one of flesh and blood."

"And where is, or was, that leg, sir?"

"You force me to a personal reference, Mr. Larcum. At one time, all too briefly, it composed the most valuable part of my own anatomy."

The Americans were, plainly, interested. "Chubb," said his companion, "we must come all the way to England to learn a particular as interesting as this!"

" 'Tis not mentioned in Doctor Franklin's writings, that I can vouch for," the bookseller replied.

"I can well believe it, sir," said the surgeon. "Doctor Franklin considered the making of it a mere pastime. 'Twas done through kindness of heart, out of sympathy for the young man I then was."

"Would you favour us with an account of it, Doctor?" the apothecary asked. "But first, may I ask how you lost the leg that he replaced?" He broke off. "No, I must not," he added. "The story is known, of course, to your friends, here."

"On the contrary," Ostiff put in. "We've yet to hear it, though the tale has been promised, many's the time. Dogbody, no further excuses! We have you on the hip at last! We'll not set you down until you've Doctor Franklin's leg to stand upon!"

"Needs must, then," said the surgeon, with a smile. "But my long reluctance to give you the tale, friend Ostiff, has been three parts shame. For never was leg lost in a more humdrum fashion. B'gad, here am I, an old Navy surgeon, afloat through all our wars during the past half-century, supposed to have suffered my loss in some gallant action, when the truth is . . ."

"Out with it, Doctor!" said Balthus. " 'Twas no disgrace, I'll lay to that."

"It was, Ned, and it wasn't. . . . Well, if you must know, I was brought down by a gamecock, and an English bird at that!"

"A cock!" the gunner exclaimed.

"You've no cause to feel dishonoured, Doctor," said

Murgatroyd. "Where's the cocks to equal our English breed? They are compact of spirit, and would stand up to the ravening wolves of Russia, if it came to that."

"So they would, Inky, so they would," the doctor replied, his eyes twinkling. "But, uncommon though it was, you'll admit 'twas a poor way to lose a leg. I've no wish to dwell upon it."

"But ye'll not deny us the rough particulars?" said Balthus.

"Ned, I will not. I'm bound to give you those for the sake of what comes after, for 'twas not the leg I was born with whose loss I mourn, but Doctor Franklin's improvement upon it. . . . Will Tunn!"

The landlord, who knew the surgeon's tastes and habits to a nicety, was already returning from the bar with a small glass of the latter's favourite rum. Having scrutinized its colour, smelled and sipped of it, the surgeon proceeded.

"I must revert to a time, Mr. Larcum, less pleasant for Englishmen to recall than for yourselves, across the Atlantic: the years just precedent to the unfortunate American War."

"And, in my estimation, sir, as unhappy for ourselves," the apothecary observed. "Our nations belong together. For the separation, we have His Majesty George the Third to thank, and him alone!"

Doctor Dogbody nodded. "Did you know, sir," he then asked, "that, in the month of March, 1764, when the scaffolding for fixing His Majesty's statue at the Royal Ex-

change was struck, it was discovered that the sculptor
had put the sceptre into the wrong hand?"

"Indeed, Doctor?" Mr. Chubb exclaimed. "A truly
prophetic error! It was always in the wrong hand in his
dealings with the American colonies."

"Being an Englishman of England, Mr. Chubb, I cannot go all the way with you there. He was a great man,
but possessed the defects of his virtues to a remarkable
degree, and never more so than in his stubbornness,
which is the obverse side to firmness of mind. He knew
not when to yield and thus brought the greater part of
his colonial empire to ruin. But we are digressing. I was
about to say that, in the year 'seventy-two, I was a young
man, surgeon's mate of the *Griffin,* sloop of war, then on
the West India station. It was in the course of a voyage
home to refit that I met the cock.

"I'd met him times enough before; he was the pet of
the whole ship's company. We'd a pair of them in the
Griffin; they had the run of the decks, turn and turn
about, for they'd have murdered each other if loosed at
the same time. They were kept to defend the *Griffin's*
honour against the cocks of other ships, and well they
succeeded!

"One day, whilst at play with the smaller of the two,
the little fellow gave me a dig in the calf of the leg with
his spur. I was not even aware of it at the time, and it
was not till some hours later that I noticed the rent in
my stocking and the small wound beneath. I gave no
heed to it, though I was careful to mend the stocking,
one of my secondbest pairs.

"The neglect was to cost me the leg. I spare you the details. 'Tis enough to say that we had a long and wearisome passage home, with many sick on board. I'd no time to look after myself, though by now the leg was paining me damnably; the scratch had taken infection which was working inwardly. The result was that, when at last we put into Portsmouth, I had to be carried ashore to our naval hospital."

The surgeon broke off for a taste of his Port Royal.

"Mr. Larcum," he then asked, "you have, perhaps, heard of one of our famous herbalists and pharmaceutists, Doctor Amos Quittichunk?"

The apothecary, who was just then sipping his negus, set down his glass with an air almost of reverence.

"Heard of him! Doctor Quittichunk?" he exclaimed, softly. "The friend of Linnaeus? The author of the *Vegetable Statics?* Have I the honour of speaking to one who has, perhaps, spoken to him — who may even have known him?"

"Sir, you have," the surgeon replied. "It was my superlative fortune to have met him at this time. The friendship — for I flatter myself I may so term it — then begun continued until the Doctor's death, in 1802."

"Doctor Quittichunk! Doctor Quittichunk!" the apothecary repeated, as though trying to bring home to himself the honour he so evidently felt at having met one who had been in the great herbalist's presence. "The maker of the vulnerary water! . . . Doctor Dogbody, I would, I think, give both of *my* legs to know something of the history of that remarkable preparation!"

The surgeon's face beamed. "Sir, you shall have it, willingly, without the loss of either, for it was upon my own person that the styptic from this water was first tried. As it chanced . . ."

"Begging your pardon, Doctor," Balthus interrupted; "an old seaman like myself can make no easting across the vulnerary waters till he knows what they are."

"Ned, forgive me. B'gad, Mr. Larcum has made me forget that we're not all herbalists here. A vulnerary water hath the property of stopping all kinds of bleedings, even those occasioned by the rupture of arteries or larger blood vessels. The dressing, or *pensement,* as the French term it, to which the vulnerary water is applied, is often called the styptic. Am I correct in this, Mr. Larcum?"

"You could not have stated it more accurately," said the apothecary. "But you are speaking of vulnerary water in its perfection. There is, or was, but one of that description: Doctor Quittichunk's, which is no longer obtainable. Why is this, Doctor Dogbody? Why have the faculty been deprived of a pharmaceutic of such inestimable value?"

" 'Tis in the pith and marrow of my story, sir, as you shall see," the surgeon replied. "To return, for a moment, to my humble self, by the time I reached our naval hospital here, the infection in my leg had spread in alarming fashion, from knee to ankle. Nevertheless, I clung to the limb, hoping it might yet be saved; but within forty-eight hours it became clear that further delay would cost me the entire limb instead of the half of it, and, perhaps, my life. Therefore, having first been fortified with near a pint of neat rum, I was whisked away to the operating chamber.

"You will remember, Mr. Larcum, that, at the period of which I speak, nothing was more coveted by the faculty than a vulnerary water whose efficacy, in amputations, could be counted upon. Doctor Quittichunk had, for years, been working toward the perfection of one, and had arrived so nearly at his goal that he was willing for a trial of his preparation to be made. He had come down from London for that purpose. I knew nothing of this, of course, at the moment. I had never, then, heard of Doctor Quittichunk, and, half-stupefied by the rum I had been given, delirious with the fever of the infection, I thought I saw the gamecock perched on my throbbing leg and crowing with exultation.

"The operating chamber was filled with people, for the chief naval surgeons then in Portsmouth were present to witness the experiment. Doctor Timothy Ward, of the hospital, was to perform the amputation. He was a huge man, with arms and chest like a boatswain's and a face like a butcher of the King's beef, which he was, in fact, but a great surgeon, nonetheless. In my feverish condition, he looked three times his natural size.

" 'Young lustyguts,' said he, when I was laid on the operating table, 'you'll remember this day as the proudest of your life.'

" 'That's as may be, sir,' I managed to reply, 'but I'll never call it one of the happiest.'

"He gave no heed to me. I was naught to him save a

body for his knives and saws to work upon. He stepped back to regard me better, feeling of my arms and shoulders with a kind of relish. 'Full of the vital juices,' said he. 'We couldn't have a better specimen. He'll bleed well, I'll be bound. You *will* bleed, lad, hey?' he added. 'Mind you do, or I'll have the other leg as well!'

"I was then given a piece of tough shoe leather to set my teeth in, one that had been chewed by many another poor fellow in my fix before that day. I seized the rod above the table. The surgeon took up his knife, felt the edge with his thumb; then, setting it to the leg, just above the knee . . ."

"You can spare us that," Ostiff interrupted.

"You'll not have the details?" the surgeon asked, with an air of surprise.

"We'll grant the limb off. Lead on to the Franklin leg."

"Aye, Doctor," said Murgatroyd. "Drop the old leg into a lacuna of the tale and proceed."

"Very well," said the surgeon, regretfully; "but, by your squeamishness, you deprive Mr. Larcum of an account of the action of the vulnery water, for I was perfectly conscious throughout the operation. What between the numbing effect of the rum I had drunk and my professional interest in an amputation performed so skillfully, I scarce remembered it was my own leg I was being deprived of. But you can imagine my astonishment, and that of the onlookers, when the *pensement* of the vulnerary water was applied to the stump. The bleeding was arrested as though by magic. A few drops only stained the dressing, and all save Doctor Quittichunk himself called the water a complete success. For him, nothing short of perfection would do.

"I need not tell you, Mr. Larcum, or you, Mr. Chubb, that Doctor Quittichunk was an honoured friend of Doctor Franklin. As you know, Mr. Franklin was in England at this time, as a representative of your American colonies. Interested in every branch of the sciences, he had accompanied Doctor Quittichunk to Portsmouth to witness the trial of the vulnerary water, and 'twas my privilege to meet them both on this occasion, for they stopped over a day to see how I did. They were kindness itself to me, and in the little conversation I then enjoyed with Doctor Quittichunk, he was, it seems, impressed by some slight knowledge I had of the pharmaceutics. He did me the honour to call it remarkable in so young a man. He wished to perfect me in this, and the end of it was that he asked for and received the loan of me from the Navy for the space of one year. As soon as I was able to hobble with a crutch, I was carried to London and installed in Doctor Quittichunk's dwelling, which stood on the Duke of Bedford's New Road, in Lamb's Conduit Fields.

"At that time, Lamb's Conduit Fields was still open country, yet we had London at our doors. Here Doctor Quittichunk had his gardens, his warm-beds, everything needed for his experimental labours, and within his dwelling, his herbaria, which I need not say were the envy of botanists in every part of Europe.

"What a happy time it was for me! What days, what

nights, I passed in that hallowed spot! Consider the privilege it was for a young man standing on the threshold
of life, though on but the one leg, with the boundless domains of human knowledge stretching out and away before him, to be led by the hand from that threshold, into
the nearer purlieus of those domains, by Doctor Amos
Quittichunk, Doctor Benjamin Franklin, Doctor Carolus
Linnaeus . . ."

At mention of the name of the great Swedish botanist,
Mr. Larcum overturned, in his excitement, his glass of
negus, and the wine spread over the table like a small
lake and dribbled from the edges onto various laps and
knees. The apothecary was profuse in his apologies as
Will Tunn and Tom Tapleke, who had just returned on
duty, hastened to repair the damage.

"Gentlemen, I beg your indulgence for my clumsiness,"
Mr. Larcum repeated as they seated themselves again.

"Tut, Mr. Larcum," Dogbody replied, genially. "We
are none the worse for a Roman libation, poured out to
the memory of a great man."

"It may well be called such," said the apothecary. "But
a man? Linnaeus? He was a very god, sir, among botanists! And you have known him! You have seen him,
talked with him!"

"London was honoured with his presence at this time.
Both he and Doctor Franklin were all but daily guests
at Doctor Quittichunk's. It was indeed a meeting of the
gods when those three were in company, and I was privileged not only to listen to their conversation, but, at
times, to make my own modest contributions. 'Twas Lin-

naeus who had put Doctor Quittichunk in the way of his improved vulnerary water. This was a matter of frequent discussion betwixt them. What would you say, Mr. Larcum, was the basis of the preparation? Not an apothecary on this side has ever guessed it, nor come anywhere near it."

"I shall not hope to do better," Mr. Larcum replied; "but I have sometimes wondered if the foundation might not have been the liquor expressed from the leaves, or fruit, of some genus of the dicotyledonous polypetalous plants whose order was founded by Linnaeus himself."

Doctor Dogbody gazed at the apothecary in admiration, rose, bowed, and resumed his seat.

"Gentlemen," he said, "you heard me say that, in the whole of England, there are not two apothecaries of Mr. Larcum's eminence. I wish to amend that statement: there is not one! Sir, you are right. 'Tis the Heracleum. The genus embraces some eighty species of perennial herbs, with alternate leaves and generally white flowers, in compound umbels. They are native to the temperate regions, in general, though found as far north as Kamchatka."

"We have one species in America," said Mr. Larcum, "vulgarly known as the cow-parsnip, or hogweed, eaten by some of our Indian tribes. It is my knowledge of this plant which led me to suppose that some member of the genus might have served in the vulnerary water."

" 'Twas the guess of genius, sir. My compliments once more. To proceed: under Doctor Quittichunk's guidance,

I was to learn more, in a month, of the order *umbelliferae* . . ."

"Ye'll not forget, Doctor, the Franklin leg is to come?"
Balthus put in.

"Curse ye, Ned! I'm but three months out of Portsmouth Hospital at the moment. Will ye not give a man
time for his stump to heal?"

"Pay no heed to him, Doctor," said Captain Murgatroyd. "It's been load and fire with Balthus for half a
century. He'll have a tale go *bang!* like his thirty-two-
pounders."

"No, Captain, not that," said Balthus; "but are we
under way? It's heave and set as far as I can tell."

"Be damned to ye, Ned! The leg's dead to leeward,
never doubt it. Where was I, Mr. Larcum? This rascally
gunner's blown me off soundings."

"You were speaking of the *umbelliferae,* sir."

"Precisely. . . . Doctor Quittichunk was not satisfied
with the action of the Heracleum in the vulnerary water
because, as I have said, it fell a little short of perfection.
That little was enough to make him consider it a failure.
One evening while Doctor Franklin was present, the discussion of it was resumed.

" 'No, no, Linnaeus! It won't do! It won't do at all,'
Doctor Quittichunk remarked, as he paced the floor. 'I
must better it, but how? How?'

" 'This I will tell you, my good friend,' Linnaeus replied. 'The liquor needed will certainly be found in one
of the *umbelliferae.* What do you think, Doctor Franklin?'

"Mr. Franklin was seated before the fire listening to the conversation with that air of grave, benevolent interest so characteristic of him. Though he made no pretense to eminence in botany or pharmaceutics, his unsurpassed intelligence and profound common sense made instructive whatever he might have to say on any subject. Appealed to now, he smiled, and, with a nod in my direction, 'Why not ask our young friend, here?' he asked.

"Doctor Quittichunk stopped short in his restless pacing. 'Damme, why not indeed?' said he. 'Dogbody, my lad, speak up! Where, in the tribe *Peucedanum*, order *umbelliferae*, will I find the plant whose juices are to replace those of the Heracleum in my vulnerary water?'

"I was so taken aback at being appealed to in that presence that, without a moment's thought, I blurted out the first thing that came into my head.

" 'Though the genus to which the Heracleum belongs has hitherto been found only in the higher latitudes,' said I, 'may it not be that a sub-tropical or semi-tropical species exists, perhaps where a sourer, spongious soil would give its juices the increased astringent quality which the Heracleum lacks?'

"A wilder hazard was never ventured by a greater fool, in a more learned company. The silence that followed convinced me that I had damned myself forever. I dared not look up; I could have sunk through the floor for very shame. Then came a shrill whoop from Doctor Quittichunk: 'Linnaeus! He's hit it! The lad's hit it, has he not?' In amazement I raised my eyes, to meet the glance of Linnaeus himself, resting upon me with a warmth of approval there was no mistaking.

" 'He has, Quittichunk,' that great botanist replied. 'Which goes to show that men like ourselves may reflect so deeply upon a problem as to miss the one road leading to its solution. There must be — nay, there *is* such a species: I'll stake my reputation as a botanist upon it! Moreover, I'll tell you where it will be found: in the Kingdom of Naples, on or about the slopes of Mount Vesuvius. Young Dogbody, my compliments, sir! You have in you the making of a great herbalist. A supposition of such genius is proof of the fact.' "

The surgeon paused, gazing into the contents of the cone-shaped Venetian glass before him, twirling it lightly by its stem.

"You will forgive me, gentlemen," he went on, "for speaking of a matter so complimentary to myself. Mine had been a hazard at a venture for which I deserved no credit whatever. But you will know how praise from so illustrious a man warmed the heart of the youth I then was.

"It has ever been my observation that the truly eminent have in their characters something childlike which comes to the surface in moments of great exhilaration; and now that I had, unwittingly, put them upon the scent, Linnaeus and Doctor Quittichunk were like a pair of boys together. They skipped about the room, embracing me at one moment and Doctor Franklin the next; then, with great eagerness, they brought from the herbaria all of Doctor Quittichunk's dried specimens of the dicotyledonous polypetalous plants and spread them out on the floor to be studied together. Amazing as it may seem, Doctor Linnaeus, by a process of pure ratiocination, proceeded, then, to describe in advance the plant which he predicted would be found on the slopes of Vesuvius. The event proved that he had made not the slightest error.

"And now, Ned, all in good time I come to the leg, for it was on this very evening that I was measured for it by Doctor Franklin.

" 'Quittichunk,' he remarked, smilingly, 'our young friend here deserves a memento of this occasion, and I can think of none that would be more useful to him than a leg to replace that he has lost. I shall furnish him one.'

"Doctor Quittichunk, who was on his knees beside Linnaeus, looked up absent-mindedly. 'Yes, yes, Doctor. To be sure, the lad must have a leg. Of course, of course,' he remarked, and at once resumed the discussion with his learned confrere.

"Doctor Franklin then asked me to lay bare my stump, which he studied and measured with the greatest care, feeling gently of the severed muscles and tendons, and making notations in his pocketbook. He was as deeply occupied, as lost to his surroundings, as his two friends near by. Being young, and ignorant at that time of Doctor Franklin's genius, I thought only that he was taking uncommon care in his measurements for a wooden peg which he meant to order for me in town.

"Well, sir, not a word more was said of the leg during

the next three weeks. Meanwhile, Linnaeus had returned to Sweden, but Doctor Franklin came as usual to visit us, though less frequently. As my stump was now perfectly hardened, I longed for the promised leg and spoke of it to Doctor Quittichunk. 'Patience, lad,' said he. 'Mr. Franklin is a man of the greatest affairs. He may have forgotten his promise; in any case, we mustn't speak of it. You do well enough with your crutch for the moment. Never fear: we'll have you furnished with an excellent peg before setting out for Naples.'

"I'm obliged to confess that we did Doctor Franklin the greatest injustice in supposing that he might have forgotten. One afternoon he appeared with a parcel, wrapped in brown paper, under his arm. 'Twas the promised leg."

Doctor Dogbody halted in his narrative and sat with his hands clasped lightly on the table, gazing abstractedly at his thumbs, which he twirled, first in one direction, then in the other. His audience waited in silence, and at last Balthus said, "Well, Doctor?"

The surgeon shook his head. "No, Ned. Don't ask me to describe it. 'Twould require the genius of Doctor Franklin himself. The leg was a miracle, no less: in shape and colour precisely like its fellow of flesh and blood. 'Twas hollow, of course, and within was the mechanism: the wires to correspond with the tendons; the springs, of intricate complexity, to perform every function of the muscles. That a human brain could have conceived it was all but incredible. Granting the conception, that human hands could have fashioned it passed the bounds of the most enlarged belief. Yet it was done. Imagine it: a man immersed in the greatest of public affairs, sought after by the highest personages in the learned, fashionable, and political worlds; and yet, in the space of little more than three weeks, in his fleeting leisure moments, he had fashioned this . . . this . . . words fail me: there *are* none to describe so great a marvel."

"How was it attached to the stump?" Ostiff asked.

"That part was simplicity itself, and yet it was a deceiving simplicity. The leg sprang into place as though it were the one I had lost, perfectly restored, nor could the point of union be detected save by the closest scrutiny. Two buckles held it. 'Twas a matter of thirty seconds to remove and replace it."

"You're not saying there was toes?" Balthus inquired.

"There were, which I could flex as readily as those on the other foot, and with nails to correspond."

"There was calf, ankle, and all? 'Twould serve ye to walk with?"

"To walk with? To leap, to dance, to run with! Where it met the stump was a kind of porous, membranous cushion. What it consisted of I know not, but I believe it was charged with the electrical fluid. Be that as it may, by means of it the impulses carried by the muscles and tendons of my stump were, in some way, communicated through this membrane to the wires and springs, so that they acted as though at the bidding of the former. The articulation of the joints was a marvel of ingenuity. The leg lacked naught but sensation, and at times even that was not wanting. I could all but feel the blood coursing to and from the extremities. And over all was a covering of some curious soft leather, tinted a perfect flesh colour, and which adhered to the member as smoothly and closely as the authentic skin of its fellow."

"God's rabbit!" the gunner exclaimed. "With such a leg, ye might well be content to have lost the other."

"Content! I would not have exchanged it for a dozen of the old! The moment it was attached I ran to my bed-chamber to fetch a stocking and my left shoe, which I had thought never to wear again. Oddly enough, the stocking I seized upon chanced to be that I had worn when wounded by the cock, marked with the mended rent. Then, as whole a man as I had ever been, I fell upon my knees before Doctor Franklin, tears in my eyes, unable, in my excess of gratitude, to say one word."

" 'He'll do now, eh, Quittichunk?' said the Doctor. You would have thought he had done no more than whittle out a pretty knickknack to please a child. 'Couldn't have young Dogbody stumping over the slopes of Vesuvius on a peg. He'll need his old agility there, I'll warrant.' Then, excusing himself, — he was to attend a meeting of the Royal Society that afternoon, — he hastened out to his coach, which was awaiting him at the bottom of the garden.

"During the brief visit, Doctor Quittichunk had been as speechless as myself. Genius that he was, as botanist and herbalist, — and I would place him next to Linnaeus in these respects, — he had no mechanical ingenuity; he could not even have fashioned the simple frame for one of his warm-beds. The very pattern of modesty with respect to his own gifts, his delight in another's knew no bounds. His rejoicing on this occasion was as great as my own."

"Would you be good enough to describe him, sir?" Mr. Larcum asked. "I don't see Doctor Quittichunk's corporality."

"You would scarce have seen it had you been in his presence, sir," the surgeon replied. "He was about four feet high and delicate to a degree; there was little more body to him than to an astronomical line. But he was all compact of energy, and though well into his eighties, he could wear out men not the half of his age."

"In his eighties!" said Mr. Chubb. "And you say that he lived until 1802?"

"He did, sir, to the age of one hundred and fourteen, and was busily at work in his gardens the day before his death. I was about to add that he was bald as an egg, through his own wish, for he had invented an unguent to remove his hair, not wishing to be troubled with the cutting of it. He wore a wig in company.

"Now that I had my leg, Doctor Quittichunk would lose no time in setting out for Naples, and here, Mr. Larcum, I will beg your leave to drop the events of the journey behind. Though replete with adventures and incidents of the greatest interest, amongst which we all but lost our lives in a blizzard in crossing the Alps, I must pass them by, else I shall have Mr. Balthus calling me a laggard again."

"Proceed at your own pleasure, Doctor," the apothecary replied. "But first, will you satisfy my interest upon one point? The wished-for species of the *umbelliferae* was found, of course?"

"It was, sir. We made the entire circuit of Vesuvius and had all but despaired of success when, by pure chance, we stumbled upon a tiny plantation, not more than a dozen paces in extent. It was, unquestionably, all that remained of the species, all others having been destroyed in former eruptions of the volcano."

"How did the plant differ from the Heracleum?"

"It was almost identical, but the leaves of the male herb, which alone were used in the making of the vulnerary water, instead of being thin, like those of the Heracleum, were from a sixteenth to an eighth of an inch in thickness, and filled to fatness with the creamy liquor which both the doctor and Linnaeus had agreed ought to be, and would be, found in the species. These were collected with the greatest care, as well as the broadly ovate, strongly compressed, wing-margined seed pods, found only on the female herb. We returned with these to Naples where the juices were expressed from the leaves and carefully bottled. Then, with our precious freight of seeds and liquor, we set out on the homeward journey. But before leaving, Doctor Quittichunk arranged to have twenty tons of Vesuvius earth shipped home to him by a merchant vessel.

"We returned through France, and halted at Paris to see Doctor Quittichunk's friend, Monsieur l'Herbier, an apothecary of great distinction. You know of him, I presume, Mr. Larcum?"

"I do indeed, sir. Was it not he who wrote the treatise on the medicinal virtues of the hemlock?"

"The same; and who proved, by experiments upon himself, that the thorn apple, — the *pomme épeneuse* of the French, — the henbane, and the wolfsbane, then considered poisons, might be taken inwardly, not only with safety, but with advantage.

"And yet he was, at times, overzealous; he had not Doctor Quittichunk's patience and caution at the pharmaceutics, and would try out his medicaments too hastily. He was in a peck of trouble at the time of our visit, and the reason was this. The celebrated Madame d'Albon had a lovely daughter, a girl of eighteen, who had been attacked by a malignant fever which occasioned the falling-off of all her hair. The matter was kept secret, of course, and as the hair seemed not likely to grow again of itself, Monsieur l'Herbier was consulted. The despair of mother and daughter served as both challenge and spur to the great apothecary, who prepared a decoction based upon the powder of boxwood, and with this he washed the girl's head. Unfortunately, in his eagerness to see the result, Monsieur l'Herbier neglected precautions to secure the face and neck of Mademoiselle d'Albon from the lotion. The result was that, while hair of an enchanting chestnut color sprang forth luxuriantly upon her head, the face and neck were also covered, wherever, through carelessness, drops of the lotion had fallen. In this state the unfortunate young lady was at the time of our arrival."

"God's rabbit!" said Balthus. "A queer sight she'd be if there was much of it spilled about."

"So she was, Ned. 'Twould have been comical in the extreme had it not been, at the same time, so truly pathetic. And the worst of it was that the young woman was engaged to be married, and the event was at hand. Meanwhile, she was forced to remain hidden in Monsieur l'Herbier's dwelling, whilst he worked with feverish haste to discover some counter agency to repair the damage. He knew, of course, that he was ruined forever unless he could restore the once lovely girl to her former charms. Thanks to Doctor Quittichunk, this was perfectly accomplished. The doctor prepared a depilatory of the resin of the larch tree, mixed with that of mastiche, with which he had removed his own hair, and after three applications Mademoiselle d'Albon was restored to the beauty originally hers.

"The gratitude of mother and daughter was, naturally, boundless. Doctor Quittichunk was showered with favours, and we were asked to the great ball in honour of the coming nuptials. At this event, we found a principal topic of conversation to be the invention of an artificial limb called the Laurent leg, which had been made by a Monsieur Laurent, Chevalier of the Order of Saint Michael. One of Madame d'Albon's guests, Comte d'Epinay, who had lost a leg at Quebec, was present at the ball, wearing the Laurent limb.

"He was the first to display it in France and was the sensation of the evening. Generals, admirals, and great personages from Court crowded around him to examine the mechanism. There was a kind of rod came out of the thing, with a handle to it, and this had to be moved up and down at every step, to make the ankle joint work. The joint went click-clack loud enough to break your eardrums; for all that, it was a leg of a sort, and could be walked with. Monsieur Laurent himself, the inventor, was present at the ball, a fellow with a hawk nose, eaten up with vanity and conceit at the success of his invention.

"In order to display it the better, a minuet of four couples was arranged, in which the Comte d'Epinay danced with Madame d'Albon. I was asked to take part, and was honoured with the company of her lovely daughter as my partner. The clicking of the count's ankle joint made an abominable racket, and he needed one hand to work the lever at the side; nevertheless, he managed his figures with considerable adroitness. All present were lost in admiration, and, at the conclusion of the minuet, compliments were showered upon both the inventor and the user of the limb. . . . And then . . ."

Doctor Dogbody paused for a sip of his Port Royal; set down his glass, drew forth his handkerchief with great deliberation, and touched his lips.

"Don't tell us, Doctor, that you were foolish enough to speak of the Franklin leg?" Captain Murgatroyd put in.

"Inky, I was . . . and did. Mind you, I was then a young man, reckless and impulsive, and as proud of everything English as men of our nation have the right to be. Furthermore, I had danced with Mademoiselle d'Albon, and although few words had passed between us, we were placed, in that brief time, in a position of perfect mutual esteem and understanding. I divined at once her loathing for the Chevalier Laurent, to whom she was, in fact, affianced, — he was thrice her age, — and her despair at thought of marriage with him. She felt and deeply appreciated the sympathy I dared not express. And there was, I suppose, a kind of youthful vanity on my part: a desire to astonish, and to be looked upon with the interest accorded to the Comte d'Epinay. Even so, I would, I think, have kept silent had it not been for a remark made by Laurent to an officer seated beside him. The latter had complimented him to excess on his invention, and Monsieur Laurent had then told him that a copy of the leg had been sent to England. He knew me to be English, and added so that all could hear: 'We have deprived many of the English of their legs in our past wars, General, and will deprive more of them in the future. It is a matter of charity to furnish their invalids with substitute limbs, the more so since they lack the intelligence and the skill to provide them for themselves.'

"B'gad, 'twas too much for me! 'Monsieur Laurent,' said I, 'we have better limbs of artifice in England than those Frenchmen are born with,' and with that I rolled down my stocking, loosed the fastenings in the wink of an eye, removed my leg, held it forth for a moment, and as quickly replaced it.

"The company were speechless with amazement, and I realized at once what a fool I'd been. The leg was as good as lost. Unwittingly, I had been a traitor to my country, for not only would the French seize it, they would copy and furnish it in tens of thousands to their hosts of one-legged and no-legged soldiers and seamen whom our excellent English gunners, such as Ned Balthus here, had deprived of their members in the last war. In the next war — for there is always a next war with France — these would be thrown into the conflict in better state than whole men, and so great a reënforcement might well turn the scales of victory in their favour.

"Thanks to the presence of mind of Mademoiselle d'Albon, we were saved. She had not forgotten the debt of gratitude owed to Doctor Quittichunk, nor the unspoken sympathy that had made itself felt between us during the minuet.

" 'How wonderful!' she exclaimed. 'Monsieur Dogbody, you must dance the next minuet with my mother. Meanwhile, you and Doctor Quittichunk have not yet seen the conservatory, and I know the doctor's great interest in flowers.'

"Then, taking our arms, she led us from the salon with the ease and self-possession characteristic of French ladies in moments of emergency and danger. But once we were beyond view of the company she seized our hands and ran with us through a dozen passages, then out and across the park to a little private postern at a distant part of the gardens. And it was well she did, for the hue and cry was raised at once. There was scarce time for a word, but at the little gate reserve was banished. The lovely girl embraced the doctor and myself with all the ardour of her fresh young nature, and, taking a little pair of silver scissors from a reticule she carried at her wrist, she snipped off a tiny lock of the beautiful chestnut-coloured hair restored to her with such lavishness by Monsieur l'Herbier. This she pressed into my hand; then, 'Fly!' she whispered, and herself vanished in the darkness of the gardens.

"B'gad, fly we did! Doctor Quittichunk, for all his eighty years, fairly soared away before me, but I was right at his heels. Luckily for us, the streets of Paris were as badly lighted at that time as those of London, which is to say, there was scarcely a lamp in a half-mile. We had left hats and coats behind, and the doctor soon lost his wig. But there was a dim winter moon shining behind the clouds, and by the light of it, reflected upon the doctor's bald head, I was able to keep him within view. He was dressed in his usual black, and, save for his head, was a part of the darkness itself; but that was like a ball of St. Elmo's fire floating on before me, up courts and alleys, around corners, across bridges . . . b'gad, before the night was over I'd reason to know the value of the Franklin leg we were fleeing to save. The precision of its action, the perfection of the balance between the impulses given to coils, wires, and springs, made it, in sober truth, superior to its fellow of flesh and blood, and, unlike the other, it was tireless. Had I possessed a pair of them I could have run across France and the whole of Europe to Petersburg, and returned home by way of the Baltic.

"However, there was no need for such a roundabout journey, though once we came within an ace of being caught. In the maze of unfamiliar streets we lost our way, and had, evidently, doubled on our tracks, for we again found ourselves in the very quarter from which we had fled. As we paused to take bearings anew, we heard close at hand a sound there was no mistaking, the horrible click-clack of the Laurent leg. We had barely time to conceal ourselves in an entryway when there appeared a company of a dozen men, the Comte d'Epinay struggling hard to keep abreast of them, though they moved at a snail's pace on his account. They were preceded by servants furnished with *flambeaux* whose light blinded them, else they could scarcely have missed seeing us. Fortunately, they passed, and having, at length, eluded all of our pursuers, we hastened to our lodgings, and, with our precious cargo of seeds and vulnerary liquor, left Paris, in disguise, before dawn. We reached London three days later.

"Curiously enough, the Laurent leg was there before us, on display at Chelsea Hospital, where it was greatly admired by the virtuosi. A day or two later there appeared in the newspapers an announcement of a visit to be made by His Majesty at Chelsea for the purpose of viewing the leg. The doctor felt, and I, foolishly, agreed, that England should know of the Franklin leg; therefore, we set out for the hospital on the day of the royal visit.

"Though a private citizen, Doctor Quittichunk was known to and respected by the fashionable world, and had been more than once honoured in the houses of the great. As it chanced, we arrived at Chelsea well before the royal visitor and were at once admitted by the surgeon-general. We took our places amongst the other guests in the great hall where the Laurent leg was on display. By good fortune, the Duke of Bedford, known to the doctor, was present, and the latter begged the favour of a moment's conference. His lordship could not credit what the doctor assured him was true, that I was wearing a leg not my own, nor would he be perfectly satisfied until I had been escorted to an antechamber where it was my privilege to set his doubts at rest.

" 'Doctor Quittichunk,' said he, 'not a word of this to anyone for the moment! His Majesty has been on pins and needles to see the French leg. He will arrive directly, and, by God, we'll have something to show him when he comes!' He then gave me some instructions as to how I should behave. 'Get you back, now, to the hall,' he said. 'Keep me within view, and come forward when I bid you.'

"We did as directed, taking our places amongst the throng of notables who awaited the King. He arrived within the half-hour and was met by the surgeon-general and his staff. His Majesty was then in his thirties, his character well set, showing the forthright, dogmatical qualities and the bluff, hearty manners which distinguished him as a monarch and endeared him, as a man, to his people. Conversing with the surgeon-general, he came slowly down the hall toward the table where the Laurent leg reposed on a cushion of velvet.

" 'A French leg, what, what?' I heard him say as they passed.

" 'It is, Your Majesty,' the surgeon-general replied, 'and wonderfully ingenious.'

" 'Ingenious, is it? What? What? Damn my eyes! Must I put French legs on British soldiers and seamen? Can't have that, Surgeon — what? What? Such legs might carry my subjects off to serve against me.' He glanced quizzically at the surgeon-general as he said this, and the rest of the conversation was lost to me.

"His Majesty was seated whilst the Laurent leg was attached to the stump of an old Chelsea pensioner chosen to display it and practised in its use beforehand. He managed the contraption well enough, and the ankle joint went click-clack, click-clack. 'Twas thought a marvel by the company.

"I was near enough to hear what was said by His Majesty, whose attention was fixed on the display. There was a scowl of reluctant admiration upon his face. He was impressed, but the fact that it was a French invention rankled with him. The Earl of Chatham was standing at his side.

" 'Clever, Pitt — What? What?' said the King. 'But, damn my eyes! British subjects, French legs! Can't have that, can I? What? What? Where's my own inventors?'

" 'They've not been idle, Your Majesty,' Mr. Pitt replied; 'but I'm bound to admit that, thus far, they've not been able to equal the Laurent leg.'

" 'Numbskulls, what?' said the King. 'No brains. Let a Frenchman beat 'em. Can't be helped. Must have it, French or not. Have it copied. War with my damned Americans coming soon. Need legs in thousands, tens of thousands, before it's over. Have it copied, what?'

"The King was about to rise when the Duke of Bedford came forward and said: 'May it please Your Majesty, we have a leg of British manufacture superior, I believe, to this one.'

"The King's face lighted up. 'British, what?' he said. 'Then why the devil have I been shown a French one? Where is it, Bedford? Fetch it at once!'

"At a sign from the duke I then stepped forward, bowed deeply when opposite His Majesty, walked a few paces beyond, returned, bowed once more, and sank on one knee before him. The King looked from me to the Duke of Bedford with a nettled, puzzled expression upon his face.

" 'Who's this jackanapes?' he said. 'Fetch my British leg, Bedford.'

" 'The young man is wearing it, Your Majesty,' was the reply. At a nod from the duke I then rose, and, with the utmost respect walked to and fro before the King's seat. The company were dumbfounded and His Majesty stared at me completely incredulous. 'Come here, sir,' he commanded. He stooped and felt of my legs. 'Damme, what's this, Bedford?' he exclaimed, his face flushing with anger. 'His legs are as sound as my own!'

"I made haste, then, to put down my stocking, but the King was still deceived. It was not, indeed, until the leg was detached and in his hands, and I stood before him on my one leg of flesh and blood, that his doubt was removed. Then, gentlemen, I received the surprise of my life, and a sorry one it was. The old pensioner had, meanwhile, removed the French leg, which was restored to the cushion upon the little table. The King strode across to it, took it up, and thrust it into the surgeon-general's hands. 'Away with this!' said he. 'Burn it, bury it, or throw it in the Thames!' Then, tucking the Franklin leg under his arm, he marched down the hall to the entrance where his coach was waiting. But he halted midway to call back: 'Surgeon, give the young monkey a crutch to get home with. This leg is mine, what?' And out he went."

Doctor Dogbody paused to drain his glass.

"God's rabbit!" Balthus exclaimed, with a chuckle. "The shoe and stocking with it, Doctor?"

"Aye, Ned. The leg clothed and complete; and there was I, standing on my inferior leg of flesh and blood, steadying myself with a hand on Doctor Quittichunk's shoulder. . . ."

At this moment the door to the taproom was pushed slowly open, and there entered what appeared to be a small cone-shaped mound of snow. The snow was toppled off at the entrance and a bit of a lad emerged from beneath, his head bound round with an old shawl, and wearing a seaman's canvas jacket whose skirts dragged on the ground. Spying the surgeon, the lad called out, in a shrill voice: "Mrs. Quigg's compliments, sir, and she'll not answer for the gravy and the crust of the pigeon pasty unless ye come to dinner directly."

"What the devil!" the surgeon exclaimed, drawing forth his watch and consulting it hastily. "Come, splinter, and warm yourself whilst I get my hat and coat."

The lad approached and stood by the fire, the snow still upon him melting rapidly till he appeared of an even more diminutive stature; but he was well clothed and dry beneath the canvas jacket.

"Gentlemen, my apologies," said the surgeon, as, with Tom Tapleke's aid, he struggled into his greatcoat. "I'd no notion it was dinnertime."

"But why not have it here, Doctor?" Will Tunn urged. "If ye'll please to step into the kitchen and see what I've got on the spits . . ."

The surgeon shook his head. "Tunn, I cannot. Nor can I," he added, "ask ye all to dine with me. There's but the one small pigeon pie. Mrs. Quigg, my landlady, has gone to a deal of trouble with it on my account. I'd not wish to disappoint the good woman."

"You've carried us on wings, Doctor Dogbody," Mr. Chubb said, graciously. "It was the intention of Mr. Larcum and myself to propose that we all dine together."

"Were it possible, nothing would please me more, sir."

"But ye're standing on the one leg at Chelsea, Doctor," Balthus protested. "What became of the other? Ye can tell us that before ye go?"

The surgeon's eyes twinkled. "What! In a word? Be damned to ye, Ned! 'Tis the tale I was leading up to. But no," he added. "I owe ye the finish, no doubt."

"Aye," said Murgatroyd. "Go *bang* with that, for Balthus's sake."

The surgeon seated himself once more, holding his cocked hat on his knees. "So I will, Inky. In truth, there's little that remains to be told. I never saw the leg again. The King had it sent to Mr. J. Harrison, him — you'll remember, Ostiff — who won the great prize of Parlia-

ment, for his clock to determine the longitude. A genius
he was at the delicate mechanics; if anyone could have
copied the leg 'twould have been Mr. Harrison. After
keeping it a fortnight, he admitted that the mechanism
was beyond his guessing, and, to his honour be it said, he
refused to destroy the leg in the hope of learning its secret. He returned it to His Majesty, who was bigoted
enough to believe that anything an American could make
— even such a genius as Doctor Franklin — any Englishman could make, or, at least, copy. And he was, past question, provoked at Mr. Franklin for having invented a leg
for a nobody named Dogbody, a young surgeon's mate,
instead of offering it directly to himself. The long and
the short of it was, he would have it taken apart to discover the secret, and there was the end. Nothing was discovered save the ignorance of the man who did the King's
bidding."

"May I ask one question, Doctor?" said Mr. Larcum,
as the surgeon was about to rise. "You have yet to say
why Doctor Quittichunk's vulnerary water is no longer
obtainable."

"So I have, sir. 'Twas the great tragedy of the doctor's
life, and, undoubtedly, hastened his end. The plants, fed
with earth from Vesuvius, throve splendidly in his warm-
beds at Lamb's Conduit Fields. But in the great frost of
'eighty-two, when the cold was even beyond that of this
present December, every plant was killed. Doctor Quittichunk returned, of course, to Vesuvius, for a further
search, but the spot where the little plantation had been
was found buried deep in lava. Nor was any specimen
ever again found."

"So you were both great losers, with nothing to show, at the end, for so memorable an association," said Ostiff, musingly.

"The doctor had his Vesuvius earth, which he then used for other purposes. As for myself . . ." the surgeon smiled with an air of half-sad, half-pleasant recollection, "I have my memories of the Franklin leg. Nothing can deprive me of those. And I have one small memento of the time when I wore it — the lock of Mademoiselle d'Albon's hair."

"You kept it?" asked Murgatroyd, glancing up with interest.

The surgeon nodded. Drawing out his watch, he opened the case at the back and took from it a bit of folded paper, well worn, which he passed to the captain.

"I did, Inky. I scarcely know why, but I did. A lovely, charming girl she was. I heard, later, that she had refused at the last moment to marry Monsieur Laurent and entered a convent."

Balthus was craning his neck to peer over Captain Murgatroyd's shoulder as he opened the paper to examine the contents.

"Chestnut-coloured, ye said the hair was, Doctor?"

"You'll not judge of its colour then by what you see now," the surgeon replied. " 'Tis ravaged by time, Ned. Here, let me have it back. I should not have displayed such a keepsake."

A moment later he rose, buttoning his coat briskly.

"Come, splinter," he said, taking the small boy by the hand. "Boreas roars, but he'll not keep us from our pigeon pie."

V

RULE BRITANNIA

THE evening was a busy one at the Cheerful Tortoise, and Will Tunn's staff of servants were at the stretch, caring for the wants of the numerous company, above and below. In the taproom all the tables were occupied; the Argand lamps were blurs of mellow light in the haze of tobacco smoke, and a lively hum of conversation filled the air. Tom Tapleke shuffled from table to table on his flat feet, resentful of the unaccustomed activity, while Hodge, who had been pressed into the taproom service for the evening, made rapid zigzag sorties, answering the calls of thirsty patrons. With his bandy legs twin-

kling under him and his fusty wig askew, he resembled an
elderly and disreputable gnome who had strayed into
the place by accident and was frantically seeking some
means of escape. Will Tunn, delighted at seeing custom
pick up, strolled among the tables exchanging greetings
with his guests, all the while keeping a watchful eye
upon the two pretty barmaids busy at spigots and decan-
ters behind the high zinc-covered bar. He halted at the
table where Doctor Dogbody, Mr. Ostiff, Ned Balthus,
and Captains Runyon and Murgatroyd were seated. Mr.
Ostiff glanced up indignantly.

"How now, Tunn?" he remarked. "Is it first come,
last served at the Tortoise, and we the props of the
house?"

The landlord was profuse in his apologies and immediately hurried away to attend to their wants.

Doctor Dogbody had been gazing from time to time at
a gentleman in the uniform of a merchant captain who
was seated alone at a table on the far side of the room.

"Ned," he remarked, "I'll take my oath I know the officer yonder."

"It's like enough," the gunner replied. "He's the cut
of an old Navy man."

"An admiral, surely, in such a rig," said Runyon, with
an air of disapproval. "Or a nabob, no less."

The stranger was, indeed, handsomely dressed in broadcloth of robin's-egg blue, richly embellished with gold
braid, with lace ruffles of the finest material at his cuffs.
His white hair was tied with a ribbon of the same colour
as his coat.

"Aye, Runyon," Captain Murgatroyd replied; "he'll look so to an American, no doubt. There's none of your Yankee plainness and poverty in the India service. They'll have their captains dressed as befits their station. Shouldn't wonder if he commands the *Hindostan:* she came in this morning. Four months from Calcutta."

"He's the same advantage as yourself, Dogbody," said Ostiff. "A leg off just above the knee, and on the same side."

"You don't tell me," said the surgeon, craning his neck for a better view.

"I was here when he came. A handsome peg he's wearing if ever I saw one. Ivory it looks to be, inlaid with silver and gold."

At this moment the officer in question turned in his seat for a casual view of the company. Dogbody stared hard at him. "Damn my bones and blood!" he exclaimed. " 'Tis Dick Rodd!" Immediately he sprang from his seat and crossed the room to where the captain was sitting. His companions looked on with interest at the meeting which then took place; indeed, the attention of all the company was suddenly fixed upon the two old fellows who stood with hands clasped, beaming at each other as though scarcely able to credit their good fortune at the chance encounter. Nothing more nautical in appearance could have been seen in the whole of Portsmouth. Then Dogbody linked his arm in that of his companion and marched him across the room to his own table.

"Gentlemen," he announced, "you've heard me speak times without number of my old friend Dick Rodd."

"Captain Rodd, you rogue," his friend replied. "You'd deny me my rank, would you?"

"What you will, Dick, what you will," the surgeon replied, airily. "B'gad, had you left it to me to kick you upstairs I'd have made a handsomer job of it. You'd have stopped in the Navy and been Lord High Admiral by this time."

He then proceeded with the introductions, whereupon the company took seats again. "Now, Dick, bring me up to date," said Dogbody. "And first, ye renegade, what are ye doing in the merchant service?"

"He asks me that!" Captain Rodd replied, addressing the company in general. "Gentlemen, it was this same rascally surgeon who maimed me as you see me now. I'd a scratch on the leg, a mere nothing, and before I could draw breath to protest, he'd deprived me of the scratch and the leg with it."

"Tut, man," said Dogbody. "You'd not grudge a surgeon the practice of his trade? If ye recollect, 'twas a slack time with us when I took the limb. I'd the need to keep my hand in."

"I harbour no ill feelings, Dogbody. You might have the right leg as well, if I was as sure to get as handsome a peg to replace it as I have for the left."

"Whalebone, Captain?" the gunner asked.

"No, Mr. Balthus. Elephant's tusk. Dogbody, have ye ever seen such a work of art? The carving and inlay were all of a year in the execution. The leg is worth a prince's ransom. As a matter of fact, 'twas an Indian prince that gave it to me."

" 'Tis a pretty kickshaw. I wouldn't cheapen it, Dick, since ye seem to prize it so highly."

"Sour grapes!" said Captain Rodd, with a grin. "And small wonder, with such a common-looking thing on your own stump. You couldn't have bought it, surely?"

" 'Twas a gift, like your own," said the surgeon, stretching out his peg and regarding it with a complacent air. "I'd not exchange it for a dozen elephants' tusks."

"And who from? Some of your Scotch friends, I doubt not?"

"Ye really wish to know?"

"Aye; but first I'd learn how a sawbones managed to get sawn, for once, in his turn. Would ye bear with me, gentlemen?" he added, with a glance at the others. "I've not seen this fellow in better than twenty years. His history since we last met is a blank to me."

"With pleasure, Captain," Ostiff replied. "We are as curious as yourself. The doctor has been with us these four months past, but not a word will he say of his lost leg. Wild horses will not drag the tale from him."

"Nonsense, friend Ostiff," the surgeon replied, with a deprecatory wave of the hand. "What could be duller, in a seafaring, war-faring race like ours, than the tale of a missing leg? As far as interest goes, ye might as well ask Ned Balthus here what food he was wont to eat on banyan day."

"Damme if ye get off with that excuse," Captain Rodd replied. "You chopped off my leg, you villain! I'll have yours, now, in retrospect."

"You'd force me to it, would you?"

"We'd be pleased to learn, first, of your own loss, Captain," said Runyon. "The doctor will then be bound to oblige, in his turn."

"I can tell you that, sir, in scarcely more than a breath," Captain Rodd replied. "Dogbody and I were serving on the *Bedford* at the time. The *Bedford,* the *Prince Frederick,* and the *Magnanime,* under the command of Lord Howe, in the latter ship, were sent to reduce a fort on the little island of Dumet, on the French coast. The place was of no consequence, but there was excellent water upon it, wanted for servicing our fleet, then on blockade duty. The fort was silenced without the loss of a man, but one of their salvos shattered the *Bedford's* mizzenmast, and a splinter from the mast grazed the calf of my left leg. I would have bound up the little wound with my handkerchief and gone about my business. As it chanced, this butcher, Dogbody, was on deck at the moment. For all my protests, he, with his dressers and loblolly boys, seized and bore me to the after cockpit, and before I could have said 'Oh,' my leg was in his meat tub. Mine was the only casualty on our side."

The surgeon smiled. "You'll mind, Dick, how we carried you ashore, on the evening of that day, and buried the leg below the fort, with you looking on? You might give me credit for that, at least. 'Tis not every man who has the honour of witnessing his own partial interment. Did you know that the place is called Rodd's Island to this day, by Navy men?"

"So I've heard," the captain replied. "I've often thought to go back there and fetch the bones. They'd make a pretty keepsake for my grandchildren. I remember the very spot where you laid them."

"Bones? Bone meal is what we buried, and well ye know it! I've never seen a worse-shattered leg. You've me to thank, Dick Rodd, for a stump to set a peg on. Most surgeons would have had that, as well, in the state it was."

"I'll give you your due, Dogbody. It may have been more than a scratch I had. Now then, where's your own leg? Did ye buy an island with it?"

"I made a better bargain than that, sir. As in your own case, France has it, and a pretty penny it cost them!"

The surgeon paused to draw out his snuffbox, laid a train of the powder along the back of his left hand, snuffed it in with one deft movement, and replaced the box in his pocket.

"Dick, did ye ever know Bob Fingott?" he then asked.

"Fingott . . . Fingott . . . The name's familiar. A lieutenant, wasn't he? And a perfect ass?"

" 'Twas the reputation he bore, and I'll not say without some cause," the surgeon proceeded. "But for all his lack of judgment and his madcap ways, a better friend and comrade never trod the deck of a King's ship."

"Mind you, I never knew him personally, Dogbody. I don't remember that I ever set eyes on him. But I've heard mention more than once of a Lieutenant Fingott. Always in hot water, I believe. Court-martialed four times, or was it five?"

"Six," the surgeon corrected, "and came through with

flying colours every time. I was his fellow culprit before
the fifth court, and more than proud of the company.
B'gad, I'd sooner be hung with Bob Fingott than sit at
the Admiralty Board, bedecked with all the stars and
garters in His Majesty's gift of disposal. Near enough I
came to that end at the time I speak of."

"When was this?" Captain Rodd asked.

"In 1809, and Basque Roads was the place. You'll recollect, Dick, what happened there in the month of April,
in that year. Lord Gambier's Channel fleet had eleven
French ships of the line bottled up before Rochefort, to
say nothing of frigates, sloops, and bombs without number. And there were ourselves, outside, in the Roads,
under the command of Rear Admiral Robert Stopford,
doing what brave men could to taunt the enemy out to
battle. For all their numbers, the French squadron, under
Admiral Allemande, lay where they were, week after
week, moored in two compact lines, as close as they could
get under their batteries on the island of Aix, in Rochefort Harbour. 'Twas an all but impossible thing to get
at them with ships of any draught. But to be certain of im-
munity, they'd erected booms and impediments of every
description. And there they lay, snug and safe, as they
thought."

"There is this to be said for Admiral Allemande, Doctor," Captain Murgatroyd put in. "The French had some
new ships of the line building in Rochefort Harbour at
that time. The admiral was waiting till he could add
them to his strength."

"So he was, Inky," the surgeon replied. "I cast no reflections upon his courage. All I say is that we were tired of waiting till he would consent to come out."

"As I remember it, Admiral Wiliaumez was in command of the French fleet, then at Rochefort," said Ostiff.

"Under Admiral Allemande, Ostiff, as Admiral Stopford was under Lord Gambier, on our side. 'Twas Wiliaumez who got the blame for what we did to them, as it was Lord Gambier who reaped most of the glory with us, over Admiral Stopford's head, but 'twas the latter who deserved the credit.

"Well, having cooled heels and keels in Basque Roads for an unconscionable time, it was decided that we must, somehow, drive the enemy from their lair or destroy them where they lay. Admiral Stopford called a conference of his ships' captains on board the *Caesar,* in which ship I had the honour to be surgeon. Bob Fingott was one of the *Caesar's* lieutenants. A most gallant project was there formed for destroying the enemy by means of fire-ships, transports of light draught, loaded with explosives and combustibles, which should be sailed in amongst them. There is no need to tell old Navy men of the hazardous nature of such a project: hazardous in itself, and for this additional reason, that, by the laws of war, men taken by the enemy on such an expedition suffer death. For this reason it was to be a volunteer affair.

"Bob Fingott was one of the first lieutenants to volunteer, and the first to be accepted by Admiral Stopford. You may think this strange, in view of Fingott's reputation throughout the service, but Admiral Stopford knew what he was about. Bob was sure to go wrong in carrying out whatever orders, but, by a kind of genius, he invariably mounted on his mistakes to the most brilliant successes.

"There were to be twelve fire-ships and three explosion-ships, sailed in by a crew of five men each, in charge of a lieutenant. The lieutenants were to have the choosing of their own crews. Immediately after the conference on the *Caesar,* Fingott called me aside.

" 'Dogbody,' said he, 'was there ever such glorious luck? Now then, I want your advice as to the four men to go with me.'

" 'Four?' said I. 'I thought the number was five.'

" 'So it is,' said he, 'but I've already chosen the first,' and he put his forefinger, like the muzzle of a pistol, against my breastbone.

" 'Thank you kindly, Bob,' said I; 'but I'll not be burned up or blown up for any lieutenant in His Majesty's service. Furthermore, ye know damned well they'll never permit a ship's surgeon to volunteer for any such expedition as this.'

" 'They?' said he. 'What have *they* got to do with it? I'm to choose my own men, and, by God, you're to be one of them!'

"Well, the long and the short of it was that I let him win me over. He'd the most engaging, peremptory way with him, and I loved the man, of course. B'gad, had he wished to set his mind to it, he could have persuaded a Scotch parson to leap with him into the fiery pit. I knew this was about what it would come to, in my own case, with such a leader. 'Bob,' said I, ' 'twill be as much as my commission is worth if the matter is discovered. I'll be broke and dismissed the service as sure as sunrise.' But he had a ready answer to every objection I could make. It was to be a night expedition, of course, and we'd be either killed, captured, or safe back well before daylight. In the latter case, he'd pawn his honour to get me aboard the *Caesar* once more, and no one the wiser."

The surgeon paused to taste his grog, and Murgatroyd took advantage of the opportunity to remark: "I believe I once met Fingott, at Christmas time, in the North Sea. A short fellow, wasn't he, and none too tidy about his person?"

"*Believe* you met him?" said the surgeon. "Damme, you could never be in any doubt, if you had! As for his person, he was short and dirty as a winter's day. Ye'd have had a merry Christmas, if he was of the party."

"We did that! And at the end of it, Fingott swum back to his own ship for a two-pound wager. A calm still day it was, but cold as Greenland. Such a bath would have killed another man."

" 'Twas Fingott, certain. There's nothing he wouldn't do for a wager. When we were serving together in the *Marlborough,* at the time of the Duke of York's visit to Spithead, Fingott got to the very top of the vane of the mainmast, and stood there upon his head, waving a little Union Jack which he held in his bare toes. At so great a height he looked no larger than your little finger. He was a mid at the time, and such a prank would have gotten anyone else into a peck of trouble. But His Royal Highness was so taken with the lad's daring, damme if he didn't get Bob his lieutenant's commission for it!"

"How was your fire-ships fitted out?" Balthus asked, fearful lest the surgeon should branch off on one of his long digressions.

"Where's the need to tell an old Navy gunner of that?" said Dogbody. "Ye must have prepared fire-ships yourself, more than once."

"So I have," said Balthus, "and never twice the same."

"In truth, Ned, 'twas a matter of great interest to me, for I'd never seen it done till then. Two of the vessels, the *Thomas* and the *Whiting,* old transports of three hundred and fifty tons, were fitted out by the *Caesar's* men. For the *Thomas,* narrow troughs were made, with others to cross them, and in these were laid trains of quickmatch. In the square openings of these troughs were put the combustibles: open casks of resin, turpentine, and coal tar. Tarred canvas hung above, fixed to the beams, and great loose bundles of tarred shavings. Four portholes were cut on each side for the fire to burst through, and thick ropes of twisted oakum, well tarred, led from each of the ports to carry the fire up the standing rigging to the sails and mastheads. B'gad, nothing was wanting to make a very furnace of each vessel, the moment they were set aflame.

"The *Whiting* was to be an explosion-ship. In her hold there were stowed, upright, thirty-six barrels of gunpowder, of ninety pounds each. The heads of the casks were out and on each was placed a ten-pound shell, with a short fuse, in order to burst quickly. A canvas hose filled with prime powder was laid for a train from the barrels through a small hole in the ship's quarter, to the outside. It was there she was to be touched off, with a fuse to burn from twelve to fifteen minutes to give the men in her time to get well away in their boat before the explosion.

"The preparations were of the most thorough description. Lord Cochrane, who was to command the expedition, was a very genius at this work and left nothing to chance.

"On the eleventh of April, all was in readiness: three explosion-ships and twelve fire-ships completely equipped, and their little crews eager to be off. The night could not have been more perfect. The tide was making, the sky overcast, and the wind fresh from the north. At eight o'clock the signal was made to weigh . . ."

"Pawl there, Dogbody," Captain Rodd interrupted. "I'll not have the details scanted at this rate. You were not to go without convoy, surely? And what was the order of your going?"

"I should have spoken of that. We were not, of course, sent in without support. With us went the sloops *Aigle, Pallas,* and *Unicorn:* they were to lie near the Boyard shoal, to receive the boats returning from the fire-and-explosion ships when the work was done. The *Indefatigable* and the *Foxhound* were to lie near the island of Aix, to protect the *Aetna,* bomb, whilst she threw shells into the batteries there. The *Emerald, Dotterel, Beagle, Insolent, Conflict,* and *Growler* were to make a diversion on the east side of Aix. All these latter vessels were fitted with Congreve rockets, to spread terror and confusion amongst the enemy. The *Lyra* and *Redpole* were sent ahead of all to anchor, with lights showing, the first on the Boyard side, the other on the Aix side. They were to serve as a guide to the channel to the rest that followed. Lord Cochrane, in the *Impérieuse,* was to act as circumstances would permit, but going in as far as possible to take up the men escaping in the boats, in case they should miss the vessels told off for rescue. There was the order of it, Dick. Is all clear now?"

"Aye, proceed," said the captain.

"There is one particular I have not yet mentioned. The French had placed, amongst their other obstructions for safety, a heavy boom across the channel to the inner roads where their ships of the line were moored. That had to be broken. To effect this, the old *Mediator,* frigate, also equipped as a fire-ship, was to lead the way, crashing through the boom and opening up the channel for the ships of light draught that followed.

"Fingott got me aboard the *Thomas* at dusk without a soul aware of the fact save our little crew. The four others, all of the *Caesar,* were a quartermaster's mate and three seamen. One of these latter, Runyon, chanced to be a countryman of yours in our service, a brisk lad, Jack Ellis, known as Yankee Jack to his shipmates.

"Fingott was tearing to be off, but we had to wait our signal. The *Mediator* went first, then the three explosion-ships, then the fire-ships in a particular order, each one about half a cable's length from the next ahead. We were fifth in the line, following the third of the explosion-ships.

Fingott had put the lot of us, in the *Thomas,* in French uniforms stole from amongst the effects of some prisoners we had in the *Caesar,* off the *Jalouse,* frigate, which had struck to us the week before. As I've said, men taken by the enemy on a fire-ship expedition suffered death. Very well, said Fingott. Since we would run no greater risk by doing so, we'd go disguised as Frenchmen, and we might well meet with opportunities denied to the others. He spoke French near as well as myself, and was dressed in a captain's outfit. Mine was that of a lieutenant of marines, and the fellow must have had an admiral's belly. However, I stuffed out waistcoat and breeches with a feather pillow and the rig did well enough."

"Was ye cool, Doctor?" Runyon asked.

"At this time? B'gad, no! I was shaking in my shoes, but I'd the vanity not to let Fingott see it. But mind you, Runyon: scared as I was, there was an exhilaration in the venture to have made a very sheep happy to be a part of it. Fingott was in his glory. He'd no imagination, not an atom. I doubt if ever the man knew the least tremor of fear. He had the wheel at the start, and was humming 'Rule Britannia' to himself in his deep bass voice.

"The place where our fleet lay was a good fifteen miles out, which gave Bob plenty of room for starting his mischief.

" 'Dogbody,' said he, presently, 'we'll be first in, what d'ye say? Show the lot of 'em a clean pair of heels.'

" 'Not with my consent,' said I. 'Damn your eyes, Bob! Stick to orders for once. We're to keep fifth place.'

"He clapped me on the back. 'Never fear, old cock! I'll earn ye more glory in the next three hours than ye'd hoard up in fifty years as a sawbones.'

" 'I've no wish to have it in a lump,' said I. 'Be prudent, Bob, for God's sake!'

"I might have saved my breath. There was no reasoning with such a madcap, once he'd made up his mind. The *Thomas* was a fast-sailing little vessel, and Fingott had been ordered to use none but his headsails so as to be sure to keep his place. But nothing would do, now, but we must hoist more, and we began to surge forward. There never was a blacker night, at the start, but each vessel had a light showing astern to guide the one behind her. We were scarce two miles on our way when we passed the explosion-ships. What they thought I don't know. They may have believed us some French merchantman slipping in unawares of what the British were up to. In any case, not a hail did they give as we passed. But Captain Woodridge, in command of the *Mediator,* had sharper eyes. We passed almost within spitting distance, though we were a mere shadow, and he guessed what was up.

" 'What ship is that?' he roared through his speaking-trumpet. 'Is it you, Bob Fingott?'

"No reply from Bob save a low chuckle. Then, gentlemen, we were treated to the most accomplished explosion of blasphemous rage it has been my privilege to hear in more than sixty years at sea. But it trailed away behind us and became inaudible. The *Mediator* had all sails set, but she was deeply and heavily ballasted for the sake of

the great boom she was to break, and she'd not yet full
way on her."

"Damn his soul!" Captain Rodd broke in. "Was Fingott so great a fool as to endanger the success of the entire
expedition?"

"He was, Dick. And he feared neither man, beast, devil,
nor Admiral Gambier himself. I reminded him of the
boom ahead and asked if he thought we'd break it with
our little three-hundred-and-fifty-ton transport. 'Never ye
fret about that, Dogbody,' said he. 'The boom will be
well sunk for ships of deeper draught than this. I'll take
my oath we'll pass over it with a foot or two to spare.'

"By this time we could see, far ahead, the lights of the
Lyra and *Redpole,* marking the way for us. As soon as
they came within view, commanders had only to hold a
course midway between them, and they'd be right for
the channel where the boom was fixed."

"Ye fetched over it?" Balthus asked.

"I'm coming to that," said the surgeon. "We're not
there yet. You'll recollect, Dick, how the harbour of
Rochefort lies, with the Ile d'Oléron enclosing it to the
west and south? When you've passed the Antioch Rock,
off the northern tip of Oléron, there's another ten miles,
or thereabout, before you fetch the island of Aix. Fingott said he knew the place better than the palm of his
hand and held his course with the utmost confidence, all
the while quizzing me for being a sour old bachelor, as
he called it. Unless I made haste to wed, there'd be no
children for me to tell my tales to as an old man, above
all, the story of the glorious night of April eleventh,

when Lieutenant Robert Fingott was first in with his
fire-ship and destroyed the entire French fleet. Presently
he left off his banter, and I could see he was worried.

" 'Where's the blasted boom?' said he. 'Ought to be
hereabout. Blast me if I don't believe we've sailed over it!'

"We hadn't long to wait to know where the thing
lay. The words were scarce out of his mouth when we
struck it.

" 'Twas no honest, downright, shattering blow that
tells ye the worst at once. The thing played with us as
though it had a kind of intelligence. Fingott had not
been far off in reckoning how deep it would lie, but he
was just wrong enough to do us all the damage necessary.
The little *Thomas* slipped up on it, heeled over to starboard, and there we stuck. Then the boom swung back
slow and we slid along a bit more till we were slightly
down by the head. This gave us hope that she'd inch
along over it, for the wind was fresh and coming from
right aft, and our mainsail had the full good of it. We
began to slip down, ever so slowly.

" 'We'll make it, lads! By God, we will!' said Fingott.
'Half a minute more and we'll be clear. Dogbody, what
d'ye say now? Was I right to take the chance?' "

The surgeon paused to draw out his silk bandana, and
blew his nose loudly. "I'd no need to answer that question, gentlemen," he then resumed. " 'Twas answered for
me by a frigate of fourteen hundred tons."

"God's rabbit!" Balthus exclaimed. "I was about to
ask ye, Doctor, what space ye had with the *Mediator*
right astern."

"About thrice the length of this taproom, Ned, at the moment when we cleared the boom, for clear it we did. Will ye believe it? In the excitement of getting off we'd clean forgot the frigate. 'Twas Jack Ellis that spied her first. 'Hold hard!' he yelled; then we all saw her. The sky was clearing to seaward, and there she came, seething down upon us, her sails seeming to reach the very stars. She had way enough on her now, b'gad! Fingott put his helm hard over, and much good it did him! The *Mediator* struck the boom, lifting the great beams clear of the water and tearing them apart with a rending and crashing of chains and timbers. On she came as though the impediment had been so many ropes of straw. There was no room to stand clear of us. Out went my feet from under me; I saw all the stars in the mind's firmament, and when I came round I was lying in the bottom of our jolly boat, with Jack Ellis spilling some of Fingott's flask of brandy over my chin.

" 'What's this, Jack?' said I. 'Where are we, and where's the *Thomas?*'

"His reply was lost in a shuddering roar that Vesuvius could scarce have made, in full eruption. The first of the explosion-ships had been touched off, not half a mile from where we lay. By the light, I saw the *Thomas* near by, settling by the stern. Down she went as I looked at her, with all her combustibles intact. Then the second of the explosion-ships blew up. We bobbed about in our little boat with burning wreckage falling on every side. The men had their oars out, awaiting Fingott's orders. He sat with the tiller under his arm, staring at the spot where the *Thomas* had sunk, blood streaming down the side of his face from a cut he'd got.

" 'Dogbody,' said he, 'we've disgraced ourselves forever!'

"I could have spared his generosity in sharing the blame with me, but I said nothing, and waited to see what he'd do next."

"What! Not a word?" said Captain Rodd. "You were a blessed saint, Dogbody, if you'd so firm a command of your feelings. Damn his blood! I'd have had the last drop of it if he'd gotten me into such a mess!"

"No, Dick. Not if you'd known Fingott. 'Twas at just such a moment, when bogged to the chin in a mess of his own making, that his guardian angel took him by the hand and raised him out of it. The man was a genius at falling on his feet.

"He got to those feet now, in the stern sheets of the jolly boat, and looked about him. We were about a mile to the west of Aix. I wish it were within my power to give you a picture of Rochefort Harbour as we saw it then. 'Twas a spectacle truly awe-inspiring. The third of the explosion-ships now blew up, whilst the fire-ships, with flames roaring hundreds of feet into the air, were drifting in every direction. Land and sea for miles around stood out in clear relief in the awful light. The French batteries on Aix were in full action, endeavouring to sink the fire-ships and the convoy that had followed us in, and these latter were replying as hotly with shells and Congreve rockets. A more infernal sight could scarce be conceived. 'Twas fit to mimic the Day of Judgment.

"Fingott wiped the blood from his face with his coat-sleeve and took the tiller. 'To the oars, lads,' he said. 'Break your backs! Our luck's been out thus far, but, by God, we'll better it before the night's done!' The men pulled with a will, and Fingott steered us straight for the French fleet. The instant we were under way he was his old self again. 'Dogbody,' said he, 'how's the feather belly? Full of courage?' He was alluding to the pillow I had under my borrowed French waistcoat and breeches.

" 'Lead on,' said I. 'I'd as soon be killed or taken by the French as be flung out of His Majesty's Navy in disgrace. Ye promised me glory, Bob Fingott. If ye miscarry a second time, I'll smother you with that same belly!'

"We proceeded into the midst of a scene of the wildest confusion. One of the fire-ships had run afoul of the *Océan,* a one-hundred-gun ship, which was all aflame, her men pouring out of her like rats. The ships on either side were being unmoored in frantic haste; we saw the *Aquilon* and the *Tonnerre* already free and drifting toward the Palais Shoal, where they soon grounded and heeled over. The sea all round their fleet was alive with boats rushing about like water spiders on various errands. No notice was taken of us, and Fingott steered right on. He was awaiting the inspiration of the moment, and presently spied it through flame and smoke: a ship of the line anchored a good half mile from where the fleet lay. We found a six-oared boat alongside, empty, and a boarding ladder let down as though for our convenience. 'Twas the *Varsovie,* a brand-new ship, though not yet in commission. She was lying there to take in her guns.

"We made the painter of our boat fast and followed Fingott up the ladder, not knowing what we'd find the next moment. We found no one. 'Twas such luck as would come only to a Fingott, but aft, in the ward room, still smelling of gilding and new paint, was a detachment of ten marines, under a lieutenant, all stretched out on the bare deck, asleep. On guard duty, and snoring through all that uproar!

"There was Fingott's chance. As I've said, he was near as perfect in his French as myself, and even better skilled to speak the argot of their Navy. We roused them out, and Fingott gave the lieutenant a dressing-down would have done credit to a post captain. They were scared as rabbits at having been caught asleep, and must have thought the end of the world had come when they saw what was taking place outside. They never doubted us French. Fingott drove them before him to the gangway and told the lieutenant he was to report at once with his men aboard the *Aquilon*. They sprang into their boat and off they went.

"Not a moment did we lose. We rushed down to the main gun deck where a dozen new thirty-two-pounders were already in place. Fingott seized a swab, plunged it into a bucket of tar, and this was set aflame. Down he led us into the bowels of the ship, and, with that flaring torch to light us, we gathered up shavings, oakum, bits of new boards and beams left by the shipwrights, and within twenty minutes we had the ship burning fiercely in half-a-dozen places. 'Twas a crime, no less, for she was a splendid ship, but we did it for Old England's sake, to

say nothing of our own. By the time we cleared out,
nothing could have saved her.

" 'Bob,' said I, as we scrambled into our boat once
more, 'there's glory enough for the six of us. We'd best
push home now whilst we've whole skins.'

" 'Home!' said he. 'We've only just started.' He was
rapt clean out of himself with so huge a success and
thought no more of our safety than he did of his own.
For all that, I'd never have believed he was daft enough
to do what he did next.

"We passed three frigates, still at moorings, but he
gave them scarce a glance. He was so flushed with success
that nothing less than a ship of the line was game for
us. The *Foudroyant* lay next.

" 'Lads,' said he to the seamen as we made toward
her, 'the surgeon and I are going aboard yonder. Do you
lie close by within hail. If we fail to appear within
twenty minutes, make the best of your way out to one
of the rescue ships.' Then, with a nod to me, up the side
he went, as cool as though he were the captain himself,
coming aboard after a night in town.

"Everything was in confusion on deck, for rockets
and bombs from our sloops were bursting on every side.
Wounded men were being carried below and some still
lay as they'd fallen. Fingott strode aft with me at his
heels. We found a lieutenant in charge of the quarter-
deck. 'Where's your commander?' demanded Fingott.
The lieutenant stared hard at him. 'He's been hit, sir,'
he then said. 'You are in charge of the deck?' asked Bob.
'I am, sir,' replied the other. 'Then slip your cables

without an instant's delay!' said Fingott. What he hoped to do was to get the *Foudroyant* adrift and grounded where she could be destroyed at leisure, and damme if he didn't come within an ace of succeeding! But a Congreve rocket, fired at that moment from one of our sloops, did for the pair of us. The thing came flaming over and burst almost upon us, and a fragment of the iron casing ripped open my belly. Or, to be more exact, it ripped open what would have been my belly had I been as fat in the middle part as the French lieutenant whose uniform I wore. The result was that I was damaged only in the feathers, but these flew out in a blinding cloud."

The surgeon paused to glance at Captain Rodd.

"I'm coming to the leg, Dick," he resumed, "but 'twas the belly that went first. Large as the pillow was I was stuffed with, ye'd never have believed there could be such a mort of feathers in it. They came and they came, and when I thought I was all but emptied, another cloud greater than the last would be teased out by the wind, which was still blowing fresh, and whirled aloft and about the decks.

"We were lost from that moment. I knew it and Fingott knew it. Nevertheless, we stood our ground, trying to make it appear that nothing was amiss and that all wounded men, upon occasion, were as like as not to bleed feathers.

"'*Tonnerre de Dieu!*' Fingott roared, when he could see once more. 'Do ye stand there gaping, Lieutenant? Unmoor, I say! Slip your cables at once, sir!'

"The fellow spat out two or three feathers that he had inadvertently drawn in with his breath. 'By whose authority?' he then replied.

" 'That of Admiral Wiliaumez,' said Fingott. 'I've come from him this instant.'

"But it wouldn't do. He had no more than spoken when a voice at our backs replied: 'From *me,* sir? *I* am Admiral Wiliaumez.'

"We turned quickly, and there in truth was the admiral himself, who had just emerged from the companionway with the *Foudroyant's* captain, the latter's head bound round with a bloody cloth.

"Fingott saw that the game was up, but he lost none of his self-possession. With a faint smile, he drew his borrowed French sword, and, with great dignity, tendered it by the blade to the admiral. 'Then I am your prisoner, sir,' he replied. 'Lieutenant Robert Fingott, of His Majesty's ship *Caesar.* . . . Surgeon F. Dogbody, likewise of the *Caesar,'* he added as I proffered my blade, and with it another storm of feathers, largess for the entire ship's company."

"Damn your eyes and feathers, Dogbody," Captain Rodd broke in, with a chuckle. "A wonder it is that the pair of you were not guillotined as you stood, with your own swords. Well you deserved to be!"

"We expected no less," the surgeon replied; "but the French honour reckless courage as well as ourselves. We were secured at once, of course, but treated with the utmost courtesy. As my hands were being tied behind my back, Admiral Wiliaumez stepped forward to inspect my wounded middle part, thrust his hand into the aperture, and drew forth the tattered pillow. Then, gentlemen, followed a white storm that even surpassed the earlier ones. 'Twas like the fairy tale of the mill that makes the sea salt: there was magic in the pillow; its contents seemed to come from an inexhaustible supply. With the utmost gravity, the admiral handed the not-yet-emptied casing to a midshipman, who made haste to carry it to leeward and toss it over the bulwark. The admiral turned to me, and I could see that he maintained his composure with some difficulty. 'Surgeon Dogbody,' said he, 'I wish the wounds of my own men were of as light a nature as this.' He then gave orders that we were to be carried aboard the *Calcutta* and placed under a strict guard."

"The *Calcutta*? Was she not destroyed in the Basque Roads affair?" Captain Murgatroyd asked.

"She was, Inky, but not until the day following the running-in of the fire-ships. All of these latter had miscarried save the one that burned the *Océan;* nevertheless, Admiral Stopford's purpose had been well served. The French had been forced to unmoor, and on the morning of April twelfth, all save two of their ships were aground on the Palais Shoal, some of them helpless and exposed to our further damage. Admiral Stopford ordered the *Caesar* and the *Theseus* into Rochefort Harbour, and the *Caesar* was able to get close enough to the *Calcutta* to effect her destruction. 'Twas then that Fingott and I, with the *Calcutta's* men, were treated to a dose of British ball from our own ship that I shudder to think of to this day. My leg went in one of the first salvos, and this time

I bled something worse than feathers! Fingott was wounded as well, though not gravely. The end of it was that the *Calcutta* was abandoned, a complete wreck, and the pair of us were taken to the naval hospital in Roche-fort.

"With your leave, Dick, I will now pass over the next four months. They were not, in truth, eventful for pris-oners-of-war. Fingott never lost his spirits, but I was sad enough, at times, knowing what we had in prospect as soon as we had recovered from our wounds: the final wound of all, either strung up at a yard arm, or stood up against a wall, facing a firing squad. We hoped for the latter, but never doubted it would be one or the other. Fingott was up and about long before myself. There never was such a man to make friends with no matter whom. He knew everyone in the hospital, from the chief surgeon down to the girls who brought the bread, and was on first-name terms with most of them. At last, when I was able to hobble with a crutch, we were ordered be-fore a naval court.

"We were tried on the *Foudroyant*, Admiral Wiliau-mez himself presiding. The examination was as brief as it was fair and unprejudiced. We made no attempt to defend ourselves, but freely admitted our part in the fire-ship expedition. The evidence having been heard, we were dismissed to await sentence.

"A quarter of an hour later we were again escorted to the admiral's great cabin. Court and spectators rose as we entered, and stood in deep silence, awaiting the words of Admiral Wiliaumez. He was a man of noble bearing, with a countenance grave, serene, and commanding. He stood with his hands resting lightly on the table before him. The interval seemed endless to me. Then he spoke.

" 'Lieutenant Robert Fingott — Surgeon F. Dogbody: Having heard the evidence in support of the charges made against you, and having heard your own freely offered testimony which confirms that evidence, and having maturely and deliberately weighed the whole, this Court is of the opinion that the charges have been proved. It doth, therefore, judge that you shall die.'

"He paused, and we waited in numb despair to learn whether we were to suffer the ignominy of being hung, or whether we were to be accorded the melancholy honour of a firing squad.

" 'But,' continued the admiral, — and never has that small word produced in me so profound an emotion, — 'but . . . it is neither the desire nor the intention of this Court to hasten that judgment. On the contrary, it is the wish of my officers and myself that it may be carried out only through natural causes, in the fullness of time, when you are as distinguished in years as, by your courage and hardihood, on the night of April the eleventh last, you are ennobled by the honours which your grateful country will, doubtless, confer upon you. Lieutenant Robert Fingott — Surgeon F. Dogbody: I sentence you to be returned to that country with all the honours of war.' "

"What! Ye was let off?" Balthus exclaimed.

"You may well be astonished, Ned. Imagine our own amazement at the moment. I was so shaken with relief and joy that the crutch I balanced with slid from under my shoulder and down I went before the assembled Court! As I was helped to my feet, or, better, my foot, Admiral Wiliaumez smiled and remarked that I'd best be furnished now with another feather pillow for the reverse side of my anatomy, which set them all to laughing."

"Nonsense, Dogbody!" Ostiff remarked. "You tell us that a court-martial in an admiral's ship was as informal as this comes to?"

"It was, Ostiff, but I'd be the last to say it was a common thing. It could never have happened with us, for British officers stand too much on their dignity. The French are vastly our superiors in the gracious art of unbending, upon suitable occasions. They excel us in magnanimity to an even greater extent. Can you imagine a British court that would forgive two officers of an enemy nation that had stolen into one of our very harbours and destroyed a ship of the line? 'Tis not conceivable. They might have called them brave fellows, but they'd have hung them like dogs."

"There was pride in it, to my thinking," said Ostiff. "The French wished to belittle Admiral Stopford and the fire-ship expedition by making it appear that they considered you harmless and not worth the hanging."

"Never, Ostiff, never," the surgeon replied. "Say what you may, you'll not lower my opinion of that most noble action. 'Twas pure magnanimity."

"How were you sent home?" asked Runyon.

"Admiral Wiliaumez fulfilled his promise to the letter.

The following day we were brought once more on board the *Foudroyant,* where, to my infinite surprise, I was presented with the leg that I wear at this moment, the gift of the admiral and his officers.

" 'Surgeon Dogbody,' said the admiral, in making the presentation, 'you have been deprived of a leg by your own countrymen. Accept this substitute, the gift of your country's enemies, and may it bring you to France, under more happy auspices, when we are again at peace.' He then paused, and a smile in which grimness and humour mingled crossed his face. 'But you are not to try our good nature too far,' he added. 'Should you venture amongst us again whilst our nations are at war, we will require the return of our gift. And not only the leg, sir! Though you should come adorned, or stuffed, with the feathers of all the plucked geese of Arcady, they will not suffice, a second time, to save your head.' "

"I should think not, indeed," said Murgatroyd, with a laugh. "It was undoubtedly the pillow that saved you, Dogbody."

"So I believe," said the surgeon, "though Fingott would never acknowledge this. Had I not bled feathers in so astonishing and seemingly inexhaustible a fashion, which touched Admiral Wiliaumez's sense of humour, the pair of us would have been dead these nine years. I have since had an affection amounting to idolatry for both ducks and geese. I would not taste the flesh of the noblest bird of either species that Will Tunn might roast upon his spits."

"Did ye wear the peg home?" asked Balthus.

"I did; it was attached to my stump there and then. When Fingott and I had made our grateful *adieux* to the admiral and his officers, four longboats, under a flag and manned by seamen in their dress uniforms, conducted us out to Basque Roads where our fleet still lay. We were, of course, thought to be dead by our comrades, and you can imagine the amazement in the *Caesar* as we approached that ship, with a band of music playing in the leading boat. Our comrades swarmed on the yards and lined the bulwarks, and, as we came on deck, wild cheering burst forth from all ranks. But it was soon silenced. Captain Woodridge, who had taken in the *Mediator* on the night of April eleventh, was now in command of the *Caesar,* and what did he do but clap us under arrest the moment our French escort was gone! We were, later, court-martialed, as I've said, and it was no thanks to Woodridge that we were not dismissed the service. As it was, Navy discipline demanded that we be found guilty of disobeying orders and sentenced to be reprimanded.

" 'Twas Admiral Stopford himself who delivered the reprimand, in the privacy of his own cabin. He ushered us in, and locked the door behind him; then he brought out a bottle of his best French brandy. Having filled our glasses, he raised his own.

" 'Lads,' said he, 'God bless you! Here's to Old England, and to Surgeon Dogbody's feather belly!' "

" 'Twas a handsome way of letting ye down," said Balthus.

"Was it not? He kept us with him a full hour, for he

wanted all the details of the burning of the *Varsovie,*
and I took pride in showing him my new peg."

"I'd have spared calling his attention to such a clumsy-
looking thing," said Captain Rodd. "The poorest carpenter's mate in our service could have made you a
better one."

The surgeon stretched out his peg, regarding it fondly
for a moment. "Hodge!" he called.

The little waiter was still bustling about the taproom
on his tasks, though the place was half empty by now.
Setting down a tray of glasses on the bar, he hastened
to the call.

"Unstrap my peg," said Dogbody.

Hodge had performed this service more than once for
the doctor when he wished to rest his stump. He knelt
down and quickly loosed the straps, whereupon Dogbody
set the peg upright on the table before the company.

"I'll show you, Dick, why I prize it so highly, beyond
its associations," he remarked, with a glint of triumph
in his eye. " 'Twas not the gift of an Indian prince, to be
sure, but I fancy it nonetheless."

The cylindrical part of the peg, next the stump, was
of plain polished oak. The surgeon pressed a tiny button
that appeared to be a knot in the wood itself, and immediately two panels slid back revealing a pair of mer-
maids, their bodies of ivory, their tails of gold, upholding
a curved balcony, of exquisite workmanship, with a little
gateway of filigree gold midway along it. The surgeon
waited while a hidden mechanism whirred within. The
gate then opened, and two little figures, dressed in the

uniforms of English naval officers, came stiffly out from a sculptured niche and stood upon the balcony while a music box, likewise hidden, tinkled 'Rule Britannia.' The music ceased; the little figures turned about and marched to their niche; the gateway closed behind them, the wooden panels slid back into place, and the leg appeared as it had before.

Balthus was the first of the company to break silence.

"God's rabbit!" he exclaimed, bringing his fist down with a hearty thump. "I never saw the beat of that, for a peg!"

"It does well enough for an old Navy surgeon," said Dogbody, with a glance at Captain Rodd.

VI

THE HAPPY RETURN

THE hour had gone seven when Will Tunn's favoured patrons, having dined abovestairs, descended to the tap-room, each of them wearing the look of content and solid well-being which a dinner at the Tortoise never failed to bring forth. The meal had been of Captain Murgatroyd's ordering, in honour of his friend John Honeywood, Esquire, of Hertfordshire. Mr. Honeywood had the appearance of a plain hearty countryman. He was solidly built, and his face, ruddy with health and out-of-doors living, had now an added glow, caused by the two bottles of excellent port he had drunk at dinner.

His manners were easy and affable, and it was evident that he approved of Captain Murgatroyd's friends as heartily as they approved of him. All were present upon this occasion, and as soon as they were seated at the accustomed table, the landlord himself came forward to attend to their further requirements.

"Inky," Doctor Dogbody was saying, "I'd not known until this evening that you are a native of Hertfordshire."

"Born at Webwyn," Captain Murgatroyd replied. "Mr. Honeywood and I first saw the light within a few hours of one another, and in the same village."

"You've been to Ware, of course?"

Murgatroyd nodded.

"And have seen the great bed?"

"A time or two, in my younger days, but Honeywood tells me that it has been removed from the old Crown Inn."

"Aye," his friend replied, "the inn was pulled down long since, to make room for a gentleman's seat. The bed now stands in Rye House."

"What bed is that?" Balthus asked.

"You tell me, Ned Balthus, you've never heard of the great bed of Ware?" said the surgeon. "The one mentioned by Shakespeare? 'Tis the oldest in the whole of England. I am right in this, I think, Mr. Honeywood?"

The other nodded. "The oldest and the largest. Twenty-six butchers and their wives have slept in it at one time."

"God's rabbit!" said Balthus. "And slept well?"

"I'll not take my oath as to that," said Mr. Honeywood. "But lie in it they did, from dark to dawn. 'Twas
done for a wager, which was a tun of ale."

"But why butchers, sir?" Captain Runyon asked.

"It happened long ago, sir, when King William was
on the throne. The butchers were part of a delegation
on their way to London to complain of the price paid
them for beef. They, with their wives, or those said to
be their wives, bedded on the great couch for the one
night. The fact is well known and authenticated."

"What are the lines in Shakespeare, Dogbody?" Ostiff
asked. "I'd forgotten the bed was mentioned by him."

"You'll find 'em in *Twelfth Night*," the surgeon replied;
"in the scene where Sir Toby is egging on Sir Andrew
Aguecheek to write the challenge for the duel." He then
quoted, readily: " 'Taunt him with the license of ink. If
thou thou'st him some thrice, it shall not be amiss; and
as many lies as will lie in thy sheet of paper, although
the sheet were big enough for the bed of Ware in England, set 'em down. Go about it.' . . . But the bed will
hold more than fifty-two, Mr. Honeywood," he added.
"Counting children with adults, I've seen one hundred
and four lying in it at the same time, at head and
foot."

"God bless me!" the squire exclaimed. "When, sir, and
under what circumstances?"

The surgeon was silent for a moment; then he said:
"I should not have mentioned it. The tale is of small
interest, and I'd be loath to trouble you with it."

"Concerned with the loss of your leg?" Ostiff inquired.

The surgeon was again silent, then he nodded with an air of great reluctance. "It is. I'm bound to admit it."

"We've got him at last!" Ostiff exclaimed, triumphantly. "Honeywood, there's a secret in the doctor's life, connected, we are convinced, with this same missing leg, for the bare mention of it shuts him up like a clam. I believe we are now on the right track. With your help, we'll make him stand and deliver."

"Then deliver he shall," Mr. Honeywood replied. "Surgeon Dogbody, you'll not deny one of the King's magistrates? I'll have you summoned, else."

The surgeon smiled. "No secret, gentlemen," he replied. "None whatever, for the tale itself, though you'll force me at the outset to confess a thing I'd vastly sooner keep hidden. Murgatroyd alone is privy to it."

"Me?" the latter replied. "What thing, Doctor?"

"You came near enough to giving me away some months back, at this very table. You recollect? 'Twas the afternoon we met, after your return from Russia."

Murgatroyd shook his head, still mystified.

"My name, Inky. . . . My given name."

"Damn my eyes! So that's it!" said Murgatroyd, with a hearty laugh. "Ostiff, this explains everything! Small wonder we've not heard the tale of the missing leg, if his Christian name's bound up with it."

"Never call it a Christian name," said the surgeon, ruefully. "B'gad, 'twas not one to be wished on a dog!"

"There's an odd thing, Doctor," said Balthus. "I've known ye close to fifty years, and I've yet to hear it."

"And with reason, Ned. I'm anything but proud of it."

"F . . . there's a sight of names begin with that letter. . . . Would it be Francis? . . . Frederick, then?"

The surgeon shook his head. "I'd have no great cause
to resent either of those."

"My guess is Ferdinand," Runyon put in. "You were
called Ferdie as a boy."

"Worse than that — much worse." The surgeon drew a
sharp breath. "I may as well out with it at once, for ye'd
not guess it in a hundred tries. 'Tis Feadle."

"Good God!" said Ostiff.

"I quite agree, sir. Do you wonder that I sign myself
plain F. Dogbody?"

"Better Feadle than Ferdie," Balthus replied, loyally.

"No, Ned. Mine is the very nadir of names. 'Twas fixed
upon me, with the best of intentions, by my mother.
She'd an uncle, Isaac Feadle, a Bristol shipowner, and as
rich as a dozen supercargoes, but her hopes came to
naught. The only money the old rogue ever gave me was
a shilling when I was first carried to see him as a lad of
six." The surgeon paused, adding reflectively: " 'Tis odd
to think that my leg was sold for that shilling. Had I but
known it, the limb was as good as off from the day of
my christening. . . . Mr. Honeywood, you are familiar,
no doubt, with the events of our British slave trade?"

"I know next to nothing about it, sir, save that the
abominable traffic has been stopped. When was it? Half
a dozen years back, if my recollection serves."

"You are right, sir. The bill abolishing the trade passed
both Houses and received the royal assent on the twenty-
fifth of March, 1812. I have been told by no less a man

than Sir William Wilberforce himself, the great humanitarian who laboured so long toward that end, that the
happy result was hastened by events in which I played a
modest part: I and my friend Tom Achins. Like myself,
Achins comes from an old seafaring family. Unlike myself he numbers amongst his ancestors one only a little
less illustrious than Sir Francis Drake."

"Achins? Achins?" said Balthus. "I fancied I knew the
names of our great English seamen, but call me cut if
ever I've heard that one before."

"You have, Ned, scores, hundreds of times. 'Tis the
ancient style of the name 'Hawkins.' Tom Achins was in
the direct line from old Sir John, but he reverted to the
antique spelling of the name. 'Twas typical of the man.
Proud as he was of his descent, he'd carry no honours
save those he could win for himself. And there's this to
be added: he could never forgive his illustrious ancestor
for the one blot he fixed to the family escutcheon; for,
as you will remember, Mr. Honeywood, Sir John Hawkins was the first Englishman to engage in the traffic in
slaves.

"Now, sir, I must carry you back to the autumn of
'seventy-one. I'd been paid off out of the *Valiant* three
months before, and enjoyed myself no end, ashore, after
a dozen years steadily in the service. But I ran through
with my savings in short time and then was ready enough
to go to sea again. But with the country at peace, Navy
ships were being laid up rather than put into commission. There were hundreds of men out of the service in
my own fix. So I began to look about for a berth in a

merchantman. I went to Plymouth, Portsmouth, and up and down London River, and finally set out on shank's mare for Bristol to see what might be offered there. 'Twas on the course of this journey that I met the Russian Wonder."

"What wonder was that?" Balthus asked.

"The most prodigious eater ever heard of, Ned. I first got wind of him as I walked westward toward Bristol; apparently he was a little ahead of me, going in that same direction. A man from Whitechapel had him in charge. The Russian was a bear in human form, close to a fathom broad and half again as tall. He could eat a bushel of cherries, stones and all, at one meal, or the entire carcass of a sheep. But it seemed he was not in the least particular about the nature of his repast. He would consume what other men would on no occasion attempt, breaking with his teeth and masticating earthen or glass vessels, or flints. He was making a great stir in his progress and hundreds flocked to see him eat, which was always done for money, of course. I heard of him all the way along and caught up with him at Bristol. On that day his keeper had announced that the fellow was to ingurgitate the entire contents of a tin standish."

"A standish? What may that be?" Runyon asked.

"You must have the article in America, under another name, no doubt. 'Tis a convenience for holding writing materials: ink and well, sand, sealing wax, paper, and the like. The fame of the Russian Wonder had gone before him and the half of Bristol had gathered to witness this latest exhibition of his powers. The standish and its contents were provided by a Bristol merchant who had wagered with the fellow's keeper against the accomplishment of the meal."

"And he won; I'll lay to that," said Balthus.

"So I would have thought, Ned. So certain was I it could not be done that I bet my last two pounds against its performance, and lost. The fellow began with the sand, as much as you could have held in your cupped hands. He then drank off the ink and followed by crushing with his teeth, masticating, and swallowing the glass well itself. Pens, a full ream of paper, and three sticks of sealing wax followed. A candle and candlestick came next. There chanced to be a penknife on the standish, and this was swallowed at a gulp, to finish the meal."

"Nonsense! It was an imposture, surely," said Ostiff.

"No, Ostiff. I saw the meal with my own eyes, and there were judges present, comprising those who had laid the largest bets against the meal, to see that no trickery took place. No, the thing was done, to the amazement of all present, and the Russian appeared none the worse for it.

"But this is, of course, beside the tale. I mention it only because, as I have said, I lost to the fellow's keeper the last two pounds I had in the world, save one shilling. That shilling, oddly enough, was the one given me by my great-uncle, Isaac Feadle, so many years before. At my mother's suggestion I had always kept the coin as a pocket piece, for a warning — not that I needed it — against the vice of avarice.

" 'Twas this same day that I chanced to meet Tom

Achins in a tavern by the waterside. A happy meeting that was, for we'd not crossed tacks in five years and I'd clean lost sight of Achins. He was never a Navy man, but had worked his way up in the merchant service, and when I'd last seen him was captain and owner of a fine brig, trading between London and the West Indies.

" 'Dogbody,' said he, 'if there's one man in the whole of England I'd rather see than any other at this moment, 'tis yourself. What brings ye here?'

" 'To this tavern?' said I. 'I've come in to spend the last shilling I've got in the world, Tom lad,' and with that I drew forth the coin and rapped on the table for the waiter.

" 'Put it back in your pocket or I'll wring your neck,' says Tom. 'This is my treat.'

"And a treat it was, and in the course of it we posted one another with respect to our goings and comings since we'd last met. He told me that he'd lost his brig in the great fire at the Shadwell Dock, in London, and he'd been forced to begin all over again.

" 'And what is it now, Tom?' said I.

" 'I'm first officer of a slaver,' said he.

"Had he told me he was picking pockets or the proprietor of a bawdyhouse I could not have been more taken aback.

" 'You in a slaver, Tom Achins?' said I. 'There never was a stauncher opponent of that dirty trade, in the old days, than yourself. Well I remember how you'd abuse the memory of your great ancestor, Sir John, for being the first that took part in it.'

" 'And still do,' says he. 'But I'll see it for once, at first hand, the better to fight it in future. Dogbody, if I've an aim in life, beyond caring for my good wife and my five children, it is to undo, in my own person, the harm Sir John Hawkins did, in his, when he started buying and selling our fellow creatures.'

"But there was more to the matter than this. Achins loved ships better than his life, and he'd spied one, the *Happy Return,* lying in the Avon, that took his heart at first sight. He was bound to sail in her and had signed on as first mate, having been told she was engaged in the ebony and ivory trade. It was only later that he'd learned the ebony and ivory were negro slaves. All this he explained to me in great detail, and he went on to say that the *Happy Return* was one of a fleet of five owned by an old rogue and miser, one Isaac Feadle. I had some explaining to do then, and hard work I had convincing Achins that this same Isaac Feadle was my own greatuncle. The end of it was that Tom was bound I should come with him on this voyage, and I was more than willing, granted I could persuade Uncle Isaac to carry a surgeon, for once. I called to see him the same afternoon. I'd not laid eyes on him since the time my mother had carried me to see him, but I remembered him well enough. He was a little pinched-up man, around eighty, with not a hair on his face or head, and eyes the colour of a bad sixpence. He didn't remember me, and was none too pleased when I told him who I was. I had to prove the relationship, which I did, at last, to his complete dissatisfaction.

" 'Well,' says he, 'and what brings ye to Bristol? What d'ye want now?'

"This roused me, b'gad, though I'd the wit to keep my temper. You'd have thought, from the way he spoke, that I'd done nothing, my life long, but pester him for favours.

" 'Nothing, Uncle Isaac,' said I, 'save that I've always wished to return the shilling you gave me the time my mother brought me to see you, as a lad of six. I've no doubt it was ill spared, so I've kept it for you, and here's the very coin.'

"With that, I laid it on the table. He took it up, turned it over in his hand, peered at the date; then, damme if he didn't pocket it! However, 'twas a good move on my part. It stirred his interest, and he began to ask questions. I said naught of my friendship with Achins, but let him know I was a Navy surgeon, temporarily ashore, who'd made a lifelong study of all the fevers, dysenteries, paludisms, and the like, common to tropical countries, and of the means for combating them. I got my berth as surgeon, for one voyage, on the *Happy Return,* at the wage of one pound, three and six, per month.

"Achins was as curious as myself about our shipmates for so long a voyage, for they'd not joined yet, but we were all on board within the week. The captain's name was Maggard, a Liverpool man who began to show his true colours before we were out of Bristol Channel. They were, in truth, all of one colour, various shades of black. A more accomplished scoundrel, in his human relations,

I have yet to meet, but he was, of course, a thorough seaman. The second officer might have done well enough under a better commander, but he was weak in character and took his cues from Maggard. The supercargo was an animal named Gloach; both Maggard and he had been in my uncle's employ for years. As for the crew, half were what you'd expect on a slaver, but the other half were decent lads, most of them from Navy ships. Amongst these was Daniel Wegg, the boatswain, a fine old seaman and a true Christian.

"Achins and I messed with the captain and supercargo. The food was not fit for dogs, — trust Uncle Isaac for that; 'twas his practice to buy up job lots of old Navy stores for his ships, — but Maggard wolfed it in as though the victuals were of the choicest. He'd hubble in great lumps of rancid fat and gristle, crack bones with his leathery jaws, and suck out the marrow with noise enough for a dozen litters of pigs. The bread was full of maggots, but little that mattered to Maggard. He'd shake them out on his plate, make a butter of them, then, with the blade of his knife, he'd scoop it up with a relish . . ."

"We'll dispense with that, Dogbody," Ostiff interrupted.

"So you may, Ostiff," the surgeon replied; "but *I* couldn't, nor Achins. We had to look on three times per day. I'm not what would be called squeamish, having messed with gross feeders and to spare, in the King's ships, but the worst of them were veritable epicures compared with this Maggard. The supercargo was a good match for him, and their conversation was of a piece

with their table manners. For the most part, it was concerned with . . . No; I'll leave that, as well, and wish ye
over the sea as I wished myself a dozen times a day during that voyage.

"When we raised Bonny, on the west coast of Africa,
for all it was one of the worst fever holes and death traps
on the continent, I'd have called it paradise itself, after
being cooped up with Maggard and Gloach for so many
weeks. It was not much to look at, offshore, and even
less when you got there. There was naught to be seen of
men or their habitations; only the long low coast, and
coming off the land the smell of mud and heat and rank
vegetation. The pinnace was hoisted out and rigged, and
sent over the bar to Bonny. Maggard went with it to
make his arrangements with King Pepple, from whom
the slaves were bought. He returned next morning in a
black mood. Two other slavers were lying at Bonny, and
they'd bought up all the negroes Pepple had on hand.
We'd have to wait for ours."

"Were there many English ships in the trade at this
time?" Mr. Honeywood inquired.

"Indeed yes, Mr. Honeywood. We English have been
the greatest traffickers of all Europe in human flesh and
blood. At the time of my visit to Bonny the trade was at
its height. French, Dutch, Portuguese, and Danes were
all engaged in it, but the bulk of the business was in our
hands. The annual number carried away in English ships
was above twenty thousand.

"We worked through broken water and anchored off
Bonny that same afternoon; then we fired old Pepple a

salute, for he was as vain as he was black, in skin and heart, and 'twas necessary to feed his vanity, else not a slave would be forthcoming. He was rowed out to us presently by some of his retainers. I'd never before seen such a lump of flesh; he would have weighed all of twenty-five stone. He was dressed in a heavy gold-braided uniform and a cocked hat some captain had had made to his order, and wear it he would, for all the sweltering heat of the place. He spoke little English, but he and Maggard understood one another well enough. Pepple was not yet ready to 'break trade,' as they say; first he'd have to go upcountry to replenish his stock. Our traffic with these blacks was conducted in a unit of value called a 'bar,' which is five shillings in trade. Their principal wants are brandy, muskets, powder, and ball, and they hold a prime slave at a hundred bars' worth of these commodities. Our brandy was of the vilest kind, but even then not raw and hot enough for these savages. Gloach had a method of making it more acceptable. Out of each puncheon a third of the contents was pumped. Half a bucket of cayenne pepper was then stirred into the remainder and the missing brandy replaced with water. The mixture was allowed to stand for a fortnight, when it was hot enough to have pleased the devil himself. Pepple would drink two quarts at a sitting. He was fit to match the Russian Wonder I spoke of.

"He was off with his gang of desperadoes the following morning. Maggard sent Achins with him, and Tom was willing to go, for he wished to see the worst evils of the traffic at first hand, whilst he had the chance. The other slavers at Bonny sailed within the week, and the *Happy Return* was made ready to receive her cargo. Sails were unbent and stowed away, the topgallant masts sent down, and the topmasts struck. A roof of matting was then raised over the entire ship, giving her the appearance of a great floating barn. After this, the decks were cleared of all lumber, and a strong barricade built across the deck, amidships, and another in the 'tween-decks. During the voyage, the males were to be kept forward of these barriers and the females and children abaft.

"Then followed ten weary weeks during which our slaves were brought down to us in small companies, by Pepple's soldiers. They belonged to the tribe of the Eboes; my uncle would have none but these, for, although a strong, well-made people, they were gentle in disposition, easily handled, and greatly coveted by the West India planters. They brought two pounds per head above the negroes of other tribes.

"My horror and indignation grew apace as I saw these poor folk brought in, men, women, and children linked together with great collars of wood. Many of the women had babes in their arms, and the faces of all were marked with grief and terror. They were herded aboard and below decks, and, for all the unbearable heat of that fever hole, Maggard would allow them but an hour a day on deck. I remonstrated with all the weight of anger and common sense behind me, and much good it did. There was nothing Maggard loved so much as to inflict torture on the helpless.

"Achins returned with the last of the negroes brought

down, and never have I seen such a change in a man. He would not consent to talk of what he had seen, but if he hated the traffic before, you'll guess how he viewed it after more than two months in old Pepple's company.

"The ship was quickly made ready for sea. Pepple came off to receive the last of his booty of brandy and muskets, and we then saw him depart once more for the interior. He was dead drunk and carried in a litter, in the midst of a procession of two hundred naked warriors, whooping and yelling and brandishing spears and muskets in response to our farewell salute. The place was now a complete solitude, save for ourselves, and the following day the *Happy Return* sailed from the abominable place, with three hundred negroes below decks. I flattered myself that I had well earned my monthly wage of one pound, three and six. I had paid strict attention to the health of the crew, with the result that we lost but one man. The death roll in a slaver, during a two- or three-months stay, was from ten to twenty, and often this latter number was far exceeded.

"I pass over the first fortnight of our voyage toward the West Indies. I would not harrow your feelings. Thanks to the inhumanity of Maggard and Gloach, the ship was hell afloat. You would have thought that greed alone would have persuaded Maggard to use the slaves well; they were a valuable property in which he, as captain, had an interest. Nothing of the kind: he loved cruelty better than his pocketbook. Achins and I, together with the decent members of the crew, did what we could to offset it, but that was little enough.

"Then a mysterious thing happened. I was sent for in haste one morning and found Maggard in his berth, so weak that he was unable to rise and scarce able to speak.

" 'What's this I've got?' he asked, in a frightened whisper. 'Surgeon, am I going to die?'

"He had often boasted that he'd never known a day's illness and was immune to all the dangers of the African climate. And he may well have been, for this, I was soon assured, was none of the known diseases of Africa. I was at a loss to assign it a name. His limbs were as cold as ice, his pulse a mere flutter. I saw at once that he had only a few hours to live. He died at midday, in fact, and on that same afternoon, from the same mysterious cause, we lost the supercargo and nine of the seamen. No ministrations of mine were of the slightest avail."

" 'Twas heathen magic, like as not," said Balthus. "The negroes had a witch-doctor amongst them."

"It may well have been, Ned. Certain it is that all the deaths were of men who had followed the captain's lead in brutal treatment of the negroes. We heaved the bodies overboard without ceremony, and not the ghost of a sigh of regret or sorrow was heard amongst those remaining, for any one of them.

"A happy ship we were from that day; the change was truly remarkable. Achins was now in complete charge. The seamen liked and respected him. As for the slaves, it was touching indeed to observe their response to humane treatment. Their feeling toward Achins bordered upon adoration. Our passage toward the West Indies was slow indeed, for the ship's hull was foul with barnacles and weed. Slow as it was, Achins and I begrudged every league of salt water left astern, for it brought us that much nearer the day when we must sell these poor creatures into bondage, and we had both seen enough of life on the West India plantations to know how cruel that bondage could be.

"'Dogbody,' said he, one evening when we were pacing the deck together, 'say the word and we'll 'bout ship: take them all home again.'

"'Much good that would do,' said I. 'Pepple and his men would have them again within a month's time.'

"'So they would,' said Achins, gloomily. 'And there's our duty to your uncle to be considered. We're in his pay, and bound, in honour, to fulfill our trust.'

"'I care nothing for that,' said I. 'I'd be recreant to that trust with joy in my heart, if we might save these poor creatures. But I see no way in which it can be done.'

"'Nor I,' said Tom. 'No, we must go through with it, but there's one thing we can do: we'll creep to our destination slower than a crippled snail. We'll delay the evil day as long as possible.'

"He then told me that he knew of a little island near Grand Caicos where we would heel down the ship to clean her before proceeding to Jamaica. It was a rich little place, he said, abounding in every kind of tropical fruit and nut, and, best of all, a complete solitude. We'd give our poor charges a last taste of freedom before carrying them into slavery."

The surgeon paused to taste his grog, and Runyon remarked: "It was one of the Turks Islands, as like as not?"

"No, Runyon, it lay to the north of those. What the place was called I couldn't say, but it was all that Achins had claimed for it. There was one small landlocked bay on the west side, with beaches of pure white sand all round, and a stream of clear cold water flowing down from the interior, in cascades of fairylike beauty.

"The island was, indeed, a veritable paradise, and I wish that you might have witnessed the joy of our negroes as they came ashore. We gave them perfect freedom and they built for themselves little houses of thatch that suited the landscape as though they were a part of nature itself. Rising from the mirrorlike bay were lawns and groves and champaigns over which we wandered like children in the days of the world's innocence. Birds of an infinite variety filled the air with their music. As for the fruits, we had the golden orange in quantities past belief, the pineapple, the mango with its smooth rind, the succulent plantain, the coconut filled with its cooling nectar. Oysters better tasted than any I have ever found elsewhere abounded in the lagoons, and fish of every description could be had for the mere casting of a line. I doubt if the Garden of Eden could have been so fair a spot. Alas! Like the Garden of Eden, it had a serpent."

The surgeon paused and held up his little finger.

"One," he added, "and no larger than that. We had been two months in the place and had seen no reptile of any description, and it was not until we were about to proceed to Jamaica that this one appeared."

"And bit ye?" Balthus asked.

"It did, if so slight an accost may be called a bite," said

the surgeon. "Achins and I were sitting on a rock at the border of the bay, with our bare feet and legs dangling in the water. 'Twas a favourite spot with us; we could look down thirty fathoms, through water as clear as air, into the coral forests, of incredible beauty, below. The shadow of impending departure lay heavily upon our spirits, and we had little speech. Presently I noticed a tiny water serpent rising gently from the depths and coming in our direction. As the shafts of sunlight struck him, his little form threw off rainbow tints, blues, and greens, crimsons and tawny gold. We watched him, fascinated, so graceful were his movements, so innocent his appearance. He swam between Achins's legs, circled my own, then, returning, he gave me the tiniest conceivable peck on the left ankle. The nibble of a minnow would have seemed rude and brusque by comparison. The result was unlooked for."

"Poisonous?" asked Murgatroyd.

"Poisonous! Inky, that small worm had in its fangs, if fangs they were, a concentrated venom beyond anything I would have believed possible. Within ten minutes I was helpless. Within half an hour I realized that it was a matter of my leg or my life. Achins himself, who was a good rough ship's doctor in his own right, performed the amputation under my direction, and so benumbed was I by the poison that I felt no twinge of pain.

"As the event proved, 'twas the worm of Providence. Achins asked nothing better than an excuse for further delay in our voyage, and he now decided that we should remain on the island until I was restored and my stump perfectly hardened. Happy months they were. Our little company of negroes and whites was like an ideal community in the golden age of mankind, if ever there has been such. We English came to realize how many virtues and accomplishments the negroes had which were denied to us. Amongst others, they were gifted with prodigious memories and a power of mimicry that was truly astonishing. They could copy the voice and manner of any one of us, and they learned to sing our English songs better than ourselves. Wegg, our boatswain, a devout member of Mr. Wesley's church, taught them innumerable hymns, and because they learned them so readily and sung them with such enthusiasm the good old fellow fancied he had made Christians of them all.

"The months rolled by, and at last we could find no shadow of excuse for remaining longer on the island. The negroes were ready enough to go, for they had come to regard Achins as a kind of loving father whose only purpose in life was to lead them from one paradise to another, nor could we find it in our hearts to disillusion them. They would discover the truth soon enough. 'Twas best to keep them in ignorance until the last moment.

"But Providence was not done with us yet. We were not thirty leagues from Kingston, our destination in Jamaica, when we were struck by a hurricane of such appalling violence that we could do nothing but scud before it, under bare poles. Scud, do I say? Damme, there were times during that storm when it seemed to me that we were blown clean out of the water and carried along above the waves in that mighty torrent of air. We lost

both main and mizzenmast, though neither had a rag
of sail on it. But there never was a sturdier ship than
the *Happy Return,* and under the handling of such a
seaman as Achins, she carried us through in splendid
shape. On the tenth day, wind and sea abated; on the
eleventh we were proceeding under the foresails alone,
in a westerly direction. The sky was still heavily over-
cast, and Achins had not been able to determine our position; but he reckoned that we must be nearer England
than Jamaica, and as the wind was fair for home, he decided that we must proceed as we were.

"The next morning I was aroused in the early dawn by
one of the seamen, who informed me that Achins desired
me on deck. I found him examining with his spyglass
something that could not be seen with the naked eye.
The weather was once more beautifully clear.

" 'Dogbody,' said he, 'take my glass and tell me what
you find yonder.'

"I took the glass, steadied it against the stump of the
mizzenmast, and studied the remote object long and
carefully.

" 'Well,' said Achins. 'What is it?'

" 'What I see, Tom,' said I, 'is Land's End with the
Lizard beyond. I'm a liar. I must be a liar. We've not
been blown across the entire Atlantic in less than a fortnight. But that's what I see and I'll stick to it.'

"As the light increased and the haze of early morning
melted away, we could doubt no longer: we were, indeed, all but home. A more perfect day for such a land-
fall could not have been dreamed of or hoped for. The

sky was the pale blue so dear to English hearts, and once the sun was well up, the air was as pleasantly warm as I have ever felt it off our coasts. Our Africans had been kept, of necessity, below decks during the entire period of the storm. We now brought them up, though not without misgivings as to the effect the shrewd air of our higher latitudes might have upon them. Their dress was of the scantiest; some of the men wore the flimsy Osnaburgs provided for slaves in those days. Others were clad in their own quaint native costumes, which left something to be desired by way of covering. The women were as variously clad, or unclad, and the small children had only their little kirtles of dyed grasses. We expected them to congeal and rush back to the warmth of the 'tween-decks. On the contrary, the brisk air and the wan sunshine had an effect upon them as of some heady wine. They laughed and sang and leaped and danced, and ran about the decks with an excess of vigour that brought home to me clearer than ever before the virtue there is in our English air.

"Achins and I stood by the bulwark, taking pleasure in their pleasure. A file of small children marched past, engaged in one of their African pastimes, and each one of them sucking an orange. Of a sudden Achins seized my arm.

" 'Dogbody!' he exclaimed. 'Look! They're eating oranges!'

" 'I see nothing strange in that,' said I, 'considering the amount of the fruit we put aboard at the island. There must be fifty or sixty tons of it in all.'

"We had, in fact, loaded up with oranges before setting out toward Jamaica, chiefly as an excuse for further delay. But they were of such a splendid quality that Achins hoped to dispose of them at Kingston at sixpence the hundred.

" 'But . . . damn your eyes, Dogbody!' said Achins. 'Don't you realize what we've got here?'

"He rushed to the main hatch and down the ladderway. Then, in a flash, I *did* realize. By reason of our incredibly swift passage across the Atlantic, our oranges, all of which had been picked a little on the green side, were just now coming to ripeness, to their full sweetness and flavour. And there never was such fruit. The oranges of Spain were as nothing compared with these. And yet the English, the greatest orange lovers in the world, I fancy, would pay fantastic prices for the Spanish fruit when they could get it. Unwittingly, we had carried home a cargo of all but fabulous value. I realized that our sixty tons of golden fruit would bring such showers of golden guineas into Uncle Isaac's coffers as he had never dreamed of.

"Achins came on deck again in a state of great excitement. Officers bred up in the merchant service are bound to think of trade and profits, and Achins would have been no true member of his profession had he not been elated at this unexpected turn of fortune.

" 'Dogbody,' said he, 'that old rogue, your Great-uncle Isaac, will have no cause to regret the storm which blew us home. The fruit is all in prime condition. I would not venture to guess the price it will fetch in the Bristol market.'

" 'I could wish to dump the lot of it overboard, Tom,' said I. 'Not a penny of the fortune will Uncle Isaac pass on to us. But I care nothing for that. 'Tis the slaves I'm thinking of. The moment the ship is repaired he'll send us back with them to Jamaica. Aye, as you say, we've done a noble stroke of business for my uncle.'

"Achins nodded, gloomily. 'So he will,' said he. 'No matter of doubt there. But something is gained. Bristol folk will see, for once, the flesh and blood so many of them fatten on. And who knows . . .' He brought his fist down on the bulwark. 'Damme, what am I thinking of! We'll put into Plymouth first. Where's the sense in taking oranges all the way to Bristol when the great market is London?'

" 'Why not bear away for London direct?' said I. But Achins doubted that the breeze would hold. If we got to Plymouth, the commission agents for the London merchants would see the fruit loaded into wagons and carried to Covent Garden market as fast as wheels could turn. Achins was right about the breeze. It failed at midnight, but we were then at anchor inside Penlee Head. The next morning we worked up the sound to Plymouth. 'Twas a Sabbath Day, and we warped into the basin just as folk were coming from church.

"With our Africans scrubbed and shining and swarming the decks, we expected to cause a stir, and so we did. People came and they came, pouring down every waterside street, till there was such a throng before us as I doubt Plymouth had seen since Francis Drake came home with the wealth of the Indies in the hold of his vessel. But not a hail was given us. All gazed in silence, as though in a kind of stupor.

" 'Here's a strange to-do, Dogbody,' said Achins. 'What ails 'em? Are they hostile, or friendly, or what? Damme if it don't look as though they was waiting to murder us!'

" 'Like enough,' said I. 'Remember this, Tom: Plymouth has never been a port for the slave trade. 'Tis deeply hated here. You'd best explain what's happened.'

"Achins now hailed the throng below. 'Stand back, good people,' he called. 'We've been driven from Jamaica by a hurricane, with these poor creatures, and across the entire Atlantic. I must take them ashore for refreshment. Give way! Let me have room to disembark them!'

"This, seemingly, was precisely what the crowd wished us to do. A great buzzing and murmuring rose, and they made way directly, pushing and struggling back until a wide area had been cleared. We then shepherded our charges, men, women, and children, to the *quai*. The crowd waited in complete silence until the last one of them had set foot on shore; then pandemonium itself broke loose.

"B'gad, within the next ten minutes I came as near to death at the hands of Christians, mauling me with Bibles and prayer books, as ever I'd come in His Majesty's Navy. The greater part of them had just come from the morning services and had their weapons in hand. I was so pushed

and hauled and belaboured that the fastenings of the
new peg our carpenter had made for me came loose and
the leg was lost in the melee. I hopped about on one
foot, trying desperately to keep my balance, and the blows
rained upon me from all sides. Then I was seized by so
many infuriated women that I couldn't fall, though I
was dragged every which way. One, with her bonnet over
her eye, had gotten a firm hold of my waistcoat, and was
shouting at and mauling me at the same time.

"'They're free, you wicked, wicked creature!' she
screamed. 'You didn't expect that, did you, when you
brought them ashore? But it's true! They're safe now,
every one!'

"Achins was as rough-handled as myself, and the wonder is we weren't killed. We were rescued in the end, but
I was all to pieces by that time, and had only half a shirt
to cover my nakedness. Damme, never were two innocent
men more abused, but 'twas more than made up to us
when the truth came out.

"What had happened, gentlemen, was this, and you'll
understand, now, why I called the tiny serpent the worm
of Providence. On the very day I was bitten, as I afterward learned by comparing dates, there had come before
Lord Mansfield, in the Court of King's Bench, in London, the case of an African slave brought to England by
his master, a West India planter, and who, through the
instigation of the Friends of Africans Society, claimed
his freedom for that reason. The case immediately became a *cause célèbre;* the whole of England was stirred
by it, and despite all the interest and pressure brought to

bear by the advocates of slavery, after a hearing which dragged through many weeks, Lord Mansfield, in the presence of the full bench, handed down the decision that any slave was free from the moment he set foot on our free English soil. That decision had been given only the week before our arrival at Plymouth."

"It couldn't have happened better for you, Doctor!" said Balthus. "I'll warrant ye was chaired and feasted at Plymouth, when the truth was known about yourself and Achins?"

"Feasted!" The surgeon rolled up his eyeballs, blinking rapidly.

"You recovered your lost peg?" Runyon asked.

"I didn't try," said Dogbody. "When Achins and I were entertained by the City of Plymouth, my own memento of the occasion was a magnificent peg of ebony. It was shot from under me some thirty years later, at Trafalgar, whilst I was serving in the *Téméraire,* which convinced me that I was fated to lose the limb at one time or another. I've deeply regretted its loss, for I have nothing, now, to remind me of what was, certainly, one of the most rewarding experiences of my life. . . . Nothing," the doctor added, pensively, and after another pause, "save my Uncle Isaac's shilling piece."

"But you gave that back," said Runyon.

With thumb and forefinger the surgeon fished in his waistcoat pocket and drew forth a coin which he passed to the American.

"You'll note the date of the minting, Runyon. Seventeen forty-eight, the year I was carried to see my great-

uncle by a hopeful mother. It came the second time from
my uncle's solicitors. He'd left the instructions in his
will." The surgeon's eyes twinkled as he added, "Doubtless my share of the orange money."

"And where does the bed of Ware come in?" asked
Murgatroyd.

"I was coming to that, Inky. The Society of the Friends
of Africans proved friends indeed to our charges, and no
one more so than Sir Willis Wynne, of Matching, in Essex.
He undertook the care and training, in agriculture, of
seventy-five of the number, not counting their young
children. With old Daniel Wegg to assist me, I had the
honour of conveying them to Matching, in four large
wagons provided by the Society. Our progress across the
southern counties was a veritable triumph in the cause
of African freedom. I was later informed that more was
accomplished on that journey in arousing the people of
England to the evils of the slave trade than a generation
of labour had effected theretofore. The last night of the
progress was spent in Ware, and 'twas then that our
charges, one hundred and four in number, counting the
children, rested in the great bed. A curious sight it was
to see them, two rows of heads on the long bolsters at
either end. They slept well, tired as they were, and
were viewed throughout the evening by the whole of
Ware."

The surgeon rose, and Will Tunn made haste to fetch
his hat and coat.

"Thankee, Tunn. . . . Mr. Honeywood, this meeting
has given me pleasure indeed. Gentlemen, good evening."

"Your legacy, Doctor: your shilling piece," said Runyon, taking up the coin and passing it to him.

The surgeon held it in the palm of his hand for a moment, gazing at it thoughtfully. Then, placing it on his thumbnail, he flicked it across the room with such dexterity that it plopped squarely into a glass that Tom Tapleke was polishing at the bar.

"Drink that for me, Tom," he called, and with another bow to the company he stumped across the room and out the door.

VII

ATTICA, THE TWELFTH

WILL TUNN had never more splendidly sustained the reputation of the Tortoise than upon an evening, late in
March, when the Banyan Club held one of its dinners in
the great upstairs dining room. The Banyan Club was
an informal organization, social in character, meeting at
no stated times, and its membership comprised both
wardroom and warrant officers. Captains, lieutenants,
masters, gunners, naval surgeons, pursers, and, often, seamen of yet humbler rank, as well as others connected with
the Admiralty on shore, sat down together to enjoy
evenings of good fellowship and the best food that could

be provided by the best taverns in Portsmouth. Members could bring guests, if notification were given in advance, and the one bylaw of the organization was, "No quarter-deck manners."

The afternoon could not have been more favourable as a sauce for the gustatory pleasures, with the sky over-cast and a raw east wind to sharpen appetite well in ad-vance, so that it is doubtful whether, in the history of the Tortoise, a greater amount of better food had ever been eaten by eighteen men. Captain George Trecothick, brother of Sir Nicholas Trecothick, Admiral of the Blue, presided at the long table. He was known in naval circles as George Trebleguts, and, indeed, his great solid belly surpassed in size those of three ordinary men. No officer in His Majesty's Navy was a better judge of a dinner, or more capable of enjoying and stowing it away when set before him. Nevertheless, being almost as broad as he was tall, and sturdily built, he carried himself with an ease that might have been envied by the youngest midshipman under his command.

The company had drawn up to table at five, and the hour was approaching nine when the remains of the des-serts were cleared away and all made tidy for the pleas-ures to come. Sea-coal fires burned on the hearths at either end of the room, and the light from many candles in sconces along the walls was reflected in a rich glow from bronzed or ruddy faces, all of them now bedewed with a fine digestive sweat. The toasts of fealty to King and Fleet had already been drunk, and songs rendered by various members, the others joining in the refrains with such good will that all waterside Portsmouth, within half a mile of the Tortoise, knew that the Banyan Club was in session. Presently, Captain Trecothick rose once more, glass in hand, and rapped on the table for order. The hum of conversation died away, and all looked expectantly toward their master of ceremonies.

"Fellow Banyanians," he said, "it's heave and awash, now, with the best part of the evening to come; but before we're well under way, we'll take one look astern. Damme, if ever I've et better-tasted beef, better cooked or served, than what we've had here." He raised his glass. "Lads, the Roast Beef of Old England, and if any of ye have ever been nourished by that beef, in whatever form, better than ourselves this night, let him speak up!"

The toast was drunk with loud acclamations of "Hear, hear!" and Captain Trecothick was about to proceed when there was a hesitant knock at the door and Will Tunn put in his head.

"Begging your pardon, Captain and gentlemen . . ."

"Come in, landlord, come in," Trecothick interrupted, heartily. "Ye need beg nobody's pardon, after the feast ye've set before us. What is it?"

"There's an old seaman belowstairs, sir, has had his dinner in the kitchen, that's a friend, he says, of Doctor Dogbody. He'd take it kindly if the doctor could see him for a moment."

"What name?" Dogbody asked.

"He didn't tell me, sir, but he says he served in the same ship with you years ago. He's an outpensioner of Greenwich Hospital, on his way to visit his great-grand-

daughter and his great-great-grandchildren, lives in Bot-
ley."

"His great-great-grandchildren?" said Captain Trecothick. "Damme, how old is he? But bring him up, landlord. No Navy man comes amiss here."

A moment later the landlord knocked once more, and
was followed into the room by a spry little man, as dry
as a bone, who might have been of any age between eighty
and one hundred and ten; but his round cheeks had
still a kind of childish bloom upon them, and his pale
blue eyes seemed to look out upon the world with
a child's lively interest. He halted at the threshold
and gazed doubtfully toward the company. There was
a brief silence; then half-a-dozen voices shouted at
once: "Davy Spiggott!" Dogbody and Captain Trecothick sprang up at the same moment; another chair was
brought, and the old seaman was placed at the table
between them.

"God bless my soul!" Dogbody exclaimed once more.
"Is it you in the flesh, Davy?"

"Aye, the same — what's left of me," the old fellow
replied, with a pleased smile. "And there was I, Captain
and Doctor and gentlemen, a settin' at my supper in the
kitchen, not knowin' till now there was old shipmates
abovestairs here."

Captain Trecothick stared at him as though still incredulous.

"But . . . but . . . you're a ghost, Davy!" he said.
"Wasn't ye blown up in the *Kent,* years ago?"

Spiggott nodded. "I was blown up, sure enough, but I

came down with the splinters. I was right as ever a fort-night after."

Trecothick shook his head, wonderingly. "Lads," said he, "I'll take my oath ye've all heard of Davy Spiggott, the oldest and best master-cook in the Navy. Damme, he was the oldest forty years back, when I was a mid in the *Hercules!* What's your age now, Davy?"

"I don't rightly recollect, Captain, but if I was to say a hundred and five I'd not be far off. . . . Doctor Dog-body, d'ye mind the ostriches? I ain't forgot that time, for all my memory's goin.' "

"Hold hard," said Trecothick. "Ye'll not go yarning with Dogbody till I know about the *Kent.* But first we must wet ye down. What's your fancy?"

The old man smiled wistfully as he glanced over the table. "I'd half a pint of porter with my supper," he said. "Ye'd have me shakin' a cloth if I was to take much more."

"We'll not urge ye beyond your capacity, Davy, but a sup of water-bewitched will set well atop of the porter. Waiter! Fetch it."

A small glass of weak spirits and water was brought, and the cook tasted it with relish.

"Now about the *Kent,*" said Trecothick. "Ye'll all re-member her, lads, blown up in this very harbour. I was in the *Egmont* at the time, at Spithead, and we'd just weighed for Jamaica. For all that I saw her go, I never did learn the details. Saluting the admiral, weren't ye, Davy?"

"Aye, and some sparks got into the arms chest. There

was above fifty lads lost that day, but I came down right enough, like I said."

"But you were reported killed, Davy: that I know," said Dogbody.

" 'Twas my grandpa. He was a Davy Spiggott as well, if ye recollect."

"So he was, so he was; I'd clean forgot," said the surgeon. He turned to Balthus, who was seated at his right. "Ned, 'tis all but incredible that you and Spiggott have never crossed tacks before now. I'll warrant he's served in every ship in His Majesty's Navy, at one time or another. Eh, Davy?"

"Near enough, Doctor. Us Spiggotts was born at sea, ye might say. My youngest *was* born there, on the *Panther,* when we was comin' round from Sheerness to Plymouth. My missus was aboard for the day, and was that near her time she was took short, there and then. The lad come into the world alongside one of our twenty-four-pounders. He was found to weigh seven pounds, so the gun was called the thirty-one-pounder after that."

"Weren't there four generations of you serving at one time?" asked Trecothick.

"Aye, and in the same ship, sir. We had a paper for it, from the Navy Board, and sixpence a week, over and above our pay."

"Sixpence, Davy! A handsome reward *that* was! Say what we may of the Admiralty, they know how to be generous upon occasion."

The sarcasm was lost upon the old seaman, who replied, with genuine sincerity: "So we esteemed it, sir.

The extra twenty-four shillin's a year came in handy enough, but the bonus was stopped when my grandpa was blown up."

"Now, if you remember, tell us what ships ye *have* served in, first to last."

"There's a place my head's as good as ever," said Spiggott. "I ain't forgot one." The old man paused for a relishing taste of his glass. "There was the *Augusta* for the first. Then comes the *Lancaster, Revenge, King George, Invincible, Edinburgh, Hercules, Panther, Norfolk, Isis, Hero, Acteon, Pallas* . . ." He halted for a moment and glanced drowsily around the table. "*Sapphire* . . . *Achilles* . . . . *Minerva* . . . . . *Neptune* . . . . . . *Dispatch* . . . . *Centaur* . . ."

Whether it was the mild grog he had taken, in addition to his half-pint of porter, or the excitement of the unexpected meeting, or the effort of memory, the old cook's head seemed to become heavier and heavier as he proceeded. His eyes closed. With an effort he opened them once more, smiling vaguely. "*Vanguard* . . . *Spitfire* . . . . *Triton* . . ." Then his head drooped and he went quietly to sleep, leaning against Doctor Dogbody's shoulder. There was a sofa in a corner of the room. At a nod from Captain Trecothick, the two waiters, Hodge and Tom Tapleke, carried the little man there and placed him comfortably upon it.

"Lads," said Trecothick, "we've had guests at the Banyan Club times without number, but none more deserving of the honour than young Davy Spiggott." He raised his glass. "Here's a long life to him!"

The toast was drunk with enthusiasm, whereupon a middle-aged lieutenant halfway down the table called out: "What was that about the ostriches, Dogbody?"

" 'Twas nothing, Earthy, nothing," the surgeon replied, with a deprecatory wave of the hand.

"Trecothick, does he get off with that?" the lieutenant demanded.

"He does not," said the chairman, firmly. "We've had ducks, geese, turkeys, pigeons, and other fowl in the main courses. Let the ostriches come now."

There was a clamorous assent to this proposal. Chairs were pushed back into easier positions. The surgeon protested in vain; therefore, having shown just the right amount of reluctance, he nodded a good-humoured assent. "Very well," said he. "But damn your eyes, Fred Earthy! 'Tis no mere anecdote, this. I'll have to go far enough from Portsmouth to fetch in the ostriches, and lose my leg on the way."

"Better still," said Trecothick. "But mind ye, Dogbody! If you're too long about it, we're all free to follow Davy Spiggott's example. Now heave ahead, but tell us, first, where ye start from."

"From where we sit," the surgeon began, "as near as may be, but there was no Tortoise then. The Unicorn stood on this corner in 'seventy-nine, as some of you remember. On a day in July of that year, I was having a last glass of grog in the taproom of the Unicorn, with Lieutenant Anthony, of the *Daedalus,* before we set out for India."

"D'ye speak of Harry Anthony?" Captain Mundy asked, from the far end of the table.

"The same," the surgeon replied.

"Did he have his girls with him?" said the other, with a grin.

"He did, but they were abovestairs at the moment, with Mrs. Anthony. Ye knew him, George?" the surgeon added, turning to Captain Trecothick.

"Anthony. . . . Killed at Copenhagen, wasn't he?"

"He was, poor fellow, in the *Glatton,* under Captain William Bligh, who had the mutiny in the South Sea in 'eighty-nine, when sent to fetch the breadfruit to the West Indies."

The surgeon paused for a double charge of snuff. Having dusted his fingers with great deliberation, he went on: "Lads, we're all friends here, and what's said is amongst ourselves. I speak of this because there'll be some who never knew Anthony, and I can't tell my story without mention of his girls. He had eleven at this time, the eldest past thirty, and the youngest not yet three months. Damme, there was something comical, to his friends, the way they came along, one after the other, with never a son to vary the monotony. And not one of 'em married. Harry was a younger son of a younger son, and on top of that, he'd married young, at twenty. And all his fortune was his lieutenant's pay, with sixty pounds a year Mrs. Anthony brought him. He was fifty-three at this time, and had gone into the Navy at twelve. In the thirty-odd years from his marriage, he'd not had above six months ashore with Mrs. Anthony. Admiral Collingwood himself was not more steadily in the service. But, b'gad, as sure as he went home for a week betwixt voyages, the event would be marked, nine months later, by the arrival of another daughter. Fine healthy girls they were, the kind that make the best of wives and mothers. But with not a sixpence to spare as a dot for any one of 'em, he'd never once heard the heartening music of marriage bells.

"Well, as we were off to India this voyage, with no expectation of a return for three years, Mrs. Anthony and the girls had come all the way from Bristol, in a carrier's wagon for economy's sake, to see him off. The town was more than full, for there were two hundred and fifty ships, here and at Plymouth, waiting a fair wind, half for the West Indies and half for India. My guess was there was a double purpose in bringing the girls to see their father off. With Portsmouth crowded with officers, and planters and merchants from the Indies, the parents must have hoped a two-three amongst 'em might take a shine to some of the daughters. But there'd been no such luck, and Harry was gloomy as a winter's day.

"'Dogbody,' said he, 'is there anything amiss with my girls?'

"'Amiss?' said I. 'B'gad, no, Harry! There ain't an officer in the service with a finer family.' And I meant every word of it.

"'Then why can't I get some of 'em married?' said he. He was all but desperate, thinking of such a flock to leave behind, and nothing between them and downright penury if anything was to happen to him. I felt so sorry for him, I came within a fraction of asking for one of them myself, and I could see he was hoping I might by the wistful way he looked at me. I was nearer, that moment, to the dangers of matrimony than ever I've come since, but I managed to hold fast, and Harry Anthony was not one to take an unfair advantage in friendship. He was called Saint Anthony in the service, and if ever a man deserved the title for his character, 'twas he. His one enemy was chance, or luck, or whatever you choose to call it. With no important connections in the service ashore, there was none to push him forward, richly as he deserved promotion. A lieutenant he was, and a lieutenant he remained.

"But I'll get on with the voyage. The signal to weigh had been made at dawn, but with so many ships in the harbour, and outside, at Spithead, it was close to midday before the *Daedalus* sailed. As ye'll recollect, we were at war with both France and Spain in 'seventy-nine, and there were twenty ships of war to convoy the great fleet of merchantmen. Eight of these, of which the *Daedalus* was one, were for Bombay and Calcutta, with the East Indiamen. We had Sir Eyre Coote as passenger; he was returning to India as Lieutenant General of the forces there. 'Twas Harry and I that took him off to the *Daedalus*, in the last boat, and I well remember Mrs. Anthony and the eleven girls standing by the boat stairs waving their father farewell. He stood in the boat, facing astern, and waving as long as he could make them out; then he sat beside me, his chin in his hands, the picture of misery.

" 'Dogbody,' said he, 'shall I ever see them again?' What

he added struck me as so comical that I was hard put to keep a straight face. 'If I do,' said he, soberly, 'little Patricia' (that was his youngest) 'will be out of Mrs. Anthony's arms. There'll be a new one in her place . . . and a daughter, that's sure.' "

Captain Mundy broke into a laugh. "I can hear him say it, Dogbody. There never was a man that took his family responsibilities so hard."

"Could you blame him?" said the surgeon. "B'gad, Mundy, if you or I or any of us here had such a regiment to keep on a lieutenant's pay, we'd have our sober moments, I'm thinking. But at sea he could put his worries aside and be as full of larks and high spirits as a lad of fifteen.

"We'd a wearisome four months' passage to Capetown, and to make it worse, that old martinet, Childers, was in command of the *Daedalus*. We were supposed to be the best-sailing frigate in the fleet, and carrying Sir Eyre Coote for that reason. But we were last in at the Cape; the others were well on with their watering and revictualing by the time we got there. Childers was wild about it and drove us like a slave master to make up for lost time. We had no freedom in the three weeks we'd spent at the Cape, but on the day before we were to sail, Anthony and I had an afternoon off.

"There was one pleasure we'd promised ourselves, in case we had a few hours of leisure, and that was a ride on a pair of tame ostriches owned by a Dutchman. He asked ten shillings an hour for their hire. Harry balked at that; he said he could keep Mrs. Anthony and the girls

for a week on half a pound. But I won him over by saying we'd take only five shillings' worth. If we liked it and
were out longer, 'twas to be my treat.

"We had our dinner in the town, as happy as schoolboys; then the Dutchman came in to say the ostriches
were ready. Tall powerful birds they were, with a cloth
over their backs and little bridles to guide them by. The
owner gave us a leg up and told us how to manage them.
They'd go left or right at the touch of a rein, but
when we wanted to come home we must say, 'Attik!
Attik!'

"We set off at a walk till we got clear of the town; then,
with our little sticks, we prodded the birds into a trot.
Damme, 'twas perfect, once we got used to the motion,
like floating on the air, in a series of bounds, or curves.
Harry enjoyed it as much as myself, and in the exhilaration of the ride we clean forgot the ten shillings an hour.
On we went, through draws and valleys and over rolling
plains of sand and scrub. Anthony's bird was swifter than
mine, and at last he was miles ahead. I could scarce make
him out, but by using my prod I managed to overtake
him in the end.

" 'Damn your eyes, Harry,' said I. 'At this rate we'll
come out somewhere in Egypt. Don't you think it's time
we were going back? The sun's near to setting.'

" 'I've thought it the past two hours,' said he. 'Heaven
be thanked you've caught up with me, Dogbody, for I've
forgotten the word for turning!'

"B'gad, so had I! Our great birds loped on, their long
shadows and our own loping with them whilst we racked

our memories in vain. We tried every conceivable com-
bination of sounds, hoping to hit the right word, and all
the while we were going farther into the wilderness.
We'd little notion of the way back, but the Dutchman
said we could depend on the ostriches. We'd only to give
them the command, which meant 'home' in one of the
Hottentot tongues. 'Tis a precious word, 'home,' in any
speech, and we thought it dear enough in the Hottentot,
remembering that the lack of it was costing us ten shillings an hour. In my own case, it cost far more than that,
in the end, for I gave my larboard leg for the bit of
breath that framed it."

The surgeon gazed pensively in his glass as Tom Tapleke refilled it. Then he proceeded.

"We coaxed the birds down to a walk, but they were
as fresh as when we first set out, and soon broke into their
bounding trot again. The sun had set by this time and
there was little daylight left. Presently the birds halted
of themselves, and cocked their heads as though for a
better view of something. The same instant the air was
filled with little hissing noises. Harry gave me a surprised
look.

" 'What's this?' said he. 'By God, Dogbody, we're being
shot at!'

"I was even more certain of it than himself, for I got
an arrow through the leg just above the knee. B'gad, the
blow jogged my memory with a vengeance!

" 'Harry,' I shouted, 'the word is "Attik! Attik!" ' '

"Immediately the ostriches spun round and bounded
away in the midst of another shower of arrows, fortu-

nately all of them wide of the mark. If they'd run before, they flew now. In thirty seconds we were well beyond the dangers of the ambush.

"My wound pained little, at first, and we rode at a fast clip, but after an hour it was all I could do to keep my seat. Presently, as we crossed a muddy little stream, I had to give in. We expected the birds to leg it home the moment we slipped from their backs, but damme if they didn't stand as quiet as you please. They drank from the stream, taking the water up in their bills and tilting it down their throats exactly like the fowls in a barnyard. Then they squatted down to wait for us.

"We reckoned that we must be a good fifty miles from Capetown, and it might as well have been five hundred and fifty in my own case, for I could travel no farther. I'd lost a deal of blood and suffered torments whilst Harry drew the arrow. The head had come through, fortunately, and he cut off the feathered nock-end and pulled the shaft out. Then he tore off a part of his shirt and bandaged the leg as well as he could. I wanted him to push on for Capetown and leave me there, but he'd not hear to this.

"A long night that was, but day came at last, and with it a fine fresh breeze from the north, which meant that the fleet would be unmooring and getting under way at that very moment, and ourselves marooned, thousands of miles from either India or home. Captain Childers would not delay the sailing of the *Daedalus* five minutes on our account, and with reason, for 'twas a matter of great importance that Sir Eyre Coote should reach India at the earliest possible moment. Knowing the rage Childers would be in at our absence, we also knew the report he'd make to the Admiral when he reached India. We were as good as dismissed the service. But not a word of this crossed Anthony's lips, though I knew he must be thinking of it, as I was. He was as cheerful as though we were safe aboard ship and all hands just piped to breakfast.

"Our ostriches were still squatting in the sandy clearing where we ourselves lay. Presently the cock rose, shook out his feathers, and went off at his easy lope to the top of a rise, half a mile distant. He stood there for a little time, then, to our joy, loped back and stood looking at us with an expression almost human, as though urging us to be on our way.

" 'Harry,' said I, 'you must push on, now, to the settlement, and get a cart to fetch me in.' But he'd not stir, for all my urging. Leave a comrade, alone and helpless, in a savage wilderness fifty miles from the nearest habitation? Never! What he feared was that he'd not be able to find me again. And he hoped, as I did, of course, that the wound, if no infection set in, would heal sufficiently for me to ride once more.

" 'Aye, and what are we to live on meanwhile?' said I. 'We'll do well enough for water here, but where's the food?'

"B'gad, I'd scarce spoke when the female ostrich turned her head to look at me as though she'd heard and understood. She rose to her feet, and there beneath her, in a hollow in the sand, was an egg of enormous size. Damme, the largest duck's egg ever seen would have been a pea beside it.

"We'd no flint-and-steel with us, but the crystal of my striking watch was a burning-glass, and with that Harry kindled a fire and roasted the egg. Hungry as we were, we couldn't get through the fifth part of it. We had it again for supper, and the following morning there was a fresh one laid where the first had been. The long and the short of it was that we stayed four days in that spot, but as my wound was getting worse instead of better, something had to be done. Harry agreed at last that he must try and find the settlement; so, having made me as comfortable as possible, he set off on the male ostrich, with the female trotting after. I watched them go with a heavy heart, trying not to think of the long wait ahead. The birds dwindled as they mounted the rise to the south and looked no larger than titmice when I had them for a moment against the skyline. Then, to my surprise, they turned and came speeding toward me once more.

" 'Harry,' said I, as he drew up beside me again, 'I know what you'd say, and I won't have it. I'm all right here, with water at hand, and a roasted egg will last me a fortnight if it comes to that. No; go you must, old fellow.'

"He sat astride of his ostrich, grinning at me; damme if I didn't think, for a moment, he'd had a touch of the sun. 'Dogbody, d'ye know where we are?' said he.

" 'No more than yourself,' said I, 'but give the bird his head and I'll warrant he'll find home.'

" 'So he will,' said Harry, 'for Capetown is just over

the rise yonder. We're not two miles from the Dutchman's ostrich paddock.'

"Damme if it wasn't true! We'd not been wrong in estimating the distance the birds had carried us, but we were far out in thinking we'd traveled as the crow flies. We'd ridden in great zigzags, and at the farthest point where we'd been attacked by one of the wandering bands of wild negroes we could not have been more than ten miles from the settlement.

"I was bound, then, to ride in, and did, but only just managed it. The result of the little excursion was that, a week later, I contributed to the continent of Africa the better part of as good a larboard leg as was ever thrown across an ostrich's back. A Mr. Wietjen, a Dutch surgeon of the town, performed the amputation. I must do him the justice to say that he made an excellent job of it."

"The fleet had sailed?" Lieutenant Earthy asked.

"Every ship of them, whilst Harry and I lay in the little gully, thinking ourselves in the heart of Africa."

"But how's this?" Captain Trecothick asked. "If ye lay so close to the town ye must have heard the exchange of parting salutes between the fleet and the fort."

"There were no salutes. The Dutch were short of powder when we reached the Cape and begged to be excused from saluting us upon arrival and departure. So, naturally, we didn't salute them."

"And the *Daedalus* hadn't waited for ye?" Balthus asked.

"Not an hour. Childers had gone off in a towering rage, and left word with the Dutch governor that we were to be neither helped nor harboured. We were to draw no bills on the Admiralty for food or lodging, but were to house in a warehouse belonging to the India Company, and live on some old stores that were there."

"Was it the great shed on the east side of the bay, beyond the town?" Captain Murgatroyd asked.

"That's the place. We lodged in the upper part, which was used as a sail loft. There was room enough: 'twas a good half cable's length from end to end, and empty of everything save four casks of beef and bread that looked as though they'd been there since the Cape was a town. 'Twas now that we were joined by Davy Spiggott and a carpenter's mate, James Worth, both of the *Circe,* who'd been left behind, like ourselves. They'd misjudged their capacity for the strong Cape wine our seamen are so fond of. By the time they'd sobered up the fleet was gone.

"We spent ten weeks in the warehouse, as bad off for the creature comforts as rats in a tar barrel. We'd no money, for the Dutchman we'd hired the ostriches of had cleaned us out to the last farthing, and his countrymen would give us nothing without pay. Harry and I had silver buckles to our shoes, and we traded these for some fruit and wine, but when that was gone 'twas the old stores and nothing else. But, damme, thanks to Davy Spiggott, we throve like fighting cocks. He could have served up our very shoe leather, with naught but his own genius for sauce, and 'twould have been as tasty as beef from the *Tortoise.* And there was this besides: ye'll all mind the southeast wind that blows in those parts. 'Tis called the Cape Doctor, and with reason, for more bracing, salubrious air blows nowhere. With that to sharpen our appetite, we were well content with what Davy could set before us. But there was one cask of the beef . . ."

The surgeon paused, and was so long silent that Lieutenant Earthy put in, "What of that one?"

"Earthy, I'm reluctant to say. . . . No matter; call me three times a liar, I'll stick to the facts for all that. 'Twas James Worth that opened it. Not a drop of liquor remained in the cask, having, seemingly, been absorbed by the beef itself, and that was as hard as iron: huge lean pieces of twenty to thirty pounds weight each, and gleaming with salt crystals. Even Spiggott shook his head when he saw and felt of it, and decided we'd best leave it till the last. Whilst Worth was replacing the head of the cask, he noticed some lettering stamped into the oak and called my attention to it. . . . That lettering, gentlemen, was: E–L–I–Z. R–E–G."

"What the devil!" Captain Trecothick broke in.

"George, you've taken from my mouth the very words I used when I saw the lettering. Now let me ask you a question. As an old Navy man, and your ancestors before you as far back as Harry the Seventh, you should be able to answer it. Was it, or was it not, the Admiralty custom, in Elizabeth's reign, to stamp our stores with her name?"

"I'll not take oath as to that," Captain Trecothick replied, with a chuckle. "There's been various ways of marking them through the centuries; but . . ."

"That's all I wish to know," the surgeon interrupted. "If it might have been so, then I am convinced it *was* so, and that the animals from which that beef came were driven along the lanes of England perhaps by William Shakespeare himself, as a country lad at Stratford. It is even possible that the cask was left at the Cape, through some oversight, by Sir Francis Drake, seventy-two years before the Dutch made their first settlement in the place."

"But did none of ye try your teeth on it?" Balthus asked.

"That's as may be," Dogbody replied. "I'll not be hurried beyond my gait by any ex-gunner in His Majesty's service. 'Tis enough to say, at the moment, that James Worth kept out one piece, and from that he carved me as fine a peg as was ever fitted to a stump. 'Twas hard and smooth as mahogany wood and near the same colour. I couldn't wear it yet, but Worth made me a box to keep it in against the time when my stump should be healed.

"Then came the ill wind, to Captain Brian Windle, of His Majesty's sloop of war *Fleetwood,* that was the saving of us. The *Fleetwood,* homeward bound from India, put in at the Cape with her lieutenants dead of a palludism, and poor Captain Windle at his last gasp from the same cause. Anthony and I knew him well, having served under him in the *Cambridge,* in 'sixty-nine. He died three days after reaching the Cape, but not before he had appointed Anthony to the command in his place. We were to proceed homeward without an instant's delay, for the *Fleetwood* was carrying despatches of the utmost importance.

"No time was lost, after we had performed the last rites for Captain Windle. Mr. Van Wyck, the governor, and his officers, attended the ceremonies. They couldn't do enough for us now that Anthony was again in a position of authority, and, to my disgust, he was as courteous as though we'd received nothing but good from the Dutch during the whole of our stay. I begged him to lay in a supply of ostrich eggs to bombard the fort with by way of a parting salute, but there was no winning Harry over to any deviltry. 'Twas impossible for him to bear a grudge. Contrary though it was to my own character, I admired him for it.

"I'll not dwell on the passage home. Had we been favoured at the end as we were four fifths of the way, 'twould have been the record passage from the Cape. We had clear skies and strong southerly gales all the way north. B'gad, we fairly flew, and the seamen had naught to do but hold on the slack so far as sailing went. Scarce a line was touched in a distance of better than five thousand miles.

"We were two hundred leagues past Madeira when the thing happened. 'Twas coming on for dusk, and Anthony and I, having finished supper, were standing by the bulwark. Harry was in his gayest mood and well he might have been.

" 'Dogbody,' said he, 'this cures all for us. Old Childers may do his worst, they'll give no heed to him at the Admiralty, after such a passage as we've made. I doubt if there's been the like of it since England was a nation.'

"He was not far wrong there. We were four weeks from the Cape . . ."

"Four *weeks!*" Captain Trecothick broke in. "And two hundred leagues past Madeira? Come, Dogbody! I knew the *Fleetwood*. Fast sailer that she was . . ."

"George, I don't expect you to believe me. It's not in reason you should. All I'm saying — and Davy Spiggott yonder would bear me out if he were awake — is that we left Capetown on the eleventh of January, in the year 1780, and at sunset on the eighth of February, Harry Anthony and I were walking the *Fleetwood's* quarter-deck in latitude forty-one, north, nine and some minutes west. Where does that bring us? Oporto, on the Portuguese coast, lay to starboard, though some forty leagues off."

"What was it happened?" Balthus asked.

"That's what I was asking myself, Ned, not two minutes after Anthony had spoken. My crutch flew from under my shoulder; I slid across the deck and came up against one of our long nine-pounders with a thud that left me short of breath for a good five minutes. We were doing eight knots at the time and whatever we'd struck seemed as solid as the continent of Africa, yet there was a kind of give to the thing. The ship slewed right round, and for a moment there was the greatest confusion on deck, sails slatting and banging, the master shouting his orders, and the seamen running three ways at once.

"Then we saw it. 'Twas a bull whale of enormous size that had, evidently, been lying asleep. There was a female near, with a calf under her fin. A calf, do I say? Damme, the infant of the pair was as large as the *Fleetwood,* which will tell you something of the bulk of the parents. Anthony sent the boatswain at once to sound the well, for 'twas not to be thought that we could have taken such a blow without damage. The next moment one of the midshipmen ran over to us.

" 'Sir,' he said, in a trembling voice, 'we're being at-tacked, I think. One of the whales is coming this way.'

"The infuriated whale, which had drawn off to a con-siderable distance, had turned and now came seething toward us at awful speed. He was right upon us, and be-fore an order could be given struck us squarely amidships. The impact was terrible; every man was sent sprawling once more, and the fore-topmast came crashing down, though, luckily, no one was injured by it.

"There was not a stauncher vessel afloat than the *Fleetwood,* but no ship ever built could have weathered such an encounter. The timbers along the starboard side were so sprung they were like withes in a basket. We drew tarred canvas under the hull in the attempt to fother her, and so far succeeded that we were encouraged to hope we might yet reach home. One circumstance both favoured and hindered us: the wind died away and by dawn the sea was dead calm. We pumped and we pumped, watch in and watch out. So it went for five days and nights.

"My heart bled for Anthony. Chance, which had played him so many scurvy tricks, outdid herself in this latest one. For all that, he was quiet, determined, and cheerful, heartening and encouraging all, and taking his turn at the pumps with the rest. On the morning of the sixth day he held a conference of the ship's company whilst the watch on deck continued the weary work at the pumps.

" 'Lads,' said he, 'we're flogging a dead horse. Had we been favoured by a slant of wind, we might have reached home, but fortune is against us. You've done all that men can do to save the vessel, but there's nine feet of water in

the hold and with the best will in the world she can't
float much longer. I must now think of your safety.'

"He then gave his orders. Mr. Lumpitt, the master, was
to command the longboat, Mr. Gregg the green launch,
and Mr. Twentytooth, the red. They were to proceed to
Oporto, then about thirty leagues distant. He himself,
with five men, in the jolly boat, would make direct for
England with the despatches.

"Preparations for departure were quickly made. All the
stores were under water, but one large and one small
cask of beef had been gotten on deck, and there was a
sufficiency of fresh water in the scuttle butt by the galley.
The beef in the large cask was shared out to the company
to go in the longboat and the two launches, giving them
food and to spare even though they should have to row
the thirty leagues. Those to go with Anthony in the
jolly boat were James Worth, Spiggott, two seamen, and
myself.

"Toward noon, all but the jolly boat's crew left the
ship. Spent as the men were, they gave their commander
a hearty three-times-three as they set off. Then the oars
were gotten out, and we watched them crawl away over
the quiet sea until they were lost to view.

"We were to have gone immediately after, but when it
came to the point, damme if Harry could do it! He kept
putting it off and putting it off, making little excuses to
himself and us for further delay. So it went till nightfall,
when a fresh westerly breeze struck up. All sail had been
set for just such a breeze, and the little *Fleetwood* felt
and answered to it as best she could, for all her bellyful

of sea water. She moved at about two knots, reason enough for our staying with her as long as she'd float. To our surprise, we found that the leaks had not gained above three inches in the last eight hours. This set us to pumping once more. Knocked up though we were, we'd have pumped our insides out to please Harry Anthony. Damme, if I'd had as many legs as a centipede, I'd gladly have given the lot to have seen him get his first command into Plymouth or Portsmouth.

"But chance hadn't done with him yet. The next morning, when Davy Spiggott opened the little cask of beef we were to live on, he found it packed with bones. Some scoundrel in the Tower Hill or the Deptford Victualing Yard had stolen the beef and covered his villainy in this way. He'd not even had the decency to put in fresh bones; these looked as though they'd been dug from the kitchen middens of Saxon London. Nevertheless, Spiggott boiled them, and we drank the water, and managed for that day. Soon we'd no longer the strength to pump. 'Twas as much as we could do to steer, and the need for that was soon gone. It fell calm once more, with a fog so thick we couldn't see the bow of the ship from the quarter-deck.

"The only cheer we had was a little cag of rum Anthony kept in his cabin. Spiggott made us two gallons of hot grog to keep the cold and the fog out of our bones. B'gad, we didn't stint ourselves, and in an hour's time we were as merry as crickets. We sang songs and told stories and drank death and desolation to the rogue who'd stolen our beef.

" 'Lads,' said Anthony, 'this calm won't last. There's a

deal of nourishment in good rum, and what's left in the little cag will see us home. This day week, at the latest, I promise ye shall sit down to the best meal of roast fresh beef and potatoes Plymouth can furnish, with veal pies, and tarts and custards and puddings and whatever else your fancy calls for. Till then, damme, we must pinch in our guts and let them growl as they may.'

"We were all with him. At the moment, merry as we were, we felt we could sail the jolly boat thrice the distance, if need were. Of a sudden James Worth turned to me. 'Doctor,' said he, 'your leg!'

" 'Never ye fret about that,' said I. 'The stump's still a bit on the tender side, but the rest of me's as tough as an old lanyard knot. I'll outlast the five of ye, if it comes to that.'

" 'I'm not thinking of the stump,' said he. 'The peg, Doctor! The beef peg!'

"Anthony set down his glass with a bang. 'Damn my eyes!' said he. 'Why haven't we thought of it before! Hopping Giles, fetch me that jury-leg and be quick about it!'

" 'What, ye cannibals!' said I. 'Would ye dine off your surgeon that's been father and mother to the lot of ye these many weeks?'

" 'That we would!' said Harry; and, b'gad, I was willing enough to set my own teeth in the beef if Davy Spiggott could manage to soften it by roasting or boiling. I'd never yet worn it, and now 'twas fetched from the box I kept it in. We all went to the galley where a hot fire was made and water boiled whilst Worth blunted the teeth of three saws, cutting the leg in sections, for we decided that soup would go farthest, if soup could be made of such petrified meat. We sat from ten in the evening till the dawn of day, whilst the water boiled away and was replenished, and the lumps of beef lay in the bottom of the pot, as whole and hard as when Davy Spiggott placed them there. He'd prod them now and again with a long fork, but the only result was the bent prongs. He was about to admit himself beaten when, as though by magic, the beef fell away in small bits, and these, in turn, dissolved into a rich broth. We were standing over the pot, breathing in that heavenly aroma, when we noticed that a film of water was spreading in tongues, and bays, and promontories, over the galley floor. So intent had we been on our soup we'd all but forgot we were at sea, in a sinking ship. The water was now lapping in at the scuppers. There was no time to lose.

"The jolly boat was ready, chocked up on even keel on the foredeck. We had our parcels in her, and two *barriques* of water, and the rum, and now Anthony made haste to fetch his box of despatches and the ship's papers. With one of the seamen to help, Spiggott carefully lifted the pot from the fire and set it gently down in the bottom of the jolly boat."

"What's this?" said Trecothick, as the surgeon paused for refreshment. "Was ye going boating on the deck of your ship? You've not put your skiff over the side yet."

"There was no need, George. The ship was bound to settle gently, with the logs of larota wood we had below.

We could float off in the jolly boat as she went under."

"Larota wood? What's that?"

"I thought I'd mentioned it. The larota is a tree that grows in scattered parts of India, with a trunk as straight as that of a pine. The wood is of a tough, fibrous nature, yet so light that a log three feet in diameter and twenty feet long can easily be carried by two men. The sap, it seems, draws innumerable small air bubbles in with it, and the cells of the wood form around these. We had twenty logs of it aboard, being sent home to the Admiralty in the hope that the wood might be found useful in shipbuilding. We'd cursed them often enough during the voyage, for they were in the way, but they proved a boon in the end. Without them, we'd never have been able to keep the ship afloat so long. But now their buoyancy was being slowly overcome by the immense weight of water as the vessel filled.

"We took our places in the jolly boat, and not long after we were floated gently up and over the bulwark. The *Fleetwood* sank on even keel, with scarce a ripple, going down with infinite slowness. At another time we'd have watched her with heavy hearts, but we were still merry from the grog. Furthermore, our interest as seamen was deeply engaged in so strange a sight. The hull was now a mere shadow below, yet the masts as they followed made perfect right angles with the surface of the sea.

" 'Lads,' said Anthony, 'here's a sight I'd never have believed possible. My advice to all of you is to say naught of it hereafter, else ye'll be set down for as great liars as

Munchausen. . . . Blast me! What's that? 'Tis Effie, sure as the world!'

"Effie was our cat, and a great pet with all. We'd looked high and low for her, but not high enough, for there she was, clinging to the vane of the mainmast. With a touch of the oars the jolly boat was brought alongside and Effie jumped into Worth's arms. A joy it was to have rescued her.

"Ten minutes later the mainmast vane itself glimmered and vanished beneath the sea. We were alone in our tiny boat in that great solitude of waters, but not without comfort.

" 'Now, Davy, breakfast,' said Anthony, rubbing his hands. 'We'll soon know whether beef, like good rum, improves with age.'

" 'Twas then broad day, or would have been save for the fog. That lay so thick on the sea we could look no farther than fifty yards beyond the boat. Davy took the lid from the pot, and the rich broth sent up a steam that made our bellies quiver with anticipation. A pint each was quickly ladled out, and no time was lost in tasting it. Harry took a long noisy sip, then looked up with an expression of pleased astonishment.

" 'Damme, here's richness!' said he. 'Dogbody, if the rest of your anatomy's as good as this, we'll finish ye off before we reach home.' "

The surgeon paused for a sip from the little glass before him, tasting the contents with relish, as though it were the broth drunk so many years ago.

"George," he resumed, "you were asking, a while back,

if men have ever been better nourished by English beef
than ourselves here, this night. Yes . . . once, and those
were the six in the *Fleetwood's* jolly boat. A more heartening broth was never drunk by half-famished men. All its
original goodness and flavour seemed to have been held
in suspension in the beef, in its hardened state. Damme,
it made very lions of us, for energy and courage. If — as
I am convinced it was — the cask from which it came had
been left at the Cape by Francis Drake in his glorious
voyage around the world, I can well understand how and
why the seamen of Elizabeth's time made England the
Mistress of Oceans. Davy stirred the broth well before
dishing out our second helping, and in doing so he
brought up in his spoon the reefer's nut with which the
end of my peg had been shod. That, curiously enough,
was as hard as ever. Boiling had had not the least effect
upon it."

"The reefer's nut? What is that, Doctor?" Captain Runyon inquired.

" 'Tis the core, the centre of the hard bread issued to
our Navy ships," the surgeon replied. "The seaman is not
yet born with teeth and jaws strong enough to crack one."

"True enough," Captain Mundy put in, with a laugh.
"Our Navy cooks manage to crack and crumble them, Mr.
Runyon, twixt hammer and anvil. Boiling will then have
its effect. The flour is excellent for puddings, and as the
nuts are impervious to maggots, they are highly prized. I
don't wonder, Dogbody, that the carpenter's mate shod
your peg with one. 'Twould have lasted your lifetime.
You should have treasured it for a keepsake."

"So I did," said the surgeon. Leaning back, he fished in his breeches pocket and drew out a greyish disc, about two and a half inches in diameter and of the same thickness. One side had been hollowed out to the depth of half an inch, leaving a collar whose purpose seemed to have been to fit over the end of the peg proper. With a glint of triumph in his eyes, the surgeon passed this down the table for examination. The conversation became general for a moment while the disc was handed round; then Captain Trecothick, with a question, brought the surgeon back to his tale.

"We knew exactly where we were," the latter replied. "At least, Anthony did, and he was never half a mile out in his reckoning. According to his calculation we had two hundred and fifty leagues between ourselves and Plymouth. There was not a breath of wind, but heartened and refreshed as we'd been by the broth, the oars were gotten out and we started to row for home as blithely as though we had Penlee Head in sight.

"We'd not been rowing ten minutes when Anthony called out, sharply, 'Rest!' He was staring intently into the fog. We turned to stare as well. A great shadowy bulk loomed high above us into the mists. 'Twas a huge ship, her sails hanging limp from the yards. Then we lost her and half doubted we'd seen her, but a moment later there she was again.

" 'Hold hard, lads,' said Anthony, quietly. 'Dogbody, what is she?'

" 'We were singing "Spanish Ladies" last night, Harry,' said I, 'and here's one before us or I'm much mistaken.'

" 'What d'ye think, Worth?'

" 'She's the look of one, sir,' said Worth.

" 'In that case we're as good as taken the minute the fog lifts,' said Anthony, glumly. He reached under the thwart for the tin box containing the despatches from India. 'I've orders to destroy these at all hazards, in case of capture.' With a bit of line he bound the box round securely. 'Dogbody, pass me the iron lid of the pot. That'll sink 'em.'

" 'Don't be hasty,' said I. 'You'll not scuttle 'em at once, Harry?'

" 'I'm not such a fool as that,' said he, 'but I'll have all in readiness. Now, lads, pull up to her. We'll soon know if our luck's in or out.'

"We were not thirty yards off, and the fog was so thick we were certain we had not yet been seen. For all she was a merchantman, her sides were pierced for a double row of gunports. A handsome ship she was, around a thousand tons burden, but with the dingy look of a long passage about her.

"Not a sound of life did we hear as we approached. As we came under her stern we saw the name, *Sancta Inez*, beautifully carved, with cherubs and angels hovering over and around it, and little seraphim with their cheeks puffed out as though they were blowing her on her way, but they weren't making much of a job of it. She lay as motionless as though rooted to the ocean bed. We'd no longer any doubt as to her nationality. Anthony sat with the despatch box on his lap, the pot lid fastened to it, ready to heave it overboard. We crept soundlessly along to the bow, no man speaking. A fouler ship's hull I've never seen. Barnacles a good four inches deep showed at the waterline, and long streamers of weed and grass swayed gently to and fro. Of a sudden came the sound of shrill barking right above us. A little terrier thrust his head through a scupper; he'd caught sight of Effie, who was arching her back and spitting at him. The dog was a pitiful bag of bones. A moment later he left off as though exhausted. Nothing more happened. To say that we were puzzled is to say little.

" 'What the devil,' said Anthony, in a low voice. 'Where's her people, and what's that boatswain's chair doing over the side?'

"The seat, fixed to a single stout line, floated at the water's edge, and at that point we saw that a small area of weeds and barnacles had been cleared from the hull.

" 'It might be a starving ship, sir,' one of the seamen remarked. 'I've heard tell of men drove by hunger to eating barnacles as a last thing.'

"Anthony shook his head. 'A thousand-ton vessel and all her stores gone? 'Tis impossible.' He got to his feet and passed me his despatch box. 'Mind this, Dogbody, and be ready to heave it over at a word from me.' With that he took off his boots, and, seizing the line, walked up the ship's side, seaman fashion.

"We waited a matter of ten minutes, perhaps, though the time seemed much longer; then he reappeared above. 'Make the painter fast, lads, and come aboard,' he called. He threw down a coil of small line. 'Spiggott, bend that on to the pot handle and steady the pot whilst I draw it up.'

"The soup went first, Harry leaning out and drawing it up with such care that not a drop was spilled. We then followed. Emotions of joy, relief, and pity seized our hearts as we clambered over the bulwark. A score of men, frightfully emaciated, lay about the deck, too feeble to move. Their eyes looked larger than human in the wasted sockets as they turned them upon us in mute appeal. The small terrier lay nearest, by the side of his food pan, which was licked clean.

" 'This little chap will have a sup of broth if I do naught else,' said Spiggott, and he ladled some into the bowl. The dog lapped it up with fierce eagerness; then, damme if he didn't fly at Spiggott like a baby lion! We liked his spirit, though we couldn't say much for his sense of gratitude; but he was Spanish and recognized his country's enemies by instinct. But when he made for Effie she gave him such a clawing he was glad to fly for safety.

"Meanwhile, Anthony, who had gone aft, returned to where we stood. 'Lads,' said he, scarce able to believe his own words, 'the ship is ours. There's above a hundred poor creatures here, all in a pitiable state from disease and starvation. They can make no resistance. We must do what we can for them, but first I want all the small arms collected, lest some amongst them might yet have the strength to do us a mischief.'

"This was soon done; then we carried the Spaniards into the great cabin, and one of our seamen was placed as a guard over them. If we'd believed ourselves unlucky, what could we say now, comparing our luck with that of the Spaniards? We learned from one that spoke English that they'd left the Manillas sixteen months before, under convoy. Whilst crossing the Indian Ocean they'd become separated from their ships of war in a succession of gales that drove them as far south as latitude forty-eight. Thereafter they'd had nothing but misfortune, and in all that time not one vessel had they sighted. Most of their stores had been spoiled by sea water, and scurvy added to their misery. Nevertheless, by dint of courage and perseverance they'd won to where we found them. But when the weather fell calm their last strength was gone and hope with it.

"We'd six gallons of broth left in the pot. Interest urged that we keep it for ourselves, but humanity demanded that we succour our country's enemies, now in our hands. In my small medicine case I still had two packets of Doctor Quittichunk's anti-scurvy tablets. These I dissolved into the broth, and with Spiggott to help me fed the Spaniards, a spoonful each, at a time. 'Twas the saving of them. There was such virtue in both the broth and Doctor Quittichunk's tablets that every man of them revived wonderfully. In fact, they began to buzz like a nest of revived hornets, so that we had to keep them under lock and key and a strict watch over them. For ourselves, we lived upon the remains of Anthony's little cag of rum, mixed with water.

"And now, gentlemen, I am home at last, after a ride that began on an ostrich's back, in the deserts of Africa, and ended in the *Sancta Inez,* which was tided up the Avon to Bristol by the longboats of one of our Navy ships, in the midst of such a crowd of cheering spectators as the town has rarely seen in her history."

"Home!" said Trecothick. "Damme, did ye fly the two hundred and fifty leagues? And why Bristol? I thought ye was to make for Plymouth?"

"The getting home was nothing, George. We were no more than aboard the *Sancta Inez* when the breeze came fresh from the south. And Anthony being a Bristol man, 'tis not to be wondered at that he should wish to take such a prize to his home town. The word of his coming flew up the river before us and all Bristol was there to meet him, his girls standing in front. Little Patricia, who'd been in her mother's arms when he last saw her, was now standing on her own little feet. Harry waved and waved, his heart too full for words, as we warped in to the dock.

" 'I don't see Mrs. Anthony,' he said, anxiously. 'And where's Helen?'

"His noting Mrs. Anthony's absence was natural enough, but I wondered he should miss one of his girls in so great a company. The waterside was so filled with people we could scarce get ashore; then I lost sight of Harry for a bit. He was fairly smothered in the midst of his daughters. At last he managed to get back to where I stood.

" 'Dogbody,' said he, laughing and crying in the same breath, 'did ye know we've been gone nine months, almost to the day? Mrs. Anthony's lying in again. I'm going straight home and I want you to come with me.'

"B'gad, 'twas useless to protest. The girls seized my arms and swept me away with their father. All save the baby had Grecian names: Hero, Ariadne, Helen, Juno, Electra, Antigone, and the like. As I looked from one to another, I thought how well the names suited them. There were no great beauties amongst them, but all had a freshness and vigour that made me think of the women of the classic eras.

"They lived in a dingy house in a shabby part of town, but 'home' was written all over it. Harry ran ahead and up the steps and was met by Helen, his oldest daughter, who was on the lookout. It could not have happened better for Anthony. The new baby had come not half an hour before, and Mrs. Anthony was doing well."

"Another daughter?" Captain Mundy asked.

"It was, and Harry took as much joy in the news as though Mrs. Anthony had brought him a pair of sons. It rounded out the dozen, and with the prize he'd brought home, he'd no need to fear the future. But he didn't know the extent of his fortune at the moment. When the ship was examined by the Navy Board, they found a strong room filled with silver, in bars, and chests of minted coin to a fabulous amount. My own cut was enough to have bought me a landed estate, but I squandered it, of course. I never could stick to money."

"And what of Anthony? He got his girls married?" Captain Murgatroyd asked.

"Every one, and well married, too. Oddly enough, their own families ran to sons as readily as that of their parents had to daughters. Splendid boys they are. I've met some of them. Were they serving together, they could man a ninety-gun ship. The little daughter, born the day we got home, is now the mother of six."

"What was her name?" someone asked.

"Had she been my daughter, I'd have called her Inez," Captain Trecothick said.

"Ostrichia would have been better," said Lieutenant Earthy. "And the name would have gone well with the next youngest, little Patricia."

"She received a far better name than either of those," said the surgeon. "Attica. 'Twas I that suggested it. Mrs. Anthony was partial to Greek names. But we never told her that this one had a Hottentot root."

Doctor Dogbody was about to add a word more when Davy Spiggott, asleep on the sofa, opened his eyes, sat up abruptly, and looked about him with a dazed, wondering expression.

"*Mercury,*" he resumed . . . "*Repulse, Fleetwood, Ramilies, Aurora . . .*"

He broke off and regarded the company with an abashed smile.

"I ain't been asleep?" he asked.

VIII

APRIL FIRST ON APRIL SECOND

The sun had set in a cloudless sky, flooding the streets of Portsmouth with golden light. Seamen on shore leave from ships in the harbour, as well as many of the towns-people, were abroad, enjoying the sweet bland air of early spring, and it was not until the lamps were being lit that Doctor Dogbody entered the taproom of the Cheerful Tortoise, then beginning to fill with the customary after-supper patrons. Captains Runyon and Mur-gatroyd, Mr. Ostiff and Ned Balthus, were already there, in the company of two gentlemen whom Murgatroyd now introduced to the surgeon. The first, Mr. Sawbridge, was a London merchant. The other, Mr. Rasmussen, was a Dane who owned a fleet of vessels trading between Copenhagen and various English ports, as well as to the Baltic.

"I doubted that we'd have you with us on so fine an evening, Dogbody," said Ostiff when the introductions had been concluded. He then turned to the visitors. "Gentlemen, you see before you the most confirmed pedestrian in the whole of Portsmouth. Ten or fifteen miles of an afternoon are nothing to him."

"If you'd spent better than half a century walking the decks of ships, friend Ostiff, you'd find it hard, upon coming ashore, to fit yourself to a pair of sitting breeches," the surgeon replied.

"You'll have a respectable mileage behind you, sir, after so many years at sea," said Mr. Sawbridge.

"So I have, sir," said the surgeon, his eyes twinkling. "Oddly enough, not a week ago I was making a rough estimate of the whole, and I dare say I've come pretty near it. From the year 1766, when I went to sea as a lad of fourteen, until five months ago, I have walked, on the decks of twenty-nine ships, ranging from bombs, sloops, and cutters, through frigates to ships of the line, a distance of three times around the earth at the equator, with an additional circumference at about latitude forty-five. B'gad, had it all been in the same ship I'd have worn her deck planking through a dozen times over."

"And how much of that distance was covered on your own two feet?" Murgatroyd asked.

"Before I was fitted with a jury-leg? You should be able to guess that," said the surgeon.

"Guess it? How?"

"You mean to say I've never told you when and where I lost the other?"

"Do you call that a fair question?" said Ostiff. He turned again to the guests. "Gentlemen, Doctor Dogbody, by his own admission made just now, must have seen something of service in an active career covering more than fifty years, but none of his friends ashore know what it may have been. As for his missing leg, I'm convinced there was something more than strange connected with the loss of it, for he's deaf and dumb on that point."

"And why not, Ostiff?" the surgeon replied. "Had your life's work been the hewing-off of the limbs of other men, the loss of your own would be no subject for comment. A barber's tale of an occasion when he had his own hair cut might be expected to interest fully as much."

"I would willingly chance the lack of interest, sir, if you'd be pleased to favour us," Mr. Sawbridge said.

Mr. Rasmussen warmly seconded the proposal, whereupon Captain Murgatroyd said: "Then let's have it, Dogbody. The duller the tale, the more ready we'll be for bed, after."

The surgeon hesitated, then shook his head, slowly. "Damme, you don't know what you ask. . . . If I tell it, I must refer to an event that will be painful for Mr. Rasmussen to recall."

"For me, sir? In what way?" the Dane replied.

"It is curious that the matter should have been broached on this particular evening," said the surgeon. "I will reply to your question, sir, by another: What day are we now? I mean, what day of the month?"

"Tuesday, the second, are we not?"

"Aye, the second of April. Ned Balthus, has the date any significance for you?"

"Can't say it has, Doctor. Not as I know of."

"B'gad, here's a Navy gunner has fought so many battles he's clean forgot one of the most glorious! Chiefly glorious, sir," he added, with a glance at Mr. Rasmussen, "because of the brave, determined, and skillful foe who opposed our seamen on that occasion — your own countrymen."

"I take you now," Mr. Rasmussen replied. "The battle of Copenhagen, of course."

"So it was," said Balthus; "April second, 1801. Fancy my not recollecting the date!"

"I'll say this, Mr. Rasmussen," said Dogbody. " 'Twas Nelson who won us the victory. Had you possessed so great a genius on your side, there'd have been none of us left at the finish on *either* side. Even with Nelson, 'twas a near thing for us."

Mr. Sawbridge was leaning forward in his chair. "Doctor Dogbody," he said, "you could not have hit upon an event more calculated to interest Mr. Rasmussen and myself than the battle of Copenhagen. I was in Denmark at the time, looking after my interests there, and a guest in Mr. Rasmussen's house. We witnessed the battle and all Copenhagen with us. I'd no mind to crow over my friend here at the close, for, as you say, 'twas touch and go till the last moment."

"It was indeed," said the Dane; "and since we had to be trimmed, we were pleased it was Nelson himself who did the trimming."

"What brought Denmark in against England at that time?" Mr. Runyon asked. "I never did understand the politics of the business."

"There was no real sense to it, Runyon," said the surgeon. "Mr. Rasmussen will agree that there was right and wrong on both sides."

"So there was, sir. Our differences chiefly concerned matters of trade, unfortunate indeed between two countries so long united by ties of blood and friendship."

"The Emperor Paul, of Russia, was largely responsible," said the surgeon. "You may remember, Runyon, that he had formed the second armed neutrality, with Denmark as one of the contracting parties. The confederacy held the principle that property at sea was protected by the flag of a neutral; in other words, that free bottoms made free goods. You will readily see what recognition of such a right would have meant to England, then at war with the half of Europe. No enemy's property, from that moment, could have been detected. As Lord Whitworth said, if such a principle were admitted, a neutral might have afforded protection to enemy commerce in all parts of the world. 'Twould only be necessary to find a neutral state, however small and contemptible, to cover that commerce and contraband with its flag."

"A pity it was," said Ostiff, "that so bloody a battle as

that of Copenhagen should have to be fought over so mean a cause. What ship were you then serving in, Dogbody?"

"I was surgeon in the *Monarch,* Captain Mosse, and Balthus here was banging his twenty-four-pounders in the *Amazon,* frigate."

"The *Monarch?* You don't tell me, sir!" said Mr. Sawbridge. "Was she not the second of our ships of the line, anchored during the battle near the channel to the inner harbour?"

"She was, sir."

"Rasmussen, you recall her?" asked Mr. Sawbridge.

"Do I not!" his friend replied. "We were in an upper chamber at my house, Doctor Dogbody, where, with the aid of my great telescope, we had a clear view of the battle. The guns of all the ships and batteries, both ours and yours, were splendidly served, but Sawbridge and I particularly remarked the firing of those in the *Monarch.* There was one tier that seemed to have been commanded by the devil himself, so rapid and destructive was the fire."

"On the lower gun deck?" the surgeon asked.

"So it was!" Mr. Rasmussen replied. "Who was in charge there, Doctor? The fellow must have been a perfect genius, and as cool as he was brave. I've often wondered whether or not he survived the action."

"Wasn't they under Lieutenant Teddar's orders?" Balthus asked.

"They were and they were not, Ned, if you understand me."

"Can't say I do," said Balthus. "Don't see how it could be the two at once."

"No more could Philip Teddar himself, but so it was," said Dogbody. "A stranger thing has never happened in His Majesty's service." He was silent for some little time, then he said: "Well, gentlemen, I see you'll have the tale, and I'm bound to oblige because of the anniversary. This day sixteen years ago I bade farewell to my larboard leg, but that had little to do with Lieutenant Teddar's part in the battle of Copenhagen. You knew him, didn't you, Ned?"

"Not well, though I was six months in the same ship with him."

"After Copenhagen?"

"Aye. Under Captain Wainright, in the *Hotspur*."

"Teddar was liked in the *Hotspur?*"

"That's putting it small," said the gunner. "The men worshiped him, for all he was one of the silent kind. I never heard him say more than three words at one time to anyone."

"Sober in his habits?" asked the surgeon.

"Sober! He wouldn't have taken a sup of ale, to say nothing of spirits, had his life depended on it. He'd a text from the Bible on the wall of his cabin: 'Wine is a mocker, strong drink is raging.' He lived by it, too."

Dogbody nodded. "Aye, that was Teddar, after Copenhagen. Even before it he was never a toper, but now and again when disturbed in his mind he'd cure himself by getting blind drunk. Blind, do I say? Damme, frozen, petrified, dead! A log of wood had more life in it than Phil Teddar in the depth of his cups. His bosom friend at this time was Lieutenant Sidney Thone, likewise of the *Monarch*.

"Thone was the damnedest practical joker in the Navy, though I'll say this for him: there was never anything cruel or mean in his pranks. He showed a kind of genius in the least of them. Had he used the abilities spent in these games to get on in the service, he'd have been an admiral long since. As it is, the last I heard of him he was still a lieutenant.

"Now, gentlemen, I'll take ye to Yarmouth Roads, in the month of March, 1801, where our fleet was gathered under the command of Admiral Sir Hyde Parker. There'd been no announcement as to where we were bound, but 'twas generally believed we were to go against Denmark. And what made all ranks content was the knowledge that Nelson was second-in-command. Admiral Parker, though an officer of distinction, was unqualified, by age and infirmities, for such a responsibility. He was the favourite of a party at home; but the King, the Earl of Saint Vincent, and the nation looked to Nelson for the success of the expedition.

"Weeks had been spent in getting the ships ready for sea, and never was a fleet more ready than ours by the first of March. 'Twas perfection itself, thanks to Nelson's management; and, thanks to his goodness of heart, wardroom and warrant officers had a bit of freedom ashore when all was in readiness on shipboard. Some of the lieutenants took rooms in the Yarmouth taverns. Thone had his turn, and 'twas then I learned he'd been busy at more than ship's duties during those weeks.

"I had a day off myself, and chanced to meet Thone on Yarmouth High Street.

" 'Dogbody,' said he, 'what are ye doing ashore?'

" 'I'm out for a little gapeseed,' said I. 'D'ye grudge one of His Majesty's best Navy surgeons the chance to stretch his legs?'

" 'Never in the world,' said he. 'You're the very man I wished to meet. Come along to the Three Magpies and we'll wet ye down.'

" 'Who's your company?' said I, for I knew Thone of old, and his companions were like to be too gay for such a sober steady fellow as myself.

" 'There's a proper answer to an offer of hospitality!' said he. 'Come and see. If ye must know, there's none but Phil Teddar.'

" 'Teddar was aboard ship when I came in this morning,' said I.

" 'That may be, but he's not now,' said Thone. 'He's sitting in my room at the Magpies, as pleasant for a companion as the pains of death. I came out to look for someone I could talk to.'

"He went on to say that Teddar was in one of his glum moods. I knew what was amiss with him, for he'd opened his mind to me aboard ship: he hated the thought of England fighting the Danes. He wasn't alone there; hundreds of men in the fleet felt the same, but Teddar took the prospect harder than most. 'Twould be fighting our own flesh and blood, he said, which was close to the truth, for there's a deal of Danish blood in Englishmen's veins.

"Well, up we went to a pleasant chamber on the first floor, front, at the Magpies, and there sat Teddar at a little table covered with a flowered cloth, looking out the window to seaward. His back was toward us and he gave no heed as we came in. He'd his left elbow propped on the table, and rested his chin in his hand. The fingers of the other hand were clasped around a glass of grog that stood by him.

" 'What cheer, Phil?' said I. B'gad, there was no cheer at all so far as he was concerned. He didn't so much as look round, and not a word did he say.

" 'Give no heed to him, Dogbody,' says Thone. 'Let him mope it out, the swab, since that seems to be his fancy. Draw up here by the fire and we'll be merry by ourselves.'

"B'gad, merry we were; I don't know when I've enjoyed an afternoon more, for all Teddar's glumness. 'Twas perfect weather for indoors, with a cold rain falling. In the Magpies' best sitting room, with a bright fire going and a table spread with good cheer, Thone and I were as snug as mice in a wheat stack. He ordered up smoked fish and ham, a kidney pie, cold beef and mutton, with greens and roast potatoes. We had pickles and jellies and the best of soft bread and fresh butter, and the pair of us tucked into a hearty meal, whilst Teddar, by the window, bogged himself still deeper in the dumps, if anything. It grieved me to see a young man — he was less than half my age, as was Thone — missing all the good of such an occasion. Presently I turned my chair half round to bring him in view, and there he sat, just as he was when we'd first come in.

" 'Phil,' said I, 'stop your gabble, will you?'

" 'Ever know such a chatter-basket?' says Thone. 'Once he starts talking there's no stopping him. He's got tongue enough for three sets of teeth.'

"But there was no cajoling Teddar. He didn't stir; you'd have said he was not even aware of us. I was a bit puzzled at Thone. He sat grinning and hugging his knees. I couldn't see what there was to grin about. Then he leaned over to me, speaking in a low voice.

" 'Have ye noticed?' says he. 'He's not even tasted his grog! You're the one to stir him out of it. Have a try, anyway.'

"I was bound to bring him to reason if the thing were possible, so I strolled over and stood behind his chair.

" 'Come, Phil,' said I; 'ye'll not change our orders by sitting like a wooden image looking over the sea toward the coasts of Denmark. It's not our part to criticize the decisions of His Majesty's ministers. Go we must, and fight we must. The Danes, I'll warrant, like the business no better than ourselves, but they'll serve their guns like devils, for all that, when it comes to action. We must do the same. Cheer up, lad! Damme, we may all be dead in a fortnight. Don't spoil one of your last days ashore.'

"With that I laid a hand on his shoulder, and if I'd laid it on the shoulder of a skeleton I couldn't have had a greater shock or a queerer one. It was not flesh and blood I felt beneath his coat, but something as smooth and hard as polished wood. I jumped back and whirled around to Thone, who was rocking back and forth in his seat, pounding his knees with both fists. If ever I've seen a man happy, 'twas that rogue of a junior lieutenant.

" 'It's perfect! It's perfect!' said he, scarce able to contain himself.

" 'What's perfect, ye devil?' said I. B'gad, I was ready to throttle him I was so taken aback, and if any of you have ever been deceived by a dummy ye'll know how I felt."

"A dummy? God's rabbit!" said Balthus, with a grin.

"Ned, that waxen image, for it was of wax, was Teddar's very identity. B'gad, it resembled him more than he resembled himself, if you understand me. During the two hours Thone and I sat in its company, I never for a moment doubted 'twas Teddar there by the window."

"But where had Thone got such a figure?" Runyon asked.

"Ye may well ask, Runyon. You've not, perhaps, heard of Madame Tussaud, a Frenchwoman, who had her wax-works in London, in the Strand? In fact, she still has it there, with a greatly increased number of figures over what she had sixteen years ago. 'Twas she that made the image of Teddar. You must have seen her exhibition, Mr. Sawbridge?"

"More than once," the latter replied, "though I've never chanced to meet Madame Tussaud herself. A remarkable woman, by all accounts."

"She is indeed," said the surgeon. " 'Twas her uncle,

John Curtius, a physician of Berne, in Switzerland, who taught her as a young girl the art of modeling in wax. So adept was she that her fame soon spread over the whole of Europe. She was commissioned to model many of the great personages at the French Court before the Revolution, and was sent for to stay at the palace in Versailles to instruct Madame Elizabeth, sister of Louis Sixteenth, in the art. During the Terror she was commanded by the Republican government to model the heads of the most eminent victims of the guillotine, directly after the heads had been struck off. In the year 1800, I think it was, she begged and was granted permission, by Buonaparte, to come to England, and has since lived in this country."

"But how did Lieutenant Thone contrive to get so perfect an image of Teddar?" Murgatroyd asked. "It must have been done with his knowledge?"

Dogbody shook his head. "Teddar knew nothing about it, though he sat for his portrait many's the time. Whenever Thone knew that he and Teddar were to have a few days' shore leave, at Plymouth or Portsmouth or London, he would have Madame Tussaud on the spot, to study Teddar, unbeknownst to himself, and to make her sketches from life."

"A pretty penny that must have cost," said Ostiff.

"Two hundred and fifty golden guineas, and 'twas no more to Thone than tuppence would be to ourselves. His people own the half of Essex. He was willing to go to vast trouble and expense to carry through one of his jokes, but it was not for the mere pleasure of taking *me* in that he'd planned this one. Before the fleet sailed, there was to be a festive evening ashore for some of the officers of the *Monarch* and the *Ganges*. Teddar was certain to be absent, for he'd small talent for the social pleasures and never went abroad in much company. Thone's plan was to have his image at the gathering, and he promised himself, with good reason, that he could hoax the lot of 'em."

"And did he?" asked Balthus.

The surgeon turned to give the gunner a glance of such distinct disapproval that the latter made haste to add, "But go your own gait, Doctor. I've no wish to bustle ye on beyond it."

"Damme, no! Ye'd merely scuttle me, Ned Balthus, before ever I've quit Yarmouth Roads. 'Tis a story I'm telling. I'm obliged to follow the events as they fell out.

"As I've said, Thone was overjoyed with his success at the rehearsal. 'Dogbody,' said he, 'beside myself there's no man in the fleet knows Teddar better than you do. If I can hoax you I can hoax 'em all. 'Twill be All Fools' Day and no mistake, on April first.'

"The evening of the first had been set for the jollification ashore, and Thone was on pins and needles for the day to come. I told him that if he must play his joke, he'd best urge the others to set the date ahead, for the fleet was in readiness and awaiting orders, but he was bound to wait. He took near as much pleasure in the prospect as in the execution of his tomfooleries, and 'twas generally believed that we'd not leave Yarmouth before the middle of April.

"And then — March twelfth, I think it was — came Admiral Parker, posthaste from London, and went immediately aboard his flagship, when the fleet signal to weigh was made. Damme, some of us had not even time to get our washing from on shore.

"Admiral Nelson had his flag in the *St. George,* Admiral Parker was in the *London,* and Rear Admiral Totty was in the *Invincible,* but that ship was lost before ever we got to Denmark. She sailed after the others, though the same afternoon. The wind was blowing strong from the southwest, and the *Invincible* went aground on the flood tide, on a sandbank called the Ridge, off Cromer, where she soon after sank, in the darkness and horror of a tempestuous night. Captain Rennie and above four hundred of the crew were lost. The remainder, about two hundred, were picked up by colliers and fishing vessels. You'll not have forgotten that night, Ned?"

"That I've not," said the gunner, soberly. "Many an old shipmate was lost in the *Invincible.* 'Twas thought a dark beginning for Copenhagen."

"None of us in the *Monarch* was harder hit than Phil Teddar. His youngest brother was a mid in the *Invincible* and was first reported drowned. Teddar took the loss of the ship as an ill-omen for the success of the entire expedition, and called it a judgment in advance upon the King's ministers for going to war with Denmark. He didn't know till a month later that his brother was safe. The lad was picked up by a Swedish fishing boat and carried ashore to Gothenburg.

"Now, gentlemen, I'll waft ye over the North Sea,

through the Skagerrack, down the Cattegat, and on to Copenhagen. As we passed through the narrow channel betwixt the island of Zealand and the Swedish coast, we met a heavy fire from the batteries of the Cronenberg Castle, but little damage was done, and Admiral Parker conducted the fleet on to an anchorage about five miles from the island of Hven, whereupon himself, Lord Nelson, and Admiral Graves went in a small vessel to reconnoitre the position of the enemy's fleet and defenses before Copenhagen. It was decided to make the attack from the south, and Nelson volunteered to conduct it, for which purpose he shifted his flag from the *St. George,* of ninety-eight guns, to the *Elephant,* a seventy-four having a lighter draught, and therefore better adapted for the service."

The surgeon paused to taste his grog. "I'd not be superfluous," he added. "You're all familiar, I take it, with the details of the preparations?"

"Not I, for one," said Runyon.

"Then ye'd best wait, Runyon, till my friend Captain Brenton completes his Naval History of our times."

"Brenton?" said Ostiff, with a shrug. "Damme, he'll never have finished at the rate he's going. He's slower at his task than a carrier's wagon."

"And with reason, Ostiff. Captain Brenton will be certain of his facts before he sets them down."

"That's as may be," Ostiff replied. "There's one thing he *is* dead certain of: his own view of every matter. I can't abide the man. How far along is he now?"

"Near the end of his first volume. Oddly enough, I had

the honour of a visit from him not a fortnight ago, at my lodgings at Mrs. Quigg's. He had just then completed his chapter on this very battle of Copenhagen, and 'twas my privilege to set him right upon various small points of it."

"Then set me right for the larger ones," said Runyon, "for I've never yet heard a first-hand account of the battle."

"Aye, let's have 'em, Doctor," said Balthus. "For all I was there, I'd take joy to hear the particulars over again. And little enough I saw at the time save what could be spied through the gun ports of the *Amazon*."

"Very well. The broad particulars you shall have. For the first, there's no need to tell Mr. Rasmussen of the difficulty of the approaches to Copenhagen."

"Indeed no," said the Dane. "The greater part of my countrymen, the best seamen included, expected to see the most of your ships stranded on the mudbanks before the action was well begun."

"We've Nelson to thank for the contrary," said Dogbody. "With the assistance of Captains Riou and Brisbane, he had been at great pains to sound and buoy the channel. This done, he proceeded with the ships under his immediate orders to Draco Point, where he issued his instructions to his captains and made ready for the attack. Admiral Parker was willing, no doubt, to be out of it. He was to act as a reserve, lying with eight ships off the north end of the Middle Ground. Each ship and vessel under Nelson's orders had a particular duty assigned. The gunboats were to be placed so as to rake the enemy's hulks. A flat-bottomed boat, well manned and armed, was to be stationed on the off side of each ship to act as the occasion might require. Four launches, with anchors and cables in them, were to be in readiness to give assistance to any ships getting aground. The command of the sloops and frigates was intrusted to Captain Riou, of the *Amazon,* and well he fulfilled that trust! He was killed at Copenhagen. England might better have lost a dozen first-rates than to have lost Captain Riou."

"Well may ye say so, Doctor," Balthus put in. "He'd have been a second Nelson had he lived."

"No, Ned. He'd have been second to no one. He'd have been Riou and no other, as distinguished as Nelson, I verily believe, but in his own way.

"The Danish line of defense might well have been pronounced capable of resisting any naval force brought against it. They had six sail of the line and eleven floating batteries mounting on one side from eighteen eighteen-pounders to twenty-six twenty-four-pounders, one bomb ship, and innumerable gunboats. They were supported by the fort on the island of Amac and the two Crown batteries. These latter deserve particular mention for they consisted of artificial islands raised on piles above the mudbanks near the arsenal, and mounting eighty pieces of heavy cannon, nearly flush with the water. I need not tell old seamen that such batteries are the most dangerous and destructive that ships can come against. Being low and stationary, their fire is deadly in the extreme, and the men in them are spared the toil and confusion that is the seamen's part, in action, in clearing away the wreckage of masts and yards and rigging falling upon the decks of ships."

The surgeon drew forth his silk bandana and blew a blast so unexpectedly loud that Mr. Sawbridge gave an involuntary start in his chair.

"Inky," he then resumed, turning to Murgatroyd, "as an old Navy captain, with innumerable sea fights behind you, have you ever forgotten, amongst others, certain nights-before-action when everything was in readiness and your ship's company had little to do but wait for the coming of day?"

"Such occasions have been few in my experience," Murgatroyd replied. "It rarely chanced that we were given time for perfect readiness."

Dogbody nodded. "And in my own as well, but Copenhagen was one of these. Thanks to Nelson's thoroughness, every conceivable emergency to which ships are liable in action had been foreseen and provided for. In the *Monarch*, not even Captain Mosse, who would improve upon perfection itself, could find anything to criticize or alter in our preparations. Therefore, at an early hour on the evening of the first, having called the ship's company together, he gave us a brief account of Nelson's orders for the battle and the part the *Monarch* was to play in it. He then dismissed all but the watch on duty, urging the others to get what rest and refreshment time permitted.

"We were a healthy ship, thanks to the short passage from Yarmouth. I had not one man in the sick bay. As my own preparations for the bloody work to come had been as thorough as those in the other departments, I saw to it that my surgeon's mates and loblolly boys were in their hammocks before retiring to my own. My small cabin was off the wardroom. I stretched out there, fully dressed, but damme if I could sleep for thinking of the day to come. The surgeon's part in a great action is least to be envied of any in a ship's company, for he is shut away with his assistants from all the glory and excitement of battle. He sees naught but the human wreckage swept in to him from every deck. Aye, I could well picture myself, a few hours later, stripped to the waist, smeared with blood worse than any butcher, whilst scores of splendid fellows, torn to pieces by balls and shells and splinters, lay huddled on the canvas-covered chests, awaiting their turns for such help as human skill could afford them. And little enough that was, times without number."

"You are a man of sensibility, Doctor Dogbody," Mr. Sawbridge remarked. "How you have weathered half a century's service as a naval surgeon passes my comprehension."

"By first performing the most difficult operation upon myself, sir," the surgeon replied. "By cutting out my bowels of compassion. Damme, you must have none, else you are lost and useless in a ship of war."

"And you found it possible so to command and harden yourself?"

The surgeon glanced across the taproom.

"Mr. Sawbridge, if at this moment, as we sit here, a ball from a thirty-two-pounder were to crash through the wall yonder, and to remove the mark of the old sabre cut on Mr. Balthus's cheek by taking his head with it, whilst his trunk spouted blood over the lot of us, I could sit without flinching. Old friend that Balthus is, I could regard him, for the time necessary, as naught but a fountain of gore that would presently empty itself. I could forget the times without number I had heard the familiar oath, 'God's rabbit!' issuing from that head. I could forget that I had ever lifted a friendly glass in the man's company. The thought that his severed gullet would never again be soothed and refreshed at my expense would cause me neither pleasure nor sorrow."

"Ye'd best get on with your story," said Balthus, gruffly. "There's no cause to be so bloody-minded now that our wars are past and done with."

"Done with! And old Boney still alive, gnawing his pudgy fingers at this moment, as he paces deep channels through the turf at Saint Helena? Done with! Damme, Ned Balthus! To-morrow's post may bring us word that he's landed at Marseilles, with the whole of France flocking to his banner once more."

"And you'd wish to return to service in that case?" asked Ostiff. "A valetudinarian like yourself?"

The surgeon's eyes snapped. He turned abruptly toward the bar. "Tom!" he called. "Fetch the decanter! My own, with the Port Royal!" Tapleke made haste to answer the summons. "Fill my glass to the very brim," said the surgeon. . . . "More yet. Now drop by drop."

The drawer poured slowly until not one drop more could have been added, and the skin of the liquor seemed to extend slightly above the rim of the glass. Taking the glass by the stem, Dogbody then held it at arm's length, so steadily that no tremor from his hand passed across the surface of the liquid. He then set it on the table before him, glancing triumphantly at Ostiff. "There, sir, is the best of answers to the libel of valetudinarianism. Let me see you do the like."

"No offense, Dogbody," Ostiff replied, with a grin.

"I should hope not, indeed! Because you've both feet in the grave, you'll not stretch out a palsied hand to draw me in with you! Damme, no! I'll see the infant son or daughter of the Prince Regent upon the throne of England. I'll be walking the decks of Navy ships for another two decades, at the least. I'll be cutting arms and legs from English seamen now in their cradles, and with as skillful and steady a hand as I have at this moment."

"No offense; none whatever," Ostiff repeated.

"In the churchyard at Egg Buckland, near Plymouth, there is a tombstone to the memory of my grandfather. The inscription reads as follows: 'Sacred to the memory of Robert Dogbody, the only man of this parish who has ever seen at one time his great-grandfather and his own great-great-grandchildren.' I come of an active, long-lived family."

"I've never doubted it, Dogbody. All I meant to say . . ."

"And a prolific one as well, save for myself who lacked the leisure to wed at a suitable age and so never wedded at all. But none did better in this respect than the grand-parent of that same Robert Dogbody, who had by his first wife nineteen children, by his second seventeen. Before his death he was grandfather to eighty-two, great-grandfather to forty-one, and great-great-grandfather to twenty-six."

"And yet your name is none so common," said Ostiff. "I can't recall that I ever heard it until the day of our first meeting, in this same taproom."

"There's good reason for that, Ostiff. You'll find few stay-at-homes amongst the Dogbodys. Men and women of my family are scattered along the coasts and through the inland regions of four continents, to say nothing of those who inhabit archipelagoes in the remotest seas where the name Dogbody has often been the first word of civilized speech learned by their savage inhabitants. Were they all gathered in one place they would make a town as large as Portsmouth. In fact, there is a settlement distinguished by the name in the western part of Virginia, in America."

Ned Balthus wet a huge gnarled forefinger and held it aloft.

"We've lost the breeze," he said, "and Lieutenant Teddar with it. I don't rightly know *where* we've got to."

The surgeon sipped his brimming glass to a more convenient level and set it down once more.

"Ye can blame this thin-shanked engraver of charts for that, Balthus. No matter. The night before Copenhagen was a long one, and a short digression in speaking of it will do no harm. I'm still in my cabin aboard the *Monarch*. But I didn't stay there. Being unable to sleep, I put on my shoes again and went up to the spar deck, where

I found Mr. Keepus, the master, standing in the darkness by the mainmast. The night was clear, though a thin haze, high up, dimmed the light of the stars. The air was nipping cold, and the master and I walked together for a little.

" 'Surgeon,' said he, 'I'd be pleased to think we'd have blood left to warm in our bodies come to-morrow night.'

" 'That's as may be,' said I.

" 'Aye,' said he.

"There was a great silence upon the waters. The *Elephant,* Nelson's flagship, the *Defiance,* and the *Edgar* lay nearest us, black and shadowy in the starlight. We had boats out on guard patrol, lest the enemy should attempt to do us a mischief in the darkness. We watched one pass, as soundlessly as though it were Charon's ferry on the Styx.

"Presently I returned to the after cockpit for a last look round to make sure that all was in readiness. It would be my own scene of action on the morrow. A dismal hole it was at the best of times, and looking more than ever dank and dismal by the light of a single lantern. Here the senior midshipmen were berthed, and the master's mates, and my own surgeon's mates, and their mess table would be my operating board during the action."

"What helpers had you, Doctor, at such times?" Mr. Sawbridge asked.

"That depends, sir, upon the size of the ship and the number of men she carries. In the *Monarch,* with a crew of five hundred and ninety, I had three surgeon's mates and five dressers, or loblolly boys as we call them. But in action, of course, there were additional assistants: the purser, the stewards, the chaplain, the captain's clerk, and other noncombatant members of the crew."

"And you were forced to work in that dark hole, in the lowest habitable part of the ship?"

"A ship of war, sir, is, first, a ship of war. All else is subordinate to that function. And the after cockpit, being on the orlop or lowest deck, is safest from enemy fire. As for the darkness, that was overcome as well as might be by the light of many candles, in sconces and lanterns, on the operating table itself and arranged around the bulkheads. You are interested, Mr. Sawbridge, in such details?"

"In a reluctant manner, sir," the other replied. "I was thinking how little landsmen like myself know of the life and duties of our guardians at sea. I had never before known in what part of the ship the surgeon carried on his duties."

" 'Twas not always in the after cockpit," the surgeon replied, "though it was the customary place during action."

"And what furnishings had you there?"

"For one, a portable stove for the heating of water, oils, and the like. Our saws and knives are warmed at it as well, and we thus prevent a little of the torture that would, otherwise, be increased by the contact of cold steel against raw flesh and bone. By the side of the operating table are ranged the empty kids, filled soon enough with amputated limbs, and others containing water for the cleansing of sponges, and for the surgeon and his mates to wash their arms in. Close by, on chests covered with a cloth, are the supplies of styptics, bandages, tourniquets, and newly sharpened knives and saws, under a good light."

"That'll be enough," said Balthus. "Ye've brought the very stench of the hole back to me."

"Damme, if he don't describe it with a kind of relish," said Ostiff.

"With relish? Never, sir! The place was hell afloat, during action, but landsmen should know it, Ostiff. I'd like well to have all the king's ministers, of whatever nation, looking over Navy surgeons' shoulders in the midst of battle. B'gad, we'd have fewer wars, in that case.

"But 'twas all peaceful enough on the night of April first, and the cockpit was filled with the hammocks of sleeping men. I went up for purer air, and as I came out on the main deck, I met Lieutenant Thone.

"'Dogbody,' said he, 'I've searched the ship over for you. There's the devil and all to pay! Phil Teddar's drunk!'

"'What!' said I. Had he told me that Captain Mosse was drunk, I could not have been more stunned and incredulous. As I've said, Teddar would, upon rare occasions when low in his mind, take to the bottle and drink himself helpless, but this had never before happened at sea. With Thone I went immediately to his cabin, forward of the wardroom, on the starboard side. He had a candle burning in a small lantern, and there he sat, with one emptied bottle of spirits on the floor beside him, and another, all but emptied, on his table. We managed to crowd in and shut the door after us. I took Teddar by the shoulders and shook him roughly.

" 'Phil!' said I. 'Have ye gone clean mad?'

"He raised his head and gave me a dark, dazed look.

" 'Brother lost,' said he. 'Whose fault? King's ministers. Rascals, rogues! Send us fight Danes.' And not a word beyond these could we get out of him.

"There was only one thing to do. I went down to my dispensary and mixed in warm water the most nauseating draught conceivable, and hurried back with it. Teddar was so dazed that he took the glass I offered, thinking it his own, and drank half the contents before he realized what it was. Then he made a wry face, got to his feet, and poured the rest of it over my head. Damme, I was a fortnight getting the smell of the stuff out of my hair; but he, after drinking a good half-pint of an emetic would have turned the stomach of an ostrich inside out, never so much as belched. All I accomplished was to make him sensible of our presence. He had another full quart of brandy which I tried to get hold of, but he seized me with a grip of iron and thrust me out the door, Thone after me. We dared make no noise, lest we should waken the officers in the adjoining cabins, and there was one amongst them who would have been only too pleased to carry the news of Teddar's condition straight to Captain Mosse.

" 'He's lost, Thone,' said I. 'Lost and ruined. He'll never be fit for duty to-morrow.'

" 'But we can't leave him as he is,' said Thone. 'We must rush and gag him and carry him on deck. Damme, the mere smell of the stuff he's poured over you makes me squeamish. If we could get another pint of it down his gullet . . .'

" 'Can you see us doing it?' said I. 'He's got the strength of a draught horse.'

" 'We could try,' said he.

" 'Aye, and rouse the entire ship's company, aft. A bright suggestion *that* is!' Thone knew it as well as myself.

" 'And this is the first time we've been under Nelson,' said he, in a miserable voice. 'And Phil was to be in charge on the lower gun deck to-morrow. Dogbody, he'll not survive the dishonour! He'll kill himself when he knows!'

" 'He's done that already,' said I. 'We've seen the end of Phil Teddar's career.'

"We were desperate with worry, but there seemed to be nothing we could do to save him.

" ' 'Twas this very night,' said Thone, 'that I was to have had my fun at the Magpies with his dummy.'

" 'Aye, 'tis the first of April, sure enough,' said I. 'And a fine Fools'-Day joke he's played on himself! . . . What'd ye do with it?'

" 'With what?' says Thone.

" 'The dummy, of course. Did ye leave it at the Magpies?'

" 'No,' says Thone, 'I've got it in a chest in the sail-room. Thought there might be a chance for the lark aboard ship.'

" 'You tell me the image is here,' said I; 'in the sail-room of the *Monarch?*'

" 'Where else?' says Thone. 'Would I put it in Nelson's cabin, in the *Elephant?*'

"Will ye believe it? Thone was so confirmed a player of pranks, for no reason save that of his own amusement, it never crossed his mind that one might now be played in sober earnest. *He* saw Phil Teddar's effigy in one situation only, as he had planned it for the Yarmouth jollification. In one of those flashes of inspiration that come, who knows how, *I* saw it playing a man's part in the battle of Copenhagen."

"Come, come, Dogbody," said Ostiff. "You don't tell us . . ."

"I tell you nothing, sir, save what happened through my own instrumentality, that of Thone and one other. The moment I suggested the plan, Thone was as convinced as myself that we could carry it through, granted that chance would look kindly upon it. He wrung my hand warmly.

" 'By God, Dogbody,' said he, 'we've saved him!'

" 'That's as fortune wills,' said I. 'Now go directly to George Pote, rouse him quietly, and bring him to the sailroom.'

"Pote, gunner's mate in the *Monarch,* honoured the decks Phil Teddar trod upon; I knew we should have a loyal ally in him. We three met in the sailroom, with a single candle to light us, and there Pote was told the whole of the business. No words of ours could convince him of the practicability of what seemed so mad a plan; but when the chest was opened and the effigy brought forth and seated upon it, we'd no need of further persuasion. Teddar's own father would have believed 'twas his son who sat there, silent and thoughtful, expending his breath only in his quiet breathing."

"Breathing!" said Balthus.

"Haven't I spoken of that? Within the body of the image was a noiseless mechanism, wound by means of a keyhole under the left arm. This caused the breast to rise and fall in a manner as natural as in life itself. To give further reality, the head could be turned in whatever life-like position, and both arms and legs were jointed, the fingers as well, so that the effigy could stand or sit, or assume whatever posture common to living beings. A surgeon may be said to know the human figure if anybody does. This similitude lacked naught but brains and viscera and the power to bleed. 'Twas the latter which worried us.

" 'Dogbody,' said Thone, 'if he's hit to-morrow, we're done for with him. He'll fly into a thousand pieces.'

" 'And Mr. Teddar's done for without him, certain, Mr. Thone,' said Pote. 'We're obliged to chance it. I'd be pleased to take a flogging through the fleet if so be we could save his honour.'

"For the rest, our plans were as complete as forethought could make them. 'Twas past one in the morning when Thone and I returned to our cabins. On the way we looked once more into Teddar's. He had finished the third bottle and lay on his cot with no more apparent life in him than his dummy had.

" 'God help him if we miscarry,' said Thone.

"I locked his door after us and carried the key away in my pocket.

"Had Nelson ordered the weather for April second, it could not have been more perfect for his needs, with the wind at south-southeast. At nine o'clock the masters and pilots who had been called aboard his flagship for the final conference returned to their own ships, and the signal for action fluttered out at the masthead of the *Elephant*. Ship by ship we got under way, Captain Murray in the *Edgar* leading. A noble sight it was, twelve ships of the line, their great sails bellying to the breeze as they fell into place and headed for the channel between the shoal called the Middle Ground and Saltholm Island. As soon as we were under way, Captain Mosse left the quarter-deck of the *Monarch*, with his fourth lieutenant, two midshipmen, and myself to accompany him on his final tour of the ship. There is no need to speak of my anxiety as we descended to the lower gun deck."

"Wait, Dogbody," said Captain Murgatroyd. "You've not yet told us how you managed to get the dummy in place, unbeknownst to all."

"I'll not stop for that. 'Tis enough to say the thing was done; and there now stood Philip Teddar, in all but the flesh, on the larboard side of the deck. George Pote stood near him, and I knew by his glance that he was sweating blood like myself.

"Captain Mosse halted at the foot of the companion-way, looking about him with that eye for detail which is second nature to a ship's commander. All was in readiness: the decks freshly sprinkled with wet sand, the tubs of water by the guns, the match tubs furnished, and the cheeses of wads, and the rope rings filled with the ball that was to work such havoc against the Danish ships soon to be opposite the *Monarch*. The gun crews stood by their pieces, stripped to the waist for action, with their black handkerchiefs bound around their foreheads. Every head, including one that had nothing in it but air, was turned toward the companionway where our captain stood, looking about him with the silent approval of a commander who knows he has a ship's company worthy of his pride and trust.

"'Well and good, lads,' Captain Mosse called out. 'You've an hour yet to breathe easy. Carry on, Mr. Teddar.'

"With that he turned and mounted the companionway once more. My heart mounted with him, from the mud flats nine fathoms beneath the ship, and resumed its rightful place in my left breast. Nothing would have been more customary than that he should have called Teddar to his side for a final word; but the lad's good angel was with him. B'gad, I am convinced it had taken housing for the day in the dummy itself."

"'Carry on' . . . aye, but how was it done?" said Murgatroyd. "A lieutenant in charge on the lower gun deck, or on any deck for the matter of that, has something more to do than stand in a natural attitude."

The surgeon shook his head. "Not in Teddar's case. What you say would be true of ten thousand officers in ten thousand and five, but he was one of the exceptions.

And he had his men so well trained that they knew his will without a word given. I'll leave it to Balthus, who has served under him, if he were not able to command by his presence alone."

"So he could," said the gunner. "I never saw his beat there. I mind an action we had in the *Hotspur,* in Batavia Roads, with the *Phoenix,* a Dutch frigate. We fought her an hour and twenty minutes before she struck, and I'll take my oath Lieutenant Teddar never opened his lips from first to last."

"Precisely," said the surgeon. "We'd no fears with respect to his silence, but to make all safe, Pote explained to the gun captains that Teddar, who'd been out on duty the whole of the week before, helping to sound and buoy the channel, had caught a quinsy that deprived him of his voice. The men were to have any orders that might need to be given through Pote himself.

"I was on the spar deck during the last hour before action, as the fleet was coming up to take station opposite the Danes. There was a solemn hush over land and sea. In the distance stood Copenhagen, that queen of cities, her spires and pinnacles gleaming in the morning light, and her banners streaming out to the breeze. Through our spyglasses we could make out throngs of townspeople back of their defenses, crowded at windows and balconies and along the walls of distant ramparts. As we rounded the south end of the Middle Shoal, the *Russel* and *Bellona,* seventy-fours, took the ground in such a position as to render their later assistance nearly ineffectual. The *Agamemnon,* of sixty-four guns, also grounded, entirely out of range, so there were three of Nelson's best ships useless to him before a shot was fired; but they served as a warning to the others, which steered more to the south-west and came to their appointed stations in splendid order. We anchored by the stern, as was done at the battle of the Nile, half a cable's length apart, and each ship a cable's length, on an average, from the Danish ships and batteries.

"And now, gentlemen, I bring ye to the moment: to one of the hardest-fought and bloodiest engagements in naval history. And the first cannon that bellowed out in that engagement, destroying the peace of the bright April morning, were those on the lower gun deck of the *Monarch*."

"Forgive me for interrupting at this point, Doctor," said Mr. Sawbridge, "but I should like to know whether the popular report is true that Nelson disobeyed Admiral Parker's signal to withdraw from action."

"It is perfectly true, sir. As I have said, Admiral Parker was an elderly man at this time, and with the timidity of age upon him. After a more deliberate view of the enemy's force, he supposed that Nelson would be over-matched and so recalled him from action. And he had the courage and generosity to take this great responsi-bility upon himself rather than place the decision upon Nelson's shoulders as he might have done. But Nelson refused to acknowledge the signal flown from Admiral Parker's ship. He regarded it through his telescope, which he placed at his blind eye, and never was willful blindness more triumphantly vindicated by the event. Nelson's action was entirely consistent with his own maxim: 'When in doubt, fight.'

"As I have said, the *Monarch's* guns were the first to speak. This was at five minutes past ten. Within half an hour the first part of our fleet was engaged, and at twenty past eleven the action became general. The *Monarch* was exposed to the fire, not only of the ships opposite her, but to that of the Crown batteries as well. 'Twas an awful day for the surgeons of whatever ship, but worst for us. We could not keep pace with the frightful human wreckage brought down to us. I'd no time to think of Teddar, stupefied in his locked cabin, or of the one that stood in his room on the gun deck just over my head. Captain Mosse was killed outright, early in the action. About an hour after it became general, George Pote came down with an ugly oaken splinter through the flesh of his forearm. He was so blackened with smoke that I scarce knew him. One of my dressers removed the splinter and bandaged the wound and Pote returned to duty at once, but he had time to shout, 'All goes well, Surgeon,' and I knew that Madame Tussaud's Teddar was still at his post.

"And there, gentlemen, he remained, throughout an action that lasted four immortal hours. I'm telling you now what I learned afterward. Every deck of the *Monarch* was a shambles of the dead and dying, and none more so than the lower gun deck where some of the crews were replaced three times over; but, by a miracle of chance, Teddar the Other received no hurt. Pote told me that his quiet breathing and his air of complete serenity and calm so inspired and encouraged the men that they fought as never before. The two Danish ships opposite us were the *Holstein* and the *Zealand;* both were silenced by the *Monarch,* and her guns were then trained on the ships that lay on either side.

"I need not tell Mr. Rasmussen or Mr. Sawbridge how, a little after two in the afternoon, when the entire Danish line of defense had been silenced, Nelson sent a message, under a flag, to the Crown Prince of Denmark, informing him that he had been commanded to spare Copenhagen when she no longer resisted. His terms for a cessation of hostilities were accepted. The Danes had surpassed themselves; they had done all that brave men could. Ours was the day, but the glory of it was equally divided. And now I leave all else and come back to Teddar.

"I have called Thone his bosom friend, and well he proved it on this day of days. Toward the end of the action, though himself suffering from a severe flesh wound in the thigh, he had the forethought to take a strip from his own bloody drawers and repair with this to the lower gun deck where the tumult of battle still continued. The faithful George Pote was his accomplice. Choosing their moment, they rushed with concern to where Teddar the Other yet stood, took him in their arms, quickly removing the concealed fastenings that held him in place, and at the same time tying the bloody cloth around his forehead. Then, before the others knew what had happened, they bore him tenderly away, ostensibly to the after cockpit, but in reality to the sailroom, where they hastily packed him in Thone's chest and closed and locked the lid. B'gad, the timing of the thing was perfect! Next, with the bloody cloth and a piece of jagged iron from a burst gun, they repaired to Teddar's cabin.''

Balthus leaned forward in his chair. "I'd like to have made one at that meeting," he said. "In what state did they find him?"

"Asleep, Ned, peacefully as, though more heavily than, a child, and as innocent as a child of what had transpired during the previous sixteen hours. Without a moment's hesitation, Thone took the splinter of iron, made a deep ragged cut on Teddar's forehead, and bound the wound with the bloody cloth. Even with that, they had difficulty in arousing him. He opened his eyes, stared at them, then raised himself to the side of his cot.

" 'What's this?' said he. 'Damme, have I been asleep? What time is it?'

" 'Asleep!' says Thone. 'By God, lad, if ye call it sleep I'd be pleased to know the secret of it! Ye was knocked out when Inches' gun burst, but 'tis only a scratch.'

"Pote now put in a word. 'Mr. Teddar, sir, may I shake your hand? There's not a man of us left but covets that honour.'

"Teddar put his hand to the bandage, wet with Thone's blood as well as his own. 'What's this?' he repeated. 'What's happened?'

" 'The battle of Copenhagen, no less,' says Thone. 'Ye played a man's part in it, Phil, and there's none but Dogbody, Pote, and myself that knows ye were drunk. The secret's safe with us, lad.'

"At that Teddar leaped to his feet and rushed from the cabin. He returned a moment later, Thone said, with a look of despair on his face would have melted a heart of stone. He believed he'd disgraced himself forever, but damme, if they didn't convince him that, to the contrary, he'd never appeared more sober, and had covered himself with glory! He couldn't have doubted when he'd refreshed himself a little and returned to duty. He had naught but respectful admiring looks from all ranks. His own men, what were left, gave him a hearty cheer, and Mr. Bullitt, the senior lieutenant, in command after Captain Mosse was killed, complimented him in the warmest terms. Teddar believed now, but you'll guess the shame in his heart. He had fought through a great action, so drunk that he had no recollection of it.

"But the worst, for him, was to come. That evening, a little after eight o'clock, a boat from the *Elephant* came alongside. Little was a visit expected, least of all from Nelson himself, but 'twas he who made his way aft through the wreckage, and none knew better than he the honour there was in such a mess. Lieutenant Bullitt was on the quarter-deck with Thone and Teddar beside him. Nelson strode up to him followed by three officers of his staff.

" 'Lieutenant Bullitt,' said Nelson, with that courtesy and magnanimity so characteristic of him, 'I ask your indulgence for a surprise visit, but I could not pass the *Monarch* without coming on board for a moment, at least. You are now the senior officer?'

" 'I am, sir,' said Bullitt.

" 'Then, in behalf of His Majesty, the Lords of the Admiralty, Admiral Parker, and myself, I thank you, in the room of your lamented commander, for as gallant an action as was ever fought by a ship under my orders. Your losses I already know; they surpass those of any other ship in the fleet, but you and your men have won immortal honour.'

"Nelson paused and then added: 'I would make no distinction amongst your subordinates; all are deserving of the highest praise. But I should like to know who was in command on your lower gun deck.'

" 'Lieutenant Teddar, sir,' said Bullitt.

" 'He survives?'

"Lieutenant Bullitt bowed, indicating Teddar, who stood to leeward of him with the bloody bandage around his head. Admiral Nelson strode across and took his hand.

" 'Mr. Teddar,' said he, 'accept my thanks on behalf of your gun captains and crews. A warm-sided ship was the *Monarch* this day. The *Holstein* and the *Zealand* learned it to their cost.' With that he turned and, with another bow to Mr. Bullitt, departed as quickly as he had come."

"God's rabbit!" said Balthus. "You was there, Doctor?"

"No, but Thone was, and I had the details from him."

"And what did Lieutenant Teddar do, sir?" Mr. Sawbridge asked.

"Had he known the truth, sir; had he even guessed that a waxen hand merited the pressure from Admiral Nelson's fingers that his own had received, he would have expired where he stood, from very shame. But that he never knew."

"I should think he might have expired in any case," said Ostiff.

"No, Ostiff. Teddar was no weakling. Bitterly as he reproached himself, he was not one to sink under his remorse. His lesson was learned, and well learned. I know of no officer who later distinguished himself to a greater degree, though in a quiet way, and when, after Trafalgar, he was again publicly complimented, though not by Nelson, he richly merited the honour. He was killed in command of the *Java* in 1812, after a splendid action in which he forced a seventy-four to strike to him."

"You've told us nothing, sir, of the loss of your leg," said Mr. Rasmussen.

" 'Twas a small matter, sir. In the midst of so many lost limbs, one more or less is of no consequence save to the man concerned. The very last shot fired by your great Crown battery carried a ball that must have been marked and ticketed: 'For Surgeon F. Dogbody.' That ball entered the *Monarch* at the waterline, whilst I was in the midst of an amputation, and performed one upon my own anatomy as speedily, though not as neatly, as I myself could have done it."

"What became of the dummy?" asked Runyon.

"For anything I know to the contrary, it still marks the spot where the *Monarch* was anchored during the action. Thone and George Pote scuttled it the same night, with an eighteen-pound shot to hold it fast to the mud flats of Denmark."

"What were the *Monarch's* casualties on that day?" Ostiff asked.

"Close to one in three of the ship's company: fifty-five killed and one hundred and fifty-six wounded."

"Dogbody, for once I've caught you in an error of fact," said Captain Murgatroyd. "I know those casualties by heart. The number of killed is correct, but your wounded were one hundred and fifty-five."

"No, Inky. One hundred and fifty-six is the total, despite the Admiralty figures. Curiously enough, the dummy *was* hit, though neither Thone, Pote, nor myself discovered it at the time. He lost his little finger."

The surgeon fumbled in the pocket of his waistcoat and brought forth what was, unquestionably, a finger of wax, broken off at the first joint. This he passed to the company.

" 'Twas given to me," he added, "by a wounded gunner from Teddar's deck who had the cot next to mine at the naval hospital. We'd been talking of Copenhagen, and he reached down and fished in the ditty-bag beneath his cot.

" 'Surgeon,' said he, 'what d'ye make of this queer bit of handwork? I found it up against the bulwark afore I was wounded.'

Doctor Dogbody's eyes twinkled as he finished his glass.

"I didn't tell him that he'd best ask Madame Tussaud about that," he said.

IX

FEADLE AND FOSTER

THE rain had slackened to a drizzle at the hour in the
late afternoon when Mr. Ostiff and Ned Balthus entered
the taproom. As they cleaned their shoes on the mat by
the doorway, Balthus glanced across to the table in the
far corner of the room.

"Will ye look yonder, Mr. Ostiff!" he exclaimed. "The
Doctor's smoking!"

Their friend, alone at the table, had, in truth, so great
a cloud of smoke wreathed about him that he appeared
but dimly in the midst of it. He was evidently finding
the greatest enjoyment in his pipe, and acknowledged

the greetings of Ostiff and Balthus with no more than a slight dignified inclination of the head.

"A mucky day," Balthus observed.

"Aye," said Ostiff. "An old-clothes day I'd call it. I'm no more surprised at the pipe than I am to see our friend tricked out in such handsome toggeries for rainy weather. Blessed if I knew he had 'em!"

The comment evoked no response from their companion, who was indeed richly dressed. He gazed absently before him as though he had not heard the remark. Observing that he appeared to be preoccupied, the other two seated themselves at the opposite end of the table, where they were joined, shortly, by Captain Runyon and Captain Murgatroyd.

"What's this? What's this?" said Murgatroyd, with a glance at the smoker as he hung hat and coat on a wall-peg near by. "Damme, have we renounced snuff? Have we acquired a new habit in our dotage?"

Ostiff gave him a wink. " 'Tis said there's no teaching old dogs new tricks," he remarked. "I've heard a certain old dog that shall be nameless here say as much himself. But he seems to have needed no teaching. You'd swear he'd been burning the weed for years."

"And good weed it is, if I'm a judge," said Runyon, sniffing the air with relish. "The best old Virginia."

"Trust our friend to find whatever scarce luxury," said Ostiff; "even one that he's known nothing about till now."

"I'd be pleased for a fill of that same Virginia," said Balthus. "This shag I'm smoking ain't but little better'n chopped hay."

These oblique remarks seemed to miss their goal. Their companion at the end of the table smoked quietly on as though ignorant that he was the object of them.

"Come, Dogbody," said Ostiff. "Because you're so lavish with your smoke, ye needn't be so sparing with your breath. How long have ye been at it?"

The other glanced up with a start. "You were speaking to me, sir?" he asked.

"Your name's Dogbody, I believe? Come back to the Tortoise from wherever you were. How long since did you take to the pipe? I'd supposed you wedded to snuff."

"I'm surprised, sir, that you should suppose anything whatever concerning myself. Since you ask, I may say that I've smoked for the past forty years. Now may I put a question in my turn? How came you to know my name?"

Ostiff smiled. "That *is* curious. I fancy I must have heard it at one time or another in this same taproom. What's got into you to-day?"

"He's dazed his wits with the smoke," said Murgatroyd. "Ye shouldn't go it so hard at the first, Dogbody. You're like to be sick as a dog." He grinned. "In case you're feeling squeamish, I'll remind ye that the necessary-house is along the passage, yonder to the left."

The other gave the company a glance of astonishment, opened his mouth to reply, but remained silent. Then he rose, with a slight stiff bow to Murgatroyd. "I was about to ask one of you to oblige me with that direction," he said, and, turning abruptly, he walked to the passage indicated.

Ostiff and Balthus stared after him with glances of such

stunned bewilderment that, observing them, Runyon and Murgatroyd turned their heads. Their eyes widened and their chins dropped simultaneously. Tom Tapleke, who was lounging behind the bar, sprang to life on the instant, and, running to the middle of the room, stood with his hands on his hips, gazing down the passageway, then looking to the company in the corner as though for confirmation of what he saw. It was, certainly, Dogbody whom their eyes beheld, but with his peg-leg on the right side instead of the left.

"God's rabbit!" Balthus exclaimed, and had scarcely spoken when the street door opened and, as though by some miracle of legerdemain, there entered the same Dogbody, apparently, but with the peg in its accustomed place, attached to the stump of the larboard leg. The company in the corner were still staring in the opposite direction when his brisk, "What cheer, lads?" caused them to whirl about to confront him.

The only reply was another "God's rabbit!" from Balthus, uttered in so awestruck a voice that the surgeon glanced in a puzzled manner from one to another of them.

"What's amiss with the lot of ye?" he asked. "Have ye seen a ghost?"

Balthus, Runyon, and Murgatroyd continued to stare at him, but Ostiff managed to reply: "Something stranger than that. You'll see it yourself, directly."

A moment later the other Dogbody appeared at the end of the passageway. The surgeon's head was jerked back as though an invisible hand had given it a sudden tilt by the chin. He drew down his bushy eyebrows and gazed at the approaching figure with an air of unbelief. The other stopped short, no less astonished.

"Damn my liver and lights!" the surgeon exclaimed. "Foster, as I live!"

"Feadle!" cried the other. "Is it possible!"

Doctor Dogbody was the first to recover from his surprise. He stepped forward and took the newcomer by the shoulders.

"Possible? Damme, why not? Did ye suppose me under the sod, ye rogue? Have ye been searching me out in churchyards?"

The stranger nodded. "Where else?" he asked. "We must all follow the course of nature, Feadle, and old as ye are . . ." He nodded once more. "I've just come from a visit to the family plot at Egg Buckland. I made certain I'd find ye there, under a stone."

The surgeon turned to the others. "Gentlemen, this brother of mine was at nurse when I first went to sea, and look at him now! He's twelve years my junior, and if there's an honest man here, let him say which of us looks the younger."

"I'd take oath ye was twins, Doctor," said Balthus, "and so ye'd be with the pegs on the same side."

Ostiff shook his head, wonderingly. "Was there ever such a man as this surgeon?" he asked. "Who'd have guessed that he had a brother?"

"Why shouldn't I have a brother? Other men have brothers; there's often a dozen in the same family. What's so remarkable about that?"

"But you've never once spoken of him," said Murgatroyd.

Foster Dogbody nodded his head, sadly. "I'm not in the least surprised to hear it, sir," he said. "If ever there was a man with no sense of family, Feadle Dogbody is that man's name. Never a night in the past forty-five years have I lain down to rest without thinking of *my* brother. I've wearied the ears of friends without number, talking of him, boasting about him. And here . . . damme, I meet friends of *his* not even aware of my existence!"

"Ye rogue," said the surgeon, with a grin. "If the truth could be known, I'd lay a golden pound against every time ye've thought of me, and when the account was clear I'd be three farthings out of pocket. But let me make ye known to these same friends. Captain Murgatroyd, Mr. Ostiff, Mr. Balthus, Captain Runyon: my brother, Foster, from somewhere in the wilds of America, and what he's done there these past four decades ye know as well as myself."

The company now took seats, and Tom Tapleke, serving them, was still so lost in amazement that he was all thumbs until Mr. Ostiff, with a sharp reproof, brought him back to a sense of his duties. Meanwhile, the news had traveled to the kitchen and Will Tunn hastened out to be introduced to the newcomer. He was compelled to rise a moment later to drive his kitchen staff back to their work. They had crowded into the passageway, their eyes like saucers as they stared at the two brothers, so identical in appearance there was no telling, at a distance, which was which.

"Foster," the surgeon was saying, "I've one request to make at the outset: don't 'Feadle' me."

"Why not?" his brother asked. "It's your name, ain't it? Why shouldn't I call my brother by his name?"

"I've never known a man so touchy in that respect," said Murgatroyd. "Feadle . . . it's quite a pretty name, if you ask me."

"I've spent my life trying to live it out of memory," said the surgeon, ruefully; "but crop up it will, in spite of everything."

"What would you have, then?" his brother asked. "I must call you something. . . . Damme, I know! You recollect, when we were lads, we were called Rover, Primus and Secundus? The tag went well with the 'Dogbody.' Will you have that instead?"

"Aye, anything but Feadle," said the surgeon. "Let it be Rover, by all means. . . . Now, gentlemen, would ye bear with me? I've not seen nor heard of this fellow since those far-off days. I'd like to ask him a few questions."

"Willingly, Doctor. Proceed," said Runyon.

"For the first, how long have ye been in England, Foster?"

"A fortnight, all of it spent in a search for you. I've been to London, Bristol, and Plymouth, and to the churchyard in Egg Buckland, as I've said."

The surgeon nodded. "I'm a cork tossed by the seven oceans, Foster, at rest for the moment here, but only for the moment. You're married?"

"I was, but my good wife died many years ago."

"Children?"

"Two sons in their early thirties and a daughter of twenty-nine. All three wedded, with splendid children, and thriving."

"Good. All Dogbodys should have children. I'm the one family renegade in that respect. You've been a widower for years, you say. I take it, then, that you brought up your children yourself?"

"I did, with the help of as good a woman as ever drew breath."

"And who is she?"

"*Was,* Rover," his brother corrected. "She died a twelve-month back. She was a convict."

"A convict? And you gave your young children into her charge?"

"Rover, if ever there was a saint, and a martyr to the inhuman penal laws of England, 'twas the woman who was both nurse and foster mother to those same children, and an honoured member of my family for close to thirty years."

"She was transported?"

"Aye, and the crime she was charged with was the stealing of three spoons and a silver thimble."

"God bless me! You don't say so!" the surgeon exclaimed.

"She was completely innocent of the crime; that I am convinced of. But no more of this. The matter is of no interest except to my own family. . . . You've worn well, Rover, for one of your years."

The surgeon sighed. "I'd be pleased to say the same of

yourself. 'Tis the American climate, no doubt, that's aged ye so: fevers, agues, and the like."

"Aged me? Sour grapes! I could put your head in a bag as easily now as I did when we were lads."

"And where have ye put your starboard leg? . . . Gentlemen, this brother was my veritable shadow, in boyhood. Whatever I did he was bound to do. He's not conquered the habit, I see, for all the years we've lived apart, but how he knew I'd lost a leg is beyond my guessing. I shouldn't wonder . . ."

"Now wait, Dogbody! Let me have a word here," Ostiff broke in. He turned to the other. "Mr. Dogbody, we've had your brother with us ever since his retirement from the service . . ."

"My temporary retirement, sir," the surgeon corrected. "I'll be up and away again at the first rumour of war."

"Granted," said Ostiff. "What I was about to say, Mr. Dogbody, is that while your brother will talk freely enough of most matters, he'll say naught of his missing leg. Now then, if you will consent to tell us of your own loss, we'll badger him into doing the like."

"I've no objection," said Foster Dogbody. "What d'ye say, Rover Primus? Will ye be secundus to me for once?"

The surgeon glanced gravely at his brother, then nodded his head. "Damme, so be it! I'll have no peace from these fellows, that's certain, till the story is told. Fire away, but remember: I'm to follow."

"I'll leave some bits of margin. To begin, I take it that these gentlemen know nothing of my history?"

"Nothing whatever, sir," said Murgatroyd.

"In that case, I'll cover the preliminaries in a word. Our father's brother, Bartholomew Dogbody, a planter in the Virginia colony, was childless. When he had made a careful survey of his many nephews, I was, naturally, the one chosen to fill the room of a son and to inherit his estate at his death. As Rover knows, I sailed from this very port in 'seventy, at the age of sixteen. My home thereafter was in my uncle's house, in eastern Virginia.

"Uncle Bart felt deeply the injustice of the behaviour of His Majesty's ministers toward their kinsmen overseas. Nevertheless, when these latter were goaded to the point of revolution, his loyalty remained firm. He gave his services and, in the end, his life, for the English cause. I, being young, followed his lead with the same good will.

"I chanced to be in New York, about my uncle's affairs, when the Declaration of Independence was signed, and I so abhorred that act of rebellion that I didn't wait to return to Virginia, but joined Colonel de Lancey's Loyal New York Regiment. My uncle highly approved of the action.

"As you all know, in the autumn of 'seventy-six, Lord Howe came from England with authority to settle matters in dispute between His Majesty and his American subjects. I chanced to be one of a small mounted troop sent out to escort the delegates of the Continental Congress to British headquarters, in New York. They were coming from Philadelphia, and we met their coach near the village of Brunswick, in New Jersey. I scarcely need add that the American representatives were none other than Mr. John Adams and Mr. Benjamin Franklin."

The surgeon glanced up. "B'gad, there was a privilege for a young man," he remarked. "Did you have any speech with them, Foster?"

"At the moment, very little. We met them, I remember, on the turnpike from Philadelphia, three miles south of Brunswick. They halted their coach and both Mr. Adams and Mr. Franklin got out, whereupon the captain of our troop introduced himself and produced his credentials, which were carefully scanned by Mr. Adams. Despite the calumnious reports I had heard in British circles concerning Mr. Adams and Mr. Franklin, I realized on the instant that our little troop was under the scrutiny of two great men. The impress upon us of their personalities was immediate and lasting.

" 'You are British, young man?' Mr. Adams inquired of our commander.

" 'My home is in Connecticut, sir,' our captain replied, 'but I am a loyal subject of His Majesty.'

"Mr. Adams returned his papers, giving him a smile as bleak as the autumn day. 'I trust you may live to regret it,' said he, and got into the coach again. Mr. Franklin impressed me as having the warmer nature. I remember the interest with which he regarded our escort, and he pointed out to the fellow riding next to me that his saddle-girth needed tightening.

"As he was about to enter the coach, a gust of wind made a little funnel-shaped whirl of dust and dead leaves on the highway, which began to move slowly away. Mr. Franklin was immediately intensely interested in this phenomenon, and despite Mr. Adams's protests he followed it into the adjoining meadow and on for a distance of better than a mile from where we stood, until the funnel broke and vanished. It seems that he was, just then, studying the natural causes of both whirlwinds and waterspouts, and here was a demonstration in miniature that he was bound to make the most of. Mr. Adams fumed at the delay. I remember him saying, upon his friend's return: 'Damme, Mr. Franklin! How can you be drawn aside for so trivial a thing as this? There is a political whirlwind at hand that will need all our study and our best efforts to guide it, if guided it may be.' But Mr. Franklin began immediately to speak in so fascinating a manner of the phenomena of winds that Mr. Adams was soon as interested as himself. I much regretted that the rattle of the coach prevented my hearing all but fragments of the conversation that followed.

"The same evening, Mr. Adams and Mr. Franklin lodged in the tavern at Brunswick, and to my great satisfaction I was told off by the commander of our troop to valet the pair of them. They slept in the same couch, and I was then privileged to see two great men in undress . . . damme, in actual undress as they prepared for bed. Mr. Adams wore a nightshirt of red flannel, with a tasseled cap to match which he pulled down over his ears, for it was bitterly cold and there was no fireplace in their upper chamber. Mr. Franklin had a most curious bed attire: I had never before, and I have never since, seen anything like it. A peejammah-suit he called it, an adaptation of his own of a Persian attire which he predicted would, some day, be in universal use as a bed wear for men."

"A peejammah-suit? What like was it, sir?" Balthus asked.

"There was both coat and trousers, Mr. Balthus. The trousers somewhat resembled a pair of long woolen drawers, but they were loose to the legs. I remember Mr. Adams's scorn at sight of them. Nevertheless, it was he who first got into bed and burrowed deep under the coverlets, whilst Mr. Franklin walked about the room in apparent comfort, despite the freezing air. He explained to Mr. Adams that it was a man's middle parts that chiefly felt the cold air which could circulate freely beneath a nightshirt, whereas the peejammahs conserved the warmth of the body, which made them greatly to be preferred. To demonstrate his point, he flung wide both windows of their bedchamber and stood in the icy draught with an expression of perfect serenity upon his face. Mr. Adams was horrified, and immediately leaped out of bed to close them. Mr. Franklin waited until his friend had dived beneath the blankets once more; then, with the same bland smile, he threw wide the windows a second time. At last, however, in response to Mr. Adams's earnest, wrathful entreaties, he reluctantly consented that they should be closed."

"You were there, Foster? You heard and saw all this?" Doctor Dogbody inquired.

"I did. Theirs was a huge chamber, lit by a single candle on a table by their bedside. I stood in the shadows at the far end of the room, waiting to be dismissed, but in their argument over sleeping attire and fresh air they had quite forgotten my presence. And glad I was of the

fact, for I was privileged to listen to as interesting a conversation as has ever fallen to the lot of an impressionable
young man. I deeply regretted, afterward, that I did not
make notes of the matters discussed, which ran the full
gamut of human knowledge, and beyond. Mr. Adams
spoke from the depths of the great bed. Mr. Franklin sat
in a chair near by, or walked the floor in his eager interest.

"Free Will was one of the topics, Mr. Franklin arguing
for and Mr. Adams against it. From this they branched
off to speak of the writings of Monsieur Voltaire, admired
by Mr. Franklin as much as they were abhorred by Mr.
Adams. As for Mr. Rousseau, they acknowledged his in-
fluence upon contemporary thought, but agreed that it
was a pernicious one, and Mr. Adams, in particular,
snorted at the doctrine of the nobility of the savage.

"But what chiefly interested me was their discussion of
the future of the American continent. Doctor Franklin
described it as it would be in years to come: the forests
conquered, the swamps drained, the farms, hamlets,
towns, and cities of a free and happy people scattered over
the vast prairies and plains of the still trackless western
regions. Mr. Adams seemed much more doubtful of the
felicity of those future Americans.

" 'We will win political liberty for the generations to
come,' said he, 'but can we, Mr. Franklin, endow them
with the wisdom to profit by and enjoy it?'

" 'I think so, sir, I think so,' said Mr. Franklin.
'L'homme est bête,' as the French say, but I do believe
that, in our western world, the way is clear, or will be

soon, for a new approach to human happiness. It can be, and must be, achieved.'

"Mr. Adams shook his head. 'The wish is father to that thought,' said he. 'Mr. Franklin, vast as our continent is, I greatly fear that it is not vast enough for human stupidity and for human avarice. I foresee a time when it will be covered with swarms of rats and locusts in the shape of men. They will be indifferent to their heritage. They will be so eaten up with greed as neither to think of nor care for the welfare of their children's children. Money will be their god. They will plough all the grasslands under in their eagerness for money crops. Eventually, endless clouds of dust from eroding soil will fill the air over the prairies, and our forests, which seem so immeasurable now, will be laid waste, and the lands where they stood, sterile and barren.' "

"What an absurd prediction!" said Captain Runyon. "A thousand years hence we Americans will have made scarcely an impression on those grass and forest lands."

"So, I gathered, Mr. Franklin thought," said Foster Dogbody. "He predicted that wise legislation on the part of a Federal government, which he already foresaw, would bring it to pass that, by the year 2000, settlement should extend no farther than to the central regions, along the great Mississippi River, leaving one half of the continent for the use of the generations beyond."

"Was nothing said of the war at hand?" Mr. Ostiff inquired.

"Scarcely a word, sir, if my recollection serves. Their silence on this matter convinced me that both of these great men had no shadow of doubt as to the outcome. Their minds were at peace there, and I knew, as I listened to their conversation, that Lord Howe had come from England on a fruitless errand. The Americans would have complete political liberty and nothing else."

"How long did the conversation last?" Captain Murgatroyd inquired.

"I would not venture to say, sir, with exactness, though it must have been a good two hours. At the end, Mr. Adams was so incensed by a remark of Mr. Franklin's on the subject of conjugal felicity, or, rather, the frequent lack of it, that he turned from him with a snort, pulling the bedclothes up about his ears. A few moments later he was snoring loudly. Having made certain that he was asleep, Mr. Franklin tiptoed to the windows and opened them once more. Damme, I was all but congealed without them open and I hardened to an icicle within thirty seconds. Nevertheless, I froze at my post, resolved to get the full good of so interesting and intimate a scene. To my astonishment, Mr. Franklin then took his journal and his writing materials from his portmanteau, seated himself at the table, snuffed the candle, and began to write with as much apparent comfort as though it were a night in midsummer. Presently I was taken with a fit of sneezing, whereupon Doctor Franklin glanced up quickly.

" 'What's this?' said he. 'Young man, I supposed you in bed hours ago.'

" 'I was waiting to be dismissed, sir,' I replied.

" 'Damme, there's discipline!' said Doctor Franklin. 'And you've been standing in the corner all this time?'

" 'Yes, sir.'

" 'Did you hear what I said about the peejammahs?'

" 'Yes, sir,' I replied.

"Mr. Franklin rose from the table and approached me, emphasizing his words with an outstretched forefinger.

" 'Young man,' said he, 'I will not live to see it and you may not. But mark me well! The time is coming when nightshirts such as Mr. Adams is wearing will be as obsolete, for bed apparel, as the chamber-pot under that bed will be for a night convenience. Peejammahs will replace the first. As for the second . . .' He hesitated. 'I do not yet foresee what the improvement made upon it will be,' he added, 'but you can take this as certain: the improvement is coming as surely as water obeys the law of gravity. . . . Go now and take your rest, and if your somewhat exaggerated sense of duty earns you a cold in the lungs or head, I have some drops of my wife's preparation that will cure you before you can cough twice.' "

"Did you need 'em, Foster?" the surgeon asked.

"Yes, and they were all that Mr. Franklin had claimed for them."

"What could he have meant by that strange comparison?" said Ostiff.

"I could not hazard a guess, sir, but I've no doubt he already saw, in the mind's eye, some invention to come which would add to the comfort and convenience of life."

"What's more convenient than a chamber-pot?" Balthus remarked, gravely. "Don't see how you could improve on that. Our grandfathers used 'em. So will our great-grandchildren, if you ask me."

"Proceed, Foster," said the surgeon. "Damme, we're getting off the subject. There's a pair of legs to be lost before the evening's over."

"So there is," said his brother. He smiled. "Gentlemen, my apologies. The Dogbodys need something more than elbowroom for the telling of a mere anecdote. 'Tis a family trait. Rover, you'll not have forgotten our Great-uncle Daniel?"

"That I've not," said the surgeon. "You recollect the year we spent our school holidays with him, at Hum-shaugh?" He turned to the others. "The very evening of our arrival," he explained, "Uncle Daniel began telling Foster and me the story of the hen that crossed the road. We were three solid months in his house, and gentlemen, I give you my word: every evening during those three months we had a chapter of the tale, and we had to leave in the autumn without hearing the end of it."

"The end?" said Foster Dogbody. "Damme, if ye remember, when we came away Uncle Daniel had not yet brought the hen out of the thicket on the near side of the road. He was a true Dogbody, loath to bring anything to a conclusion, his own life not excepted. He was ninety-eight when he died."

"Ye've robbed him of ten years, Foster," said the surgeon reproachfully, "and of those he most enjoyed."

"I've a clear recollection of the number. 'Twas ninety-eight."

"Your memory's going, no question of that. He was one hundred and eight years, three months, and four days precisely, on the evening of his death. The parish record of Humshaugh is there to prove it."

"Be that as it may: a fine figure he was of the old English yeoman. But where had I gotten to?"

"Ye was still in the tavern at Brunswick, sir," said Balthus, patiently.

"So I was, and, not to take a leaf from my Great-uncle Daniel's book, I'll whisk ye away from there in a word, and through all the fatigues and dangers of the American War. 'Tis enough to say that I fought on many fields. I doubt whether any soldier in His Majesty's forces shed more blood in more places than myself: Saratoga, the Brandywine, Monmouth Courthouse, Yorktown — Dogbody blood, from flesh wounds, enriched the soil of a dozen battlefields, but I shed no limbs upon any of them. It was left for the country in whose behalf I spilt the blood to deprive me of the leg itself.

"At the end of the war I found myself in New York with thousands of other impoverished loyalists, dependent upon the King's bounty, such as it was. My Uncle Bart was dead, killed at Bemis Heights, and his estates were confiscated by the Federal Congress. I had the clothes I stood in and no more.

"You are all familiar, I take it, with the miserable fortunes, after the war, of the American loyalists. Some were taken in the King's ships to the Canadian wilderness and left there to fend for themselves as best they could. I was amongst these, but after four years of misery I left the accursed place and returned to England, arriving at Plymouth in the spring of 'eighty-nine. Where were you at that time, Rover?"

"In 'eighty-nine? Surgeon of the *Intrepid,* on the India station."

"I tried to get wind of you, with no success. Meanwhile, a sorry time we loyalists had of it, cold-shouldered and ignored at every turn."

"Nonsense, Foster! His Majesty's ministers were deeply concerned about the loyalists. That I know."

"We were not entirely ignored, to be sure. Common decency required that some notice be taken of us, but they were slow enough in getting anything done. Meanwhile, we were free to starve with what decorum we could manage. There was a plan to colonize the lot of us at Botany Bay, in New South Wales, but nothing came of it."

The surgeon glanced up quickly. "In Botany Bay? So there was: I recall it now! And you wanted to go there?"

"Yes; I was greatly interested in the project, but it fell through, as I've said. 'Twas decided to make a convict settlement there, for England could no longer dump her riffraff on the American continent. Why do you ask?"

"No matter. Proceed," said the surgeon.

"The proceeding was downward, Rover. Like all the American refugees then in England, I became more and more dingy and down-at-heel. At last, in desperation, I set out for York on a borrowed horse, thinking there might be some of our Uncle Daniel's kin still living in or about Humshaugh."

"They are scattered to the four winds," the surgeon put

in. "There's not a Dogbody left in the whole of York-shire."

"So I learned. I was none too merry, as ye'll guess, as I turned southward once more, riding through the dusk of a winter evening, with eleven shillings and sixpence to see me to London and no prospects of whatever kind when I got there. I came to a bit of an inn on the York road, a humble place for the accommodation of carriers, post-boys, hostlers, and the like, and there I put up for the night. Had I but known it, my leg was then dangling by a thread.

"In the middle of that same night I was routed out of bed by four constables. There'd been a coach robbed near by, and I was identified as the highwayman by one of the robbed passengers. I was dragged from my bed, ordered to dress at once, and half an hour later I was placed in the midst of a mounted patrol to be taken to York for trial at the next assizes.

"Damme, 'twas the last straw! There was I, a loyal Englishman who had lost everything but life in the King's cause, with that life now in jeopardy at the hands of those I had fought for. 'Tis a Dogbody trait to resent injustice. The night was pitch dark, with wind and rain. I bided my chance, and when it came I knocked the constable on my right from his horse, turned my own, and, giving it the spur, galloped at a furious pace down the road we had come. I was hotly pursued, of course, the constables firing their pistols at random. As luck would have it, the ball from one caught me directly behind the knee; never-theless I kept my seat and managed to escape. Shortly after dawn I pulled up at another inn on a little-traveled road which may well have been a resort for highwaymen, for not a question was asked of me, nor did my lack of money deprive me of entertainment. I was treated with great humanity, and when it became clear that my leg must come off, a man was sent for who performed the amputation as well as any London surgeon could have done it. There I lay until fully recovered, whereupon I returned to London. Having had enough and to spare of England, I worked my passage to America on a merchant vessel, began life anew in the western part of Pennsylvania, and with such success that I may now look back with composure upon the vicissitudes of the past."

"Foster, this is beyond all credence and belief!" Doctor Dogbody exclaimed, as his brother brought his story to a close.

" 'Tis nothing of the kind," the other replied, warmly. "I have given you the facts without the least embellishment. The one incredible thing is that a loyal Englishman who had sacrificed his fortune and shed his blood for king and country should have been rewarded for his services, upon returning to that country, by being hunted down as a common thief. And had I not escaped as I did, there is no doubt that my bones would be mouldering beneath a gibbet at this moment."

"You mistake me," said the surgeon. "I doubt no word of your story, but . . . damme, so strange a coincidence all but passes the bounds of the conceivable! Now tell me this: was it the year 1790 that you were taken on the York road?"

"It was."

"And the exact date was November the twenty-first of that year? And the inn where you were taken was called the Cock and Fox?"

Foster Dogbody glanced at his brother. "How the devil could you know that?" he asked.

"Because, my dear brother, I came so near to hanging in your stead that my throat has been sore ever since."

"God's rabbit!" said Balthus.

"You never made a truer observation, Ned Balthus. A rabbit I was, pursued by the hounds of the law with a malevolence that all but ended me, and never until this moment have I known that there was reason behind the persecution."

"What are you saying, Rover? You don't tell me that you were apprehended in my place?"

"Precisely. In September of the year 'ninety, I returned home after four years on the India station. The country being at peace, I came ashore, on the one leg, to be sure, but well content to have lost the other in the King's service."

"How's this?" said Runyon. "Your leg's off before ye start!"

"Aye, Runyon: lopped off with as pretty a left-handed swing with a two-handed sword as was ever made, with one hand, by a six-foot Sikh. 'Tis no matter for the leg, for the story I have to tell greatly exceeds in interest the one I had thought to relate. I came ashore, as I've said, and found a thousand pounds in prize money awaiting me at the Admiralty office."

"And there was I, likewise in England, without two ha'pence to rub together," said Foster Dogbody.

The surgeon nodded. "And your own fault, too. You should have kept in touch with me. I had scarcely set foot on land in ten years and I now resolved to make the most of the opportunity. I traveled like a nabob, in post chaises, through all the southern counties, visiting old friends; then I struck out for the north, meaning to tour the highlands of Scotland which I had never seen. Little I dreamed, Foster, that you were on this side of the Atlantic."

"Just when was this?" his brother asked.

"In the March of 'ninety-one."

"And I had only then begun to hobble about with a crutch. I well remember, 'twas the twentieth of March that I set out for London from the inn where I had lain concealed, riding in a carrier's wagon."

"Damme, 'tis as certain as sunrise that we passed one another on the way, for it was on March the twenty-fourth that I was overtaken by darkness at the Cock and Fox."

"Did ye sleep in a chamber on the first floor, front, facing the road?"

"I did. At least, I would have slept there had I not been routed out in the same manner as yourself, just as I was preparing for bed."

"By a constable with red hair?"

"Brick red, and with but one front tooth in his upper jaw."

"Rover, 'twas the very man who seized me!"

The surgeon nodded. "And he was fully convinced that he had you once more. A brazen reckless fellow he thought me to have the courage to return to the place. Despite my indignant protests, he, with his four assistants, bound me hand and foot. At dawn I was carried in my own hired chaise and flung into the prison at York."

"You didn't long remain there, surely?" said Ostiff. "An old Navy man would have small trouble in establishing his identity."

"Say you so, Ostiff? B'gad, had you been in my place, you'd have discovered that York is far different from the seacoast towns. Her citizens scarcely know that England has a navy. The worst of it was that I had no papers with me, and the gold in my money belt was, of course, thought to be the loot from my robberies on the highways. 'Tis a common practice, it seems, for lawless characters to protest that they are seamen traveling to and from the coast towns, and not the least credence was given to my story. Furthermore, there had been an unusual number of robberies in Yorkshire and none of the robbers caught. There was a great to-do about it in the papers, and the authorities were bound I should suffer the final penalty as a sop to public outcry."

"And did ye?" asked Balthus, adding hastily: "I mean to say, was ye convicted?"

"Tried, convicted, and condemned to die on a gibbet, Ned Balthus, and I have known from that day how small a chance for his life an honest man may have when the law is determined to condemn. I was positively identified as the highwayman in question, though no word appeared in the evidence as to whether the man had one leg or two. I was, of course, regarded as the most consummate liar. My very indignation and my air of complete probity worked against me, for they were considered the arts of an accomplished villain.

"I pass over the next two months, during which time I looked death more and more closely in the face. Two other wretches were to hang with me, and York prison, an unspeakably vile and filthy place, was crowded with unfortunate creatures, both men and women, awaiting transportation. Amongst the latter was a girl of twenty for whom my heart bled. She was a domestic servant and had been convicted of stealing from her mistress. The evidence was strongly against her, but she as strongly and tearfully protested her innocence. I believed implicitly the story I heard her tell in court. If ever I have seen an honest woman it was that poor girl. She was the very pattern of modesty and goodness.

"I scarcely need say that I escaped hanging. I give you the details in a word. Three days before that set for my execution there came to York Captain Dudley Mitchin, who'd commanded the *Medusa,* a seventy-four, when I was serving in her. Mitchin was one of the best of men, but he had a vice that sorted oddly with his character: he couldn't resist a gallows day. When ashore, he'd travel from one county to another to witness executions. He had, I believe, the most complete collection of the dying confessions of condemned men to be found in England.

"Having come to York for the June hangings, Mitchin had heard that one of the three wretches who were to climb the ladder to bed, as the saying goes, stubbornly clung to the assertion that he was a surgeon in His Majesty's Navy. His interest was aroused, and he asked for and was granted permission to visit the prison, where he found me with the hangman's noose all but about my neck. I scarcely need add that, in my case, the date of execution was stayed. A messenger was sent posthaste to London, and within the week my innocence was completely established.

"I returned to London in Mitchin's company, and never shall I forget that delightful journey, in fine weather: cuckoos, skylarks, and nightingales singing from every bough, giving voice to my own joy and gratitude for the inestimable gift of life. Damme, 'twas worth having lived within the shadow of a gibbet to have that sense of gratitude so quickened, and that joy so immeasurably increased. Well would it be if misanthropes and all peevish, carping, complaining folk could have such an experience as mine. The world would be a happier place if they, in their tens of thousands, could escape hanging, as I did, by minutes.

"Curiously enough, upon reaching London I learned that a transport, the *Lady Juliana,* which was to carry two hundred women convicts to Botany Bay, was then fitting out in the Thames, and that a surgeon was wanted for her. My experience in York prison had aroused my interest in, and quickened my sympathies for, all poor creatures within the clutches of the law. I now resolved to see, if possible, in what state they were banished from their country, and, as well, the place of their banishment. I applied for, and was given, the post of surgeon to the *Lady Juliana*. It seems that no one else would have it.

"I was warned that I would find the officers and men in a convict transport far other than those I was accustomed to in Navy ships; and so I did. The better class of seamen are loath to serve in such ships; therefore, the Home Office, which has these matters in charge, sweeps up from the waterfront whatever riffraff can be persuaded to sign on the transports. The one concern is to get rid of the convicts, emptying the jails for an endless stream of newcomers. What become of the old they care not, so long as they leave England."

"Why is it, Dogbody," Captain Runyon put in at this point, "that you English have such enormous numbers of convicts? For the past century and longer you have been dumping them upon us, in America. Since the Revolution we no longer permit this and you must find room for them elsewhere. But why should you have so great a criminal class amongst you?"

"I can answer that question in five words, Runyon: 'Empty sacks cannot stand upright.' Poverty, starvation, and the unspeakable social conditions of our country in general, compel thousands to steal or die."

"My belief is that our land-enclosure acts account for the greater part of them," said Ostiff. "The evil goes back over a period of three centuries and has reached its height within our own lifetimes. We have a new class of landlords concerned only in getting all the wealth from the land into their own hands. This they accomplish through

the parliamentary enclosure-bills, by means of which tens
of thousands of small farms are taken from their former
tenants and turned into pasturage for sheep and horses.
The small farmers become either landless labourers, at
starvation wages, or vagabonds."

"Well may ye say it, Ostiff," said the surgeon. "The old
class of yeoman farmers is fast disappearing with us.
Their children drift to the cities, where want drives them
into crime."

Captain Murgatroyd nodded his head, soberly. "Doctor
Goldsmith has judged us, once and for all," he said.

> "Ill fares the land, to hastening ills a prey,
> Where wealth accumulates, and men decay.
> Princes and lords may flourish, or may fade,
> A breath can make them, as a breath has made;
> But a bold peasantry, their country's pride,
> When once destroyed, can never be supplied."

"So it is, Inky," said the surgeon. "What would have
been, in earlier times, the daughters, wives, and mothers
of a flourishing peasantry were brought on board the
Lady Juliana as convicts."

"But some was harridans, like enough?" said Balthus.

"Harridans!" The surgeon rolled up his eyes. "Ned, ye
never saw such a lot of reckless, desperate, impudent
women as most of 'em were, but made such, I do believe,
by England herself. Nine tenths of the *Juliana's* women
were young, from eighteen to twenty-five. The plan was
to mate them up with men convicts already at Botany
Bay.

"There was one in a class by herself — a Mrs. Living-

ston; at least, she went by that name. A more beautiful
creature could not have been found at one of the King's
levees. She was said to be the natural daughter of a very
great personage indeed, and I could well believe it, for
her intelligence and strength of character equaled her
beauty. She had been mistress to a noble lord who was so
eaten up with jealousy on her account that his life was
complete misery. In one of his fits, he had, wrongfully, I
believe, accused her of robbing him of five hundred
pounds and a gold watch. She was convicted, and sentenced to transportation for fourteen years. The fellow
repented of his act at leisure and moved heaven and
earth in an attempt to get her off; but once the wheels of
the law begin turning there's no stopping them, and his
efforts were useless. So deeply he regretted his action that
he came to the ship with chests and boxes without number, filled with elegant apparel and supplies of every sort
for Mrs. Livingston's use. He also engaged a private cabin
for her. But although she accepted these favours as her
right, she would not be reconciled and treated him with
the greatest coolness and contempt. She chose as her maid
for the voyage the poor girl I had seen convicted of theft
at York Assizes.

"We left London early in July. I fully expected that our
transport would belie her ladylike name the moment the
chalk cliffs of England were below the horizon. Transports filled with women convicts are, commonly, no better
than floating bawdyhouses during their voyages, and ours
might have been with a different ship's company. A more
miserable lot of miscalled seamen were never gathered in

one ship; even the most common and abandoned of the women would have naught to do with them. For some reason — to save expense, perhaps — no marines were sent with us as guards; nevertheless, the women were as quiet and orderly as you please. We had Mrs. Livingston to thank for it. She took complete charge of the females, organized them into messes, and provided for their amusements and distractions on board. They had the greatest respect and admiration for Mrs. Livingston; her lightest word was law. It was, 'Ladies, come up for your pork,' or, 'Ladies, come up for your grog,' for those who wished it had their small tot morning and evening. Damme, I all but forgot the women were convicts. You might well have thought we were carrying out the wives and daughters of the clergy, so exemplary to outward seeming was their behaviour.

"We proceeded southward with calms and light winds marking the passage, until we were not far off the Canaries. One morning at dawn I was aroused from sleep by a knocking at the door of my cabin.

" 'Come in,' said I.

"The door opened, and there stood Mrs. Livingston, with a brace of pistols in her hands, and backed by three stalwart women, one with a musket, the bayonet fixed, one with a cutlass, and the third with an iron bar in her huge fist.

"I sprang from my hammock on the instant. 'What's amiss, ma'am?' said I, little dreaming of the truth of the matter.

" 'Make haste to dress, Surgeon,' she replied, quietly,

'and these ladies will escort you on deck.' Then, with a nod to her subordinates, she left me.

" 'These ladies' were a trio of giantesses, any one of which would have made any two of us here present. Mrs. Grogan, a convict for life, from Liverpool, carried the iron bar.

" 'Is it pirates, Mrs. Grogan?' said I, for we were not then far off the Barbary coast.

" 'Faith and b'Jazus, it is,' said she: 'two hundred women pirates! We mean no harm to ye, Surgeon, but if ye lift yer little finger against us, it's this bit of iron I'll be layin' along yer skull, so soft ye'll wake up with the blessed saints!'

" 'Never with the saints, Mrs. Grogan,' said I.

" 'Come along now, Surgeon darlin',' said she, with a grin; 'and let ye be aisy in yer mind, for it's chose out ye are, along with the master and boatswain.'

"I didn't know what she meant by that, but I made haste to obey orders. B'gad, there was naught else I could do with three such guards alongside. Any one of 'em would have topped the Colossus of Rhodes, and Mrs. Grogan was a match for a dozen men. Some of you must have heard of her under the name of the Woolton Wonder. 'Twas she who had the great fight with George the Brewer, the champion of Liverpool, in 'seventy-six, and knocked him out in the thirtieth round. Never has a man taken such a beating with bare fists. It ended him.

"I was marched on deck, where I found Captain Lush and the entire ship's company gathered to one side, and fifty women drawn up on the opposite, muskets at the ready. We had on board a quantity of powder and ball and three hundred stand of arms being sent out for the New South Wales Corps. Through the captain's negligence, the women had gotten possession of all this, and the ship was now in their hands. I was ordered to stand at one side with Mr. Crofte, the master, and Given, the boatswain, the only decent members of the crew. We were kept apart from the rest.

"A chair had been placed for Mrs. Livingston at the break of the poop, and there she sat, perfectly cool, with another fifty women, under arms, on either side. As always, she was splendidly dressed, as handsome and elegant a figure as ye could find in any portrait by Sir Joshua Reynolds. For some little time, she regarded captain and seamen with an expression of perfect indifference and contempt. Then she spoke.

" 'Captain Lush,' said she, 'as a ship's commander you are a disgrace to His Majesty's service. As a man you are a disgrace to the human race. You are a bawdy old villain, sir, or would be if you had the courage of a rabbit. Since we left England you have entirely neglected your duties that you might have time to peep from holes and corners and make sly advances to these virtuous women. You have yourself to blame for losing your ship. As for your men, with the exception of three, the master, the surgeon, and the boatswain, they are worthy of such a captain as yourself. . . . Take off your clothes!'

" 'Mrs. Livingston, ma'am,' said Lush, in a trembling voice, 'I admit I may have forgot myself with so many handsome women aboard. I may have looked where I

shouldn't have, now and again, but I humbly crave pardon, and I promise to mend my ways in future.'

" 'Take off your clothes!' Mrs. Livingston repeated,
sternly. 'There is to be no future for you in this ship.'

" 'You'll not flog me, ma'am?' said he, imploringly.

" 'Flog such a thing as yourself?' said she. 'Where would
be the satisfaction in that? We mean you no hurt unless
you are so foolish as to offer resistance, but do as I've
commanded, and your men as well.'

"Mrs. Grogan now skipped forward, brandishing her
weapon over the captain's head.

"'Strip, ye forked radish,' said she, 'or I'll undress the
under side of your skull-pan; and faith, if I did, 'tis
naught but a bad smell I'd be lettin' out to the blessed
air of heaven. Strip, ye chitty-faced, Drury-Lane ague!'

" 'Mrs. Grogan!' called their leader.

" 'Yes, me lady?'

" 'They may keep their drawers.'

" 'Faith, and to be sure, me lady. 'Twould be no treat
to ony of the daughters of Eve to see the Nature's mistakes with no rag to their skinny bodies. Keep the drawers,
ye makeweights, them that have 'em, but off with the
rest, or it's arsy-varsy ye'll go and we'll peel 'em from ye!'

"B'gad, strip they did! Two or three had the spirit to
resist, but not for long. Mrs. Grogan and the special
guard of Amazons made short work of 'em. I blessed my
stars, as did the master and the boatswain, to have been
spared such an ordeal. Damme, 'twas as comical a sight
as ye'd see in a lifetime to behold that mangy lot lined
up in their next-to-nothings. The more brazen of the

women laughed and hooted at them, making more than
pertinent remarks, but Mrs. Livingston brought them to
order with a word.

"The clothing was gathered in one large heap, for
boiling and washing. Some of the women then brought
forth the men's fresh garments, but not for them. The
captain's slop-chests were likewise emptied and all was
sorted into neat piles: shirts, jerseys, trousers, and the
like. This done, the women awaited further orders. Mrs.
Livingston sat with her chin resting lightly in the palm of
her hand, letting her glance travel slowly along the ranks
of seamen.

" 'During our passage thus far,' she resumed, 'these
honest women have been annoyed past bearing by your
furtive spying upon their privacy. Some of you have even
had the courage and the effrontery to solicit their favours, and well have you merited their rebuffs. Though
creatures of flesh and blood, endowed with all the softer,
warmer feelings of their sex, they would have been desperate indeed to have yielded to any blandishments of
yours.'

" 'Mrs. Livingston, ma'am, allow me to speak,' said
Lush. 'There's no woman in this ship can say I've offered
her an insult.'

"At this a saucy-eyed, buxom lass stepped out to confront him, her hands on her hips.

" 'Oh, ye wretch!' said she. 'And what would ye call an
insult? Didn't ye coax and whisper me into your cabin
the night afore last? And didn't I go? For it's long I've
been shut away and a poor choice is better than none.

And wasn't I with ye a full half-hour? And didn't I come out no happier than I went in?' She turned indignantly to Mrs. Livingston. 'Me lady, if there's a Domine Dolittle in the ship, 'tis the creature that calls himself a captain!' "

"The young hussy!" said Murgatroyd, with a chuckle. "It's plain, Dogbody, that, amongst the virtuous gentle-women, there was a sprinkling, at least, of somewhat tar-nished ones."

"What would ye expect, Inky, in a convict ship?" the surgeon asked, gravely. "We had all kinds, to be sure, as ye'll find all kinds in any hamlet, town, or city in Eng-land."

"What had Mrs. Livingston to say to that?" asked Run-yon.

"She was all composure, Runyon, though some of the women were truly shocked at the brazenness of the young vixen. Others, with Mrs. Grogan, broke into roars of laughter. I leave you to imagine the feelings of Lush.

" 'Sure, Molly, and what would ye expect from the cribbage-faced trapsticks?' said Mrs. Grogan. 'Did ye look at the lathy limbs of him! Veal will be cheap: calves fall. I'll take me oath, he's had no good of his socket-money from the day he called himself a man!'

" 'Silence, Mrs. Grogan!' said Mrs. Livingston.

" 'Yes, me lady,' said the latter, with an elephantine attempt at a curtsy.

" 'We will have no more of these accusations, for none are needed,' said Mrs. Livingston. 'All the ship's com-pany, save the three honourable gentlemen yonder, are under a blanket indictment for peeping and spying.' Her

smile was glacial as she added: 'Before we bid them farewell, we will treat them to one honest peep in the full
light of day.' "

Doctor Dogbody broke off and was so long silent that
Balthus asked: "What did she mean by that?"

"Exactly what she said," the surgeon resumed. "B'gad,
Ned, queer things and odd things have happened in
King's ships, but I'd never seen the like of this before.
She ordered the women to change into the seamen's dress,
there before them; but those whose modesty forbade it
were to go below to make the exchange.

"All this had been prearranged, of course. Then,
damme, if near a hundred of the women, mostly of the
younger sort, didn't down petticoats and off blouses there
and then! They took their time about it, too, taunting
the men meanwhile, and assuming postures something on
the under-side of modesty. Presently all stood in their
shifts, and some would have gone the whole distance had
not Mrs. Livingston, for reasons of her own, forbade it.

"She waited until all had clothed themselves in the
seamen's dress. She then ordered a little lacquer-wood
chest to be fetched from her cabin, and took from it a
handsome captain's uniform, made, evidently, to her
order. A rug was spread before her; then she herself began disrobing as quietly as though she were in the privacy of her own bedchamber. Garment after garment was
removed and handed to one of the older women, who
folded and laid them in the lacquer box. At last she stood
in naught but a little shift of cobweb silk that reached
to her knees."

"Good God!" said Ostiff. "You don't say . . ."

"Wait, Ostiff. I *do* say, and that wasn't all. She stood with her back to the seamen. Turning her head with a most ravishing smile for Lush, she loosened a ribbon at her comely shoulder and the last little garment slid to her feet."

"God's rabbit!" said Balthus. "She was the most brazen hussy amongst 'em!"

"No, Ned. Ye might well have thought so, but the truth was otherwise. In the course of a long life, in which I've met my share of women, I've never known one more modest in word and deed than Mrs. Livingston. But she could be bold when occasion required. 'Twas painted-grape nourishment she offered that parcel of Peeping Toms, and well they deserved it!"

"What of yourself, Rover?" Foster Dogbody asked. "You closed your eyes, of course?"

"I did not. A man of my profession, Foster, is skilled to look with composure upon whatever sight disturbing to other men. And let me add this: there was nothing wanton in the act, as there was nothing meretricious in the view of that superb creature whose beauty Helen of Troy herself might well have envied. 'Twas a vision for the statuary and the artist."

"And what then?" Murgatroyd inquired.

" 'B'gad, 'twas but the first half of the punishment. After the feast of painted grapes, with the women all in seamen's costume, and Mrs. Livingston herself in her splendid captain's uniform, with a little rapier at her side, Lush and his crew were compelled to don the

females' garments. Those that offered resistance were
soon persuaded by Mrs. Grogan and the Amazons. 'Twas
she who dressed the captain in her own petticoat, so
much too large for him that she fastened it under his
arms, and even then it trailed the deck. Damme, much as
he deserved the indignity, I could find it in my heart to
pity the rogue. And to top all, he was forced to put on a
frowsty old bonnet that looked as though it had been
knocking about the dust bins of London for a century.
Mrs. Grogan tied the strings of it for him, and for all her
great size she minced about him with the comic likeness
of a ladies' milliner. But he was no odder a sight than
the rest.

"Mrs. Livingston permitted the women to have their
sport for a bit, and Mrs. Grogan was not one to miss the
full good of it. A fine figure of a seaman she made, or
would have made in clothing large enough to fit so huge
a frame. She walked up and down before the transformed
seamen.

"'Will ye look at 'em, lads!' said she, addressing the
other women. 'B'Jazus, was there ever such trumpery
wenches seen in the worst nugginghouse in Crooked
Lane! But sure, it's a fine lady is this Mrs. Lush! Black's
the white of her eye! Will ye look at her, now! Ain't she
the modest fusty-luggs — as demure as an old whore at a
christening! . . . And here's a likely lass, or was in her
day. Many's the green gown she's had in the lanes and
the cow lots. . . . But, lads, mind this one! She's as common as a barber's chair, I'll take me oath! She's prayed
with her knees upward for twenty year. There's no

heels to the wench's boots and she'll fall on her back at the wink of a tinker's eye. . . . Doll Cudlip! Is it yerself, chickabiddy? And where've ye been since ye made the belly-plea at Newgate, for the sivinth time, to me certain knowledge? But ye'll be hanged yet, ye wagtail!'

" 'Mrs. Grogan!'

" 'Yes, me lady?'

" 'That will do!'

" 'Faith, and it will, me lady. Away with the lot of 'em! There's not one would make a dacent sweetheart to honest hearty lads the like of ourselves.'

"The longboat and the larger of our two launches were now put over the side, furnished with food and water for a fortnight. Lush and his men were forced into them and we soon left them astern. We were fifteen leagues east of the Canaries, and as the weather was fine, with a light breeze from the north, they could have had no trouble in making the land; but I've never heard, from that day to this, what became of them."

"Were none kept to work the vessel?" asked Murgatroyd.

"None save the master, the boatswain, and myself, but the loss was not felt, Inky. Mrs. Livingston, or, I should now say, Captain Livingston, was as good a navigator as any in the service, though where she learned it I couldn't say; she was nearer to true reckonings than the master himself. The latter, with the boatswain, she set immediately to work, instructing the ablest of the women in the seamen's duties. We were favoured in the weather, and at the end of a fortnight we had a far better ship's company than we'd left London with."

"And where were you bound this while?" Runyon asked.

"Not to Botany Bay, to be sure. Mrs. Livingston well knew the danger she ran from meetings with the King's ships. She was determined to get herself and her charges ashore as soon as possible. The course was west and a little north, and 'twas her good fortune to cross the Atlantic without speaking an English vessel, though we passed half-a-dozen Americans.

"We ran into Delaware Bay and came to anchor in a lonely cove well up the west side of Cape May. Here Mrs. Livingston was set ashore with two of her men, for they were still in male attire. She was well supplied with money of her own, and touched no penny in the ship's strongbox. She was gone for three days, and upon her return immediately disembarked her entire company save the master, the boatswain, and myself. They were again dressed in their proper garb, for they had two outfits of clothing provided by Government. Mrs. Livingston kept close watch whilst they gathered their little bundles and examined each one as they left the ship. She made the natural thieves amongst them disgorge the articles they would have stolen. Mrs. Grogan had, in a sailcloth, a load that would have broken a horse's back, but she had to leave it. I was both astonished and not astonished, if you understand me, to see the docility with which she obeyed her leader and left it all behind.

"At last all were ashore, and Mrs. Livingston herself

was ready to leave the ship. She was again dressed as a lady and a lady she looked, as lovely as she was charming. She called the master, the boatswain, and me into the cabin for a final word.

" 'Gentlemen,' said she, 'I sincerely regret leaving you, and I say this in no spirit of mockery. You have been model prisoners, and, having been a prisoner myself, I understand the difficulty of that position. Before I go I have one question to ask, and I put you upon your honour for the reply. Will you, or will you not, remain quietly here, communicating with no one, for the space of five days?'

" 'What do you mean to do, ma'am?' said I.

" 'That is a fair question, Surgeon, and deserves a straightforward answer. In this new country, with its boundless apportunities, I mean to see that the unfortunate women I have brought here are given the chance to live the decent honest lives forbidden to them in England. Some of them will make excellent wives and mothers, and I have no doubt that opportunities to assume the pleasures and responsibilities of wedlock will not be wanting here.' She regarded us with a grave smile. 'Others, such as Mrs. Grogan and my corps of special guards, are not, perhaps, what would be called marriageable women; but they will, I think, easily fend for themselves.'

" 'No doubt of that, ma'am, none whatever,' said I. 'But marriageable or not, they'll take husbands if their fancy runs that way.'

"Mrs. Livingston nodded. She was silent for some time,

then gave a wistful little sigh. 'A few of us, I fear, are no better than we should be.'

" 'Never include yourself in that class, Mrs. Livingston, ma'am,' said the master, gallantly. 'And what are the best of us, if it comes to that? If all them was transported that should be transported, there'd be more churches emptied than prisons. There'd not be a score left in the seats of Parliament, and I won't say even His Majesty's Privy Council would have all present at its next meeting.'

"Mrs. Livingston gave him a charming smile, half gay, half wistful.

" 'You comfort me, Mr. Crofte,' said she. 'After all, one does what one can, and my particular talents . . .' To my chagrin she left the sentence unfinished. But a moment later she remarked, with the same charming smile: 'And I know of no better land than this in which to be no better than one should be. . . . But you have not yet answered my question.'

" 'Speaking for myself, ma'am,' said I, 'I readily promise to remain quietly here for the space of five days, or longer, if that would please you better, and there's my hand on it!'

" 'Thank you, Surgeon,' said she. 'Five days will be sufficient. Mr. Crofte?'

" 'Ye have my promise, ma'am, with hearty good will, and I wish ye and the ladies all the happiness ye so well deserve.'

" 'Mr. Given?'

"The boatswain, a splendid honest fellow of thirty, hesitated before he spoke. 'For the promise, ye have it, ma'am, and welcome; and I'd go farther if summat could be brought to pass is my heart's wish.'

" 'And what is that?'

" 'There's one amongst your company as I'd take to wife to-morrow, if so be she'd have me; and I'd stay here with her and fend for her with joy. 'Tis Jenny, the young woman from York. I offered, but she'd not hear to it, ma'am, though she said she liked me well enough. But if you was to speak for me . . . ?'

"Mrs. Livingston shook her head. 'It's useless, Boatswain. Jenny has told me her story. She was promised at home, and on the point of marriage when accused of theft by her mistress, and tried and convicted at York Assizes. The girl's heart is broken. Time will heal it, perhaps, but she'll never marry: that's certain.'

" 'But please to tell her this, ma'am: when I'm home again I'll make it my duty to clear her name, if so be as I can, for she's as innocent of stealing the three spoons and the silver thimble as my own sisters. And please to tell her, if ever she do change her mind and'll have me, I'll come the minute she sends word. She's to direct to T. Given, at Ditchin Hills, near Hartland, in Devon. And I'd wish her to have this keepsake to mind her of me.'

"The boatswain took from his finger a little ring of pearl-shell which Mrs. Livingston promised to give the girl. Then . . ."

"Rover, by all that's wonderful, tell me that girl's name!" Foster Dogbody broke in.

"I have: 'twas Jenny," said the surgeon.

"Aye, but her family name?"

"That I never heard, Foster. The poor girl was in low spirits throughout the voyage and scarce spoke a word to anyone save Mrs. Livingston. I knew her family name no more than she knew mine."

"Then I will tell you what it was and who she was," said his brother: "Jenny Lowe — no other, Rover, than the good woman who reared my small children with all a mother's tenderness and love."

"I know, Foster," said the surgeon, quietly. "I was convinced from the moment you spoke of her that she of your household must have been the Jenny of the *Lady Juliana*. Furthermore, I recognized the ring on your little finger as the one Given had sent to the girl, in Mrs. Livingston's care."

"So it is," said Foster Dogbody. "The last request the good woman made of me, on her deathbed, was that, if ever I went to England, I would take the ring to a certain T. Given, if he could be found, and let him know that she'd never forgotten his kindness to her. And I promised I would."

"That promise can never be fulfilled, Foster. Given is dead, long since, and he died unwedded: that I know. After he'd cleared Jenny's name, as he promised he'd try to do, he went all the way to America on a search for her, but without success."

"He cleared her name, you say?"

"Within the year. He went to the village where the girl had been living, and by patient, dogged effort found the real culprit. The three spoons and the silver thimble, together with other small articles, were discovered in a magpie's nest."

"I never heard the beat of this for a queer thing," said Balthus. "And to think that ye both knew the girl! Wide as it is, 'tis a small world, certain. Did ye never hear tell, Doctor, what became of the lady?"

"The last I saw of Mrs. Livingston, Ned, was on that same afternoon when the master, the boatswain, and I rowed her ashore. A lonely spot it was, lonelier then, no doubt, than it would be now: the shore seemed to be one great forest. The others had already vanished into it. After a word of farewell, Mrs. Livingston turned to follow a dim footpath that wound amongst the great trees. We stood looking after her in silence, and I knew that the others felt the same ache in the heart as myself.

" 'Surgeon,' said the master, 'if she'd turn, now, and crook her little finger at me, I'd follow her to the ends of the earth.'

" 'Aye, but she won't. She's not for us, Mr. Crofte,' said I.

"We worried as to how she and the women would manage in such a wilderness, but we found, later, that the forest-land was no more than half a mile deep. Beyond were the farms and hamlets of a well-settled country.

"We did better than keep our promise. We were, perhaps, negligent of our duty as officers in a King's ship, but we felt that a higher duty was concerned here. We wished those poor women to have the chance they'd well earned for themselves, so we lay hidden in the cove for a fortnight. Then, in the jolly boat, we rowed up the bay to

the town of Wilmington, and what should we find when
we got there but His Majesty's frigate *Calypso,* which had
sailed from London only the week before the *Lady
Juliana.* She'd come to America on some official errand
connected with fisheries, and her captain, Dennis Kelly,
was a friend of mine of twenty years' standing. Though
commanding an English ship, Kelly was first of all an
Irishman, and if ever there was a friend of the abused
and downtrodden, 'twas himself. He was more than surprised to see me.

" 'Dogbody,' said he, 'what the devil are ye doing here?
I'd supposed ye picking posies and nosegays in Botany
Bay by this time. And where is that splendid fellow, Cap-
tain Lush?'

"I knew that Kelly was to be trusted, so I told him the
whole story, and he was pleased as only an Irishman can
be pleased at anything that happens to the domestic dis-
comfiture of England, though he'd fight the King's enemies with the best will in the world. He took charge of
the *Lady Juliana,* of course, and sent her back to England, where the matter was so carefully hushed that no
word of the women's mutiny was ever seen in the public
prints. Kelly said that the purpose of his life, in future,
would be to find Mrs. Grogan and give her fifty pounds
and a gold shillelagh for putting petticoats and a bonnet
on that King's bad bargain, Lush."

"And did he?" asked Balthus.

"I believe not, Ned. But, curiously enough, I myself
had the pleasure of seeing her again, ten years later, when
surgeon of the *Venerable,* Captain Samuel Hood, one of

the squadron under the command of Admiral Saumarez. I had just been appointed to the *Venerable,* and joined her shortly before the battle of Algeciras Bay. At the beginning of that action, whilst we were hotly engaged, there came down to the after cockpit a huge fellow, wounded in the forearm.

" 'Surgeon,' said he, 'will ye take this bit of iron from me arm, and I'll hasten back to me duties.'

"Where, I thought, have I heard that voice before? I looked at the fellow, but he was so blackened by smoke and powder that I could make little of his features. But when he stretched out that brawny arm, I knew that I'd never but once seen its fellow, for might.

" 'Damn my blood! Mrs. Grogan!' said I, speaking before I thought, but there was so much noise and confusion that my words were, fortunately, lost save to the lady herself. A jagged piece of metal had been driven deep into the muscles of her forearm, but she thought no more of it than if it had been the smallest of bird-shot. I was given a bold, steady, quizzical look.

" 'Was ye speakin' of Mrs. Grogan?' said he, for he was a man in all but sex. 'Sure, Surgeon, she's well and hearty, and 'twas meself that promised, if iver I run acrost ye, I'd greet ye kindly for her. Make haste, now, to pluck out the bit of iron, and when we've licked the Frenchies yonder, as sure's me name's Tim McCann, we'll gut a quart-pot in the old trollop's honour.'

" 'Has she any of it left, Tim?' said I as I probed the wound.

" 'Divil a rag, Surgeon darlin',' said he, with a grin, 'but we'll enj'y the grog none the less for that.'

"And so we did, later, though 'twas half-a-dozen quart-pots on Mrs. Grogan's side, for she could hold her liquor as safe as a hogshead. A merry meeting we had.

" 'Tim,' said I, 'd'ye mind how Mrs. Grogan bedeviled the poor creatures in the *Lady Juliana,* with their petticoats and bonnets and all?'

" 'Bediviled, would ye call it?' says Tim. 'Sure, Surgeon darlin', she praised them to the heights of heaven beyond their desarvin'. 'Twas a pity she was hushed by the lovely lady, for she was jist at the pint of her second wind.'

" 'Where'll she be now, Tim?' said I. 'Mrs. Livingston, I mean.'

" ''Tis the Grand High Admiral she'd have made, Surgeon, save for the cursed luck of her womanhood.'

" 'I'd be pleased to know that she is well and happy,' said I.

" 'Let ye not be grievin' for the lady,' says Tim, 'she is, and all, I'll take me oath. The divil of a fall will she have save on her two little feet. Not a fortnight after we left ye, Surgeon, in the deep forest, she was ridin' in her carriage in the city of New Yark, with a grand magistrate on one side, and His Honour, the Mayor, on the other, but which of thim won her I couldn't say. 'Twas five golden sovereigns she gave me, the very day, and wished me well.'

"Tim then gave me the story of Mrs. Grogan's wanderings since last we'd met. In the ten years she'd carried a score of names, both in and out of prison.

"And now, Foster, I'm through, and the next time you're taken for a thief, let it be on your own side of the Atlantic. But I've one question to ask."

"What is it?" Foster Dogbody replied.

"Don't take it amiss. We're all friends here, and what happened was long ago. Ye can speak frankly. Did ye, or not, rob the coach on the York road?"

"Me? Rob a coach? You thing, you!"

"You were the black sheep of the family, lad; and desperate and angry as ye were at the time, with no money and no prospects, ye might well have been tempted. And myself being so positively identified . . . damme, 'tis scarce conceivable that we've a twin, unknown, who did it."

"Black sheep! If there was one of that description amongst the Dogbodys, 'twas he who bore, and bears, the distinguished name of Feadle!"

The surgeon held up his hand. "Foster, in heaven's name, not *that* name! There, we're quits, ye rogue! Now tell me, where have ye lodged?"

"Near by, at the Dolphin."

"Ye might much better have come here, but no matter for that. Kinship requires that I offer you hospitality at Mrs. Quigg's."

"I'll not discommode you, Rover?"

"What if you do, lad? 'Tis but once in half a century."

The surgeon rose briskly, followed by Foster Dogbody.

"Gentlemen, good evening to ye." With a glance at his brother, the surgeon then leaned toward the company, speaking in a more than audible whisper. "Now that ye've heard both stories, ye may still have a suspicion as to the culprit on the York road. But for old friendship's and his brother's sake, give him the benefit of the doubt!"

X

THE GREENWICH PENSIONERS

THERE were seven in the company in the favoured corner at the Tortoise on that mild midsummer evening. Will Tunn's faithful "props" were all present, and had with them Captain Oliver Tucker, an old friend of Doctor Dogbody, and Mr. Timothy Dwight, Secretary to the Society of the Sons of Ancient Britons, who had been introduced to the others by Mr. Ostiff. Captain Tucker, a half-pay officer living in retirement in the country near Portsmouth, was in his late sixties, though he looked younger. His grey eyes were of the colour of North Sea water, fogs, and easterly gales, and his hearty voice was better suited to the wide air of mid-ocean than to the confines of a taproom, however spacious. Mr. Dwight was a short plump man, and dressed with extreme neatness. His white silk stockings fitted his smooth calves like another skin, and the kindliness and good humour of his expression was added to by a pair of steel-rimmed spectacles which he frequently removed to polish with his handkerchief. There had been a lively exchange of conversation between the various members of the company. Presently, in a momentary lull, Doctor Dogbody turned to the secretary.

"Mr. Dwight," he said, "I have, of course, long known of the Society of the Sons of Ancient Britons, but this is the first time I have had the honour of meeting one directly connected with it. Would you be good enough to tell me what the purpose of your organization may be?"

"With pleasure, sir," the other replied. "We are one part genealogical and two parts humanitarian and benevolent."

The surgeon nodded. "And the benevolent purposes are turned in what direction?"

"Wherever ancient Britons are to be found, sir, in need of our ministrations. We strive, constantly, to enlarge the scope of our work. For example, I have only this week come from a visit to Greenwich Hospital, where, it was hoped by members of our board, some small services might be rendered the old seamen living in retirement there, despite the fact that the pensioners are under Government's care."

"By God, sir," Captain Tucker put in, "ye'd have found

some ancient Britons at Greenwich! Prime old seadogs, eh, Mr. Dwight?"

"They are indeed, sir," the latter replied. He sighed and shook his head. "But I discovered that there is little we can do to improve their condition."

"You're not saying they are neglected, Mr. Dwight?" Captain Murgatroyd asked.

"No, no. They want for nothing, of course, in the material sense. And that which they do want it is not within the power of our Society to furnish them."

"And what is that, sir?" Mr. Runyon asked.

"Their youth, Mr. Runyon. Or, better, perhaps, the heyday of manhood: their old life of stirring action in His Majesty's Navy. I was very sensible of the tedium with which the days pass in their retirement."

"There ain't nothing to beat seamen for grumbling," Ned Balthus remarked. "We're all of a piece there, old or young."

"You surprise me, Mr. Dwight," said Ostiff. "I had always supposed that the Greenwich pensioners are thoroughly contented in so snug a berth for their latter days."

"They bear their lot well enough, to be sure. But my conviction is that the poor old fellows are bored to death; some, perhaps, without knowing it. For all their advanced years, they still have a power of life in them, which makes the monotony of their existence particularly hard for them to bear."

"You have diagnosed their trouble precisely, sir," Doctor Dogbody remarked. "I recall an experience I once had with Greenwich Hospital pensioners. B'gad, 'twas an extraordinary one, and it taught me that there is no such thing as a superannuated British seaman."

"When was that, Doctor?" Balthus asked.

"All but forty years ago, but I'd not wish to trouble the company with an account of it on this occasion."

"I, for one, should greatly like to hear it, sir," said Mr. Dwight.

"Aye, let's have it, Dogbody," Captain Tucker added. "We'll not have ye whetting our interest, then putting us off, this way."

"I was thinking of yourself, Nolly, for I should have to mention, at the outset, a name that would set ye to bellowing like a bull."

"Me? What name?" Captain Tucker asked.

"You're bound to have it?"

"Damme, why not? I can think of none that would have the effect ye say."

"Lord Sandwich."

Captain Tucker straightened himself with a jerk and leaned forward, his brown muscular fists clenched on the table.

"Sandwich, is it?" he roared. "Dogbody, would ye speak of that rogue in the company of decent seamen?"

"I knew it: I should not have been tempted," said the surgeon, innocently. "Damn your blood, Nolly! Ye needn't share the secret with the whole of Portsmouth."

"Secret?" roared the captain once more. "Where's the secret about it? He was known for a rogue to the whole of Europe! There never was a greater villain in a position of high public trust! The most formidable enemy the

British Navy has ever had to meet was the British Admiralty itself, under the administration of that scoundrel, Sandwich!"

Mr. Dwight was, plainly, shocked at this outburst. "You astonish me, Captain Tucker," he said. "I have some recollection of a parliamentary inquiry made at the time into Lord Sandwich's administration at the Admiralty, but I had believed it due to his political enemies. Was he not exonerated?"

"No, sir, he was whitewashed, and a murky job they made of it! Mr. Dwight, for barefaced corruption and incapacity, the Sandwich administration at the Admiralty is unique in the annals of our history. Offices in the service were bought and sold like so much cheese. Naval stores were stolen right and left, all merit neglected, and half-starved seamen sent out to fight the battles of their country in ships so rotten they could scarce swim. Dogbody knows it as well as myself. There's not a seaman, afloat or ashore, but knows it!"

"We'll bear off on the other tack," the surgeon remarked. "Nolly, ye've a voice like a Thames bargeman. Ye'll be heard from here to London!"

Captain Tucker, having rid himself in a blast of his sudden flare of temper, now gave a rumbling laugh like the dying thunders of a spent storm. "Proceed, Dogbody. I've done," he said.

"No more outbursts?"

"None, I promise. Heave ahead."

"Very well, then; but there is more than a suspicion of the truth, Mr. Dwight, in what the captain has said of

the state of our Navy during the Sandwich administration. He headed the Admiralty Board from 'seventy-one
to 'eighty-two. I need not remind you that, for the greater
part of that period, we were at war with France, Spain,
and the American colonies.

"In the autumn of 'eighty, I was appointed surgeon to
a seventy-four-gun ship, the *Repulse,* recently commissioned, and then lying in the Thames at Greenwich. I
joined her the day my orders came, and found, to my
surprise and pleasure, that she was commanded by an
old friend and former schoolfellow, Captain Hugh Didd."

"Not Patience Didd?" Captain Murgatroyd asked.

"The same. As Murgatroyd knows, he bore the nick-
name because he was, past question, the most long-suffer-
ing and even-tempered officer in His Majesty's Navy. He
would accept the disappointments and delays so common
in the service, and more than ever so at this time, with an
equanimity that was, truly, saintlike. *But* there was a
point at which even the patience of Patience Didd could
be exhausted. When that was reached, there was no man
so determined and daring in his action, or so reckless
of whatever consequences to himself that action might
lead to.

"Well, I congratulated myself no end at having been
appointed to a new ship, and one, as I thought, all but
ready for sea; but Didd informed me that my joy was
somewhat premature. The *Repulse* had been lying at
Greenwich ever since she'd come from Deptford Shipyard,
three months before, and was still waiting for her guns.
Didd had managed to get eighteen twenty-four-pounders

from the Woolwich Arsenal. Not another one was forthcoming, for all his efforts to hasten matters.

"As for the ship, it needed no practised eye to see that
she was about as seaworthy as a butcher's basket. She was
built by the yard, as the saying went of many of our ships
of this time. Didd told me they had pumped the Thames
through her half-a-dozen times since she'd come from the
yards."

"You astonish me, Doctor Dogbody," Mr. Dwight remarked. "I am no seaman, but is it customary for a new
ship to be in such a state?"

"I'll answer that question for you, sir," said Captain
Tucker. "It *was* customary, during the Sandwich administration. Our ships were built by the yard, as Dogbody says, and at a cost that would have been dear for
the quarter-inch. We hadn't a score of sound vessels afloat
in the year 'eighty."

"Well may ye say it, Nolly," said the surgeon; "but for
shoddy, the *Repulse* topped anything I would have believed possible. 'Twas as much as we could do to keep
above water in the Thames. I didn't like to think how
we'd manage in a seaway, granted that we ever got to sea.

"But we were not there yet, and, as the days and weeks
passed, I could see that even Didd's patience was wearing
thin. Of the seventy-four guns needed, he'd managed to
get the number up to twenty, with four carronades for
the quarter-deck. We were short of men as well. The *Repulse's* full complement was five hundred and twenty, of
which number we had no more than two hundred, the
half, pressed men, as sullen and rebellious as such men

usually are at first. There was a large number of Americans amongst 'em sent to us off merchantmen captured at sea. We had only ninety, all old Navy men, who could be counted upon.

"I will now leave the ship for a moment, to speak of one of those curious chances that play so large a part in human affairs, afloat or ashore. It was my custom, during this long interval of waiting, to attend the Sabbath service at Greenwich Hospital. I enjoyed meeting and talking with the old seamen there who had served England in past generations. I might almost say, in past ages, for some were in their nineties, and better than a dozen had passed their hundredth year. It was heartening, too, to see octogenarians, even centurians, so spry and hale physically. Mr. Pinney, the chaplain at Greenwich, and himself approaching eighty, told me that of the eight hundred men then at Greenwich, only seven were bedridden.

"One Sabbath morning I set out for the service at Greenwich in the company of one of our midshipmen, a lad of fourteen named Sherr, who had, surprisingly, asked to accompany me. Had I known him better, I would also have known that he was up to some mischief, but he had only recently joined the ship, and was as innocent in manner and appearance as a pocket saint. He told me that he had already spent a few hours off duty in roaming about the walks at Greenwich Hospital.

" 'You couldn't do better, lad,' said I. 'Cultivate the acquaintance of those old seamen. There's more authentic naval history in their stories and anecdotes than you'll find in all the books.'

"'But aren't they frightfully bored with life now, Surgeon?' said he.

"'You've noticed it, have you?' said I. 'So they are, lad, just as you will be bored with inactivity, if you survive to their age, which is far from likely.'

"'I suppose not,' said Sherr. 'Old seamen are very scarce, aren't they, Surgeon?'

"'They are and all,' said I. 'Any man in the service who lives to see his fiftieth birthday deserves a Navy medal for the achievement. He's well earned it, if only for his agility at dodging balls, bullets, and oak splinters.'

"'It strikes me the old Greenwichers would ask nothing better than the chance to be dodging 'em again,' said Sherr. 'They seem so tired of idleness. It's a pity something can't be done to liven 'em up.'

"We walked on in the faint April sunshine, young Sherr chatting in his engaging innocent way, and reached the chapel just before the beginning of the service. The pensioners were coming along from the halls and dormitories, some with empty sleeves pinned up at the shoulder, some on crutches, whilst peg-legs past counting beat a ceaseless tattoo on the paved yard. Sherr and I stood at the entrance to watch them pass. 'Twas a privilege merely to gaze into the faces of those old fellows who had fought for England's glory in every corner of the Seven Seas. There was one amongst them, Dan Ruggles by name, who'd been a gunner in the fleet under Sir George Rooke, at the time he seized the treasure ships at Vigo, early in the reign of Queen Anne. Mr. Pinney, the chaplain, whom I'd known years before, had told me about him:

he had passed his one hundred and fourth birthday, and though he'd lost the use of his legs, he propelled himself vigorously along in a curious little chair on wheels. B'gad, he seemed immortal in his energy and high spirits, for, unlike so many of the others, he rose superior to tedium. I shouldn't wonder if he were still speeding about the halls of Greenwich to this very day.

"Young Sherr and I took places in the pew reserved for visitors — there were no others present on that day — and the service began. The chaplain was an excellent old fellow, though not what would be called an inspired preacher. He read his sermon, and on that particular morning he repeated one I recalled hearing twenty years before, in mid-Atlantic; I was then a loblolly boy in the old *Shoreham,* bound for Quebec, and Pinney was our chaplain."

"God's rabbit!" Balthus broke in. "Ye remembered a sermon heard twenty years before? I'd not known ye was that devout."

"There was reason for it, Ned. I was a bit of a lad, then, and had been mastheaded for an hour that Sabbath morning, in freezing December weather, as a punishment for some prank. To top it off, Captain Needham had then ordered me to attend the chaplain's service and bring him a full account of the sermon, afterward, under pain of going aloft for another hour if I failed in the charge. A more anxious listener never hung upon a parson's words. It was curious indeed to hear those same words once more, after so long an interval, and under such different circumstances.

"However, on this second occasion I was not under the same compulsion to attend, and I observed that the pensioners were getting as drowsy as myself. Heads began to droop, and presently most of them had disappeared behind the backs of the pews. I was all but asleep when I was pulled up by a sharp *fs-s-s-st,* close beside me, and a momentary glare of light in the dusky chapel. Turning my head, I saw young Sherr on his knees before his seat, but in no attitude of devotion. He had my enameled snuffbox which for convenience I had left on the prayer-book shelf in front of us. The young rogue had mounded on the lid of the box a generous pinch of gunpowder he'd brought with him tied up in his handkerchief, and had just touched it off. The smoke rolled up in an undulating cloud and spread itself widely in the lofty vaulted chamber.

"B'gad, the effect was immediate. . . . No, I'm wrong there: 'twas not immediate, for none save myself had noted the flash, and it was not until the smoke had spread that the result became apparent. Mr. Pinney, who was reading his sermon, glanced up, peered out into the dusky chapel, at the same time wrinkling his nose like an old war horse. Heads reappeared above the backs of the pews, and faces were turned upward where the smoke had spread like a canopy about halfway to the vaulted roof. There was a stirring and scraping of crutches and wooden pegs and an increasing buzz and murmur arose from all sides.

"I was vexed enough to have shaken young Sherr out of his jacket, there in the midst of the service, but it was next to impossible to assume and hold an expression of decent severity in the presence of the young imp. He gave me a cautious sidelong glance, so droll in its mingled innocence and appeal that 'twas all I could do to keep from grinning like a very accomplice."

"For all that, Dogbody, ye should have taken him over your knee and trounced him with a prayer book," Captain Tucker remarked, with a grin.

"I was more than tempted," the surgeon replied, "and for a double reason. I'd only just bought my snuffbox, in London, and there was a pretty fancy on the lid: old Triton with his wreathed horn reposing on the back of a whale, with a view of the sea beyond. The flash of powder had smudged the picture hopelessly, though I'll admit that the colour of the sea had been a scarcely credible blue, and the fumes of the powder had darkened it to a hue more typical of our northern waters.

"Sherr's prank scuttled the service. The chaplain tried to carry on, but he'd halt in the midst of a sentence to sniff the air once more; then he'd hem and haw for a new start and halt again before he was fairly under way. The pensioners, all fully awake now, made no pretense of listening. The old familiar smell of powder smoke had carried them far enough from Greenwich, and the place was in what might well be called an uproar for a Sabbath service. The old fellows tried to keep their voices down, but you could hear 'em plain enough. In the pew directly behind me I heard some of 'em speaking of the taking of the *Havannah* and the amount of prize money awarded all ratings afterward. One said the seamen's cut was thirteen-and-fourpence, whilst another held it was fourpence above that. B'gad, ye'd have thought the *Havannah* had only just been captured and shillings and pence of the prize money still in their pockets. They got so hot over the amount I thought they'd come to blows."

" 'Twas thirteen-and-eight for common seamen," said Balthus. "I recollect that, for my uncle was there, and he always grumbled over the difference between Lord Albemarle's share, which was twenty thousand pounds, and the seamen's cut."

"And well he might have, Ned. But that's the Navy: the pounds go aft and the farthings forward when it comes to prize money.

"But I'll not linger in the chapel. The moment the chaplain had worried through to the end, I took young Sherr by the arm and straight up to him to make his apologies. For all the years he'd been in orders, Pinney could never break himself of the habit of swearing, and small wonder; the shepherd of a flock of eight hundred old seamen would be hard put to display an example of perfect abstinence in this respect. He gave us a cordial greeting.

" 'Dogbody,' said he, as he hung his surplice in his little closet, 'you're the best parishioner I've got; you come round to service as regular as banyan day. But damn my eyes if it wasn't as much as I could do to get through this morning! One of my old villains has played a merry trick on us.'

" ' 'Twas no old one, Chaplain,' said I, 'but the young imp who stands before you. He wishes to make his apologies.'

"The chaplain held up his hand, protestingly. 'We'll

dispense with 'em,' said he. 'The lad's done a service for the lot of us. I wonder, Surgeon, you've so far forgotten what a limb of Satan you yourself were at his age. Damme, you were mastheaded a dozen times, as I recall it, on the voyage to Canada.'

"Young Sherr gave a grin at this disclosure, and I was forced to admit that I might not have been an example of perfect decorum in my younger days.

" 'I should think not, indeed,' said Pinney, with a chuckle. 'Say no more on the head of apologies. I love lads of spirit.' He broke off, smiling, as he nodded toward the entrance of the chapel. 'Look at 'em, Surgeon! Blast me if it's not the first time in my long incumbency here I've seen the old rascals reluctant to leave the chapel.'

"It was indeed an odd sight to see the pensioners lingering in the aisles and about the door, breathing in the, to them, delightful and memory-stirring aroma of powder smoke. Some who had gone out returned for a further whiff. Lethargy had vanished; one and all, they were as lively as fleas on a dog's back.

" 'I dote on 'em, Surgeon, every man Jack in the place,' said Pinney, fondly. 'They're the salt of the earth, and young Sherr's prank has brought a welcome savour back to the salt. Damme, no! I'll have no apologies. None!'

"The chaplain was, in fact, so pleased that he insisted on our staying for their midday dinner, and 'twas past two before he would consent to let us go. I can't recall an occasion that I enjoyed more than that one."

"How was the vittles? The same as in Navy ships?" Balthus asked.

"Damme if I could tell you, Ned. I don't remember what we ate, but the food was, probably, no worse than we are accustomed to at sea. I noticed, however, that the men at our table ate almost nothing, but there was good reason for that. They had been well nourished on Sherr's whiff of smoke. They were so pleased with the lad and made so much of him, I feared they'd turn his head.

"Now, gentlemen, I'll whisk ye in a breath over the next few days. They were no more than repetitions of numberless earlier ones, with Captain Didd pacing the quarter-deck of his idle ship, awaiting orders that never came. I could see that he was fast reaching a state of desperation, and, to divert his mind, I told him of Sherr's prank at Greenwich chapel. At another time he would have enjoyed it hugely, but, worried as he then was, I succeeded in bringing only a wan smile to his face. 'Damned young rascal,' he said. 'Good lad, though. Make a first-class officer some day if ever again we have a navy.' Then he fell to pacing the deck once more, so beside himself with despair and mortification at the endless delays in getting ready for sea that he could think of nothing else.

"At last he decided to go up to London, to try the expedient of getting the ear of someone at the Admiralty who would take notice of our situation."

"And much good that did him, I'll warrant!" Captain Tucker remarked, with a snort. "I tried the same thing a time or two, at the period. Never managed to see anyone above the rank of a clerk."

"So it was with Didd," said the surgeon. "He was kept

waiting in an anteroom for two hours and had to come away without accomplishing anything. I was about to say that he was gone overnight, and during his absence fifty of our pressed men escaped. They'd laid their plans well and had gotten clean off before the absence of any was noted. I can't say I blamed them, for they were all Americans. To be pressed into our service to fight their own countrymen was an outrage they were too spirited to endure.

"This was the news Didd came back to, after his Admiralty visit, and the very next day came an order, signed by Lord Sandwich himself. B'gad, 'twas brief enough; I can quote the exact text: '*H.M.S. Repulse* being now ready for sea, you will proceed at once to Spithead, arriving there not later than the 4th, ult.'"

"What's this, Dogbody?" Mr. Runyon asked. "You mean to say that affairs were as topsy-turvy in your service as this comes to?"

"They were, Runyon, I regret to say," the surgeon replied.

"I'll bear ye out in that statement," said Captain Tucker. "They were that bad, Mr. Runyon, that the very heads of the Navy Board were ignorant of the ships we had ready for service. Reports and despatches were filed away unread, and orders sent out that might well have driven ship's commanders to suicide. Who was in command at Portsmouth at the time, Dogbody? Admiral Kempenfelt, wasn't it?"

"Aye, of the *Royal George,* though we were not yet attached to his squadron. Ye'll know the effect of so mad an order upon Captain Didd. He guessed the reason for it when he noted, in the papers of the same day, an announcement of a royal visit to be paid the Channel fleet at Spithead on May the sixth. This was, apparently, a surprise to the Admiralty, and desperate efforts were being made by the First Lord to assemble the fleet in time for His Majesty's inspection. Didd well knew that no excuses would avail him. The blame, in case of failure, would be passed on to him. Go we must, somehow; and b'gad, go we did!"

"With a crew of one hundred and fifty when ye needed three times the number?" asked Balthus. "And with only twenty guns for a seventy-four?"

"Will ye give me a moment to reach that point? Damme, Ned Balthus, d'ye suppose Captain Didd was not turning that problem over in his mind until he was dizzy at sight of it? He remained in his cabin for eighteen hours, eating nothing, seeing no one, whilst his officers prowled anxiously about the decks, more than half expecting to hear a pistol shot, the signal that he'd solved the difficulty in the only way that seemed possible. I had no fears of that kind. I'd known Hugh Didd from boyhood. Despite his private opinion of the Admiralty Board, the sense of loyalty was second nature to him. I was convinced that he would appear at Spithead with his ship, to all outward appearances, completely equipped; but how he would do it was beyond my guessing.

"The review was to be on May the sixth. On the evening of April thirtieth, Didd sent for me. I found him sitting at his table with his papers spread out before him, and I saw at once that look of grim determination on his face which I knew so well of old.

" 'Dogbody,' said he, 'I wish to consult you in your capacity as a medical officer. Would there be any great risk — not to me; to the men themselves — if I were to make up my ship's company with Greenwich pensioners? Would their health be endangered by a voyage to Spithead?'

"I was so taken aback by the question that I stood, for the moment, speechless.

" 'I can see no other way out,' he added, 'and 'twas your account of young Sherr's prank that put me in mind of it. They'd come, wouldn't they?'

" 'Come!' said I. 'Hughey, they'll go wild with joy at the chance! As for their health, have no fears on that score. The old lads are as sound as the Burnham beeches. But . . . but for a naval review . . . and before His Majesty, at that . . .'

" 'The chances are that His Majesty will visit only the admiral's flagship,' he replied, adding, with more than a touch of grimness: 'Should he, however, chance to board the *Repulse,* he must draw his own conclusions as to my necessities.'

" 'But the guns?' said I.

" 'We'll have 'em within twenty-four hours,' said he. And, b'gad, gentlemen, we did!

"I know . . . Balthus here is thinking I go beyond the bounds of the possible in that statement. He's about to tell me that no ship could take in fifty-four guns in the space of twenty-four hours, granted that they were available. Nevertheless, we did. On the evening of the second of May we had the others.

"They were dummies, Ned. There chanced to be lying near us in the mud flats an old sixty-gun ship that had been used as a decoy some years before on the coast of Holland. She was furnished with wooden guns of the precise form and size of twenty-four- and thirty-two-pounders. These we placed in our empty ports, and from a distance of fifty yards ye'd never have guessed that we were not completely furnished as to armament. Our ninety loyal seamen worked like devils getting them in place. The same night our Greenwichers came aboard."

The surgeon paused for a charge of snuff, smiling with pleased recollection as he gave his nose a vigorous rub.

"B'gad, there was a sight to have seen!" he resumed. "I wouldn't have missed it for a thousand pounds. I was Didd's ambassador to Chaplain Pinney, who was, to all intents and purposes, the acting governor at Greenwich. The actual governor, one of Sandwich's political place-men, was never there; in three years he had visited the hospital but twice. Pinney never so much as hesitated in granting the request. All that worried him was how to choose four hundred from twice the number who would be tearing to go. He had a veritable riot on his hands in making the selection. However, he managed it at last, and on the evening of the second, here they came, Chaplain Pinney in the lead! They were like schoolboys on a holi-day, or, better, like schoolboys playing truant with the connivance of a popular under-master. They were bustled aboard and below decks at once, for it was hoped that the whole matter could be kept secret. But there was one Pinney had left behind who came after the others and made such a fuss at the dockside that he had to be taken aboard, wheel-chair and all: Dan Ruggles. Damme, he'd not take a score of Noes for an answer.

"We'd not a moment to lose if we were to reach Spithead in time for the review. I pass over the next forty-eight hours spent in getting out of the river. During this time our Greenwichers were kept out of sight, but they fitted into the old routine like balls in the rope rings. They were, of course, spared all heavy tasks. We had enough of our own men to work the ship; the pensioners were used to make up the gun crews, and grieved they were upon learning that so many of the cannon were dummies. The more active amongst 'em were assigned to the real pieces.

"As we were then at war with France, Captain Didd had to be prepared for any eventuality, though he promised himself that we could get round to Spithead safely by hugging the coast. As the event proved, we could not have done better, for 'twas on the morning of May the fourth, not three leagues off Beachy Head, that we met the frigate." The surgeon made a perceptible pause, adding: "The French frigate *Insolent,* of forty-four guns, as we were soon to learn."

"God bless me, sir!" said Mr. Dwight. "A French ship, and so close to our shores?"

"You may well think it remarkable, Mr. Dwight. The French had become as bold as brass at that time. They would cruise the Channel in small squadrons, even singly, with an impunity for which, as Captain Tucker knows, we had Lord Sandwich to thank. Most of their ships greatly surpassed ours in sailing qualities, and they were honestly and soundly built. They were not compelled to drag two or three hundred tons of sea water along with them, as was usually the case with us. If overmatched in armament, they could easily escape to the safety of their own shores.

"But the *Insolent* well justified her name: she showed no disposition to run, though she soon discovered that we were, to all outward appearances, a seventy-four. . . . Nolly, what would you have done in the situation, had you been in Didd's place?"

"You had twenty twenty-four-pounders, you say?"

"Aye, and the four carronades on the quarter-deck."

"With a sufficiency of powder and ball?"

"Enough for a dozen charges for each gun."

"Then, by God, I'd have tempted fortune," said Captain Tucker, "granted I could depend on my Greenwichers. I'd have given that frigate good cause to regret her name, or have gone down in the effort."

"Which is just what Didd did," the surgeon proceeded. "Damme, had he sought safety in flight, he'd have had a mutiny on his hands. 'Twas a heavy responsibility to take, but take it he did. As for the so-called invalids whose combined ages reached the surprising total of thirty thousand four hundred years . . ."

"What the devil are you saying, Dogbody?" Mr. Ostiff broke in. "Thirty thousand four hundred years?"

"I give you the all but exact total," the surgeon replied. "I'm not a dozen years off on either side. A few of the pensioners were in their late sixties, but I learned from Chaplain Pinney himself that the average age was seventy-six. We had four hundred aboard. The simple act of multiplication will convince you that the figures are correct.

"I have always been a lover of curious statistics," the surgeon added. "The collecting of them is a hobby for which my interest has grown with the years. I shall give you a few more items of a similar nature, the result of a census taken amongst the pensioners before we left the Thames. Of their eight hundred nether limbs, ninety-seven were of wood of various kinds, twenty-six of whale-bone, eleven of ivory, and fourteen of miscellaneous substances, whilst nineteen pairs of crutches served those who preferred them to pegs. One hundred and nine of the splendid old fellows bore the scars of ancient wounds, sometimes two or three to the man, received in engagements the earliest of which dated back to the closing years of the reign of William and Mary. But the most surprising result of my examination of their persons was the discovery that the action of three hundred and eighty-two of the four hundred hearts was that of men in their middle forties, at the very height of health and vigour. And all without exception beat with the same high courage."

"With the frigate closing in?" Mr. Runyon asked; "and knowing as they did the crippled state of the *Repulse?*"

"More so than ever, at that moment, Runyon. It made

one proud of one's English blood to see the coolness of the old fellows as they took their stations."

"At the dummies and all?" asked Balthus.

"The dummies and all. Every gun port was, of course, hooked up, for the victory, if it should come, would be due in large part to sheer intimidation. As for our twenty authentic pieces, the way in which our Greenwichers prepared them for action convinced me that they had lost none of their old-time skill."

"Doctor Dogbody, would you excuse a momentary interruption?" Mr. Dwight asked. "I have no notion whatever as to how such guns are fired. Would you be good enough to enlighten me?"

"I cannot do better, sir, than to refer you to Mr. Balthus, who has been in that trade the past forty years," the surgeon replied.

"I'd need a quarter of an hour for a proper answer, Mr. Dwight," said Balthus, "but I'll make it as short as the action was, with a good crew. Hooked to the beams above the guns was the tools for loading and firing. The powder ye put in with a ladle, with a long handle. The head of this shovel, as ye might call it, was shaped like a cylinder, open on one side. Ye thrust the ladle holding the powder cartridge down the muzzle of your piece and give it a quick turn to put the cartridge in place. A wad of rope yarn was then drove home against the cartridge with the rammer. Next came the ball, which ye spit on for luck, and the wad on top of that was rammed down just hard enough to hold the shot in place whilst aiming your piece. Then ye thrust the priming iron, spiraled at the end like a corkscrew, down the touchhole and into the cartridge. Next comes the priming tube, a little quill filled with the best mealed powder mixed up stiff with spirits of wine. This ye place in the touchhole so that the lower end enters the cartridge in the hole made with the priming iron. The upper end of the tube is frayed for to take the fire readily. Ye touch this off with a match on a linstock about three feet long. The gun does the rest, and the message ye send with the ball is what your fancy chooses."

"Was there no danger in the recoil from the cannon?"

"Aye, there was, for ye never could tell, from the direction it was pointed and the motion of the ship, how it would run back. The breeching kept it in certain bounds, but when your piece was hot, the recoil was that great 'twould leap from the deck to the beams above, at each shot."

"You observe, Mr. Dwight," said the surgeon, "that Mr. Balthus, a pattern of modesty, says naught of the skill needed in aiming the piece. 'Tis there our English gunners are approached by few and equaled by none."

"How do you make that out?" Mr. Runyon inquired.

"By the results of our naval engagements, Runyon, and the reason for it is our cool phlegmatic character. The French and the Spaniards are nervous and impulsive in temperament; their gunners are so eager for execution as to defeat their own ends. Ours watch like hawks and wait with patience for the precise moment when the ship begins to rise from her roll, so that the discharge, if it should miss the hull of the enemy, which rarely happens, will be certain to damage her masts or rigging.

"However, in the *Repulse* we had not yet reached the moment of action. All was in complete readiness whilst the frigate was still half a mile off. Despite crutches and wooden pegs, the old fellows stationed at the dummy guns were fairly dancing with vexation at thought of making a mere dumb show. Ye'll guess the delight of those who were to serve the authentic pieces. Dan Ruggles, who had been a master gunner in his day, was in general charge of those that would fire. He was everywhere at once in his little wheel-chair, which he guided with a skill exceeded only by the speed with which he rolled from one place to another. He drew up before me with a jerk as I was about to descend the ladder to my own post in the after cockpit. 'Surgeon,' said he, ' 'tis a day of days for us Greenwichers, but I'm done for if I get shot in the wheels,' and away he went with a cackle of glee, before I could reply.

"I regretted my obligation to go below at such a moment, and, needless to say, there was little glee in my own breast at thought of what was to come. It struck me the pensioners had forgotten, in the excitement of the moment, that guns belched something more than smoke. I shuddered, inwardly, at thought of seeing again, in their old eyes, the unforgettable look of hopeless appeal of desperately wounded men. But we were hell bent for action now. We could only abide the result.

"As it chanced, there was no shortage of men in the surgeon's department, and my assistants had all in readi-

ness below. Mr. Pinney was there as well, that being a
chaplain's post during action.

"Our dismal hole on the orlop is more than ever so
just before an engagement. Nothing can be heard there,
as the ships are closing in, save the suck and gurgle of
the water along the vessel's side, at the level of your head.
The moments then drag by, or, more accurately, time
seems to be a stagnant pool, with neither life nor movement in it, and as evil-smelling as the after cockpit itself.

"Pinney paced our confined quarters for ten minutes,
then scurried up the ladder for a peep at what was taking
place above. Back he came, his eyes shining with excitement. 'They're not half a cable's length off, Surgeon,' said
he. 'There'll be hell stirring directly!'

"Then he thought of his wards at the dummy guns and,
quite forgetting that he was or ever had been a chaplain,
he gave as pretty an exhibition of profanity as I remember
to have heard, and welcome it was, in that tense moment.
'Twas directed at the Admiralty Board and everyone connected with it, for compelling a ship's commander to put
to sea in our unready state.

" 'Dummies!' said he, his eyes blazing. 'By the . . .' No,
I'll leave that. 'Twould be useless to attempt even to
shadow an outburst of such wrathful virtuosity."

"I'd like well to have heard it," Captain Tucker put in,
with a chuckle.

" 'Twas worth hearing, Nolly. Pinney, who was a true
Christian if ever I've known one, could take all the honours in a contest in vituperation. And when he came
down to Lord Sandwich . . . b'gad, you'd have been no-

where, against him. I've heard boatswains, pursers, quartermasters, in their inspired moments. Theirs was mere talent. In his rich variety, Pinney soared to the heights of genius.

"Of a sudden, he remembered his cloth and broke off with an expression so droll and contrite 'twas as much as I could do to maintain my customary gravity. 'Surgeon,' said he, 'forgive me. I fear I'm more of a sheep than the shepherd of my flock.' 'Sheep' was hardly the word to be used in connection with so spirited a performance, but I quite understood what he meant. 'They're eight hundred to one, Mr. Pinney,' said I, 'from every corner of England, and from every branch of Navy service. 'Tis small wonder if ye've picked up, unbeknownst even to yourself, perhaps, a word or two out of the common.'

" 'Aye,' said he, 'and when I think of the splendid old fellows forced to stand at dummy guns . . .' I waited, hoping he was off once more, but this time he managed to hold himself in, though Jacob had no harder task in his wrestle with the angel.

"But, heaven be thanked, they were not all standing at dummies. A moment later the ten twenty-four-pounders on the starboard side of the upper gun deck thundered out in a broadside so perfectly timed ye could not have inserted a split second betwixt the discharges. There was a ragged response from the frigate; ye might well have thought their gunners were firing at random, but we noted, presently, that they seemed under better discipline.

"You'll know our anxiety in the cockpit where we could

hear only the uproar of action and see none of the results of it. Pinney was about to rush up again, but I ordered him to stay where he was. There would be casualties enough, I thought, without adding a needless one to the list. My gaze kept turning to the companionway where the first of the pensioners would soon be carried down to me. But none came, and I began to think that matters might be even worse than I had feared. There were none, perhaps, to bring the wounded down, or balls and great oak splinters might have been mercifully final in their action amongst the Greenwichers. Usually I am never more calm than in the midst of an engagement, but this present lack of any news of the fortunes of the day, and with no wounded to attend to when all of twenty minutes had passed . . . damme, I became as nervous as a rat in a scuttle-butt. As for Pinney, he couldn't sit still for ten seconds.

" 'Surgeon,' said he, presently, 'by God, I'm going up!'

" 'Chaplain,' said I, 'by God, you're going to rest where you are! What kind of discipline is this for an old Navy man, and a parson at that, who should set an example of coolness and obedience to others?'

" 'Only for a peep?' he pleaded. 'Damn my bones and blood! I must see how the lads are getting on!'

" 'You can hear 'em, can't you?' said I. 'Damme, if I couldn't swear they were serving ninety guns instead of twenty!'

" 'God bless 'em, God bless 'em!' said Pinney, his eyes moist with tears. 'Their pieces are that hot they'll be bucking the beams by now. Surgeon, if ye knew 'em as I do . . .' He broke off, unable, in words, to sound the depth of his affection for them.

"Then, b'gad, we were forced to forget the pensioners and think of our own situation. A film of water a quarter of an inch deep had spread over our deck. We'd not noticed at the moment, concerned as we were with the fighting overhead. Pinney stared at it in amazement.

" 'What's this?' said he. 'By God, we've been holed like a sieve at the waterline!'

" 'By French gunners? Never believe it,' said I. Nevertheless, I sent two of my lads running along the orlop on either side to spy out if we'd taken any damage. By the time they returned the water was finger-deep. Not a hole had they found. I then realized what had happened. I have said, I believe, that the *Repulse* was something wanting in seaworthiness. Captain Didd had kept men at the pumps constantly; but with the sighting of the frigate, these had, evidently, been called away for other duty. With the water sloshing around our knees at every roll of the ship, it was plain they'd have to be called back without loss of time.

"I immediately sent word to inform Captain Didd of the situation. Whilst we were waiting, the firing ceased on the instant. The ensuing silence seemed deeper than even silence could be. We stared at one another, not daring, at first, to give voice to our fears. 'Surgeon,' said Pinney, in a heartsick voice, 'if we've been taken . . .' He broke off, and we listened again. We heard the sound, very faint, of cheering. Pinney sprang to his feet, but slipped and sat down in eight inches of greasy water. He scrambled up and made a dive for the ladder, but I grabbed him by the coattails.

" 'Let me go, Dogbody!' he begged. 'By God, we've licked 'em! It's my old lads we hear! I'd know their cheers amongst the innumerable hosts at the Resurrection! Dog' body, in heaven's name! Let me go, I say! I must see how they've fared!'

" 'You'll stay here,' said I, 'where duty has placed you. We'll soon know what's happened; meanwhile we've got to move our gear out of this. Damme, Chaplain! There may be scores of men hurt. We must be prepared, now, for our part.'

"Pinney acknowledged the truth of this. I hastily packed my instruments, dressings, medicaments, and the like, whilst the others carried the kids, table, portable stove, and other necessities up to the lower gun deck. On this deck there had been naught but dummy guns. As my glance swept the place, I saw that three of them had been smashed, but there was no sign of dead, wounded, or living. The place was deserted, but we heard noise enough just over our heads. There was no holding Pinney now; he was away with the speed of a hare. My mates and I followed him up ten minutes later, as soon as we had all in readiness once more to care for the wounded."

"And what then?" Captain Murgatroyd asked, after a lengthy pause.

"Well may ye ask!" the surgeon replied. "Damme, 'twas all but incredible!"

"Ye're not saying there was none killed or hurt?" said Balthus.

"None killed, Ned, and heaven be thanked for it! Wounded there were aplenty, but they needed the services of the carpenters rather than the surgeon and his mates. Will ye believe it? There was twenty-two legs lost in the action and not a drop of blood spilled! All pegs."

"God's rabbit!" Balthus exclaimed. "There was luck that wouldn't come twice in a hundred years."

"Not twice in a thousand years could there be so extraordinary an engagement. Chaplain Pinney was all but out of his senses for joy. If he'd forgot discipline before, he threw the last shred of it to the winds now. He was pounding Captain Didd on the back as though he were a common seaman.

" 'Are they stout lads, Captain? Are they stout lads?' said he. Then away he'd go about the decks to pick up the bits of splintered legs of the old fellows who'd been hit. He gathered them in a heap, every morsel he could find; then they were all placed in one of my empty tubs that had had mangled limbs in 'em times and to spare, but never anything like this before. He meant to take them all home to Greenwich."

"You tell us, Dogbody, that no one was really injured?" Mr. Ostiff asked.

"One only of the Greenwichers, in his proper person," the surgeon replied. "Dan Ruggles. A tiny splinter of one of his comrades' legs had entered the lean calf of his authentic one; a few drops of blood stained his stocking where the splinter had entered. I had the devil's own time persuading him to part with it.

" ' 'Tain't nothin', Surgeon,' said he, 'and I wish to

carry it home as 'tis. They ain't a mite of feeling in that leg, anyway.' But at last I persuaded him to let me draw it, for safety's sake. He was more than proud of having been the only man who bled in the engagement. 'Surgeon,' said he, 'the first blood I ever shed was for Her Majesty, Queen Anne, at the battle of Cádiz, in 1702. And here I be with a few drops to spare for George the Third!'

"There never was a more contented seaman, and when ye think of it, 'twas a boasting matter to have received wounds in service, the first and last of which were seventy-eight years apart. Captain Didd, who well knew how to enter into the spirit of such an occasion, assembled the *Repulse's* company — save those again at the pumps — and we gave the pensioners as hearty a three-times-three as was ever heard on a ship of war, and three on top of those for Dan Ruggles. And there was none that cheered louder than young Sherr, despite the fact that his own wound must have pained him damnably."

"The lad was hit?" asked Balthus.

"Seared on the cheek, Ned, by a spit of flame from the touchhole of one of our own guns. He carries the powder marks to this day. And an appropriate brand it was for the young rogue.

"And now, gentlemen, I'll spirit ye on to Portsmouth. We bore up between the mainland and the Isle of Wight, and anchored at Spithead on the morning of . . ."

"Hold hard!" Captain Tucker interrupted. "Did ye, or not, tell us ye had an engagement with a frigate? Damme, what was she, the *Flying Dutchman,* that ye pass on this way, with no word more of her?"

"Ye might well have thought so, Nolly, for the speed with which she drew off from us was truly phenomenal, though she'd lost her mizzenmast in the action and was badly damaged elsewhere. When I'd first come up she was a mile distant, and she was soon hull down. At the earnest entreaties of the Greenwichers, Didd attempted to pursue her, but, waterlogged as we were, the effort was found to be hopeless."

"But why should she have run?" Ostiff asked. "Her captain must have noted that despite your appearance as a seventy-four, ye were firing but ten guns on a side."

"Aye, but those, friend Ostiff, were served by the pensioners with magnificent results. Didd himself told me that every shot went home. Even our dummies had played an important part in the victory, for evidently the enemy thought our confidence so great that we scorned to use the full weight of our armament. 'What,' they must have asked themselves, 'will our chances be if they open up with the rest?' And they didn't stay for the answer; otherwise, we would, certainly, have taken her."

"Did ye reach Spithead in time for the review?" Balthus asked.

"In the very nick of time, Ned. The Channel fleet of twenty ships, under Admiral Kempenfelt, was anchored in a single line, each ship bedecked with flags, and salutes from those farthest in were already booming their welcome to His Majesty as we crept to the outermost station, where we dropped anchor and made such hasty preparations as we could. The Greenwichers were all concealed below decks. Through our spyglasses we saw the royal barge approaching, and ye'll guess Captain Didd's anxiety at the moment. Heaven be thanked, there was a stiff breeze blowing, and the roadstead was, evidently, too rough for the royal stomach. When halfway down the line, the barge turned and made haste for the quiet waters of Portsmouth Harbour.

" 'We're saved, Dogbody,' Captain Didd remarked, with a sigh of relief.

" 'Aye, and the First Lord as well,' I replied, with some bitterness, for we had seen Lord Sandwich in the royal barge. ' 'Tis a pity His Majesty could not have boarded the *Repulse*. He would have learned something of the state of the Navy he'll never learn from the Admiralty Board.'

" 'No, no; it wouldn't have done,' said Didd. ' 'Tis our duty to shield our superiors, little as they may deserve it. And I have been very remiss, of course, in meeting an emergency as this one had to be met. There'd have been the devil and all to pay had His Majesty seen our Green-wichers.'

"He broke off to turn his spyglass on a pinnace that was putting off from the *Royal George,* Admiral Kempen-felt's flagship. It headed straight for the *Repulse*.

"I need not remind Captain Tucker and Captain Mur-gatroyd that Admiral Kempenfelt was deeply respected throughout the service, for he was just and honourable in all his dealings with his officers. Nevertheless, he was a strict, sometimes a stern, disciplinarian, and Captain Didd had ample reason for the anxiety with which he watched the approach of the pinnace. Word was quickly sent be-

low, to Chaplain Pinney, and the old lads were as scarce
and quiet as mice. We had to keep fifteen men at the
chain pumps. This left Didd with seventy-five of his own
seamen with which to attempt to make a show of five
hundred and twenty. It looked hopeless, and it was hopeless.

"As I've said, the sea was rough — the *Repulse* was
swinging her masts through a sixty-degree arc, and the
admiral's boat had difficulty in accosting. He leaped to
the ladder and then waved the boat off to wait for him.
Our men were drawn up for his reception, and Captain
Didd, in his shortage of officers, had hustled me into a
lieutenant's uniform, so that I was with him when he
met the admiral at the gangway. When the greetings were
exchanged, we followed him aft, where he turned to survey the ship with a puzzled expression on his face.

" 'You are late, Captain Didd; very late indeed, sir,'
said he. 'What is the meaning of it?'

" 'I was delayed, sir, by an action with a frigate, off
Beachy Head,' Didd replied.

"The admiral gave him a steady, scrutinizing glance.

" 'And where is that frigate, sir?' he asked.

"Captain Didd then explained. The admiral knew, as
well as any officer in his service, the state of our ships and
the superior sailing qualities of French ships of the line in
general and of frigates in particular. He said nothing
more for the moment, but continued to regard, in the
same puzzled manner, our comparatively empty decks.
He was about to speak again when a most remarkable
incident occurred. On the deck below, Dan Ruggles, un-

beknownst to us, had been having difficulties with his wheel-chair, because of the heavy rolling of the ship. Some of his comrades were trying to make the chair fast when it broke from their grasp and catapulted down the sloping deck in line with a port where one of the smashed dummy guns had been. Ruggles shot through with as precise an aim as though he'd meant to do it and fell in the sea a good twenty yards beyond the ship's side. Fortunately, the chair was of a light willow wood and floated the old seaman until some of ours could leap to his assistance. Lines were attached to the chair and he was drawn up by a dozen hands, but with the rolling of the vessel ye'll guess how he swung; we thought he'd go full circle before he could be lowered to the deck. The seamen cheered him heartily when they had him safe down. Admiral Kempenfelt witnessed the incident, of course. He stood with his hands on his hips, leaning slightly backward as he stared up at the strange sight.

" 'Captain Didd,' said he, 'I've seen queer things before now, in His Majesty's ships, but this is the first time I knew we have seamen on wheels. Who the devil is this old fellow?'

"The truth had to come out, then. Didd realized that concealment was no longer possible; therefore, he begged the admiral to retire with him to his cabin, where he made a full confession. And here, gentlemen, ends the story of the oddest experience that has fallen to my lot as a Navy surgeon."

"The end?" said Captain Tucker. "What kind of an end is this? D'ye mean to say the *Repulse* lies at Spithead to this day, with the Greenwichers aboard, and the chain pumps still going to keep her afloat?"

"We got 'em safe home, of course. Can ye take nothing for granted?"

The surgeon pushed back his chair, as though about to rise, but Captain Tucker seized his arm.

"Draw in the threads, damn your blood! Draw in the threads! Where did your captain land, after his blowing-up by Kempenfelt?"

"Blowing-up would you call it? B'gad, 'twas the pleasantest experience of the kind a ship's commander could wish for. Didd's heart was warmed to the day of his death by the mere recollection. As for the pensioners, the admiral spent the full day with 'em, and was that pleased with the company he'd have come to Greenwich with us had duty permitted."

"And what then?" Murgatroyd asked, as the surgeon fell silent once more.

"I could not have enjoyed an experience more, Inky, once we got to Greenwich Hospital. I had every care and attention. Not a day in the entire four months that I spent in bed, flat on my back, did I lack for visitors, and better company than the old lads of Greenwich a man, maimed as so many of them had been, could not have dreamt of for himself."

"What the devil's this?" said Ostiff. "Maimed, you say?"

"Didn't I speak of my unfortunate accident? . . . No . . . I did not, though I was at the point a moment ago. With the heavy rolling of the ship, one of our twenty-four-pounders that had all but worn through her breeching during the action with the frigate broke loose; 'twas scarcely an hour after Dan Ruggles's chair was hauled in. I need not tell seamen what a formidable danger a wild gun can be. Shorthanded as we were, every man's help was needed in the attempt to secure it. We succeeded at last, but at the cost of one man's leg — my own. It was so badly crushed that immediate amputation was necessary."

"I never heard the beat of that for bad luck, Doctor," said Balthus. "And so many with pegs that might have taken the damage and no one the worse for it."

"So the Greenwichers thought, Ned, but in the end I was proud to be a member of their fraternity of one-legged men. And the very first time I ever wore a peg, I clattered in with 'em to a Sabbath service at the chapel. How well I remember that day!"

"What ever became of young Sherr?" Captain Murga-troyd asked.

"He was in this very taproom not a week since, at the table yonder by the window. A happy meeting that was, for I'd not seen him in a dozen years. He now commands the *Barfleur,* which sailed for the Cape on Tuesday."

The surgeon rose and took his hat from the wall peg.

"We compared powder marks," he added, his eyes twinkling. "Those on Sherr's face are as plain to be seen to-day as the smudge he made on my snuffbox."

"God bless me, sir! The box was that you still carry?" said Mr. Dwight.

For answer the surgeon took the small enameled container from his pocket and passed it to the secretary, who examined the lid with deep interest.

"You will observe, Mr. Dwight, the recumbent figure on the back of the whale: old Triton with his wreathèd horn."

"Damn my eyes if he *ain't* smudged!" said Captain Tucker. "Dogbody, I don't wonder ye've held fast to such a keepsake."

"It has well paid for its keep, Nolly. I've carried it for thirty-eight years, this same month of April."

"There'll have been a tidy amount of snuff passed through it in that time," said Balthus; "fond as ye are of the powder."

"Just short of half a ton, Ned."

"Half a ton! Impossible!" Ostiff exclaimed.

"Eight ounces a week, friend Ostiff, fifty-two weeks in the year, and for thirty-eight years. The grand total may be easily found." Then, with a parting nod to the company, the surgeon made his way through the crowded taproom to the door.

Doctor Dogbody's Leg

WAS SET IN BASKERVILLE BY THE NORWOOD PRESS; PRINTED
BY THE ROCKWELL AND CHURCHILL PRESS ON SPECIAL PAPER MADE
BY THE S. D. WARREN COMPANY; BOUND IN LINEN-FINISH CLOTH
BY THE RIVERSIDE BINDERY AND DESIGNED BY ARTHUR WILLIAMS
APRIL MCMXL